# DOCTOR WHO™

# THE AUDIO SCRIPTS
## VOLUME TWO

## MORE OF THE FINEST
## BIG FINISH AUDIO ADVENTURES!

**BIG**
FINISH

Published by Big Finish Productions Ltd.
PO Box 1127
Maidenhead SL6 3LW

*www.bigfinish.com*

Editor: Ian Farrington
Project Editors: Gary Russell & Jacqueline Rayner
Managing Editor: Jason Haigh-Ellery

ISBN 1-84435-049-5

Cover art by Paul Burley 2003

First published July 2003

*The Eye of the Scorpion* introduction © Iain McLaughlin 2003
*The Eye of the Scorpion* © Iain McLaughlin 2001
*The One Doctor* introduction © Gareth Roberts & Clayton Hickman 2003
*The One Doctor* © Gareth Roberts & Clayton Hickman 2001
*Dust Breeding* introduction © Mike Tucker 2003
*Dust Breeding* © Mike Tucker 2001
*Charley Says* © India Fisher 2003
*Seasons of Fear* introduction © Paul Cornell & Caroline Symcox 2003
*Seasons of Fear* © Paul Cornell & Caroline Symcox 2002
*Eye of the Beetle* © Iain McLaughlin 2003
*The Eye of the Scorpion: Scripting Notes* © Iain McLaughlin 2003
*Crossroads in Time: Outline* © Gareth Roberts & Clayton Hickman 2003
*The One Doctor: Outline* © Gareth Roberts & Clayton Hickman 2003
*The One Doctor: Doctor Who and Mel's Christmas* © Clayton Hickman 2003
*The One Doctor: 'Superbrain' Questions* © Gareth Roberts & Clayton Hickman 2003
*The One Doctor: Trailer* © Clayton Hickman 2003
*Dark Rising* © Mike Tucker 2003
*Seasons of Fear: Outline* © Paul Cornell 2003
*Notes* © Gary Russell & Ian Farrington 2003

With thanks to Robert Dick and Alison Lawson

The moral rights of the authors have been asserted.

Printed and bound in Great Britain by Biddles Ltd
*www.biddles.co.uk*

# CONTENTS

# EDITOR'S NOTE

The scripts reproduced in this book are the versions taken into the studio on the first day of recording. Each script is followed by a Notes section. These sections list annotations that mark where these scripts differ from the released plays, along with comments by producer Gary Russell, who directed all four stories. Words or sentences that do not appear in the play are struckthrough. Words or sentences that were changed or added are emboldened.

# THE EYE OF THE SCORPION

## By Iain McLaughlin

It's 1999, *Doctor Who* is back in production as a series of audios, I'm a *Doctor Who* fan who earns his crust as a writer and the nice producers of these audios have an open door policy for submissions. Am I going to give it a go? Are bears Catholic? Does the Pope poop in the woods? No, hang on. That's not quite right, is it? But you get the idea. Not giving it a go was never an option, really.

Where to begin? Well, I knew from the start that I wanted to do a historical story. I've always been a fan of historicals in *Doctor Who*. I love the idea of the Doctor popping in to keep an eye on history from time to time. So, it was going to be a historical, but in which period of history would it be set? I toyed with having the Sixth Doctor meet Henry VIII, but I couldn't come up with anything other than a blustering contest between Henry and the Doctor, and the idea of Henry VIII trying to make Peri his seventh wife, so that notion got binned. I'm a great admirer of Winston Graham's *Poldark* novels (and indeed of the TV show – Angharad Rees as Demelza was one of my first crushes on telly). Now this was much more promising as a setting for a *Doctor Who* story. There could be Squires and mines, smugglers and… spot the flaw in that great idea? *The Smugglers* had already done that back in the Sixties, so the *Doctor Who Meets Poldark* idea had to go as well. Around then, on a cold and rainy October day, I was watching the Discovery Channel and on came a documentary about Hatchepsut, the female Pharoah. Two things struck me as I watched the documentary. One was that this had been a truly remarkable young woman who had become Pharaoh at just 17 despite protests and plotting from priests and politicians in her court and who had held onto power for over 20 years. The other was that Hatchepsut's ascent to the throne of Egypt was just ideal for a *Doctor Who* story. There was scope for court intrigue, political back-biting, enormous battles and a bit of romance as well. Perfect. And besides, it had always struck me as a little odd that someone who has travelled as much as the Doctor had never visited Egypt. Okay, so he popped in for a couple of episodes of *The Daleks' Master Plan*, but there had never been a full adventure set in Egypt during her pomp.

From the start, it was always going to be a story for the Fifth Doctor and Peri. I liked the idea of Peri getting to see and experience history first-hand, instead of looking at relics with her step-father. She would have the chance to see that history was alive and vibrant, about people living their lives and dealing with their problems rather than just being something she was forced to endure in museums. Why the Fifth Doctor? Because he seemed to me the Doctor who'd be most comfortable in a full-on historical story. Simple as that.

Around an episode and a half into writing it, the story wasn't working out right. It wasn't particularly bad, just a bit dull. Too much court intrigue and not enough action. I was also feeling a bit hamstrung by history. The facts were getting in the way of the story. Hatchepsut *did* become Pharaoh, she *did* have a relationship with Senenmut, her vizier, and she *did* reign for twenty-something years, all of which limited what I could do with her. The relationship between Peri and Hatchepsut wasn't working either. They should have been friendly rivals but instead they were just bitching at each other and I couldn't find a way to stop them. The whole thing just wasn't falling into place and when I found out that Paul Doherty had written a novel about Hatchepsut's ascension to the throne, that put the tin hat on it. I put the story away and tried to forget about it. Maybe it would be more honest to say I took a major huff with it. (At that point the story was called *Eye of the Beetle*, and the finished episode and a half can be found in this book's appendices.)

The answer to the problem was a lot easier than I'd imagined. If Hatchepsut was replaced with another character there would be no need to worry about getting the history right. I could do whatever I wanted with this other would-be Pharaoh. That included having her face an alien threat as well as all the political dangers she would have to deal with. That's how Erimem came to be. More accurately, that's how the character came to be. The name took longer. Egyptian names nearly always meant something. Pharaoh's names often translated as things like 'Beloved of Amun' or 'Amun is pleased'. Erimem's name – Erimemushinteperem, to give Pharaoh her Sunday best – means absolutely nothing. I spent days trying to come up with a name for her and finally it came down to either An-Ankh-Amun or Erimem. I went for Erimem mainly because it felt right for her, but also because it didn't mean anything. She was never meant to be Pharaoh, so it's possible she'd have been too far down the pecking order to get a name that meant anything.

Like Hatchepsut, Erimem was 17 when fate made her Pharaoh but that was where the similarities ended. Whereas Hatchepsut was ambitious and actively sought the throne, Erimem would be a reluctant Pharaoh. She had no interest in being Pharaoh or a god. Quite the reverse, but she was trapped by fate and her duty. Her own personal hopes and interests had to be put aside for the good of Egypt. Erimem didn't want to be Pharaoh and hated the way people treated her because of her new position.

With Erimem in place, the story came together a lot easier. To give the story an authentic Hartnell-era touch, the Doctor disappeared for an episode, leaving Peri to carry the story with Erimem acting as her companion. They seemed to work pretty well together. It was fun just to let Peri chat with someone of around her own age. When Peri left the show, we didn't really know much more about her than when she first appeared. She was a botanist, a vegetarian, she had a step-father and she was a ropy swimmer. Apart from that? Not a lot really, which seemed a shame. Giving Peri some time talking with Erimem and building the beginnings of a friendship with her seemed like a fun way of getting to know Peri better.

A completed script went in the post to Big Finish, followed by two more within a few months. I had the subtle plan of bludgeoning them into taking a script by sheer weight of numbers. If I sent enough they'd take one just to make me stop. Either that or get a restraining order. Actually, the truth is that writing *The Eye of the Scorpion* had been so much fun that I couldn't resist doing another couple. Big Finish *could* resist them though and they landed back on the mat with an ominous thud. I wasn't particularly surprised. It didn't take a brain surgeon to work out that there would have been an awful lot of people trying their hand at stories. The two Colin Baker stories were both in the envelope which had thumped onto the mat, but *The Eye of the Scorpion* had been kept for another look. It hadn't been commissioned but it hadn't been rejected yet either. The letter accompanying the returned scripts suggested tightening *Scorpion*, losing some characters and maybe giving it another go if I wanted. Who can turn down the chance to write more *Doctor Who*? Over the next few months there were various different drafts of the script. Shemek the decrepit old comedy-relief court astrologer disappeared from the script altogether along with a charioteer named Limak. The only character I really regretted losing was Rhaoubak, Erimem's mother. She and Erimem had a scene in the Palace of Concubines that highlighted how alone Erimem was. Even her own mother would only call her Pharaoh (although she did call Erimem 'my daughter' when she knew she was totally alone). It's a scene I liked a lot, but it didn't make sense to have a performer in for just one scene, so the scene was chopped and dialogue elsewhere rejigged to hint that Erimem was alienated and lonely. Some changes were made to Antranak as well, making him a darker, more driven character, probably most noticeably in the House of Death when he's quite graphic about what will be done to the would-be assassin if he doesn't co-operate. Most of that was to set up the idea that maybe Antranak really would have killed Varela to protect Erimem's position.

The biggest change was the last ten minutes of Part Four. The ending was a bit naff and not terribly *Doctor Who*. It had the Doctor isolating the parasite in Yanis and then leaving him buried underground after an offer to take the creature away from Earth was refused. I told you it was naff, didn't I? Producer Gary Russell asked for a new ending. Somewhere on my computer I had an idea about the Eighth Doctor arriving on a planet to find a woman in some sort of suspended animation. When she was defrosted she would turn out to have the memories of all the people who'd lived on the planet before the war that wiped them out. She'd eventually go a bit loopy because of the conflicting personalities inside her head. It seemed more like an incident than a story to me so I hadn't done anything with it. With a bit of jigging about, the section slotted in. The most fun in that was taking the chance to have Peri as the villain. Initially it was going to be Erimem, playing up to the idea running all through the story of her dying and not becoming Pharaoh, but it seemed like more fun to make Peri the villain.

The new ending got the thumbs up, the script was commissioned (cue for a hangover of Olympic proportions) and that was pretty much it as far as I was concerned. There were a few more changes to the script by Gary. To be honest, I didn't notice most of them until Part Four. There was a scene I had really liked in Part Four that had been cropped. It was of the Doctor sitting round the camp-fire with Erimem and telling her stories. In isolation, I still think it's a nice little scene but it would have been bad for the story as a whole if it had stayed in. It went on too long and slowed things down. Gary was right to chop it. The lines he added to a scene set the following morning about the Doctor telling stories into the night did the job far more economically than the dropped scene and still got over the idea that maybe the Doctor was telling Erimem these stories because he didn't expect her to live much longer.

In all honesty I didn't expect Erimem to live much longer either. The ending was always going to have the Doctor taking Erimem away. From the first draft, she was always going to have the chance to leave her home in the TARDIS. It made sense for her character. She couldn't be Pharaoh and she couldn't go anywhere on Earth, so the Doctor would take her away and drop her at a university somewhere where she could be herself and study, just like she wanted to. I even had a sort of half-formed idea for her meeting the Sixth Doctor a couple of years into her studies, though that never went any further than a few lines stored on the hard drive. The decision to keep Erimem aboard the TARDIS for a while was a surprise for me as much as the audience. I wish I could put it down to my immense genius in coming up with the character but I can't. I think the truth is really in the casting. Caroline Morris is perfect for Erimem. She doesn't look much like the way I saw Erimem in my head, but she gave the character so much personality that I can't imagine anyone doing a better job with her. Oddly, I can't remember how I heard Erimem's voice in my head before I heard Caroline in the role. She just sounds so right. I think Caroline is the reason Erimem's still around.

One question I've been asked quite a few times, and that should be answered, concerns why the story is called *The Eye of the Scorpion* when the scorpions turn up in Part Two, have a menacing scuttle towards Peri and Erimem and then get the rest of the story off. (I hear they were a nightmare in the green room – the water wasn't cold enough, the doughnuts didn't have enough jam, the insects weren't wriggly enough… honestly! The stunt scorpions who got trampled underfoot were a lot easier to work with, apparently.) So why is it called *The Eye of the Scorpion* and not *Doctor Who Discovers Ancient Egypt* or something? Because at one point very early on in putting the story together, Yanis was going to be descended from the early Skorpion dynasty of Egypt and would have been nick-named the Scorpion. I stuck with the title for two reasons. One was that I still thought of him waiting like a scorpion in the desert, ready to attack when his enemy showed weakness. The second reason was a lot simpler – in Part Two, Yanis saw through the eyes of the scorpions attacking Peri and Erimem. That's the title explained. You're wishing I hadn't bothered now, aren't you? Sorry.

# The Eye of the Scorpion

## CAST

| | |
|---|---|
| THE DOCTOR | Peter Davison |
| PERI | Nicola Bryant |
| YANIS | Harry Myers |
| FAYUM | Jack Galagher |
| ANTRANAK | Jonathan Owen |
| ERIMEM | Caroline Morris |
| KISHIK | Daniel Brennan |
| HOREMSHEP | Stephen Perring |
| SLAVE | Mark Wright |
| PRIEST | Alistair Lock |

# PART ONE

### 1. Ancient Egypt. Around 1400 BC.

*In the deserts outside Thebes, the wind whistles, blowing sand. YANIS, a mercenary chieftain, coughs and spits in the dust. He's big, loud and he has a permanent bad temper.*

**YANIS**        Damn this. Where is he?
*Another voice speaks – HOREMSHEP (High Priest of Horus and leader of the Council of Priests in Thebes), though he's not identified as such yet and the wind disguises his voice.*
**HOREMSHEP**   Yanis.
**YANIS**        Finally. I thought you had got lost in the sandstorm.
**HOREMSHEP**   Not this close to Thebes.
**YANIS**        A temple-rat like you could get lost in his own tunic. If I didn't need you I would tear your head from your scrawny shoulders.
**HOREMSHEP**   Are your troops in place?
**YANIS**        They fear me too much to be anything else.
**HOREMSHEP**   Good. Come with me. I found something on the way here. Something important.
**YANIS**        What is it?
**HOREMSHEP**   You will see.
**YANIS**        Hurry, then. Our plans will be ruined if you are missed in the city.
**HOREMSHEP**   Here. By my chariot. Take a closer look. Open it.
**YANIS**        That? That is worth risking everything for? I swear, if this is a trick...
*Sound of a metal hinge opening, followed by a bizarre scrabbling and scratching sound. The sound gets louder.*
**YANIS**        What?
*YANIS screams.*[1]

### 2. Inside the Temple at Thebes.

*FAYUM, a young priest is observing the stars and tutting. He is joined by ANTRANAK, head of the temple guards and Egypt's armies. They are friends but talk as if at war – baiting each other. If their tone wasn't friendly, you'd think they loathed each other.*

**FAYUM**        This is not good. Not good at all.
**ANTRANAK**    Still muttering and watching the night skies, Fayum? How are the omens? No, don't tell me – they're bad.
**FAYUM**        The gods send signs in the skies that speak only of terrible things to come, Antranak.
**ANTRANAK**    Nonsense. We are safe inside Pharaoh's own palace with my troops on constant guard. Nothing can harm us here.
**FAYUM**        We shall see.
**ANTRANAK**    Sometimes I wonder what you priests are taught. Still, the Gods' ways are not mine to question. I am only a soldier. Good night, Fayum.
*ANTRANAK's footsteps echo into the distance.*
**FAYUM**        *(Softly)* I fear we have very few good nights ahead of us.

## 3. TARDIS interior.

*The Fifth DOCTOR is giving PERI a tour of his ship. A door closes as they enter a corridor.*

**PERI**      And that's the <u>small</u> library?
**DOCTOR**      The big one's up ahead.
**PERI**      I can't believe there's more. We've been wandering these corridors for hours.
**DOCTOR**      I thought you wanted to know your way around.
**PERI**      I do, believe me, but I lost my bearings six corridors, three floors and two hours ago.
**DOCTOR**      It just takes a little getting used to, that's all. You'll know your way about in no time.
**PERI**      So you really know what all these doors are?
**DOCTOR**      Naturally. For instance, this is the main library.
*He opens the door and we hear waves crashing on the shore.*
**PERI**      The books are going to get wet.
*He shuts the door.*
**DOCTOR**      Of course, sometimes the TARDIS moves things about. Still, not to worry. A little redecorating never hurt anybody.
**PERI**      A little redecorating? You've got a lake in there.
**DOCTOR**      Yes, I know. I much preferred it where it was. Where to next?
**PERI**      I don't suppose you've got a restaurant stashed away here? My stomach thinks my throat's been cut.
**DOCTOR**      There should be a food machine around here somewhere. I haven't used it much recently.
*He is interrupted by the sound of the TARDIS lurching and being buffeted and thrown about. He and PERI are thrown about. They thump into walls loudly.*
**PERI**      Doctor?
**DOCTOR**      Grab onto something.
*More lurching and then it subsides.*
**DOCTOR**      I think it's passed.
**PERI**      It feels so hot, suddenly...
**DOCTOR**      Yes, that's a bit worrying. Come on. This way.
*DOCTOR's footsteps hurry off along the corridor.*
**PERI**      (*Mutters*) I'm fine thanks. How are you?
**DOCTOR**      (*Calling*) Peri...
**PERI**      Slow down. I don't want to get lost in this...
*Her footsteps follow the DOCTOR's through a door. The Console Room hums.*
**PERI**      How can the Console Room be here? We've gone down three flight of stairs and...[2]
**DOCTOR**      Sssh.
**PERI**      Do...
**DOCTOR**      Ssssh. Ah.
**PERI**      From that 'Ah!' I take it I don't have to ask if you know what happened.
**DOCTOR**      We've materialised. The TARDIS has been reprogrammed.
**PERI**      By who? Is there somebody else on board?
**DOCTOR**      I'm just checking. Oh. That can't be right. According to the

TARDIS, she was reprogrammed by me.

**PERI**          That's impossible. We were stuck in the middle of this flying rabbit warren.

**DOCTOR**        Yes, it does seem more than a little odd.

**PERI**          Where are we going now?

**DOCTOR**        Just a short hop it seems. A few million miles to the side and a couple of days back. Oh. We're almost there.

**PERI**          One day soon, you're gonna have to teach me how these controls work.

**DOCTOR**        (*Not entirely convinced by the idea*) Perhaps. Let's see where we are first.

## 4. Ext. The Egyptian desert.

*The wind blows, and is then interrupted by the TARDIS materialisation noise. The door opens and PERI hurries out of the TARDIS after the DOCTOR.*

**PERI**          So where are we?

**DOCTOR**        From the gravity and atmosphere (*sniffs*) I'd say Earth. No industrial by-products in the air? Definitely Earth. Egypt, roughly 1400BC.[3]

**PERI**          Oh, come on. Even you can't tell all that from the air.

**DOCTOR**        True, but the hieroglyphs on the wall of the house behind the TARDIS are a bit of a giveaway.

**PERI**          Smart guy. What do they say anyway?

**DOCTOR**        They're prayers to ward off evil and protect the house.

*A door rattles on its hinges in the wind.*

**PERI**          Whoever lived here didn't have much faith in their prayers. The place is abandoned. A few jars, some rope, bits of pottery, some clothes and an old wheel...

**DOCTOR**        (*Over Peri*) Hmm. Very interesting. (*Thoughtful*) Can you hear something?

**PERI**          Like what?

*A young woman (17) is yelling and shouting for her horses to stop. Her chariot is a runaway. She is ERIMEM. The horses snort and the chariot clatters.*

**ERIMEM**        Help me!

**DOCTOR**        Like that.

**PERI**          Her chariot's out of control.

**DOCTOR**        There's another chariot. She's being chased.

*All through we hear ERIMEM and her horses getting closer.*

**PERI**          He's more than chasing her.

**DOCTOR**        Behind the TARDIS. Quickly.

*Arrows zing through the air and thud into the TARDIS. ERIMEM is still trying to stop her horses.*

**ERIMEM**        Stop! Slow down. Stop!

**PERI**          We have to do something.

**DOCTOR**        I'm thinking.

**PERI**          Think faster. They're almost on top of us.

**DOCTOR**        He's can't drive and use his bow accurately at the same time... Grab that rope over there. Tie one end round the TARDIS.

**PERI**          What are you going to do?

9

**DOCTOR**  Take the other end to the far side of the breach in the wall and yank it tight after the first chariot is through.

**PERI**  This stuff's so slippery. It's coated with some kind of oil.

**ERIMEM**  Steady. Steady.

**DOCTOR**  Over here. This way. Peri, are you ready?

**PERI**  Nearly.

**DOCTOR**  Hurry. She's almost through. Quickly.

*The pounding of the horses is almost on top of them.*

**PERI**  There. Done. She's through. Pull it. Tight.

*The sound of the rope going taught and then a shocked yell, followed by the sound of a man in armour hitting the ground hard.*

**PERI**  We got him.

*The fallen man (a scout named KISHIK) groans. ERIMEM is yelling for her horses to stop.*

**ERIMEM**  Stop. Slow now. Stop. Whoa.

*No use. The horses thunder on.*

**DOCTOR**  Her horses have been scared out of their wits. She can't control them. Keep an eye on our friend there.

**PERI**  What?

**DOCTOR**  I don't have time to argue. Someone has to stop those horses. Tell your friend I borrowed his chariot for a few minutes.

*The sound of the reins being flicked and the chariot moving off again.*

**DOCTOR**  Hya.

*The fallen KISHIK groans and mumbles.*

**KISHIK**  Wha...?

**PERI**  I hope this isn't an antique.

*The sound of a pottery jar being smashed over KISHIK's head. Another groan and he hits the dirt hard for the second time in under a minute.*

**PERI**  Sorry.

**5. Ext. Desert.**

*Out in the desert, the DOCTOR's chariot is chasing ERIMEM's. If we could see them the horses would be sweating up a foam as they charge across the desert. Their hooves are pounding loudly and they are breathing heavily. There are two sets of chariot and horse sounds. The DOCTOR's chariot is heavier and clatters more.*

**DOCTOR**  Hya. HYA!

**ERIMEM**  WHOA. SLOW DOWN. STOP!

**DOCTOR**  I'm almost there.

*The DOCTOR's chariot sounds are merging with ERIMEM's. They are now very close.*

**ERIMEM**  Help me.

**DOCTOR**  Hang on.

**ERIMEM**  Hurry.

**DOCTOR**  You'll have to step across.

**ERIMEM**  I can't.

**DOCTOR**  Your horses are too frightened to stop. There's no alternative. I'm almost there. Just a little closer.

*On top of the horses' snorting and pounding hooves, the sound of wheels touching and sparks flying. Both ERIMEM and the DOCTOR yelp.*

**DOCTOR**  A little too close. Gently. Gently. Now. Step across.

**ERIMEM**     I can't.
**DOCTOR**     You have to. Hurry, I can't hold the chariots this close for long. Take my hand. Take it! Now jump. It's just one step. Step now.
*The sound of ERIMEM leaping over and landing on the DOCTOR's chariot.*
**DOCTOR**     Got you. It's all right. I've got you. Whoa now. Whoa.
*The chariot pulls to a stop.*
**DOCTOR**     Are you hurt?
**ERIMEM**     Stay away from me.
**DOCTOR**     It's all right. I'm not going to hurt you. Though I can't say the same for the chap I borrowed this chariot from.[4]
**ERIMEM**     Where is he?
**DOCTOR**     Back there with a friend of mine. Unconscious.
**ERIMEM**     Good. Get me away from here.
**DOCTOR**     I don't suppose you'd care to tell me why he was trying to kill you?
**ERIMEM**     You don't know?
**DOCTOR**     If I knew I wouldn't ask, would I?
**ERIMEM**     You are a stranger here.
**DOCTOR**     Well, I've been to Egypt before but I don't think I've been recently.
**ERIMEM**     Take me to Thebes.
**DOCTOR**     You haven't answered my question.
**ERIMEM**     When we are safe in Thebes, I will answer all your questions. Just get me there.
**DOCTOR**     All right. Hold on. Hup. Giddup.
*The horses pull the chariot away.*

## 6. In the desert, by the TARDIS.
*The DOCTOR's chariot pulls up by PERI.*

**PERI**       Doctor, I'm glad you're back.
**DOCTOR**     Whoa.
*KISHIK groans. Another pot smashes and he hits the ground hard again.*
**PERI**       That's my last pot.
**DOCTOR**     You enjoyed that too much, young lady.
**ERIMEM**     I hoped he would be dead.
**DOCTOR**     I think that's rather harsh, don't you?
**ERIMEM**     I owe him and his kind a hundred times worse.
**PERI**       You got her, then.
**DOCTOR**     So it would seem.
**PERI**       So who is she? And why was this guy trying to kill her? I thought he might have been a bandit but that's battle armour he's wearing.
**DOCTOR**     Yes, I spotted that as well. And whoever this is, she's too afraid to talk here. She's almost in shock. We'll take her to Thebes. She's sure she'll be safe there.[5] And we might get some answers.
**PERI**       What about him? Four of us on that chariot is going to be cramped.
**DOCTOR**     These war chariots were built for two passengers and a driver. Leave your sleeping friend there. He'll be all right in a minute or two, apart from a terrible headache.
**ERIMEM**     Others of his kind are bound to be close by now. We must leave at once.

**DOCTOR** That might be a good idea. I've had more than enough excitement for one day.
**PERI** And we still don't know what brought us here.
**DOCTOR** One crisis at a time, Peri. One crisis at a time.

### 7. The desert.
*Another squadron of chariots pulls to a stop. In one is YANIS. He's not best pleased at the DOCTOR's rescue of ERIMEM. In the far distance we hear the DOCTOR's chariot clatter away.*

**YANIS** Stop. Stop. We'll never catch them before they reach Thebes. Their archers would slaughter us as we approached. Damn you, Stranger. Where did you come from?

### 8. Thebes.
*The chariot rattles and chunters towards Thebes.*

**DOCTOR** Here we are, Peri. Thebes.
**PERI** I didn't expect it to be so huge.
**DOCTOR** Yes, impressive, isn't it?
**PERI** If Howard could see me now. He always complained that I didn't share his interest in history.
**DOCTOR** Where to?
**ERIMEM** The palace.
**DOCTOR** Are you sure? This is an enemy chariot, I don't think they'll exactly welcome us with open arms.
**ERIMEM** That will not be a problem, Doctor.
**PERI** Doctor... have you noticed the people...
**DOCTOR** ...are all kneeling?
**PERI** And bowing. And generally grovelling.
**DOCTOR** Excuse me. I don't think you told us exactly who you are.
**ERIMEM** No. I did not. Stand proud and firm. Show that nothing has happened to harm us.
**PERI** We've got company.
**DOCTOR** So I see. Whoa there. Whoa.
*The chariot halts. More chariots rattle to join them.*
**PERI** I don't like the look of those swords, Doctor.
**DOCTOR** I'm not too keen on the spears either. Best behaviour, Peri.
**ANTRANAK** Mighty one. We sing praises to the Gods for your safe return.
**PERI** Mighty one?
*When ERIMEM speaks now there is a change in her. She is strong and firm. Regal.*
**ERIMEM** Escort us to the palace, Antranak. We have a great deal to do but this is not the place to do it.
**ANTRANAK** As you command, mighty Pharaoh.
**PERI** Pharaoh?
**DOCTOR** I must be getting old. I thought I knew the names of all of Egypt's pharaohs.
**PERI** Should I be bowing or curtsying or something?
**ERIMEM** Yes, but please refrain from doing so. The chariot is quite

small – and it would be very unseemly for a friend of Pharaoh to fall off in public.

**PERI**          Whatever you say.

**ERIMEM**        I would wager, Doctor, that you did not expect anything like this when you first saw my chariot being chased.

**DOCTOR**        Er, not really, no.

**ERIMEM**        But I think the unexpected is something you are familiar with. Am I right?

**DOCTOR**        I was under the impression that divine Pharaoh is always right.

**ERIMEM**        (*Laughs*) I'm yet to actually be crowned Doctor, but when I have been, I think I would do well to avoid sparring in word games with you. Now smile and wave to the people. We have been victorious.

## 9. Yanis's Camp.

*YANIS is not best pleased. He's in a fouler than usual mood.*

**YANIS**         So. You are the spineless pig who let the whelp of a girl escape?[6] Do you have an explanation as to how the Egyptian pup escaped from a squadron of over a dozen chariots? Make your answer good, Kishik, or I will stake you in the sand and watch the buzzards feast on your eyes and innards.

**KISHIK**        It wasn't my fault, sire. I plead for mercy.

**YANIS**         Save your pleading, dung-beetle. I want answers. How did she escape?

**KISHIK**        She had a large escort. Six... No, ten chariots. We killed all the rest – we even got her driver.

**YANIS**         And still she escaped? Imbecile! Worse – coward!

**KISHIK**        No, Lord Yanis. She had help.

**YANIS**         What help?

**KISHIK**        A man with fair hair and strange clothing... And a violent girl who repeatedly struck me even when I was unable to defend myself.

**YANIS**         (*Roaring – the pretence is gone*) I know – I saw her. I saw it all. A girl should be no match for a man – or even you. Tell me about the man.[7]

**KISHIK**        I barely saw him, sire. I only know that he knocked me from my chariot as if my magic.

**YANIS**         Not magic, idiot – rope. But he handled the chariot like a true warrior. The brat's horses were running as though they had demons at their tails but he took our chariot and caught them easily. I've never seen better.

**KISHIK**        Except for you, of course, mighty Yanis.

**YANIS**         (*Sneering at the grovelling, then thoughtful.*) Of course. Even at speed he pulled the girl onto his chariot with one hand. My gut tells me he is a dangerous enemy.

**KISHIK**        Let me take a party into Thebes to kill him.

**YANIS**         If I sent anyone to do that, it would be someone I could trust to follow orders. And you were ordered not to attack the Egyptian chariots until I arrived.

**KISHIK**        But they would have escaped if I had waited any longer.

**YANIS**         What has happened is that now that unbedded whelp who calls herself Pharaoh knows that we are here and she knows that we will attack sooner rather than later. I think I should slit you open and let the dogs feed. You're worse than useless.[8]

**KISHIK**   No, great Yanis. Mercy, please. I have a wife and four children at home. Let me live. I will not fail you again. I am loyal. I have always been loyal to you.

**YANIS**   And to my predecessor. As I remember, you helped me murder him. I will let you live, Kishik, but at a price.

**KISHIK**   Anything. I'll do anything...

**YANIS**   I know you will. Come through here. My private shrine is in the back of this tent.

**KISHIK**   I am unworthy, lord.

*Sound of them moving through.*

**KISHIK**   It is dark. I can't see.

**YANIS**   Here, I'll bring a light.

**KISHIK**   What? No!

*There is an insect-like skittering sound – like thousands of insects milling about over each other.*

**KISHIK**   NO! SAVE ME!

*KISHIK screams and then is quiet – only the insect skittering sound.*

**YANIS**   At least now you may be useful.

## 10. Int. Erimem's Suite at the Palace.

*A knock at the door.*

**ERIMEM**   Come.

*Door opens and ANTRANAK enters.*

**ANTRANAK**   Pharaoh.

**ERIMEM**   You have news, Antranak?

**ANTRANAK**   Yes, Highness. I sent a chariot squadron to the area of the desert where you were attacked. The bodies of our men were recovered. They will be buried with honour and their souls will find rest.

**ERIMEM**   Good. Meanwhile, I have ordered a banquet to thank the strangers who saved me today. I will need my friend there.

**ANTRANAK**   As you command, Majesty. (*A little uncertainly*) You do these strangers a great honour with this banquet.

**ERIMEM**   No more than they have earned.

**ANTRANAK**   True. But what do we know of them?

**ERIMEM**   Only that they risked their lives to save mine without knowing who or what I was. You don't trust them?

**ANTRANAK**   I don't know them, Majesty, but they arrived at a fortunate time for you.

**ERIMEM**   For which I am grateful.

**ANTRANAK**   As am I. Perhaps I have been a soldier too long, but good luck like this makes me suspicious. Especially when my Pharaoh's safety is in question.

**ERIMEM**   (*Kindly – this is a friend*) We have all had enough bad fortune this year, Antranak. Let us celebrate what good luck we can.

**ANTRANAK**   I will be at the banquet as you wish. With your permission, I will go and prepare myself.

**ERIMEM**   Of course.

*Door closes behind ANTRANAK.*

## 11. Int. Palace outside Erimem's suite.

*ANTRANAK speaks to the soldiers on guard outside ERIMEM's suite as he comes through the door.*

**ANTRANAK**     Soldier. Double the guard on Great Pharaoh's chambers immediately.
**SOLDIER**     Sir.
**ANTRANAK**     And set others near the quarters of the pair who came into the city with Pharaoh, but don't make it obvious. There's no need for them to know we're watching them.

## 12. The Palace at Thebes.

*The DOCTOR is calling for PERI – a tad impatiently.*

**DOCTOR**     Peri, are you ready yet?
**PERI**     I'll be out in a minute.
**DOCTOR**     Do try to hurry. It's considered bad form to keep the ruler of the known world waiting in her own palace.
**PERI**     Okay, okay. Here I come, ready or not. Well? What do you think?
**DOCTOR**     You've been busy.[9]
**PERI**     Not me. I've had half a dozen servants helping me bathe, get this dress on, put this stuff on my eyes...
**DOCTOR**     Kohl. It's used to make the sloe-eye shape.
**PERI**     At least you didn't have servants trying to shave your head.
**DOCTOR**     Well, it is their custom for people to have bald heads and wear wigs. Much cooler in the heat, apparently.
**PERI**     Can we see the pyramids from here? I've always wanted to see them. And the Sphinx.
**DOCTOR**     I'm afraid not. Thebes is quite a way from Giza. If we were in the Royal Palace at Memphis it would be a different story. Shall we?
**PERI**     Is something wrong? You look a bit, I don't know – edgy.
**DOCTOR**     Just hoping my memory's playing up, that's all. I can name every Pharaoh Egypt ever had and I'm certain there was never a Pharaoh Erimem.
**PERI**     She's due to be crowned in a few weeks. You must be wrong. Maybe you just forgot her.
**DOCTOR**     Female pharaohs were a rarity, Peri. I'm not likely to forget one. Hatchepsut... Smenkhare... No. Something must happen to stop Erimem being crowned.
**PERI**     And now we have to go and have a banquet with her, knowing that she never gets to be Pharaoh? You really know how to kill an evening, Doctor.

## 13. Int. Palace at Thebes.

*There are the sounds of a crowd gathering. Low talking and muted music.*

**FAYUM**     You look worried, Antranak. Of course, you always look worried.
**ANTRANAK**     I'm in no mood for your humour today, Fayum.

**FAYUM**      I fear your mood is about to get worse.

*They are joined by HOREMSHEP.*

**HOREMSHEP**      Greetings to you both.

**ANTRANAK**      What do you want, Horemshep?

**HOREMSHEP**      Does the Priest of Horus need a reason for speaking to the head of the palace guard?

**ANTRANAK**      You never do anything without a reason. What is it this time?

**HOREMSHEP**      Nothing. What do you know of the strangers Pharaoh honours with this banquet?

**ANTRANAK**      Only what my Pharaoh tells me. That is enough – for anyone. Even the chief of priests.

**HOREMSHEP**      Of course. But still, I am curious.

**ANTRANAK**      Then question Pharaoh and leave me be.

**HOREMSHEP**      Surely you're not jealous of Pharaoh's new friends, Antranak? She has never honoured you with a banquet. But then, you haven't saved her life either.

**ANTRANAK**      I warn you, priest...

**FAYUM**      (*Butting in*) If you are so interested in Pharaoh's guests, Horemshep, why not ask them? They have just arrived.

*A little fanfare heralds the entrance of PERI and the DOCTOR.*

**HOREMSHEP**      Perhaps later. Gentlemen.

*HOREMSHEP's footsteps head away.*

**FAYUM**      Why does he constantly bait you, Antranak?

**ANTRANAK**      Because I have almost as much influence in the palace as he does and that eats away at him. But I should know better than to rise to his bait. And now I have duties to perform.

**FAYUM**      Of course.

## 13a. Int. Palace.

*The rumblings of the large gathering. Lots of chatter. Muted conversations as if we're moving through the great hall until we get to the DOCTOR and PERI.*

**PERI**      Is this party all for us, Doctor?

*Music is played – a fanfare.*

**DOCTOR**      I think we're on.

**ANTRANAK**      (*Grandly*) The great and mighty queen, daughter of the stars. Pharaoh in the eyes of the Gods and soon to be crowned, all bow to Erimemushinteperem, divine and eternal, the living god.

**DOCTOR**      (*Quietly*) Peri, kneel.

**PERI**      (*Muttering – struggling a bit*) I'd like to see you kneel wearing a dress this tight.

**DOCTOR**      Ssh.

**ERIMEM**      Rise and approach, Doctor. And you, Peri.

*Slight delay while the footsteps of the DOCTOR and PERI approach the throne.*

**ERIMEM**      The Doctor and Peri have done great service to your Pharaoh and to Egypt. As thanks, Doctor, I give you this cartouche bearing my divine name. It marks you as friend of Pharaoh and under my divine protection.

**DOCTOR**      You do us great honour, mighty Pharaoh.

**ERIMEM**        Now let the banquet begin.
*A walloping great gong.*
**ERIMEM**        You will sit by Pharaoh, Doctor.
**DOCTOR**        Thank you.
**PERI**        Absolutely, your Majesty.
*ANTRANAK speaks to FAYUM, renewing their banter.*
**FAYUM**        Nice speech, Antranak.
**ANTRANAK**        This is a strange day, Fayum. An outsider sitting at Pharaoh's right hand.
**FAYUM**        Pharaoh makes her own decisions.
**ANTRANAK**        And some do not like them?
**FAYUM**        To say that would be to admit treason. Everyone knows that divine Pharaoh is infallible.
**ANTRANAK**        Not everyone shares your opinion. I know of the split in the council of priests.
**FAYUM**        Officially, there is no split – only a... debate.
**ANTRANAK**        You will have to learn to lie better than that if you want to prosper at court.
*Back at the top table, PERI is obviously having a bit of a look round.*
**PERI**        Doctor, what's with the bug motif around the hall?
**DOCTOR**        The Scarab Beetle. Some of the priests think the beetle is sacred.
**PERI**        It's just like being at home – Mom worshipped Paul McCartney. I wish I'd brought a camera.
**DOCTOR**        And how would you explain it to the developer?
**PERI**        Never been to a toga party?
**DOCTOR**        Well, I was at a bash Nero threw once.
*Music starts up. Obviously music for the dancing girls.*
**DOCTOR**        The entertainment.
**PERI**        Dancers? Oh. They're topless!
**DOCTOR**        Well, yes I suppose they are. It's the custom. Just ignore them if it bothers you.[10]
**PERI**        Easy for you to say. You're not being letched at by that black toothed priest over there. If he asks me to dance I'll punch him.
**DOCTOR**        You'll do no such thing. That's the Priest of the Temple of Horus. He's chief of the council of priests.[11]
**PERI**        Just joking. Those other topless girls – are they the next dancers?
**DOCTOR**        Ah... well, no. Actually, they're a different kind of entertainment.
**PERI**        Singers? *(Dawn of realisation)* You don't mean... hookers? These people need a cold shower.
**DOCTOR**        You may find some of their activities offensive but remember, you're seeing them from a 20th century perspective.[12] By this time's standards, being a palace servant, even in this capacity, is quite respectable.
**ERIMEM**        Are you enjoying the banquet, Doctor?
**DOCTOR**        Very much, your majesty. Aren't we, Peri?
**PERI**        Having a great time.
**ERIMEM**        You must try the roast boar. It is absolutely excellent.
**DOCTOR**        Why not?
**ERIMEM**        *(Claps hands to SLAVE)* Bring boar for my guest.[13]

**PERI**          Is now a good time to remind you that I'm a vegetarian?
**DOCTOR**        (*Quietly*) It would be a huge insult to refuse Pharaoh's recommendation. Just push it round your plate.[14]
*Sounds of a servant dishing up from a platter. His accent is not local.*
**SLAVE**         You want more boar, lady?
**PERI**          No thanks. I don't want to pig out. That's not meant to be a bad pig joke. Sorry.
**SLAVE**         (*Confused*) Lady?
**PERI**          Never mind.
**SLAVE**         Lord?
**DOCTOR**        I don't mind if I do. Thank you.
*Sound of the slave spilling food as he serves it up. The plate scraping and the DOCTOR shifting quickly.*
**DOCTOR**        Careful.
**SLAVE**         I am sorry, Lord.
**ERIMEM**        Our apologies, Doctor.
**DOCTOR**        It's all right. No harm done.
**PERI**          (*Quietly*) The waiter's not very good, is he?
**DOCTOR**        No. His clothes don't quite fit him either, come to that.
**ERIMEM**        No more boar for me.
*Scraping on the plate.*
**ERIMEM**        I said...
*Sound of a heavy plate being thrown aside.*
**SLAVE**         Death to Erimem!
**DOCTOR**        No!
**PERI**          Doctor!
*Yells and noises of confusion and struggle, including a cry of pain from the DOCTOR.*
**ERIMEM**        You have saved me again, Doctor.
**PERI**          You're bleeding.
**DOCTOR**        (*Obviously in a bit of pain*) It's nothing much. Just a flesh wound, really. The knife only grazed my hand.
*The SLAVE laughs.*
**ERIMEM**        Tell me what is so funny, before you die.
**SLAVE**         (*Struggling – obviously being choked*) Then I will not die alone. The dagger was coated with poison. He has only minutes to live.
*Sound of someone keeling over, sending plates spilling noisily to the floor.*
**PERI**          Doctor!

**END OF PART ONE**

# PART TWO

**13a (cont). Recap from Part One.**
*At the banquet. Sounds of general banqueting.*

**PERI**      The waiter's not very good is he?
**DOCTOR**      No. His clothes don't quite fit him either, come to that.
**ERIMEM**      No more boar for me.
*Scraping on the plate.*
**ERIMEM**      I said...
*Sound of a heavy plate being thrown aside.*
**SLAVE**      Death to Erimem!
**DOCTOR**      No!
**PERI**      Doctor!
*Yells and noises of confusion and struggle, including a cry of pain from the DOCTOR.*
**ERIMEM**      You have saved me again, Doctor.
**PERI**      You're bleeding.
**DOCTOR**      (*Obviously in a bit of pain*) It's nothing much. Just a flesh wound, really. The knife only grazed my hand.
*The SLAVE laughs.*
**ERIMEM**      Tell me what is so funny, before you die.
**SLAVE**      (*Struggling – obviously being choked*) Then I will not die alone. The dagger was coated with poison. He has only minutes to live.
*Sound of someone keeling over, sending plates spilling noisily to the floor.*
**PERI**      Doctor!
**ERIMEM**      Take him to my chambers. And be gentle with him.[15]
**PERI**      You're going to be okay, Doctor. You'll get through this.
**DOCTOR**      Actually, Peri, I'm not feeling all that well.
*The DOCTOR then mutters and mumbles incoherently.*
**ERIMEM**      Antranak, torture this creature. I want to know why he tried to kill me and who sent him. Find out who dares attack Pharaoh.
*The SLAVE slumps and groans.*
**SLAVE**      You will learn nothing from me.
**ANTRANAK**      He must have taken poison himself. Already this world is slipping away from him.
**PERI**      Who are you? Why did you do it?
**ERIMEM**      Who sent you? Answer me! Who do you serve?
**SLAVE**      (*Fading*) The <u>true</u> Pharaoh.
*Sound of the SLAVE hitting the floor, followed by the buzz of whispered conversation. The comment about the true Pharaoh has got a reaction from the cheap seats at the banquet.*
**ANTRANAK**      He is unconscious. What should we do, Pharaoh?
*No answer.*
**ANTRANAK**      Pharaoh?
*There's an air of anticipation.*
**PERI**      Erimem, you have to do something.
**ERIMEM**      Discover what you can about this scum then throw the corpse into the Nile. Let the crocodiles have him. I will be in my chambers. Will you accompany me, Peri?

| | |
|---|---|
| **PERI** | Of course. |
| **ANTRANAK** | Take this filth to be tortured. |
| **FAYUM** | Antranak. |
| **ANTRANAK** | What is it, Fayum? |
| **FAYUM** | What did the killer mean when he said 'the true |

Pharaoh'?

**ANTRANAK** How should I know? I'm not privy to the thought of killers.[16]

**FAYUM** It will be the gossip of Thebes within the hour.
**ANTRANAK** I don't doubt it.
**FAYUM** Then you must discover what he meant by true Pharaoh.[17]

**ANTRANAK** I don't need a junior priest telling me what I have to do. I have been commander of the palace armies since long before you came to the royal court.

**FAYUM** I meant no disrespect, Commander.
**ANTRANAK** I know. I didn't mean to speak so harshly.
**FAYUM** The last year has seen great unrest and turmoil in Egypt.[18] The sudden death of our beloved Pharaoh coupled with the other tragedies of our royal house have caused great distress to our people. This rumour will only make matters worse. And it will be used by those in the council of priests who oppose Erimem's coronation.

**ANTRANAK** You will do what you can in council to quash this ridiculous idea.

**FAYUM** Of course. If you will excuse me.[19] I think the Doctor has need of my training as a physician.

*ANTRANAK breathes out heavily.*

## 14. Yanis's Camp.
*A tent flap opens. KISHIK enters.*

**KISHIK** Mighty Yanis, word has come from Thebes...
**YANIS** The Pharaoh girl is alive. I know, Kishik.
**KISHIK** How can you know...?
**YANIS** I know everything, idiot. I knew this plan wouldn't work. But at least Erimem's new champion is dead.

## 15. The House Of Death.
*The House of Death – the temple for torturing prisoners, sounds dank, depressing and violent. There are crackling torches, scraping metal blades and lots of agonised screams. There's the sizzle of burning flesh followed sharpish by a loud scream.*

**ANTRANAK** Talk. Tell me who sent you to kill Pharaoh at the banquet? Who is your master?
*Lots of whimpering from the prisoner but no answer.*
**ANTRANAK** You know where you are?
*No answer. A whimper at best.*
**ANTRANAK** This is the House of Death. No one leaves here alive. You are going to die here today, but I am Antranak and I am Chief of the Palace Guard. As such, the manner of your death is in my power. If you answer my questions you will die quickly and feel no more pain. You

could even take pleasure with one of the temple girls before you die. You'd like that? But if you don't answer, I will have your eyes gouged from your head. Your nose and ears will be shorn from your face and then you will be castrated. I will leave your tongue in your head so that you can beg for death and tell me who sent you. Now who is your master?

*The prisoner spits. From ANTRANAK's reaction, we'd say the prisoner spat in his face.*

**ANTRANAK**    You are a fool. But you will tell me in time. Priests, set burning coals under this vermin. Perhaps fire will burn the truth from his carcass.

*As the door closes, there are crackles and then another wild scream from the prisoner.*

### 16. Erimem's Chambers.

*PERI and ERIMEM are present as FAYUM is tending the DOCTOR.*

**ERIMEM**    What is the Doctor's condition, Fayum?
**FAYUM**    His pulse and breathing are weak, Pharaoh, like the old in their last days.
**PERI**    But he's going to be all right?
**FAYUM**    By all that I know he should be dead already. I have seen a few cases of poisoning such as this and none have survived as long as your friend.
**ERIMEM**    So he will survive?
**FAYUM**    I fear not, Highness. There is no cure for the venom and it is always fatal. He is unconscious, so at least he will feel no pain.[20]
**PERI**    There must be something you can do. What about antitoxins? Or even penicillin?
**FAYUM**    I don't understand, my lady.
**PERI**    Of course you don't. They haven't been discovered yet. Maybe if I could find the right mosses I could make some, but I don't know if they even grow here.
**ERIMEM**    Tend the Doctor, Fayum. Help him all you can.
**FAYUM**    I must attend an emergency council meeting soon but I have called for a more experienced healer to attend him while I am gone. But there is something else that seems odd. I would swear that I could make out the beating of two hearts in his chest.[21]
**ERIMEM**    Two hearts?
**PERI**    Doctor? Doctor, can you hear me? Come on, Doctor, you can come through this. You have to. You can't just leave me here.
**ERIMEM**    He can't hear you, Peri.
**PERI**    I know. I just can't believe a little scratch like that can kill him.
**ERIMEM**    Our people are skilled in the uses of poison.
**PERI**    You must be so proud.
**ERIMEM**    No, but it is a fact nonetheless. Denying it will not change that.
**PERI**    So what do we do now? Sit here and wait for the Doctor to die?
**ERIMEM**    You could tell me why he seems to have two hearts.
**PERI**    It's probably a long story.

*A knock at the door and ANTRANAK's feet entering.*

**ANTRANAK**  Majesty.

**ERIMEM**  Antranak, what have you learned?

**ANTRANAK**  Not as much as I would have liked, Majesty. The enemy charioteer we found in the desert still refuses to speak. For now, we know only that the assassin appears to have entered the palace an hour or so before the banquet began.[22]

**PERI**  How did he get in? Don't you have any security here?

**ANTRANAK**  One of the hesets saw him coming from the Palace of Concubines. She thought he was one of the eunuchs.

**ERIMEM**  If he had lived, I would have made sure that he became one and then executed him.

**PERI**  Have you asked at the... what's it called?

**ERIMEM**  Palace of Concubines.

**PERI**  That's it.

**ANTRANAK**  That is not permitted. Other than eunuchs and the women themselves, only Pharaoh may enter.

**PERI**  So you're not going to question them?

**ERIMEM**  That would be an unacceptable breach of our laws.

**PERI**  I'll go. I'll find out what he was doing in there.

**ANTRANAK**  That is not possible.

**PERI**  What if your Pharaoh says it is allowed?

**ANTRANAK**  My Pharaoh's word is law.

**PERI**  Erimem... your Majesty... let me go into the Palace. Please.

**ERIMEM**  Antranak, will you prepare an escort for us?

**PERI**  Us? You're coming with me?

**ERIMEM**  When I am crowned Pharaoh, I will be able to change laws as I see fit. For now, this is the only way you can enter the house of concubines.

**PERI**  Okay. Let's get going.

**ANTRANAK**  (*Not at all happy*) Pharaoh, I must protest...

**ERIMEM**  You have always been a good friend, Antranak. To my father and now to me. Please. Prepare the escort.

**ANTRANAK**  Thank you, Pharaoh. I will arrange a guard of my most trusted men. They will be ready within the hour.

### 17. The Palace.

*The door closes behind ANTRANAK.*

**ANTRANAK**  Soldier. Tell my personal guard to prepare themselves. They will be protecting Pharaoh herself tonight. I will join them presently. *With a shuffle of feet, the soldier goes. ANTRANAK's footsteps hurry off in another direction. FAYUM runs towards him, a little breathless. A fly buzzes annoyingly throughout.*

**FAYUM**  Antranak. Antranak...

**ANTRANAK**  Fayum? Your council meeting finished sooner than I expected. What did they decide?

**FAYUM**  I'm surprised you don't know already. I'm sure your spies had their ears pressed to the door as usual. You should take care, Antranak. If your men were caught listening to the council, you could be executed. You have a great many enemies in there.

**ANTRANAK**  I am too long in the tooth to care for such piddling laws. Besides, my spies will have heard nothing. The doors are solid wood and thicker than one of the great stones of the pyramids. Tell me what was decided – or I shall hear it from the priest of Maab in the nearest tavern.

**FAYUM**     The council decided that Erimem...

**ANTRANAK**     The Mighty Erimem.

**FAYUM**     ...as you will, cannot be crowned Pharaoh until certain questions have been answered.

**ANTRANAK**     Even the flies feel the unrest. Go on.

**FAYUM**     The question of whether there can even be a female Pharaoh is a contentious one, which has the council split in half.

**ANTRANAK**     Who is against?

**FAYUM**     Horemshep is obviously the loudest opponent of the coronation. And where the Priest of Horus goes...

**ANTRANAK**     ...the House of Isis follows. Who else?

**FAYUM**     All those you would expect to sit in Horemshep's shadow, hoping for his approval.[23] The priests of Seth, Hathor... The rest of us believe that the coronation should proceed. The houses of Osiris and Ma'at spoke loudly in favour of Erimem – the Mighty Erimem.

**ANTRANAK**     As did you? I would bet my life that you did.[24] What of the assassin's claim?

**FAYUM**     It will be investigated fully – there will be no coronation until it is. That was the compromise agreed.

**ANTRANAK**     You would delay the coronation on the dying words of a killer?

**FAYUM**     I will show you why we have chosen to delay the coronation. Come with me.

*Sound of their feet moving along the corridor.*

**ANTRANAK**     Where are we going? I have a great deal to do.

*Footsteps climbing stone stairs.*

**FAYUM**     Just to the balcony. There. What do you see?

**ANTRANAK**     Is this a game? I see Thebes. What else would I see?

**FAYUM**     No. Look closer. We are late into the night and yet the lights still burn. The taverns and inns are still filled with people. And what do you think they are talking of? 'The True Pharaoh'. Our people rely upon this palace for leadership. They will have asked questions among themselves concerning Erimem's claim.[25] Now, with this, they will be confused and in the city there will be unrest. Only when this question of another claim to the throne has been investigated and dismissed can Erimem ascend to the throne clear of suspicions and accusations of unworthiness.

**ANTRANAK**     You may be right.

**FAYUM**     I think that is the first time you have ever openly agreed with me.

**ANTRANAK**     It's late, I'm tired and I must be getting old. I'll try not to let it happen again.[26]

**FAYUM**     (*Laughing*) Please do. I would hate for both of our reputations to be tarnished.

**ANTRANAK**     I doubt anyone's opinion of you could fall any lower.

**FAYUM**     And I doubt their opinion of you is particularly high after your troops let a murderer into the palace.

**ANTRANAK**     I know that. Damn flies.

*Fly's buzzing continues.*

**FAYUM**     How are your investigations progressing?

23

**ANTRANAK**     Steadily. We are making progress.
**FAYUM**        And the Mighty Erimem? Is she safe?
**ANTRANAK**     (*A tad uncomfortably*) I must join her soon. She is planning to visit the Palace of Concubines. As safe a place as any in the palace.
**FAYUM**        I hope so. But now I wonder if anywhere is safe. Everything seems so uncertain now. Even here in the Palace of Pharaoh herself.
**ANTRANAK**     The palace is more secure than it has ever been.[27]
**YANIS**        A lie and you know it.

### 18. Yanis's tent.
*YANIS can hear the last few lines of the conversation between FAYUM and ANTRANAK, though the voices are distorted. Tent flap opens and KISHIK enters, the dialogue over ANTRANAK's and FAYUM's.*

**KISHIK**       Great Yanis...
**YANIS**        Begone, Kishik. I will not be disturbed. By anyone.
**KISHIK**       As you command.
**YANIS**        Now, where were we? Speak up, idiots.
**FAYUM**        (*Distort*) Would it not have been more prudent for Erimem to visit the Palace of Concubines in the morning?[28]
**ANTRANAK**     (*Distort*) I do not question Pharaoh's actions.
**FAYUM**        (*Distort*) Is she going, perhaps, to investigate the rumours that the assassin was seen coming from there?
**ANTRANAK**     (*Distort*) Pharaoh need not explain herself to anyone. Besides, how could I stop her? Her will is law.
**YANIS**        (*Laughing*) And soon her body will feed the jackals.
**ANTRANAK**     (*Distort*) I should be returning to Pharaoh now...[29]

### 19. Palace balcony.
*Mix mid-sentence to the ongoing conversation, now without the distortion.*

**ANTRANAK**     I should be returning to Pharaoh now...
*A fly still buzzes around.*
**ANTRANAK**     Damn this fly.
*His hand slaps.*
**ANTRANAK**     Missed. Ha!
*A metal clatter – this time he splats the fly.*
**FAYUM**        A sword to squash a fly, Antranak? Now I know we are safe.
**ANTRANAK**     (*Snorting*) It made me feel better, Fayum. Now, tend to the Doctor and we'll talk later.

### 20. Yanis's tent. Int.
*With the fly dead, YANIS can't hear any more of ANTRANAK's conversation.*

**YANIS**        Ah! You did well my little friend. You let me hear enough.
*Sound of a device being switched off – there's fumbling and cack-handed operation of the device. YANIS obviously isn't used to anything like this.*
**YANIS**        Incredible device. What other marvels are hidden here I wonder? (*Bellows*) Kishik!
*Sound of tent flap opening.*

**KISHIK**: Lord Yanis?

**YANIS** Prepare the troops. We surround Thebes immediately.

**KISHIK** As you command, my Lord. But... surely their armies will sight us before we get near the city.

**YANIS** Of course they will. But an army mourning the tragic death of that virgin brat, Erimem, will have no stomach for fighting. It will be a glorious slaughter.

**KISHIK** Erimem is dead?

**YANIS** Not yet but soon. Very soon. Prepare the troops.

*Sound of KISHIK leaving. The device is fiddled with again. YANIS still hasn't got the hang of it.*

**YANIS** I must alert more of our smallest soldiers to their great task.

## 21. The Palace of Concubines.

*The sound of a platoon of guards arriving at the Palace with PERI and ERIMEM. ANTRANAK leads the guards.*

**ANTRANAK** Halt.

*Footsteps stop.*

**ANTRANAK** Majesty, we are here. I will rouse the Palace of Concubines.

**PERI** It's enormous. How many women are in here?

**ERIMEM** My father had over sixty wives when he died.

*Thumping on solid wooden doors. A demand for entry rather than genteel knocking.*

**ERIMEM** Brides of my divine fathers. We ask permission to enter.

*No answer.*

**PERI** Nobody home?

**ANTRANAK** I believe I know the reason for the delay, Majesty. One of the palace women was found dead a few hours ago.[30]

**ERIMEM** Was it Rhaoubak? Antranak?

**ANTRANAK** No, Majesty. Your mother is well, but like the other women, she is in mourning for Varela.

**ERIMEM** Varela?

**PERI** You knew her?

**ERIMEM** She tended me when I was a child.

**PERI** Why did she kill herself, Antranak?

**ANTRANAK** I don't know. They say she had been quiet these last few days. Today she took scorpion venom while sitting in the gardens.

**ERIMEM** I am growing weary of these mysteries. But under the circumstances, perhaps we should let the women mourn tonight.

**PERI** I don't want to seem harsh but we still need to know what the killer was doing in there.

**ERIMEM** Antranak?

**ANTRANAK** She is right. We do need answers, Highness.

**PERI** If we wait it might be too late to help the Doctor.

**ERIMEM** You are right. We will mourn Varela later.

**PERI** Besides, one of the women could slip away.

**ERIMEM** Impossible. There is only one exit from this palace.

**ANTRANAK** Actually, Great One, there is a second – it dates back hundreds of years. Very few know of its existence.

25

**PERI**      Show us.
**ANTRANAK**      I would but I may not enter.
*A heftier thump on the door this time.*
**ANTRANAK**      Women, open your doors for Pharaoh Erimemushinteperem, daughter of light.
*The doors open. A slave – obviously mute – answers the door with a snivelling grunt.*
**ANTRANAK**      You took your time.
*A downtrodden grunt.*
**PERI**      He's here now. Don't scare him to death.
**ANTRANAK**      You know the hidden exit from the palace?
*A grunt that says yes.*
**PERI**      Show us where it is.
**ERIMEM**      Peri, wait.
**PERI**      What?
**ERIMEM**      I must enter first. If you had gone ahead of me, your life would be forfeit.
**PERI**      Okay. After you.
**ANTRANAK**      (*Quietly to PERI – ERIMEM isn't meant to hear this*) Hear me, girl. My Pharaoh may be walking into danger to help you enter this place.[31] I hold you responsible for her safety. If any harm comes to her, you will answer to me. Remember that.
**PERI**      If you had done your job properly, we wouldn't have to go in here.[32] You remember that.
**ERIMEM**      Peri?
**PERI**      Coming.
**ANTRANAK**      My troops will wait for you, Pharaoh.
*The doors close behind them.*
**PERI**      Which way?
*The slave grunts.*
**ERIMEM**      Show us.
*Inside the palace, there are sounds of crying. It gets louder as their footsteps head forward.*
**ERIMEM**      The women weep for Varela.
**PERI**      It's probably best that we look at this other exit first and talk to them later.
**ERIMEM**      I think that is wise. Their tears make me uncomfortable, too.
**PERI**      I thought it was just me. Do you want to see your mother while we're here?
**ERIMEM**      More than I can say, but I have seen her weep enough recently. How far to the entrance?
*A grunt.*
**PERI**      Is everyone this talkative?
**ERIMEM**      The slave's tongue was cut from his head after he was taken in battle.
**PERI**      And he's a eunuch as well? Poor guy.
*A grunt that says we're here.*
**PERI**      This is it? I don't see anything.
*A stone door swings open with a loud rumble.*
**ERIMEM**      As it should be. The exit is hidden – put here in case invaders took the palace.

**PERI**        (*Voice echoing slightly*) We'll need torches. These two will do.

*Flaming torches crackle as they're taken from wall brackets.*

**PERI**        Perhaps we should go back and collect some of your palace guards.

**ERIMEM**        The only men who can enter here are eunuchs, remember? I cannot foresee many of my troops volunteering for that duty.

**PERI**        Good point. I mean, good point, your Majesty.

**ERIMEM**        Please. Do not worry about any title. Life is much simpler and easier if people just call me Erimem.

**PERI**        That won't get my head cut off or anything? I'm allergic to decapitation. It's bad for the circulation.

**ERIMEM**        (*Laughs*) You are a strange one, Peri, but that is good. I hope I can call you a friend.

**PERI**        Who am I to say no to a Pharaoh?

**ERIMEM**        Wait here, Slave.

*Slave grunts.*

**ERIMEM**        If we do not return by dawn, sends guards after us and let Seth take our traditions.

**PERI**        Lots of guards. Big ones. With plenty of weapons.

*Another grunt. The rumble of the stone moving again.*

## 21a. Int. Thebes Palace.

*FAYUM is mixing herbs etc. with pestle and mortar. Or some such.*

**FAYUM**        I wish I could identify the poison that has taken you, Doctor. Pharaoh has told me to find a cure but I'm not sure if I can. Of course, if I don't, you'll die. Pharaoh will be unhappy. Antranak will be unhappy because Pharaoh is unhappy and so I will, naturally, become somewhat more unhappy. And then I...

*Something has shocked him*

**FAYUM**        Doctor! Doc –

*He is cut off as someone's hand goes over his mouth, he drops the bowls etc to the floor and is mumbling panic-struck...*

## 22. The passage under the Palace of Concubines.

*PERI and ERIMEM hear their footsteps echo eerily.*

**ERIMEM**        These passages must be almost five hundred years old.

**PERI**        Kind of creepy, aren't they? Claustrophobic.

**ERIMEM**        I do feel a certain... unease.

**PERI**        These tapestries are amazing. The needlework is so intricate but from the way the colours have faded they must be decades old. More maybe.

**ERIMEM**        The women must have made them up above and decorated the passages with them.

**PERI**        To make them homey, just in case? I have to say, I don't think it is working.

**ERIMEM**        There is the doorway.

**PERI**        The dust on the floor. Footprints. There's just one set of tracks – heading up the way we came, so it wasn't someone coming down here from the Palace. I'd bet my last buck those are the assassin's prints from when he came in.[33] (*Beat*) Can we talk about something else for a while?

**ERIMEM**     Tell me about you and the Doctor, Peri. Have you been married long?

**PERI**     What? We're not married!

**ERIMEM**     Are you his concubine, then? Or a slave?

**PERI**     I'm no slave – and I'm certainly nobody's concubine. The Doctor and I are friends, that's all.

**ERIMEM**     Really? That is extraordinary.

**PERI**     Men and women can't be friends here?

**ERIMEM**     No. A woman's place is to serve her man.

**PERI**     That's so... prehistoric!

**ERIMEM**     I don't understand.

**PERI**     I'm sorry. I keep forgetting where – when – I am. It's just that things are different where I come from.

**ERIMEM**     Really? Tell me. Who rules you?

**PERI**     Well, every four years the public decides who's going to run the country.

**ERIMEM**     The ordinary people? All of them?

**PERI**     Everybody. As long as they're adult, not in jail or mad. Well, then again...

**ERIMEM**     Amazing. Tell...

**PERI**     (*Cutting in – the conversation's getting awkward*) Do you mind if I ask how you came to be Pharaoh? I thought they were all men.

**ERIMEM**     Usually they are, and I think most of my council of priests believe that only men should be Pharaoh.

**PERI**     Rubbish. A woman can rule just as well as a man. Look at Margaret Thatcher. Well okay, maybe that's a bad analogy.[34] Indira Ghandi.

**ERIMEM**     I do not understand, but I thank you anyway. (*She sighs*) A year ago I wouldn't have believed this possible.

**PERI**     Why?

**ERIMEM**     Back then I was little Princess Erimem. I was sixteen years old but to everyone I was still the little girl whose nose they had wiped. My father was Pharaoh and my three older half-brothers were more important than me, so I was left to my own devices.

**PERI**     What happened?

**ERIMEM**     First, my eldest brother was killed when the axle of his chariot snapped. It rolled over and landed on him.

**PERI**     I'm sorry.

**ERIMEM**     So am I. I think we were to have married one day.

**PERI**     Your brother?

**ERIMEM**     It is tradition. The royal line must be kept pure. But first he died, and then a fever took my youngest brother less than a month later. The last of my brothers was bitten by an asp inside his own rooms at the palace. He fought the poison for five days before it took him. I think a little of my father died with each of his sons. I wasn't surprised when he died six months after my eldest brother. Only that he allowed himself to be ambushed by mercenaries while out in his chariot. But he had been taking chances like he had never done before, as if he did not care any more.

**PERI**     I'm sorry. Really.

**ERIMEM**     Thank you. Now my only living relation is my mother but now she thinks I am a god and will not look me in the face.[35] She can barely talk to me.

**PERI**     What do you think?

**ERIMEM**     I think that a god would not have needed the Doctor to save her life twice in less than a day, and a god would not feel as afraid as I feel now.

**PERI**     If it's any consolation, you're not alone there. Hey, it's broadening out.[36]

**ERIMEM**     At last.

**PERI**     What is it?

**ERIMEM**     A chapel for the women to worship their gods.

**PERI**     More tapestries. And if my step-father saw that altar he'd think he was in heaven. He could get years of work out of the inscriptions alone.

**ERIMEM**     It reaches back to the first dynasty.

**PERI**     Can you hear that?

**ERIMEM**     What?

**PERI**     Listen.

*Nothing at first, and then there is a sort of scraping sound. Very unnerving and creepy. Worse than fingers down the blackboard.*

**PERI**     That's the wind, right? Except that there's no wind down here.

**ERIMEM**     There. At the door.

**PERI**     Oh my God. Scorpions.

*The sound of the scorpions scratching and rubbing against each other is loud and freaky. It really is weird and unsettling to listen to.*

**ERIMEM**     Hundreds of them.

**PERI**     Thousands. They're everywhere. They're swarming.

**ERIMEM**     They've blocked the doorway. We are trapped.

**PERI**     Quick. Up on the altar.

**ERIMEM**     That would be sacrilege.

**PERI**     Better than the last rites. Come on. Climb up.

*Sounds of them climbing up as well as the continuous sound of the scorpions.*

**PERI**     I've never seen anything like that. I thought scorpions were solitary animals.

**ERIMEM**     They are. They even hate their own kind. Put two together and they will fight until one is dead.

**PERI**     They're not fighting now. Can they climb?

**ERIMEM**     I have never seen them do so.

**PERI**     That's something. Oh, no.

**ERIMEM**     What?

**PERI**     They're climbing on top of each other like they're making a ramp.

**ERIMEM**     I don't believe it. It will only take a few minutes for them to reach us.

**PERI**     This isn't right. They shouldn't be acting like this. They shouldn't be smart enough to do this.

**ERIMEM**     They're almost here.

**PERI**     (*Desperately thinking*) How thick are those tapestries?

**ERIMEM**     They're made of the hardest wearing wools.

**PERI**          This is probably sacrilege as well. Grab the other end and pull.
**ERIMEM**          It is stuck.
**PERI**          Pull harder. Pull.
*Sound of tapestry tearing and being pulled off the wall.*
**ERIMEM**          It's free.
**PERI**          Throw it over the scorpions.
*Sound of the tapestry flopping onto the scorpions.*
**ERIMEM**          You want us to run over the top of them?
**PERI**          Do you have a better idea? Come on.
*On top of the chittering and scraping of the scorpions we hear a set of sickly, crunching footsteps.*
**PERI**          Ugh! This is horrible.
**ERIMEM**          The tapestry doesn't reach the door.
**PERI**          It's only a few feet. We'll have to jump.
*The sound of them jumping.*
**PERI**          Made it.
**ERIMEM**          They are following us.
**PERI**          And they're blocking the way back. We'll have to follow the passage to the other way out.
**ERIMEM**          We don't know what will be waiting for us there.
**PERI**          It can't be any worse than what's behind us.
**ERIMEM**          I believe you have a point.
**PERI**          This way. I think.

### 23. Yanis's camp.
*YANIS bellows an outraged, angry yell.*

**YANIS**          Damn those witches, they have escaped.
**KISHIK**          My lord?
*Sound of KISHIK being grabbed by the gullet and choked.*
**YANIS**          Did I give you leave to speak, vermin?
*More chokings and gurglings before KISHIK is tossed aside to land loudly and painfully.*
**YANIS**          These Egyptian milksops are weak with their women. Letting them run free, doing the work of men. I'll show those women how they should be treated, before I gut them and throw them to the crocodiles. *(Even louder)* Why are we not surrounding Thebes <u>now</u>?

### 24. The tunnels.

**ERIMEM**          Is that light ahead?
**PERI**          I hope so. The torches are almost dead. Still, they've done their job. We've outrun the scorpions
*Sound of torches being chucked away.*
**PERI**          It's morning.
**ERIMEM**          I have never seen a more beautiful sunrise.
**PERI**          Me either. Where are we?
**ERIMEM**          Give me a moment. Ah. There is the palace. We must be at the base of the Western hills.
**PERI**          *(Shivering)* I wish we'd worn something warmer than these dresses. It's freezing out in the open.

**ERIMEM**     The walk will soon warm us. There – I think I see the market opening in the city.

## 25. House Of Death. Int.

*More moans and screams. The prisoner ANTRANAK ordered tortured is whimpering. He gasps for air and is obviously in a lot of pain. A priest is chanting quietly as he goes about his torturing.*

**PRIEST**     Im hishem ur tepmeram uvmet...
*HOREMSHEP startles the PRIEST.*
**HOREMSHEP**  Is this the slave who tried to murder our Pharaoh? Has he spoken?
**PRIEST**     No, Lord Horemshep. He is...
*Sounds of a knife being unsheathed very quickly. There's a cutting sound and the PRIEST gurgles as his throat is cut. The prisoner whimpers optimistically.*[37]
**HOREMSHEP**  Ssssh. Quietly. Don't be encouraged by my presence, you poor, poor fool. You are in no condition to escape, but I'm afraid you can't be interrogated either.
*The prisoner gasps – sound of the knife being stuck into him.*
**HOREMSHEP**  After all, no one leaves the House of Death alive.

## 26. Thebes.

*PERI and ERIMEM are heading back towards the Palace. The locals are vocal in their adoration.*

**PERI**       My mom could have a field day here.[38]
**ERIMEM**     How much are the dates?
**STALLHOLDER**Nothing. Nothing, Great One.
**ERIMEM**     I would not deprive you of your livelihood. One of my hand-maidens will bring your payment later. Peri...?
**PERI**       Thanks. I've never tried these for breakfast before. Can I ask a question?
**ERIMEM**     Please.
**PERI**       How do you deal with all this? The bowing and stuff.
**ERIMEM**     Not very well, apparently. My father was always scolding me for not being regal enough. I shudder to think what he would say if he could see me now, walking among the people, like a commoner. But I do wish he was here. Then I would not have this... burden of duty on me.
**PERI**       For what it's worth, you may just have invented one of the most important political tools ever – the walkabout.[39] Oh, there's Antranak. Ah, looks like we've been spotted.
*Sound of feet running towards them.*
**ERIMEM**     A pity. I could learn to like walking through the market like a normal person.
**ANTRANAK**   Great Pharaoh! You are safe.
**ERIMEM**     Obviously.
**PERI**       We're both safe. Thanks for asking.
**ANTRANAK**   When you did not return, I sent dozens of men into the catacombs. They found only...
**PERI**       Scorpions? We know. Can I see the Doctor?
**ERIMEM**     Antranak, escort us to my chambers.

**ANTRANAK**  As you command.
**PERI**  How is he?
**ANTRANAK**  Fayum is with him. When last I heard the Doctor's condition had not changed.[40] Still unconscious.
**PERI**  But not dead. (*No answer*) He's not dead?
**ANTRANAK**  Not as far as I know, although...
**PERI**  Although what?
**ERIMEM**  Tell us, old friend.
**ANTRANAK**  I fear there are those in this city who would see him dead.
**PERI**  Why? We only just got here.
**ANTRANAK**  The Royal Court is a vipers' nest. That Pharaoh has shown the Doctor and you favour makes some of the court worry as to how secure their positions are. I know a number who would think nothing of removing him – whatever it took.
**PERI**  You included?
**ANTRANAK**  I am loyal to my Pharaoh.
**ERIMEM**  And I am grateful. We are here.
*Doors are pushed open.*
**PERI**  I hope he's okay. Where is he?
**ANTRANAK**  Fayum? _Fayum_?
**ERIMEM**  He's not here.
**PERI**  Where is he? Doctor?[41]
**ANTRANAK**  I left him here.
**PERI**  He's not here now. Doctor? Doctor?
**ERIMEM**  Antranak! How can the Doctor have disappeared?

**END OF PART TWO**[42]

# Part Three

**26 (cont). Erimem's chambers.**

| | |
|---|---|
| **ANTRANAK** | Fayum? <u>Fayum</u>? |
| **ERIMEM** | He's not here. |
| **PERI** | Where is he? Doctor?[41] |
| **ANTRANAK** | I left him here. |
| **PERI** | He's not here now. Doctor? Doctor? |
| **ERIMEM** | Antranak! How can the Doctor have disappeared? |
| **ANTRANAK** | I... but... |
| **ERIMEM** | I ordered that the Doctor be attended at all times. What happened? |
| **ANTRANAK** | I will find out, Majesty. |
| **PERI** | Doctor, where are you? |
| **ANTRANAK** | I fear his whereabouts are of little importance. By now the poison will have run its course. He is dead. |

**27. Desert.**
*Sound of wind in the desert and a chariot rattling along. The charioteer is FAYUM.*

| | |
|---|---|
| **FAYUM** | Sir, this is most unusual. |
| **DOCTOR** | By now you've probably worked out that I'm a most unusual fellow, Fayum. |
| **FAYUM** | Doctor, no ordinary man could survive the venom you were poisoned with – much less get up suddenly as if from sleep and ask for breakfast. |
| **DOCTOR** | Yes, sorry about scaring you like that. There. On the horizon. Smoke from camp-fires. A good sized camp by the look of it. Pull the chariot into the oasis over there. I'll go on foot from here. |
| **FAYUM** | I must go with you. |
| **DOCTOR** | I'd rather go alone. It's bound to be dangerous. |
| **FAYUM** | Pharaoh charged me with your well-being. I cannot leave you alone. |
| **DOCTOR** | I assume I'd be wasting my time trying to change your mind? Very well. |

**28. Erimem's Chambers.**
*ERIMEM is trying to console PERI.*

| | |
|---|---|
| **ERIMEM** | Don't worry, Peri. We will find him. |
| **PERI** | But will he still be alive? |
| **ERIMEM** | He is strong. I am sure... |
| *ANTRANAK interrupts. He is agitated.* | |
| **ANTRANAK** | Great Pharaoh. |
| **ERIMEM** | What is it, Antranak? |
| **PERI** | You've found the Doctor? |
| **ANTRANAK** | Alas not. But our scouts have spied the army of mercenaries. They have surrounded Thebes to the south and the west. |

They have sent a message demanding that we surrender immediately –
or they will kill every man, woman and child in Egypt.

**ERIMEM**      Our troops?

**ANTRANAK**      Foot-soldiers and chariots of the army stand ready. As do
my Palace Guard...

**ERIMEM**      And the temple's troops? Antranak? Tell me.

**ANTRANAK**      The council of priests is split over committing its troops.

**PERI**      That's crazy.

**ANTRANAK**      Perhaps, but once Erimem, forgive me, Pharaoh has led
our troops in battle, the deliberations of the council concerning her right
to the throne will be worthless. The people will never allow a victorious
Pharaoh to be deposed.

**PERI**      So they'd rather see their city destroyed by mercenaries
than see Erimem crowned Pharaoh?

**ERIMEM**      I do not think so, Peri. They are wily and cunning. They
have waited like jackals for the moment to strike at me. Now we shall see
what they plan.

**ANTRANAK**      The council has asked that you attend the emergency
council meeting which sits as we speak.

**ERIMEM**      They summon me like I were a common serving girl.

**PERI**      I didn't think anyone could order a Pharaoh to do
anything. They must be feeling confident.

**ANTRANAK**      It is an outrage. Give me the word and my men will cut
that cabal of weasels into feed for the palace dogs.

**ERIMEM**      No. Tell the priests that I will attend.

**ANTRANAK**      But...

**ERIMEM**      Do it, Antranak, or I will have someone else deliver the
message.

**ANTRANAK**      No, Highness. I will do it. But they will regret this insult.
I swear it.

### 29. The desert.

*The DOCTOR and FAYUM are still out in the desert, talking quietly. As
they speak, we hear their movements through the dunes and over the
sands.*

**DOCTOR**      The Nile's east and they have Thebes surrounded to the
south and the west. Why not the north, I wonder? Unless you have a
garrison to the north.

**FAYUM**      A large one – at Giza.

**DOCTOR**      I thought so. Whoever's in charge of this lot isn't stupid.
If he'd sent men to the north they might have been sandwiched between
the troops in Thebes and the garrison at Giza.

**FAYUM**      We're lucky his men aren't so alert. I can hardly believe
we slipped through their lines so easily.

**DOCTOR**      Men who fight for money tend to be less attentive to duty
than those who fight for honour or their beliefs. Now I'd guess that the
camp is just over these dunes.

*Sounds of them clambering up a dune.*

**DOCTOR**      Ah, there it is. Keep your head down.

**FAYUM**      There must be thousands of mercenaries for the camp to
be this size.

**DOCTOR**      Well, look on the bright side – most of them are already in position to attack the city so they won't be here to worry about us.
**FAYUM**      That's the bright side?
*They keep moving, scrunching through the sand.*
**DOCTOR**      If they're in position I can't help wondering why they haven't attacked yet. Ah. That big tent at the centre must be their leader's. Come on. I want a look inside.
**FAYUM**      Wouldn't it be wiser to fetch help?
**DOCTOR**      Undoubtedly, but I've got this terrible feeling in my mind... never mind. We'll skirt the dunes as best we can. Stay low.
*They move on.*
**DOCTOR**      A guard. Down.
*A moment.*
**DOCTOR**      All right. Come on.
**FAYUM**      You move like a spirit, Doctor. I did not think we would live this long.
**DOCTOR**      I'm a little surprised myself. I thought the camp would be better guarded...
**GUARD**      You! Who are you?[44]
**DOCTOR**      Why can't I keep my mouth shut?
*The sound of an arrow being fired and hitting the GUARD. He gurgles, dying.*
**DOCTOR**      Fayum! Was that absolutely necessary?
**FAYUM**      He would have raised the alarm.
**DOCTOR**      From now on, use that bow only as a last resort. I came here to avoid bloodshed, not start it.
**FAYUM**      I do not understand you, Doctor.
**DOCTOR**      Just get that guard out of sight before he's spotted. He'll be missed before long. We'll have to look sharp. Quickly now. This is the one. It's empty. Inside.
*Tent flaps shut behind them.*
**FAYUM**      Look at these jewels, Doctor. From all corners of the world.[45] And so much gold.
**DOCTOR**      Evidently crime does pay. The spoils of previous campaigns, no doubt.
**FAYUM**      Doctor, the blood on this armour...
**DOCTOR**      Still fresh. This is interesting. Battlefield tents don't usually have a second room. I wonder what's through here. Very interesting indeed.
*Flap opens.*
**FAYUM**      What... oh, that stench. It's like rotting meat.
**DOCTOR**      I'm rather afraid it is. Human meat. Corpses behind this metal block. It must be a shrine of some kind.
**FAYUM**      Human sacrifice? Some of these are wearing the uniforms of our chariot squadrons. This is no way for men to die. Look at them, left for the insects to feast on. Their souls will never find rest.
**DOCTOR**      This metal block must be an altar. The markings are rather unusual, though. So is the metal, come to think of it. Definitely an alloy not developed yet. Let's have a proper look... oh, no.
*The chittering sound of bugs and insects is becoming louder. Metallic scrape as the Doctor grabs a bit of metal.*
**DOCTOR**      I've seen all I need to, Fayum. Time we were going.

35

**FAYUM**     What did you take from the altar?
**DOCTOR**     This is no time for a discussion. Go.
*Sound of a tent flap opening and of the DOCTOR and FAYUM stopping sharpish.*
**YANIS**     Leaving already? You've barely sampled my hospitality.
**DOCTOR**     If what's through there is any indication of how you treat guests, I'll pass if it's all the same with you.
**YANIS**     You must be the fair-haired giant who saved Erimem.
**FAYUM**     Show respect when you speak of Pharaoh.
**YANIS**     Did I give you leave to speak?
*Sound of a whip and FAYUM yelping.*
**YANIS**     Did I give you leave to bleed?
*Another crack of the whip. Sound of FAYUM falling over, exclaiming in pain.*
**YANIS**     Or to fall over?
**DOCTOR**     And who gave you leave to slaughter those men through there?
**YANIS**     Interesting. You are in my tent, in the middle of my camp, surrounded by thousands of my men, yet you do not fear me. You should. You really should.
**DOCTOR**     Perhaps. <u>You</u> should fear what you found in that stasis box through there.[46]
**YANIS**     Stasis box?
**DOCTOR**     Yes, you're using it as an altar.
**YANIS**     What do you know of such things, dog?
**DOCTOR**     Doctor, actually. And I know it's best not to interfere with a stasis box when you find one – especially ones with prison markings on them.
**YANIS**     You know a great deal more than you should.
**DOCTOR**     So I've been told.
**YANIS**     You are a dangerous enemy, Doctor. Too dangerous to remain alive. I shall take great pleasure in killing you myself.[47]
**DOCTOR**     Really? Danger's all in the mind, surely? But then, I imagine you've got rather a lot on your mind these days. Your thoughts, other people's thoughts.
**YANIS**     What do you mean?
**DOCTOR**     I had a rather long nap last night.[48] My mind went wandering and it sensed a presence nearby – a strong telepathic presence. The entity you discovered in the stasis box. Do you know exactly what it is?
**YANIS**     Power. Power over men. Over their minds. The power to rule the world.
**DOCTOR**     Yes, but who'll be ruling you, I wonder?
**YANIS**     No one rules Yanis! I am warlord and I will have this world at my feet.
**DOCTOR**     Rather lofty ambitions for a third rate bully.
**YANIS**     I will cut your heart out and you will live just long enough to see me feast on it.
**DOCTOR**     Not today thank you. We'll be going if it's all the same to you.
**YANIS**     You have courage, Doctor.
**DOCTOR**     I also have a little something I picked up from your stasis box there.

36

**YANIS**        What is that?

*Sounds of the DOCTOR fixing the bit of the stasis box he picked up earlier.*

**DOCTOR**        You don't know, do you? I imagine the presence in your mind recognises it. The telepathic inhibitor core circuits. A little bashed up but nothing that can't be mended by someone who knows what they're doing.

**YANIS**        Stop. Put it down.

**DOCTOR**        The little voice in your head getting nervous? Don't worry. It's perfectly harmless in the long run but if I do this...

*High pitched sound effect followed by screams and yells from YANIS and his troops.*

**DOCTOR**        It does rather tend to disorient telepaths for a while.

**FAYUM**        Let me kill him.

**DOCTOR**        There's no time for that. Come on. Come on.

*Tent flap opening. More wails and yells.*

**DOCTOR**        It's got better range than I anticipated but the effect won't last forever. Quickly. We'll take one of their chariots.

*Sounds of them leaping onto a chariot and the reins being flicked.*

**FAYUM**        Hold on. Ha! Ha!

### 30. Yanis's tent.

*The mercenaries are slowly recovering.*

**YANIS**        Up. On your feet. Up, before I grind your legs into the dirt.

*He lurches through the tent flap. The chariot is thundering off.*

**YANIS**        After them. Do whatever you have to, but bring me the fair one alive. No one kills him but me. I will do it with my bare hands.

### 31. The chariot.

*From the sound of it, the chariot is travelling at full pelt.*

**FAYUM**        We're through their lines.

**DOCTOR**        We're not free yet. I make out three, no, four chariots following us.[49]

**FAYUM**        We have a good head start but they are more experienced with these chariots than I am.

**DOCTOR**        We're still well out of range of their archers. Head for the oasis. Our own chariot is faster than this one and the horses will be fresher. They won't catch us.

**FAYUM**        Ha! Faster! Faster!

**DOCTOR**        Home, James, and never mind the horses. (*No response*) Never mind.

### 32. Erimem's chambers.

*PERI and ERIMEM are in the chamber. ANTRANAK enters.*

**ANTRANAK**        My queen, it is almost time.

**ERIMEM**        I know, Antranak. We had better not keep the priests waiting. Peri, will you come with me?

**PERI**        I thought I might go and look for the Doctor again. But I guess you could do with a friend where you're going.

**ERIMEM**        Thank you. Lead the way, Antranak.

## 33. The desert.
*YANIS is receiving reports.*

**YANIS**        Well, Kishik? Are the men in position?
**KISHIK**        Exactly as you commanded, Lord Yanis.
**YANIS**        Order them to hold position.
**KISHIK**        Hold? I thought we were to attack.
**YANIS**        Are you as deaf as you are ugly and stupid? Hold! There are many ways to win a battle. Our ally in the city will try his way first.
**KISHIK**        And if he fails?
**YANIS**        *(Brightening and cheering up no end)* Then the Nile will run scarlet as Thebes drowns in torrents of its own blood. What a magnificent thought.

## 34. The Council Chamber.
*The chamber is quiet bar a low murmur of conversation. Sound of the great doors opening.*

**ANTRANAK**    Daughter of the most high divine Pharaoh, link to the living Gods, Pharaoh in waiting, Erimemushinteperem, light of the...
**ERIMEM**      Everyone here knows who I am, Antranak, and we have little enough time as it is.
*ERIMEM sits.*
**ERIMEM**      *(Quietly)* I am glad you came, Peri. I think I have few friends in this room.
**PERI**         They look like a pack of vultures.
**ERIMEM**      Who summoned Pharaoh as if she were a slave?
**HOREMSHEP**  I did, Highness.
**ANTRANAK**    Horemshep. I hoped you would know better.
**ERIMEM**      Let him speak. I trust that you have a good reason for your actions, Horemshep.
**HOREMSHEP**  I believe that I do. Pharaoh is Egypt and Egypt is Pharaoh. Our land needs the rule of Pharaoh, the living God. Pharaoh rules all of our lives.
**PERI**         That's why you called her like a dog?
**HOREMSHEP**  *(Ignoring PERI totally)* Since the passing of her divine father, we have all believed that the Princess Erimem was the only heir to the throne of Pharaoh. But there is a doubt as to the right of a daughter to claim the position of Pharaoh, which has caused a delay in Erimem's coronation. Many days we have debated long into the night.
**ANTRANAK**    Drunk long into the night, more like.
**PERI**         And there have been female pharaohs before.
**HOREMSHEP**  *(Annoyed with Peri but still blanking her)* But that changed when the assassin stated that there was another claim to the throne.
**ERIMEM**      Does the council often listen to the claims of murderers, Horemshep?
**HOREMSHEP**  No, but this claim was too important to be ignored. So we ordered an investigation.
**PERI**         And you found something already? That's quick work, Kojak.
**HOREMSHEP**  Who is this... concubine?

**ERIMEM**    Peri is my friend. She speaks with me. Answer us, Horemshep. What is is your evidence?

**HOREMSHEP**    The proof was given to us by those who sought to hide it from Egypt. News of our investigation caused them to make a fatal mistake – by murdering an innocent woman in the Palace of Concubines.

**PERI**    Varela was murdered? We assumed she'd committed suicide.

**HOREMSHEP**    We have proof – and motive as well. The poison she took was very rare. Few in the city possess the skills required in its production and use. Tell us, Antranak, who in the palace understands the venoms of the serpents?

**ANTRANAK**    The priests of the snake gods, apothecaries, and a few others.

**HOREMSHEP**    Including certain of your guards.

**ANTRANAK**    We have experts in the venoms but... wait... are you saying that one of my men killed Varela? If you are your proof had better be undeniable, or priest or not, you will answer to me.

**HOREMSHEP**    I do not accuse one of your men, Antranak. I accuse you of the murder of Varela.

*Uproar and bedlam. HOREMSHEP speaks louder to be heard.*

**HOREMSHEP**    Of the murder of Varela and of conspiring to keep the true Pharaoh of the two lands of Egypt from the throne.

**ERIMEM**    Antranak?

**ANTRANAK**    Lies. All lies from that weasel. I'll kill him with my bare hands.

**HOREMSHEP**    Hold him.

**ANTRANAK**    Release me. Let me go.

**PERI**    I don't believe it. Erimem... (*no answer*) Erimem? Pharaoh!

**ERIMEM**    (*Shocked, shaken*) I know Antranak is protective of me. He has been ever since I was a child. And I heard him threaten you at the Palace of Concubines, although I pretended not to. But he would not do this, surely? No. I don't believe it either. And yet... I know he would do anything to protect me.

*Sound of the doors being thrown open and a commotion from outside.*

**FAYUM**    Let him pass. He carries the cartouche of Pharaoh.

**DOCTOR**    Sorry to barge in like this. Have we missed anything?

**PERI**    Doctor, you're all right.

**DOCTOR**    I will be if you let go. You're crushing my ribs.

**PERI**    I thought you were dead.

**HOREMSHEP**    As did we all.

**DOCTOR**    No thanks. I've tried death a few times. Can't say I care for it much.

**PERI**    But the poison...

**DOCTOR**    My body just put me into a deep sleep while it worked the poison from my system. Best night's sleep I've had in centuries.[50]

**HOREMSHEP**    Alive or dead, you have no place here, stranger.

**ERIMEM**    The Doctor is also here as my counsel. Join us Doctor.

**DOCTOR**    I'm honoured, Pharaoh. So, what's this all about?

**PERI**    Horemshep's accused Antranak of poisoning a concubine to make sure she didn't tell anyone that Erimem isn't really heir to the throne.

**DOCTOR**      Really? Has he said who is?

**PERI**      Not yet.

**DOCTOR**      Interesting timing for this to happen. Majesty, may I ask a few questions?

**ERIMEM**      Of course.

**DOCTOR**      Horemshep, what proof do you have against Antranak?

**HOREMSHEP**      As I have already stated, there are only a handful of people within the palace with the expertise to handle such a rare venom as killed Varela. The rooms and houses of everyone with that expertise were investigated by my palace guard.

**DOCTOR**      And the poison was found in Antranak's chambers?

**HOREMSHEP**      A vial with just enough missing to have killed Varela.

**DOCTOR**      How did he give the poison to Varela? As I recall, men aren't allowed in the Palace of Concubines.

**HOREMSHEP**      Antranak knows all the secret entrances and passages in Thebes. Even yesterday he told Erimem of the existence of a secret passage. And he was seen moving away from the Palace of Concubines only an hour before the Lady Varela was found dead in the gardens.

**ANTRANAK**      It's my duty to oversee security there, idiot.

**HOREMSHEP**      Is it your duty to murder innocent women?

**DOCTOR**      So let me get this right. Antranak slipped into the Palace of Concubines, poisoned the Lady Varela, then went back to his own chambers and hid the incriminating evidence there, ready for your guards to find? Careless of him. Almost unbelievably so.

**HOREMSHEP**      Do you call me a liar, outsider?

**DOCTOR**      No, no, no. Absolutely not. Well, not yet. Why would an intelligent man like Antranak leave the poison in his own rooms? Why not simply throw it in the Nile? Or put it in someone else's chambers? To incriminate an innocent, for instance.

**HOREMSHEP**      Ask him yourself.

**DOCTOR**      I'd rather ask you. And I'd be interested in knowing who ordered the search of Antranak's quarters. It wouldn't have been you by any chance would it?

**HOREMSHEP**      It was a council decision.

**DOCTOR**      But whose idea? Yours? Yes? Interesting. The other question is why? Why would Antranak kill an innocent woman? If he had a motive, let's hear it.

**HOREMSHEP**      Who are you to speak to Horemshep, Priest of Horus, leader of the council of...

**DOCTOR**      I'm someone seeking the truth. Who are you? Motive – if you don't mind.

**HOREMSHEP**      The reason for this cruel murder was discovered in the personal belongings of the Lady Varela. As we know, she was a wife of our beloved Pharaoh, who travelled to the west only a season ago. Among her possessions were letters written to her by her great husband.

**DOCTOR**      That's hardly surprising. What was in the letters that was important enough to cost Varela her life?

**HOREMSHEP**      The letters told of Varela's love for her husband, of her devotion to him... and of the son she bore him in secret.

*Uproar – HOREMSHEP has really played to the galleries.*

**ERIMEM**      A brother?

**PERI**      And he would claim the throne just because he's male.

**ERIMEM**     By law, all male children are ahead of females in the line of succession.

**HOREMSHEP**     Pharaoh fathered another son, older by three years then Erimem, and the true Pharaoh of Egypt. As a so-called friend of Pharaoh, Antranak knew of the child and sought to keep his existence secret so that Erimem could rule as Pharaoh – with his counsel.

**ANTRANAK**     Lies. All of it.

**HOREMSHEP**     Antranak has betrayed his duty to Egypt and the trust of his Pharaoh.

**DOCTOR**     I don't suppose you happen to know where this Pharaoh is?

**HOREMSHEP**     He is here, Doctor. In this room.

**DOCTOR**     I thought he might be. You'd better tell us who he is before the crowd gets restless.

**HOREMSHEP**     Taken from Varela at birth, he was raised by one of the priests as his own. It is ironic that he and Erimem played together as children. He recently entered this council as a respected junior member, but now we will serve him. Fayum is the true Pharaoh.

*Even more uproar.*

**FAYUM**     What?

**HOREMSHEP**     Step forward, mighty Fayum, and take the throne.

**FAYUM**     You're wrong.[51] I'm not Pharaoh. I'm just a priest.

**HOREMSHEP**     You are the son of a living god. You are our most high Pharaoh.

**FAYUM**     I'm nothing. I don't want to be Pharaoh. Get your hands off me.

**HOREMSHEP**     (*Voice a bit guttural and odd*) Embrace your destiny. This is what you were born for.

**FAYUM**     My head. It feels... there's something... a voice. Voices.

**DOCTOR**     (*To himself*) So that's how it works.

**HOREMSHEP**     You have a duty, Great Fayum. You know what you must do.

*FAYUM now speaks differently – stronger and firmer.*

**FAYUM**     I know what must be done.

**ANTRANAK**     Fayum what is this nonsense?

**HOREMSHEP**     Step down, Erimem. Step down and kneel before the true Pharaoh, the mighty Fayum, ruler of the Two Lands of Egypt. Kneel, all of you.

*General sounds of kneeling, scuffling, grovelling and abasing.*

**HOREMSHEP**     Move, girl, or be moved.

**DOCTOR**     Stay where you are, Erimem. Is this the best proof you have, Horemshep? A bottle of poison and some old letters? Hardly conclusive, are they?

**HOREMSHEP**     They are enough.

**DOCTOR**     And jolly lucky for you that they were just lying about.

**HOREMSHEP**     The Gods favour us by showing us the truth.

**FAYUM**     This is indeed the truth.

**DOCTOR**     Really? Fayum, I must say you've changed your tune. One moment you don't want to be Pharaoh, the next you have to do your duty. You changed your mind quickly – and literally too, I imagine.

**HOREMSHEP**     You have interfered enough. Stand aside or be killed.

**DOCTOR**     Why doesn't Fayum move me?

41

**FAYUM**      As you wish.

*FAYUM suddenly falls back, gasping.*

**HOREMSHEP**    What are you?

**DOCTOR**    More than a match for Fayum, it seems. Mind over matter, wouldn't you say?

**HOREMSHEP**    Guards! Kill him.

**DOCTOR**    Wait. I can prove that Erimem is the true Pharaoh.

**HOREMSHEP**    You lie!

**DOCTOR**    I leave that to the experts. You claim your proof is from the gods. Then let the gods choose who should be Pharaoh.

**HOREMSHEP**    The gods have chosen.

**DOCTOR**    Ask Ra, the Sun God, if he favours Fayum.

**ERIMEM**    Peri, what is he doing?

**PERI**    I don't know. Doctor...

**DOCTOR**    Shh, Peri.

**PERI**    But...

**DOCTOR**    Look, this is a telepathic inhibitor circuit. If I just reverse the inhibitor cache control and... there we are.

**PERI**    Doctor...

**DOCTOR**    Quiet. I need to concentrate. Now, get him to ask the question.

**PERI**    Ask your god, Horemshep – or are you scared of the answer?

**HOREMSHEP**    Great Ra, bringer of life, shine your favour on the true living god, Fayum.

*Screams and uproar.*

**ANTRANAK**    Ra is gone. The sky is dark. Ra has abandoned Fayum.

**DOCTOR**    (*Straining*) Erimem, command the sun to return.

**ERIMEM**    Doctor, I cannot...

**DOCTOR**    Do it. I can't keep this up much longer.

**PERI**    Trust him. Please. Do it.

**ERIMEM**    Very well. Great Ra, return to our skies. Bring light and life back to our lands.

*Sounds of awe and shock.*

**ANTRANAK**    Ra has returned. Only a living God can command the sun.

**ERIMEM**    I don't believe it.

**HOREMSHEP**    Don't believe them! It's a trick.

*The crowd is now behind ERIMEM. They're chanting her name.*

**PERI**    (*Quietly*) What was that? An eclipse?

**DOCTOR**    (*Quietly*) Not quite. You remember when the TARDIS was jolted then I said I'd reprogrammed it?

**PERI**    (*Quietly*) Yes.

**DOCTOR**    (*Quietly*) I just did. Telepathically. I reversed these inhibitor circuits I found in Yanis' tent to extend my range a little. Rather a useful little bit of equipment. At least now we know who brought us here.

**PERI**    (*Quietly*) You had the TARDIS block out the sun? Can it do that?

**DOCTOR**    (*Quietly*) You've no idea what the TARDIS can do when she has a mind to. She'd get to just the right distance for the right effect and, so long as it wasn't for more than a few seconds, well, instant eclipse.

| PERI | (*Quietly*) All that shaking about in the TARDIS earlier? The heat... that was just now? |
|---|---|
| DOCTOR | (*Quietly*) Yes, we're here and we were just up there, too. |
| PERI | (*Quietly*) I think Horemshep's going to have a fit, by the way... |
| HOREMSHEP | It's a trick. A lie. |
| DOCTOR | The lies are yours, Horemshep. <u>You</u> had Varela poisoned. She was an easy target – a woman depressed and distressed by the death of her husband. She would easily trust the Priest of Horus. You forged the letters found in her rooms. You planted the evidence on Antranak. You even arranged for the assassination attempt on Erimem so that you could put Fayum or anyone else you could manipulate on the throne. Then what? Murder Fayum and take the throne yourself with the help of the mercenaries outside the city?[52] |
| ERIMEM | Release Antranak. |
| ANTRANAK | Traitorous dog! The beetles will eat you alive for this. |
| DOCTOR | First things first, however. We need to know the details of his arrangement with Yanis' mercenaries. |
| ERIMEM | Is this true, Horemshep? It is. I see it in your face. |
| DOCTOR | What other reason is there for Yanis not attacking yet? The mercenaries stayed outside the city as a constant visible threat, while Horemshep here stirred up trouble inside the Palace. But there's more to it than that now, isn't there, Horemshep? |

*Sound of a sword being drawn.*

| HOREMSHEP | Indeed there is! Fayum! |

*PERI yelps as she's grabbed.*

| DOCTOR | Peri! |
| ERIMEM | Release her, Fayum. |
| FAYUM | Give us free passage from the city or I open the girl's throat to the bone. |
| ANTRANAK | You will never leave this room alive, boy. |
| DOCTOR | He means it, Antranak. Let them go. |
| ERIMEM | Do it. |
| ANTRANAK | (*Reluctantly*) Let them pass. |
| DOCTOR | Don't provoke them. |
| HOREMSHEP | Very wise, stranger. Your strength and intelligence will be of great use to us when we take the city. |
| FAYUM | We will take a chariot. Keep well back or the girl dies. |

*Doors open, PERI dragged out.*

| ERIMEM | Doctor... what now? I am... |
| DOCTOR | Confused, have a hundred questions to ask and don't know what to do next? |
| ERIMEM | Yes. |
| DOCTOR | The first thing is to mobilise every soldier you have – and every chariot. I think war's about to be declared – and I don't want Peri on their side of the lines when the fighting starts. |

(*NB: NO SCENE 35*)

### 36. The chariot.
*Peri is struggling and fighting. The chariot starts to move as:*

**FAYUM**     Ha! Ha!

**HOREMSHEP**     Stop struggling, girl.

**PERI**     Not on your life. Once you're clear of the city, you don't need a hostage.

**HOREMSHEP**     You have a sharp mind.

**PERI**     And a hard knee.

*HOREMSHEP groans as we hear PERI knee him. Probably somewhere really sore.*

**HOREMSHEP**     (*In a considerable amount of pain*) Stop!

**PERI**     Not a chance.

*Sound of PERI leaping off the chariot. She hits the ground hard. She coughs and splutters as feet run towards her. The chariot rattles off into the distance.*

**DOCTOR**     Peri, are you all right? You could have been killed jumping off a chariot moving that fast.

**PERI**     I think I swallowed half the desert. And a few cuts and bruises.[53] Nothing that kicking those two where it hurts won't cure.

**DOCTOR**     Nothing wrong with your temper anyway.

**ERIMEM**     Peri, I'm glad you're safe. Antranak, how long until all our troops can be mobilised?

**ANTRANAK**     My men are already armed and waiting. The temple guards and chariots need only a few minutes.[54]

**DOCTOR**     Good. Tell them to head for the North Gate.

**PERI**     What are you planning, Doctor?

**DOCTOR**     I'll tell you after you've let Erimem's doctor look at those cuts. The last thing we need is you catching an infection. Now, Antranak, the mercenaries outnumber the troops in the city. If we fight here, we'll lose.

**ANTRANAK**     Are you saying we should run like cowards?

**DOCTOR**     Nothing of the sort. I'm saying we should head for Giza and meet up with the garrison there. It should take a while for the mercenaries to follow us.

**ANTRANAK**     After they've laid waste to Thebes. Pharaoh, let me lead an attack on the mercenary camp. I will wipe them from the face of your kingdoms.

**DOCTOR**     You'll be slaughtered inside an hour. Erimem, you must trust me.

**ERIMEM**     You have never failed me, Doctor, but neither has Antranak. Whatever decision I make, good people are going to die.

**PERI**     Trust the Doctor, your Majesty. Please.

**ERIMEM**     Very well. Assemble the troops at the North Gate, Antranak – and no arguments. Have them ready for a hard, quick march to Giza.

**ANTRANAK**     As you wish, Mighty One. I hope you know what you are doing, Doctor.

**DOCTOR**     So do I.

### 37. The desert outside Thebes.

*The mercenaries are in position. FAYUM and HOREMSHEP's chariot clatters to a stop.*

**FAYUM**     Whoa.

**YANIS**      So you failed, Horemshep. I knew you would.

**HOREMSHEP**  I thought you would be pleased, Yanis. Now you will have your battle.

**YANIS**      And this is?

**FAYUM**      I am Fayum.

**YANIS**      I remember you. So, this pup you plan to put on the throne?[55] You should have told me, boy. I wouldn't have whipped you so hard.

**FAYUM**      That is unimportant now. All that matters is taking Thebes.

**HOREMSHEP**  And the Doctor.

**YANIS**      My troops are prepared. Only the fair-haired stranger is to be taken alive.

**HOREMSHEP**  Yes, the Doctor must <u>not</u> be harmed...

**YANIS**      No one touches him – he is mine. Attack now. I want to be knee-deep in Egyptian blood before the hour is out – then I'll bed the brat Pharaoh herself.[56] Before I open her guts to the jackals. <u>Attack</u>! I can taste the blood already.

*Cheers and yells as the troops charge. Chariots sound.*

### 38. Thebes.

*The North Gate. ANTRANAK is reporting to ERIMEM.*

**ANTRANAK**   The troops are prepared, Pharaoh, but the mercenaries are moving on the city... But the men do not want to leave Thebes unguarded.[57]

**ERIMEM**     We go north.

**DOCTOR**     And we'd better get going.

**PERI**       Doctor, wait. Are the troops really abandoning the city? The people are terrified.

**DOCTOR**     Not so much abandoning as making a strategic withdrawal, north, to Giza. I assume you're joining us?

**PERI**       You think I want to be here when those mercenaries come knocking? No thanks. I'm with you.

**DOCTOR**     I thought you'd say that. You'll travel with Antranak.

**PERI**       You've got it all planned.

**DOCTOR**     One tries.

**PERI**       Where will you be?

**DOCTOR**     Well, I'll be with Pharaoh.

**ERIMEM**     I will need the Doctor's counsel a great deal in the coming days.

**DOCTOR**     I think we'd better get moving, don't you?

**ERIMEM**     Antranak, begin the march. Open the gates. Forward!

*Great gates creak open. The chariots and soldiers move off.*

### 39. Desert outside Thebes.

*The soldiers are attacking. Yelling, screaming.*

**YANIS**      Where are they, Horemshep? You told me they would be waiting to die.

**HOREMSHEP**  Their troops are ready. Don't be so eager for battle.

**YANIS**      I live for battle, imbecile, and your Egyptian troops threaten to deprive me of it. We are within sight of their gate and they have yet to fire a single arrow.

**FAYUM**      It could be a trap. The Doctor is a cunning enemy.

**YANIS**      Kishik? Come here, dog!

**KISHIK**      My Lord Yanis, the rest of our men report the same – none of them have seen any soldiers because...

**YANIS**      Where are they...?

**KISHIK**      ...the Egyptian troops are leaving the city. They're marching to Giza.

**HOREMSHEP**      Call off the attack.

**YANIS**      But the city is unguarded. We can take it easily.

**FAYUM**      There is a greater prize than the city.

### 40. The trail to Giza.

*The DOCTOR and ERIMEM's chariot rattles along with others doing the same in the background. A chariot closes noisily. It's ANTRANAK – and he's excited.*

**ANTRANAK**      Pharaoh. Pharaoh.

**ERIMEM**      What is it, Antranak? The mercenaries?

**ANTRANAK**      Our rear scouts report that the mercenaries have ignored Thebes and are following us – with their slower chariots, they are half a day behind us.

**ERIMEM**      Doctor?[58]

**ANTRANAK**      You planned this.[59] You knew that they would follow us and the city would be safe. I misjudged you, Doctor.[60] You are a true warrior.

**DOCTOR**      Maybe you should think about strengthening our rear defences? Our chariots are faster then theirs but they might try a sneak attack. Hit and run, trying to pick off a few men at a time.

**ANTRANAK**      I will see to it now.

*His chariot clatters off.*

**ERIMEM**      Thank you. It's a great relief that Thebes is safe. Your plan worked. Why do you seem so troubled?

**DOCTOR**      Because it confirms what I suspected. They knew what we were doing. It couldn't have been their scouts. They reacted too quickly for that. I'm afraid there's a spy among us.

**ERIMEM**      Who? Tell me and I will have their heart cut out.

**DOCTOR**      I'd rather you didn't. You see, I think their spy is Peri.

**END OF PART THREE**

# PART FOUR

**40 (cont). Trail to Giza.**

**ERIMEM**    It's a great relief that Thebes is safe.[61] Your plan worked. Why do you seem so troubled?

**DOCTOR**    Because it confirms what I suspected. They knew what we were doing. It couldn't have been their scouts. They reacted too quickly for that. I'm afraid there's a spy among us.

**ERIMEM**    Who? Tell me and I will have their heart cut out.

**DOCTOR**    I'd rather you didn't. You see, I think their spy is Peri.

**ERIMEM**    Peri? You must be wrong.

**DOCTOR**    I wish I was, but I don't think so.

**ERIMEM**    Then she must be interrogated.

**DOCTOR**    Before you do anything, I think I should tell you exactly what we're facing.[62] You may find this hard to believe but I promise you that every word is true.

**ERIMEM**    Tell me.

**DOCTOR**    When I went to the mercenary camp I found a stasis box from a prison ship – it's like a cell for special prisoners.

**ERIMEM**    What kind?

**DOCTOR**    In this case, the kind who can affect the minds of others. A creature of pure mental energy. It must have been freed when the prison ship crashed.

**ERIMEM**    How can such a creature exist?

**DOCTOR**    It's like a virus – an infection, reproducing itself as it passes onto another victim. All of them linked telepathically, so that the creature gets the knowledge of everyone it infects as well as control of their bodies. One vast mind with an army of hosts. Initially, the hold will be quite weak and some of the host's personality will stay. The stronger the host mind, the longer it will take to gain control but as time passes, the host will be destroyed to make way for this creature.

**ERIMEM**    What would it want?

**DOCTOR**    The same as every other creature in the galaxy – to survive, to reproduce. Evolution has made it a parasite. It needs the lives of others to carry on living. I wondered how it was passed on – but when I saw the change in Fayum after Horemshep grabbed him I realised it must be by touch.

**ERIMEM**    Who are you to know of these things, Doctor?[63] No, Horemshep asked, <u>what</u> are you? You are not a normal man. You have fought off fatal poison and turned the sky black but I do not believe you are a god any more than I am because I don't believe in any of our gods.

**DOCTOR**    You don't?

**ERIMEM**    I believe in… real things. I have heard of men who study the stars and say that we travel round the sun not it round us. One of these men even claims that the world is round like a ball.

**DOCTOR**    Does he indeed?

**ERIMEM**    There are other men who study plants or animals or rivers, or make extraordinary devices with wood and metals. You are like them but not exactly the same. I can't explain it.

| | |
|---|---|
| **DOCTOR** | I wish I could tell you. |
| **ERIMEM** | Then do. |
| **DOCTOR** | I'm... just a traveller. |
| **ERIMEM** | Then tell me of your travels. That can do no harm. |
| **DOCTOR** | Perhaps one day I shall. For now we have Peri to worry |

about.

**ERIMEM**  Peri. This creature was passed to her by touch.

**DOCTOR**  When Fayum had her hostage. She's strong-willed, but soon they'll know everything she knows. We must make sure she hears nothing of our plans when we make camp tonight.

### 41. Antranak's chariot.
*The chariot is clattering along. PERI groans.*

**ANTRANAK**  Lady Peri, are you ill?

**PERI**  Just a little disoriented for a minute, Antranak. How far are we from Giza?

**ANTRANAK**  We will be there by tomorrow afternoon.

**PERI**  How long till we make camp tonight?

**ANTRANAK**  We will travel until dark and be gone in the morning with the first light.

**PERI**  How big is the garrison at Giza?

**ANTRANAK**  A hundred chariots and around eight hundred men. Lady, why do you ask so many questions?

**PERI**  Just curious. Do you worry that your chariots have a weak spot?

**ANTRANAK**  You have no need to fear an attack, Lady. We are well clear of the mercenaries.

**PERI**  But you must be worried that their chariots have heavier armour. Or do you have a plan for getting round that?[64]

*(NB: NO SCENE 42)*

### 43. The desert behind the advancing Egyptian army.
*YANIS, HOREMSHEP, KISHIK and FAYUM are gathered, listening to PERI's conversation with ANTRANAK.*

**HOREMSHEP**  The girl's mind is opening to us. That idiot Antranak will tell her everything we need to know.

**FAYUM**  She must be wary, Horemshep. If she asks too many questions he will become suspicious.

**YANIS**  Eight hundred men, Fayum? Is that all they can muster? Make it four thousand and they would still be slaughtered within the hour.

**KISHIK**  They will reach Giza half a day before us, my Lords.

**FAYUM**  They will use the time to prepare.

**YANIS**  Let them prepare. They will be trampled into the sand.

**FAYUM**  The Doctor must not be harmed.

**YANIS**  I will cut a channel through their troops to him myself.

**FAYUM**  What is he?

**HOREMSHEP**  Her mind is not yet completely clear to us. She is not sure but... they travel in space. If he has a craft we will be free to colonise other worlds again.

**YANIS**　　　And to conquer them.[65]

## 44. The desert. Night.
*Sounds of the camp at rest. Fires crackle and troops move around in the background. Food is being eaten and the troops talk and laugh.*

**ANTRANAK**　　Set sentries round the camp at ten paces apart and stay alert. There you are, Doctor. Do army rations agree with you?
**DOCTOR**　　I've had worse, Antranak. Not hungry, Peri?
**PERI**　　What? No.
**ERIMEM**　　You should try to eat something. Tomorrow will be another long march. And then there will be the battle.
**DOCTOR**　　(*Cutting in*) Here, try this.
**PERI**　　I said I'm not hungry.
**DOCTOR**　　I insist. Doctor's orders. It'll do you the world of good. You've been looking rather peaky. We'll discuss the battle after we've eaten.
**PERI**　　(*Chewing*) What is this?
**DOCTOR**　　Actually, it's probably best that you don't ask.
**PERI**　　(*Becoming woozy*) It tastes... it's...
*Sound of PERI hitting the deck.*
**DOCTOR**　　It's all right, Peri. The heat and travel have just got to you. Peri? Out like a light.
**ANTRANAK**　　I will help you carry her to her tent.
**ERIMEM**　　No, don't touch her. What did you put in her food, Doctor?
**DOCTOR**　　A little something I got from your physician. She'll be as right as ninepence in the morning. Well, as close as she can be in the situation.[66] I'm going to get some blankets – we mustn't move her. Would you mind explaining things to Antranak?
**ANTRANAK**　　Let me help...
**ERIMEM**　　No. Sit with me, old friend. I have a strange tale to tell you.
*The DOCTOR's footsteps head away, leaving ERIMEM's voice fading.*
**ERIMEM**　　We face a strange enemy, Antranak, like none even you have seen. A strange creature...

## 45. The desert, back a little way.
*The mercenaries are still following, but a chariot clatters to a stop. Another chariot rattles up and stops quickly.*

**YANIS**　　Horemshep, why are we stopping? If we carry on through the night we will be close enough to attack by dawn.
**HOREMSHEP**　　And the men will be too tired for battle, Yanis. We will make camp here for the night, Fayum. Pass on the order.
**FAYUM**　　As you wish, Horemshep
**YANIS**　　They would cross a river of burning oil if I ordered them.
**FAYUM**　　And finish as dead as they would if we marched through the night. We need living hosts not corpses.
**YANIS**　　Cowards. You are not fit for the prize ahead of us. Enjoy your sleep. I'll set sentries for the night. Kishik? To me, you dog, to me!
*His chariot rattles off.*
**FAYUM**　　Yanis is dangerous, Horemshep. His will is strong. Control over his mind is limited. We should kill him.

**HOREMSHEP**  In time he will be with us fully. Until then we must curb his violent ideas.

**FAYUM**  And if he continues to resist our will?

**HOREMSHEP**  Then we will remove our presence from his mind before his body is killed.

### 46. Desert. Next morning.

*The chariot clattering through the desert.*

**ERIMEM**  We should be within sight of the tombs of my ancestors any time now.

**DOCTOR**  You're remarkably bright today, Majesty, especially given how late you had me tell stories last night.

**ERIMEM**  Your stories cheer me, Doctor. They give me some hope that our cause is not so desperate. After all, we do not face, what was it, Daleks? And Cybermen? And –

**DOCTOR**  Yes, well, I think I may have said a little more than I intended. Ah. There. The pyramids. No matter how often I see them they never fail to impress.

**ERIMEM**  Can you believe they are hundreds of years old?

**DOCTOR**  They're built to last – the Sphinx even more so.

**ERIMEM**  I have often wondered whose face is on the Sphinx. My teacher believed it was Cheops.

**DOCTOR**  Definitely not Cheops – although I have heard some bizarre stories about him.

**ERIMEM**  Would it surprise you to know that I am terrified, Doctor?

**DOCTOR**  I'd be surprised if you weren't.

**ERIMEM**  Doctor, last night, you told stories of many times and places...[67] Do you really know all these things? Do you know what will happen in the battle today? (*No answer*) What will happen to me?

**DOCTOR**  Even if I knew exactly what happens today, I couldn't change it. Whoa there.[68]

*The chariot stops. They both get off, jumping onto the sand.*

**DOCTOR**  Down you come.[69]

**ERIMEM**  I will die today.

**DOCTOR**  I didn't say that.

**ERIMEM**  Your face did.

**DOCTOR**  I don't know that you'll die.

**ERIMEM**  But I will never be Pharaoh. You told Peri that you knew the names of every Pharaoh. I am not one of them.

**DOCTOR**  I'm sorry.

**ERIMEM**  It's strange – I'm not surprised. I have always been sure that I would never be Pharaoh. Perhaps I do have a destiny after all. But a different one than I expected.

*Another chariot pulls up.*

**ANTRANAK**  Majesty, your troops at Giza wait to greet you.

**DOCTOR**  So, Peri, how are you feeling now?

**PERI**  Fine now. Are those barriers the best you have?

**DOCTOR**  I'm sorry?

**PERI**  I mean, those wooden barriers won't hold off their heavy chariots for long.

**ERIMEM** They will have to. They are the best we can manage in such a short time.

**ANTRANAK** Majesty, the sentries have spotted the enemy massing just over the high dunes to the south.

**DOCTOR** Five miles or so. Resting before the attack, I imagine, which should give me just enough time.

**PERI** Time for what?

**DOCTOR** A quick stroll under the Sphinx.

**ANTRANAK** Impossible. There's no way into the Sphinx.

**DOCTOR** Actually, there is. There's a well four hundred metres directly behind the Sphinx.[70]

**ANTRANAK** Useless thing.[71] Dry as dust. A few of the locals throw scraps in it. They believe it's home to sacred cats who drank all the water in it.

**DOCTOR** I don't know about the cats but there's no water there because it's not a well at all. It's a sink-shaft used by the people who built the Sphinx. It leads under the Sphinx and branches off under the pyramids as well, come to that, but it's the Sphinx I'm interested in.[72]

**PERI** Why? What's under there?

**DOCTOR** Well, contrary to the common belief of your time, the Sphinx is much older than the pyramids, dating back to around ten thousand BC.

**ERIMEM** BC?

**DOCTOR** Another time. Anyway, the Sphinx was built by refugees from Atlantis, who placed all their knowledge in a chamber between the paws of the Sphinx – the Hall of Records.[73] We'll find what we need to beat the mercenaries and their infection down there.

**ANTRANAK** How can you know all this? These tombs are at least a thousand summers old.

**DOCTOR** Well, I am a little older than I look. Right, I'd better get started. Peri, you stay by the river. If things go badly, there'll be boats heading for safety.

**PERI** I'd rather stick with you.

**DOCTOR** Well, if you're sure...

**ERIMEM** Good luck, Doctor.

**DOCTOR** And to you. To all of us.

## 47. The desert outside Giza.

**FAYUM** If there is a weapon, he cannot be allowed to find it.

**YANIS** How can he be so old?

**HOREMSHEP** He is an alien and a time traveller.

**FAYUM** The girl has heard of Atlantis. He must be stopped. We must attack immediately.

**HOREMSHEP** The troops are still weary after the long march.[74]

**YANIS** They fear me more than death. (*Bellowing*) You've rested long enough, pigs. Rouse yourselves. We attack now!

## 48. Giza.
*ANTRANAK and ERIMEM are ready and waiting.*

**ANTRANAK** They are beginning their attack.

**ERIMEM**     Our troops know what they must do?

**ANTRANAK**     Avoid hand to hand contact with the enemy at all cost.[75] This is a dishonourable enemy. One that hides out of sight within others.

**ERIMEM**     But it is still an enemy to be defeated. If we all play our part.

**ANTRANAK**     Pharaoh, what are you doing?

*Sound of ERIMEM putting on a heavy crown – more a helmet, really.*

**ERIMEM**     I did not bring the battle crown for show and I cannot ask my men to go into battle while I watch safely from a distance. I am proficient with the bow and battle spear. You were a good teacher. I will lead the attack.

**ANTRANAK**     Your father would be proud of you.

**ERIMEM**     Only if we win the day.

**ANTRANAK**     Pharaoh? Their chariots!

**ERIMEM**     Do it.

**ANTRANAK**     Archers, ready... Ready... Fire!

*The sound of the chariots is getting closer then volley of arrows whistles away.*

### 49. The desert.

*YANIS, FAYUM and HOREMSHEP are observing the battle.*

**FAYUM**     Their archers are cutting our chariots down like cattle, Horemshep, while ours hit only those barricades.

**HOREMSHEP**     The chariots are almost too close for the archers now – and we still have enough to over-run them.[76]

**YANIS**     Kishik's infantry will break through their lines easily. And then the Doctor will be ours. Infantry, forward!

### 50. The sink shaft.

*PERI and the DOCTOR are climbing down ropes. Their voices echo in the shaft.*

**DOCTOR**     You know, this shaft is deeper than I remember. How are you doing with the ropes? (*No answer*) Peri? I asked...

**PERI**     Fine, Doctor. How much further?

**DOCTOR**     These torches don't give much light, but it shouldn't be far now. Ah. There we are. Careful. Another ten feet... five... there.

*He drops to the ground. PERI lands next to him. We hear meowing cats. One is louder than the rest.*

**DOCTOR**     Well, there are definitely cats here. Hello, puss.

*The cat spits and hisses, scratching the DOCTOR.*

**DOCTOR**     Ow. Not house-trained obviously.

**PERI**     This way?

**DOCTOR**     When it branches, we go straight on. Keep your torch up – there's no way of knowing what sort of damage time has done down here. These tunnels are millennia old. The slightest disturbance could cause a cave-in.

### 51. Giza.

*The chariots are much closer. Arrows still whistle out from the archers.*

**ANTRANAK**   Their chariots are too close for the archers to be of any effect now, Pharaoh.
**ERIMEM**   Have the archers concentrate on their foot-soldiers. The chariots are our task now.
**ANTRANAK**   Archers, target their infantry. Chariot squadrons, attack in formation now!
*The Egyptian chariots speed off to meet the attacking mercenary chariots.*

## 52. The desert.
*YANIS and his troops are charging forward. His chariot clatters forward.*

**KISHIK**   My Lord, we are winning
**YANIS**   Of course, Kishik. These Theben dogs are weak!
**KISHIK**   Forward. Cut them to pieces! Slice through – uhh
*Kishik is hit by an arrow*
**YANIS**   Kishik![77] You will be avenged! Kill them all, kill them all!
**FAYUM**   No, Yanis! We need them alive. Yanis!

## 53. The battle at Giza.
*The battle is joined. It's loud and violent. Swords clash, chariots clatter across the battlefield. Soldiers yell and scream as they are cut down. ANTRANAK and ERIMEM hold a yelled conversation as they continue fighting – thrusting with sword and spear.*

**ANTRANAK**   They are pushing us back, Majesty.
**ERIMEM**   Hold the line. The Doctor needs more time.
**ANTRANAK**   We need the foot-soldiers.[78] They could become infected but we'll be overrun in minutes without them.
**ERIMEM**   Very well. Bring forward the infantry.
**ANTRANAK**   Majesty. INFANTRY FORWARD!
**ERIMEM**   Let's hope we give the Doctor the time he needs.
*Loud yells and cheers as the infantry run into battle. Swords clash and men scream.*
**FAYUM**   Over there. It's Erimem.[79]
**YANIS**   She fights like a demon.
**HOREMSHEP**   The Doctor. Concentrate on finding the Doctor!
*YANIS roars disapproval. The battle continues. Loud and bloody.*
**ANTRANAK**   Majesty – Fayum and Yanis! They're heading for the shaft. But where's Horemshep?
**ERIMEM**   No matter, we must stop them. Go back for the infantry, Antranak! The Doctor needs my help. Send soldiers down after me when they get here.
*Sound of an arrow hitting ANTRANAK. He falls to the desert, with a cough.*
**ANTRANAK**   Majes-
**HOREMSHEP**   I fear he will be passing no messages for you.
**ERIMEM**   Horemshep, I should have expected a coward like you to attack from behind.
**YANIS**   I'll open her for the buzzards.
**HOREMSHEP**   No, Yanis. The Doctor values her life. But if she attempts to escape break her arm. Erimem, you planned to join the Doctor below. We will all go down together.

## 54. The tunnel under the Sphinx.

*Footsteps in sand and the occasional meow of a cat.*

**DOCTOR**      These tunnels stretch further than I remember. Maybe I'm just not as young as I was. Or the cats have been busy digging.

**PERI**      What are the inscriptions on the pillars?

**DOCTOR**      The potted history of Atlantis and prayers that the people and knowledge of Atlantis will be remembered.[80]

**PERI**      What wisdom? Is it the weapon you're looking for?

**DOCTOR**      There are lots of different kinds of weapons, Peri. Not far now. Ah. There we are.

**PERI**      A blank wall?

**DOCTOR**      Only to those who don't know what they're looking for. It's the door to the hall of records. Hold the torch steady.

**PERI**      Open it.

**DOCTOR**      All in good time. This door hasn't been opened in eight and a half thousand years. It's not the sort of thing you want to rush.

**HOREMSHEP**      Open it, Doctor.

**DOCTOR**      Horemshep. I was wondering when you would turn up. And you too, Fayum.

**HOREMSHEP**      Open the door. We must have the weapon.

**DOCTOR**      Hand over a weapon to a grubby little mind parasite like you – and a criminal to boot? I don't think so, somehow.

**YANIS**      Open the door or I will snap the girl's neck.

**DOCTOR**      Erimem?

**ERIMEM**      *(Choking)* Don't give it to them.

**YANIS**      QUIET!

*ERIMEM gurgles as she's being throttled.*

**DOCTOR**      All right. All right. Just don't hurt her.

**FAYUM**      Is this a trap? Tell me.

**DOCTOR**      Suddenly I don't feel all that chatty, Fayum.

**HOREMSHEP**      Then we will take the knowledge from your mind. If you resist, Yanis will snap Erimem's neck.

**ERIMEM**      Doctor?

**DOCTOR**      Quiet, Erimem. All right, Horemshep. I won't fight you. Just don't harm her.

**HOREMSHEP**      Let us into your mind, Doctor. When you are part of us, we will spread across eternity.

**FAYUM**      His mind is vast.

**DOCTOR**      Thank you.

**YANIS**      We must have his mind.

**DOCTOR**      Actually, I'm using it at the moment.

**HOREMSHEP**      With your knowledge we can spread across the planet. We can have all planets, all times. We can be supreme.

**DOCTOR**      None of you are strong enough to take my mind from me.

**HOREMSHEP**      No single one of us it is true – but for all we are many, we are one mind.

*Sort of swirling sound effect.*

**FAYUM**      And we will come together to take your mind.

**ERIMEM**      Doctor, what's happening?

*More swirling, mixed with demonic screams and wails and the chattering*

*of thousands of voices. FAYUM groans and collapses. YANIS yells and follows suit.*
**DOCTOR**     All the different fragments of the parasite are leaving the other hosts – human, insect, everything – and coming together in Horemshep so that he can take my mind.
**HOREMSHEP**     Nearly, Doctor, but I am not the host.
*With a loud groan, HOREMSHEP collapses.*
**PERI**     (*Voice distorted*) I am.
**DOCTOR**     Peri? No! This isn't how it's supposed to happen.
**PERI**     You will not fight your friend. You care too much for life. That is why you will lose.
**DOCTOR**     Let her go.
**PERI**     Do you threaten me? This one believes that you would have a plan of some kind.
**DOCTOR**     So Peri's thoughts are still in there.
**PERI**     Do you have a plan?
**DOCTOR**     An offer. Now that you've left the minds of all the people you've affected on Earth, I can take you off the planet.[81]
**PERI**     Transport? To where?
**DOCTOR**     There are any number of uninhabited worlds...
**PERI**     No. We need... I need new bodies so that I can grow.
**DOCTOR**     Worlds with non-sentient life, then.
**PERI**     How could I exist inside a blank mind? That would be worse than death.
**DOCTOR**     Would it be any worse than you've done to people here? Taking their bodies and wiping their minds? Leave Earth. Please.
**PERI**     No. (*Almost seductive*) Give yourself to us, Doctor. You can become greater than even you can imagine.
**DOCTOR**     I'm afraid you leave me no choice.
*Sound of the DOCTOR fumbling with a piece of equipment.*
**ERIMEM**     The talisman you used to block out the sun.
**DOCTOR**     The telepathic inhibitor. When I activate this, it'll disorient the creature in Peri's mind until I deliver it to the appropriate authorities.
**PERI**     (*More like PERI*) Doctor, don't. Please?
**DOCTOR**     No, you can't trick me that easily. Goodnight.
*Sound of the circuits being activated. PERI gasps and yells – but doesn't collapse.*
**PERI**     I am still here.
**DOCTOR**     Full power.
**PERI**     I am too strong for the machine. You cannot defeat me. You have lost, Doctor.
**DOCTOR**     Erimem, how are Fayum and Horemshep?
**ERIMEM**     Fayum's in a daze but Horemshep has fled.
**DOCTOR**     This isn't working quite as I planned.
**PERI**     You are beaten, Doctor. Accept the fact. I have the knowledge of thousands to call upon. Even you can't defeat that.
**DOCTOR**     Can't I? Thousands, you say? I wonder... Who are you?
**PERI**     I have no name. I am...
**DOCTOR**     I'm not asking you. I'm asking the memories you've taken. Who are you? Peri, I know you're still in there. Who are you, Peri?
**PERI**     Peri Brown.

55

**DOCTOR**          Who else? You have the memories of thousands. Who else are you?

**PERI**            *(Voice sounding different – a different personality)* Ebren.

**DOCTOR**          Who are you, Ebren? What do you do?

**PERI**            I'm a farmer. I raise sheep. I...

**DOCTOR**          Who else is there? Tell me who you are. All of you.

**PERI**            I am Ebren.. I am... *(Her voice changes as different personalities are brought to the fore)* ...Shemek.

**ERIMEM**          He was my teacher.

**DOCTOR**          Ask him a question. Anything. Quickly.

**ERIMEM**          Where did you give me my lessons?

**PERI/SHEMEK**     In the gardens, of course. You liked the smell of the flowers. And you could see what was happening in the palace. You always were one for gossip and the like.

**DOCTOR**          *(Talking over PERI/SHEMEK)* Another question, Erimem.

**ERIMEM**          What was my favourite lesson? Do you remember?

**PERI/SHEMEK**     Of course I do. You always wanted to hear more of the history of our people. You made me tell stories to you long after I should have gone home.

**DOCTOR**          *(Interrupting)* Ebren, who told you stories? Did your parents tell you stories when you were a child?

**PERI**            *(Voice switches to PERI/EBREN voice)* My father until he died, and then my mother. I told stories to my son...

**DOCTOR**          *(Over PERI/EBREN)* Ask Shemek more questions, Erimem. As many as you can think of. As varied as you can.

**ERIMEM**          Shemek, do you remember when I fell from a tree?

**PERI/SHEMEK**     *(Switching voice again)* I thought you had died, little one.

**DOCTOR**          Ebren, where do you live?

**PERI/EBREN**      On the edge of the deserts...

**ERIMEM**          Shemek, where do you live?

**PERI/SHEMEK**     In the...

**DOCTOR**          Ebren, who lives with you?

**PERI/EBREN**      My son and...

**ERIMEM**          What was your wife's name, Shemek?

**PERI/SHEMEK**     Nefral, she died...

**DOCTOR**          Peri, where do you live? Who lives there with you?

**ERIMEM**          Who are your sons, Shemek?

**DOCTOR**          Where did you go to school, Peri? Where did we meet? Ebren, tell me the names of your family.

**PERI**            *(Struggling with varied personalities all at once.)* Four sons... Shintu... Lanzarotte, I was there on vacation with my...

**ERIMEM**          What's happening to her?

**DOCTOR**          She's trying to deal with three sets of memories at once. The human mind wasn't designed to do that. Keep asking them questions.

**ERIMEM**          What city do you live in, Peri? Tell me about it. Tell me about the people. How do they choose their leaders?

**PERI**            By election every...

**DOCTOR**          Ebren, you were trying to tell me about your sons. And you, Shemek.

**PERI**            *(Struggling between personas)* I have four sons... no, three and two daughters.

56

**DOCTOR**     Which is it? Are you Ebren or Shemek? Peri, keep talking about the elections.
**PERI**     I have... we have votes every...
**DOCTOR**     Your sons! How many.
**ERIMEM**     The election, Peri.
**PERI**     There's too much.
**DOCTOR**     She can't cope with it. Time to finish it. Who else can hear me? How many of Yanis' mercenaries are there? How many more are you? Answer me. Who are you? Tell me. Tell me your names. All of you.
**PERI**     (*Voice changing constantly – becoming frantic*) Amerit, Tushka, Shemek, I'm Shemek, I'm... Corfret, no, Merenhapsut, Ebren. Peri. I'm Peri. I'm Peri Brown. I'm... Silliphar, Moeshba, Fullin, I'm...
**DOCTOR**     Who are you? Who are you?
**ERIMEM**     Where do you come from? Where do you live?
**DOCTOR**     What's your name? Who was your mother?
**ERIMEM**     What did you eat last?
**DOCTOR**     Where were you born?
**ERIMEM**     Who do you love?
**DOCTOR**     WHO ARE YOU?
**PERI**     (*Losing control – too many personalities*) I'm... I am... my children... I... I can't... too many voices. Too much.[82] I can't... Too many. Too much... TOO MUCH!
*With a loud, pained yell, PERI collapses and hits the ground.*
**ERIMEM**     Is she dead?
**DOCTOR**     Unconscious. Her mind couldn't cope with a thousand sets of memories and shut down. No, don't touch her. Keep back. At least until the inhibitor's switched on.
*Sound of telepathic inhibitor being switched on.*
**DOCTOR**     There. That should...
*A cat meows.*
**DOCTOR**     No! Shoo. Get away from her.
*The cat spits and hisses.*
**DOCTOR**     Keep away from the cat. The entity's passed a fragment of itself into that. Come here, you little brute. Ah. Missed. I need something to catch him in.
**ERIMEM**     My cloak.
*Cloak is removed and thrown to the DOCTOR. The cat spits and hisses.*
**DOCTOR**     Got it. Come on, come on. Gently. Gently.
*Cloak is thrown. The cat sounds even more agitated.*
**DOCTOR**     Got you. Calm down. I'm not going to hurt you. Just tie the inhibitor round your neck and... There. That's better, isn't it?
*The cat spits and slashes the DOCTOR – it just plain doesn't like him.*
**DOCTOR**     Ow.
**ERIMEM**     Give him to me, Doctor. You tend to Peri.
**DOCTOR**     Be careful. He's...
*The cat purrs contentedly.*
**ERIMEM**     Yes?
**DOCTOR**     Never mind. Peri? Peri? Out cold. Good. I think we should get ou – oof
*He is knocked aside*
**YANIS**     What has happened? My head is...
**DOCTOR**     The least of your worries, Yanis. Go now.

**YANIS**      You have done this to me. I will cut you apart and let the cats feed.
**DOCTOR**      Yanis, we don't have time for this.
**YANIS**      You still have an enemy here, Doctor.
**FAYUM**      And you have one here, Yanis.[83]
**YANIS**      Quiet, boy. You'll die once I've dealt with these. I can still have Egypt – when your Pharaoh is dead.
**FAYUM**      You will not harm her.
*Yanis roars, draws his sword and swings it. It hits another sword.*
**YANIS**      What? You, boy? Fighting me? I should have killed you back in my camp.
**FAYUM**      You are welcome to try again.
*Swords clash.*
**ERIMEM**      Fayum is a strong fighter, Doctor, but he can't hold Yanis for long. We must finish this quickly.
**DOCTOR**      Erimem, go. Take the cat and go. I'll bring Peri as soon as I can. Just go.
**YANIS**      I'll catch you, girl. You won't get far.
**FAYUM**      Further than you.
*Sound of a sword being stuck into YANIS – he roars.*
**YANIS**      You? You've...
*YANIS lurches hitting a pillar. The roof cracks loudly and ominously.*
**FAYUM**      The roof.
**DOCTOR**      It's millennia old. There's no telling the damage he did when he stumbled against the pillar.
**FAYUM**      I should finish him.
*Another crack.*
**DOCTOR**      There's no time for that. Go. Go.
*FAYUM's footsteps head along the passage. The DOCTOR hefts PERI and follows.*
**DOCTOR**      Up. Come on, Peri.
**YANIS**      (*Gasping in pain*) Run, pigs. I'll find you. I'll track you down and slaughter y–
*Major crack in the roof. YANIS yells as the roof collapses on him.*

**55. Giza.**
*ERIMEM and FAYUM are above as the DOCTOR climbs out of the sink-hole with PERI.*

**ERIMEM**      Doctor, when the ground shook I feared the worst. It even cracked the face from the great Sphinx... I am pleased you are both alive.
**DOCTOR**      We'll be right as rain as soon as I've had the TARDIS purge the creature from Peri and your cat.[84] What about the battle?
**ERIMEM**      The mercenaries have fled. But there has been enough death today. Let them go.
**ANTRANAK**      Even this one, Majesty? I saw Horemshep climb out of the well. I persuaded him to stay.
**ERIMEM**      Antranak! Oh Antranak, I feared you were dead.[85]
**ANTRANAK**      Merely a flesh wound, your majesty. It takes more than that to keep me down when I have a Pharaoh to protect.
**HOREMSHEP**      Majesty... Pharaoh, it wasn't my doing. The demon creature made me do this.

| | |
|---|---|
| **ERIMEM** | Send him to Thebes in chains. Let him answer to a court.[86] |
| **FAYUM** | And me? |
| **DOCTOR** | You were hardly responsible for your actions.[87] And you did save us from Yanis. |
| **ERIMEM** | You committed no crime, Fayum. |
| **ANTRANAK** | You fought Yanis? And won? |
| **FAYUM** | I'm more surprised than you are, Antranak. |
| **ANTRANAK** | I doubt that. I'll have to be careful when I argue with you in future.[88] |
| **ERIMEM** | There was no weapon below, Doctor, was there? It was just a lure to isolate the creature in one body. |
| **DOCTOR** | That would be telling. |
| **ANTRANAK** | What are your orders, Pharaoh? |
| **ERIMEM** | Doctor? |
| **DOCTOR** | Home, I think. |
| **ERIMEM** | Home. |

## 56. Thebes.

*ERIMEM's palace. Much cheering and victorious yelling. A triumphant fanfare outside. The TARDIS door opens, the DOCTOR and PERI emerge.*

| | |
|---|---|
| **PERI** | Honestly, Doctor, I'm fine. Don't fuss. You've been asking how I feel every hour on the hour since we got back to Thebes. |
| **DOCTOR** | Well, you had quite an ordeal. |
| **PERI** | And I'm fine now. |
| **ERIMEM** | I am pleased to hear it. |
| **DOCTOR** | It sounds like the people are waiting for you, Pharaoh. They're eager to celebrate your victory. |
| **PERI** | Look at the size of that crowd. |
| **ERIMEM** | I don't feel like celebrating a battle that cost untold lives. |
| **PERI** | At least now you can be Pharaoh. |
| **ERIMEM** | No. I can never be Pharaoh, can I, Doctor? |
| **PERI** | Why not? Don't tell me – history. So Erimem went through all this for nothing? |
| **DOCTOR** | You could stay and be Pharaoh. I won't stop you. |
| **ERIMEM** | I have done my duty. Egypt is safe and Fayum will make an excellent Pharaoh – though he doesn't know it yet. |
| **PERI** | But he's not really your brother! |
| **ERIMEM** | So? He will still make a better Pharaoh than I. |
| **PERI** | Where will you go? |
| **ERIMEM** | North, to one of the islands. Or perhaps Greece. No one will know me there. I can study and learn. |
| **DOCTOR** | It may not be that easy. Your face is already on coins and works of art. |
| **PERI** | We could take you somewhere. Couldn't we, Doctor? |
| **DOCTOR** | Absolutely not. It's out of the question. |
| **PERI** | Why? You said yourself, there's nowhere civilised here she can go without being recognised. |
| **DOCTOR** | Yes, but that's hardly a good enough reason for me to take her off through time and space. |
| **ERIMEM** | What will I do if I stay here? Let me come with you. Please. |

| | |
|---|---|
| **DOCTOR** | If I do, you can never come back. |
| **ERIMEM** | There is nothing to keep me here now. |
| **DOCTOR** | Oh, all right. You want to learn you say? |
| **ERIMEM** | Yes. |
| **DOCTOR** | I suppose there are a few university chancellors around |

the galaxy who owe me favours. I'm sure we'll find you somewhere acceptable.

| | |
|---|---|
| **PERI** | You'll probably wind up teaching Egyptian history. |
| **ERIMEM** | It will be impossible to get through these crowds before |

nightfall.

| | |
|---|---|
| **DOCTOR** | Oh, I think we'll manage. In here. |
| **ERIMEM** | You plan to carry me out in this blue box of yours? |
| **DOCTOR** | Something like that. In you go. |
| **ERIMEM** | Very well. Wait, I can't go without my pet. . |

*The cat purrs. Then hisses at the DOCTOR.*

| | |
|---|---|
| **DOCTOR** | If you must.[89] |
| **ERIMEM** | I... I don't believe it. |
| **PERI** | Just don't believe that the Doctor can really control this |

thing.

| | |
|---|---|
| **DOCTOR** | Thank you, Peri. I'll have you know that the TARDIS and |

I are in perfect harmony. Most of the time.

| | |
|---|---|
| **PERI** | At least I got to know whose face is on the Sphinx. |
| **DOCTOR** | I thought the cave-in damaged the face. |
| **ERIMEM** | It did. My sculptors are busy repairing the damage. |

Fayum and the council thought that my face should go on the great Sphinx but I didn't want that. Instead Peri gave them very exact images of a king to work from.

| | |
|---|---|
| **PERI** | The King. |
| **DOCTOR** | Peri, what have you done? |
| **PERI** | It won't change anything. Napoleon's troops will still use |

the face for target practice in three thousand years' time, so nobody will know whose face it was. Besides, the Sphinx is close to Memphis – and there's only one king from Memphis.

| | |
|---|---|
| **DOCTOR** | Tell me you didn't. |
| **PERI** | (*Very Elvis*) Uh-huh-huh. |
| **ERIMEM** | Elvis is a very strange name for a king. |

*Doors close and his voice is cut off. The chamber doors burst open*

| | |
|---|---|
| **ANTRANAK** | Pharaoh. We are ready to – |
| **FAYUM** | (*Breathless and excited*) Pharaoh, the people are... |

Pharaoh? Pharaoh?

*The TARDIS dematerialisation noise.[90]*

| | |
|---|---|
| **ANTRANAK** | Pharaoh? Erimem? |
| **FAYUM** | She's gone, Antranak. |
| **ANTRANAK** | She truly was a god, Fayum. |
| **FAYUM** | Oh. Now what? |

**ENDS**

# NOTES

## PART ONE

**1.** At the end of the scene, HOREMSHEP laughs.
**2.** Line changed to: 'How can the Console Room be **in** here.'
**3.** The sniff comes *after*, 'I'd say Earth.'
**4.** Line changed to: 'Though I can't say the same for **that** chap I borrowed this chariot from.'
**5.** Line changed to: 'She's **thinks** she'll be safe there.'
**6.** Line changed to: 'You are the spineless pig who let **that** whelp of a girl escape?'
**7.** Line changed to: 'Tell me about **that** man.'
**8.** Line changed to: 'What has happened **now is** that unbedded whelp who calls herself Pharaoh knows that we are here and she knows that we will attack sooner rather than later. I think I should **have** slit you open and let the dogs feed.'
**9.** There is an added, '**Erm**,' at the beginning of the line.
**10.** Line changed to: 'Just ignore **it** if it bothers you.'
**11.** Line changed to: 'He's **the** chief of the council of priests.'
**12.** Line changed to: 'You may find some of their activities **unusual** but remember, you're seeing them from a 20th century perspective.' *Gary Russell: 'It's only a little change but we thought on the day, Nicola Bryant especially, that as an educated modern girl from Baltimore Peri was unlikely to actually be "offended" – it seemed too strong a reaction to a couple of pairs of breasts! Howard's educational jaunts around the globe with his stepdaughter in tow would have opened her mind somewhat, we decided.'*
**13.** Line changed to: 'Bring boar for my **guests**.'
**14.** Line changed to: 'Just push it **around** your plate.'

## PART TWO

**15.** Line changed to: 'And be gentle with **the Doctor**.'
**16.** Line changed to: 'I'm not privy to the **thoughts** of killers.'
**17.** Line changed to: 'Then you must discover what he meant by **the** true Pharaoh.'
**18.** Line changed to: '**This** last year has seen great unrest and turmoil in Egypt.'
**19.** Line changed to: '**Now**, if you'll excuse me.'
**20.** Line changed to: 'He is unconscious **now**, so at least he will feel no pain.'
**21.** Line changed to: 'I must attend an emergency council meeting soon but I have called for a more experienced healer to **tend** him while I am gone. But there is something else that seems odd. I **would swear I could** make out the beating of two hearts in his chest.'
**22.** Deleted dialogue: '~~The enemy charioteer we found in the desert~~

~~still refuses to speak~~.' Also cut were the first two words of the next line. *Gary Russell: 'We cut this as Kishik of course is never found by Erimem's people. He goes back to Yanis, tail between this legs! On a casting note, apart from Caroline Morris, Jonathan Owen who plays Antranak was the only actor on this story I'd not worked with before, although I was familiar with his work! He won't thank me for saying this, but as a fan of terrible BBC early-Eighties soap* Triangle, *I remembered his regular stint as Peter the Purser. He is a mate of Maggie Stables and it was she who recommended him to me. He is one of a number of actors we've employed who have blown us away by the fact that the voice you hear as their character – in this case obviously Antranak – bears no resemblance to their real voice. Many good actors can change their voice for a few lines but to change it and keep it constant for two days, dropping into it at a moment's notice, especially recording, as we do, woefully out of order, takes skill and concentration. I have no doubt Jonathan will crop up in something of mine again one day.'*

**23.** Line changed to: 'All **of** those you would expect to sit in Horemshep's shadow, hoping for his approval.'

**24.** Deleted dialogue: '~~As you did? I would bet my life that you did~~.'

**25.** Line changed to: 'They will have asked **certain** questions among themselves concerning Erimem's claim.'

**26.** Line changed to: '**And** I'll try not to let it happen again.'

**27.** This switch to Scene 18 began with this line, so it is therefore distorted.

**28.** This line was said under the preceding one.

**29.** The switch to Scene 19 is here, so this line is not distorted.

**30.** Line changed to: 'One of the palace women was found dead a few hours ago **by her own hand**.' *Gary Russell: 'We changed this because we thought it was essential straight away to suggest that Varela committed suicide, otherwise it might have been a red herring, an additional layer of intrigue into a plot already overflowing with them.'*

**31.** Line changed to: 'My Pharoah may be walking into danger to help you enter this **palace**.'

**32.** Line changed to: 'If you had done your job properly, we wouldn't have to **be going** in here.'

**33.** Line changed to: 'I'd bet my last buck those are the assassin's **footprints** from when he came in.'

**34.** Line changed to: 'Well okay, maybe that's a bad **example**.'

**35.** Line changed to: 'Now my only living relation is my mother but ~~now~~ she thinks I am a god and will not look me in the face.' *Gary Russell: 'It's a tiny change, but the removal of the word "now" changes heaps about the culture. The fact is, Erimem's mother would have thought she was a god for quite a while, whereas the "now" made it sound as if it were as a result of last night's party, or Varela's death. It was during the recording of this scene that I lent over to writer Iain McLaughlin and commented on how good I thought Caroline was. He agreed. And at that moment I asked if we could keep the character as a companion. I suppose it had been at the back of my mind when reading the script but I'd not seriously considered it. Shortly after, I discussed it with Jason Haigh-Ellery and he'd pondered the same thing. As he'd introduced me to Caroline in the* *first place, I think he was doubly pleased. We both were – I'd got a top actress and a top character* and *I'd made the boss happy!'*

**36.** The word **'hey'** is said twice.

**37.** Added dialogue – SLAVE: **'My lord.'**

**38.** Line changed to: 'My **mum** could have a field day here.'

**39.** Line changed to: 'For what it's worth, you may just have invented one of the most important political **concepts** ever – **working the people**.' *Gary Russell: 'We asked Nicola (or maybe she volunteered) to go and phone her hubby, Derek, an American, to find out if "walkabout" was a term he'd heard or would expect to hear in the States. "No," came the reply – and he'd suggested "working the people". I thought it sounded more like something those topless girls back in Part One's party might do, but then, I would.'*

**40.** Line changed to: 'When **I last** heard the Doctor's condition had not changed.'

## PART THREE

**41.** Deleted dialogue: '~~Doctor?~~'

**42.** The cliffhanger ending to Part One was extended until the end of Scene 26 (see page 33). *Gary Russell: 'This was the first* Doctor Who *audio that David Darlington worked on and I enjoy doing post-production with him. He lives 15 minutes away which means unlike, say Alistair Lock or Jim Mortimore or the ERS boys, it doesn't take three hours just to get to their workplaces! This change of placement for the episode ending was his idea, and a good one.'*

**43.** Line changed to: 'Now we shall see **their plan**.'

**44.** Line changed to: **'Here!** Who are you?'

**45.** Line changed to: 'From all **the** corners of the world.'

**46.** Line changed to: **'But** you should fear what you found in that stasis box through there.'

**47.** Line changed to: 'I shall take great pleasure in killing you **personally**.'

**48.** Line changed to: 'I had **rather a** long nap last night.'

**49.** Line changed to: 'I **can** make out three, no, four chariots following us.'

**50.** Line changed to: 'Best night's sleep I've had **for** centuries.'

**51.** Line changed to: **'No,** you're wrong.'

**52.** Line changed to: 'Murder Fayum and take the throne **for** yourself with the help of the mercenaries outside the city?'

**53.** Line changed to: **'What's** a few cuts and bruises?' *Gary Russell: 'This is one of those things that needs a "well, you had to be there", but we all found the idea that Peri could swallow a few cuts and bruises hilarious. As you do. Thus we changed it to, "What's a few cuts and bruises?" I think we laugh too much at crap in studio sometimes…'*

**54.** Line changed to: 'The temple guards and chariots need only a few **moments**.'

**55.** Line changed to: 'So, this **is the** pup you plan to put on the throne?'

**56.** Line changed to: 'I want to be knee-deep in Egyptian blood before the hour is out – then I'll bed **that** brat Pharaoh myself.'

**57.** Line changed to: '~~But~~ the men do not want to leave Thebes unguarded.'

**58.** Deleted dialogue: '~~Doctor?~~'

**59.** Line changed to: 'You planned this, **Doctor**.'

**60.** Line changed to: 'I misjudged you, ~~Doctor~~.'

## PART FOUR

**61.** '**Thank you**,' is added at the beginning of the line, as in Part Three's cliffhanger.

**62.** '**Whoa, whoa there**,' added at the beginning of the line.

**63.** Line changed to: 'Who are you to know ~~of~~ these things, Doctor?'

**64.** This line begins Scene 43 and is therefore distorted.

**65.** '**Yeah**,' added at the beginning of the line.

**66.** Line changed to: 'Well, as close as she can be in the **circumstances**.'

**67.** Line changed to: 'Doctor, last night, you **told me stories** of many times and places...'

**68.** Deleted dialogue: '~~Whoa there.~~'

**69.** Deleted dialogue: '~~Down you come.~~'

**70.** Line changed to: 'There's four hundred metres directly behind **it**.' *Gary Russell: 'We decided Iain McLaughlin had an agreement with some mate that he got a fiver each time the word Sphinx was spoken in this scene. If you're reading this along with the story, you'll notice there are less spoken "Sphinx"s than there are in this script!'*

**71.** Line changed to: '**It's a** useless thing.'

**72.** Line changed to: 'It leads under **it** and branches off under the pyramids as well, come to that, but it's the Sphinx I'm interested in.'

**73.** Line changed to: 'Anyway, **it** was built by refugees from Atlantis, who placed all their knowledge in a chamber between **its paws** – the Hall of Records.'

**74.** Line changed to: 'The troops are still **very** weary after the long march.'

**75.** '**They must**,' added at the beginning of the line.

**76.** Line changed to: 'The chariots are almost too close for **their** archers now – and we still have enough to over-run them.'

**77.** 'Kishik!' is repeated. *Gary Russell: 'Kishik was one of my contributions as script editor. Iain's scripts didn't give the charioteer Yanis yelled at in Part One a name – and I think he did feed him to the dogs. Then as Yanis had other odd guards and charioteers to yell at in the script, I opted to keep him alive a bit longer to save an endless stream of faceless guards – although I did ask Iain to supply a sufficiently Egyptian name. However, he had to go at some point, so I had him die here. Yanis was actually upset – I'm not sure whether it's because he quite liked Kishak after all or because he wanted the pleasure of feeding him to the dogs at a later stage! Daniel*

Brennan, who played Kishik, had previously been in a Professor Bernice Summerfield *play, and I promised him another part as a result of that. (I often use* Benny *plays as try-outs for bigger* Doctor Who *roles. Which, on reflection, seems a little rude to the Benny range. Sorry Benny!) Similarly, as soon as I read the script, I knew who I wanted for Yanis – the fab Harry Myers who plays Adrian Wall, father to Benny's offspring in that series. Harry is a top bloke, top actor and all-round fun guy to have in the studio. One of a good number of regular Big Finishers employed for their talent and their ability to lighten my day just by turning up. As a director, trying to get all this crammed into a two-day recording, having people around who just make you laugh by saying "Good Morning" are worth their weight in gold!'*

**78.** Line changed to: 'We need **more** footsoldiers.'

**79.** Line changed to: '~~It's~~ Erimem.'

**80.** Line changed to: 'The potted history of Atlantis and prayers that the people and **wisdom** of Atlantis will be remembered.'

**81.** Line changed to: 'Now that you've left the minds of all the people you've affected on Earth, I can take you off **this** planet.'

**82.** Line changed to: 'Too **many**.' *Gary Russell: 'Nicola did this live, swapping between the alien and Peri where necessary. I always prefer to do this if possible rather record things separately as it keeps the flow going for everyone else. Shemek, later on, is* Doctor Who Magazine *journalist Mark Wyman and I can't recall who did Ebren. I've an unpleasant feeling it was me… Oh, it was.'*

**83.** Line changed to: 'And you **still** have one here, Yanis.'

**84.** Added dialogue – DOCTOR: '**Fayum, take her arm will you**?' *Gary Russell: 'We added a line in here about Fayum in case people thought he, like Yanis, was now a red mess under a few tons of Sphinx pillar! Jack Galagher, who I'd originally worked with on* The Fearmonger, *wasn't first choice for Fayum – I had planned to ask Jack to do the character of Sabian in* Primeval, *and offered Fayum to Ian Hallard. Ian, however, was on tour being a luvvie, as they do, and so I swapped the parts around and Jack got to go to Egypt and Ian went to Traken! As it turned out, I think Lady Luck smiled on me as they're both better suited to the roles they ended up with. Jack, bless him, worked and worked on his script and virtually knew it off by heart by the time he turned up in the studio. I like actors like that – you get some that just turn up, having barely skimmed the first dozen pages. Then you get ones like Jack who know the story backwards and thus have no problems with out of order recording, and know exactly what's needed for each scene. That second type of actor tends to get re-employed more than the former!'*

**85.** The order of this line and the preceding one was changed to:

**ANTRANAK**     Even this one, Majesty?
**ERIMEM**     Antranak!
**ANTRANAK**     I saw Horemshep climb out of the well. I persuaded him to stay.
**ERIMEM**     Oh Antranak, I feared you were dead.

**86.** Added dialogue – HOREMSHEP: '**But, your Majesty**, I… **you don't understand, I really**…' *Gary Russell: 'I was appalled with my own script editing here – the villain of the piece doesn't get a final line! So I asked Steve Perring to ad lib – which is red rag to a bull really! I can't recall quite how long it went on for in the rehearsal but everyone just stopped the scene and waited patiently while*

*Steve went on for what seemed like an hour begging for mercy. When he finally ran out of breath Peter, Nicola and Jonathan gave him a round of applause. I'd met Steve up in Bristol when we did* Seasons of Fear *and we all got on with him instantly. A fab actor and another one of those mood-lightening types. He, Harry and Jonathan were like the Marx Brothers on this one!'*

**87.** '**Fayum**,' added at the beginning of the line.

**88.** Line changed to: 'I'll have to be **more** careful when I argue with you in future.'

**89.** After this line, the scene switches to inside the TARDIS. *Gary Russell: 'Again, a good decision by David Darlington here to have them move into the TARDIS aurally as no one ever says, "Let's get in the TARDIS". I've always been pleased that we have post-production guys who think about things like this and thus pull my fat out of the fire. Of course, now everyone knows I'm a charlatan as a director and script-editor! Do'h!'*

**90.** The end of this scene was slightly restructured. In the finished play, Erimem's last line is followed by a cut to outside the TARDIS. The chamber doors then open as the TARDIS dematerialisation occurs, and the scene then continues largely as scripted. (The only change was FAYUM's first line becoming: '(*Breathless and excited*) Pharaoh, **Pharaoh**, the people are... Pharaoh? Pharaoh?'

# THE ONE DOCTOR

## By Gareth Roberts & Clayton Hickman

*The One Doctor* came about because we both wanted Christopher Biggins to appear in *Doctor Who*. Simple as that. It wasn't the first idea we had – that concerned a space station run by Biggins which was hosting the Intergalactic Song Contest, and was eventually reworked as our second Big Finish play, *Bang-Bang-a-Boom!* – or even the first submission we made – that was called *Crossroads in Time* (you can read it in the appendices of this book if you want) and would have seen Biggins managing a Midlands motel if it hadn't been rejected – but it was the one that finally gave us the chance to realise our ambition.

Please don't get the impression from all this that we knew Christopher Biggins, or had any sort of guarantee that he'd be interested in appearing in our play. Not a bit of it. The both of us just felt that he was perfect for *Doctor Who* and had been unaccountably overlooked during the show's run on TV. We were determined to put that right. Assuming, of course, that we could get a script accepted and persuade the man himself to do it…

We'd gone through a lot of ideas and drafts, trying to find the right story, and then Gareth suddenly remembered an idea he'd toyed with submitting to the *Doctor Who Magazine* short story competition in the mid-1980s – that the Doctor was being impersonated by somebody else. Together we fleshed out the idea of the Banto Zame character – for Biggins, naturally – and realised that he'd have to be operating in the far future when the Doctor was known as a legendary figure because of his popping up so many times in so many places. Clay thought it might be funny to call it *The One Doctor*, to make people think it was a 'special' in the vein of the *Three/Five/Two/Eight/Infinity Doctors*, when it was actually nothing of the sort. It worked, too.

Banto and Sally-Anne, his assistant-cum-girlfriend, were like the Doctor and Mel… except that they were low-rent criminals. Also, they behaved much more like normal people – they drink, smoke, fancy people – so contrasting them with the Doctor and his assistants, who don't do any of those things, was part of the fun. It was great to have Banto falling for Mel, simply because she's so utterly uncynical – unlike anybody he's met before in his sordid life. Similarly, that's why Sally-Anne falls for Doctor Who; he's solid and reliable, everything Banto isn't.

Neither of us are great fans of stories which are about the Doctor himself, his character and his history, but this one seemed like such an original idea – and there aren't many of those left after forty years of *Doctor Who*. Also, our preference is for stories which are set all in one new world, with its own set of rules and limits, giving the story a good sense of place. But the more we thought about it, the more it seemed like we should use the Banto character, teamed up with Mel, as a contrast to the Doctor, teamed up with Sally-Anne, to have fun with inverting the usual boundaries of the *Doctor Who* format. That meant starting the story at the end of a typical Who adventure, hence our naming the planet 'Generios'.

And so we cooked up a sequence of mini-*Doctor Who* adventures that we could plonk our characters down in. As Gareth had just re-read *Alice in Wonderland*, he was quite enthused with the idea of moving from place to place, but we were also keen to make sure there was a twist ending with the Cylinder – a nod to those interminable *Star Trek* probes-gone-mad – swallowing up Banto. *The Weakest Link* was at its notorious height when we wrote the script, and so it seemed the natural thing to do. It could just as easily have been *Countdown*. Back when it was on the telly *Doctor Who* used to soak up a lot of cultural references, and if it were still on now we'd surely have had stories using *Pride and Prejudice*, *Big Brother* and *Harry Potter* as their basis. Writing the *Superbrain* questions was a long and tedious business – we'd seriously underestimated how many would be needed – though it was quite amusing to watch the poor actors trying to get to grips with pronouncing all the nonsense we'd just made up. Gareth still loves *The Weakest Link*, by the way.

The idea of an enormously long-lived creature had been around for ages, but Clay's experience of waiting in for a washing machine to be delivered gave it a comic twist. The incredibly fast, short-lived creatures were probably in *Star Trek*, weren't they? Of course lots of other silly things made their way into the finished script. If you've a mind to look, you can find references to Chesney Hawkes, the Smash robots, *Blockbusters*, Ikea, *The Cucumber Song*, *Dr Where?* and the overseas print of *Carnival of Monsters* Episode Two. We recommend you don't bother.

The casting of *The One Doctor* was something we had quite a lot of involvement in. Gary Russell, who was our director as well as our producer and script editor (does the man not sleep?), was more than happy with that as it saved him a lot of effort which he could then devote to the other eight billion things which needed his attention that afternoon. Mark Gatiss was instrumental in getting us the amazing Matt Lucas, and it was at an aftershow party for the *League of Gentlemen*'s Drury Lane show that we met Adam Buxton and drunkenly asked him if he'd play a stupid robot for us. Much to our surprise he was still on for it when he'd sobered up. Mark also sounded out Lisa Tarbuck about playing Sally Anne, and she happily agreed. Unfortunately Lisa was whisked away to Montreux at the last minute by the BBC to publicise *Linda Green*, so the hunt was on for a new Sally Anne. Jason Haigh-Ellery, our other producer, found us Clare Buckfield, who turned out to be the most perfect casting imaginable. One blinding stroke of luck was that Stephen Fewell, Clay's mate and a Big Finish veteran, had recently completed a tour of *Lady Windermere's Fan*... with none other than Sir Christopher Biggins! So after a few phone calls and some gushing gratitude from us, our ambition was finally fulfiled and we had our Banto Zame. Stephen himself took on the role of the timid Councillor Potikol, whilst the wonderful Nick Pegg and the even wonderfuller Jane Goddard (doing a frighteningly convincing Anne Robinson) completed the ensemble.

It was great fun writing for Colin Baker and Bonnie Langford, because there's a lot of unexplored potential in the characters on TV, in contrast to a lot of other Doctor/companion teams, who were perhaps better worked out. Mel allows the Sixth Doctor to mellow, because Peri tended to be confrontational and negative and bring out the worst in him. Mel also gives the impression that she wants to be there, which is sadly not the case with most of the other 1980s companions. Added to that, Colin and Bonnie are two of the most dedicated actors to work for Big Finish, and they did absolute wonders with what we gave them. Hearing Bonnie nail Mel's 'never say die' speech in one take was just one jaw-dropping moment amongst many.

Of course some of our original ideas got changed along the way. The whole

*Weakest Link* segment, for example, only came about during the scripting. In our original outline – which, stupidly, sacrificed a lot of potential larks by pairing off the two Doctors and the two companions rather than mixing and matching – there was a somewhat different trial for the Doctor, based upon those particularly grating shows where twentysomethings screech loudly and Denise Van Outen falls out of her dress. In actual fact it was all rather prescient – as anyone who saw Colin Baker's appearance on Sarah Cox's twentysomething screech-fest *Born Sloppy* can attest.

One of the few major changes to the script was the loss of a scene where Banto and the Doctor have a bit of a scrap. At Gary Russell's request we changed it into a verbal duel, which was felt to be more in keeping with Colin's portrayal. But we still think this would have been rather funny…

**BANTO ZAME**    Listen, do I have to get nasty?
**MELANIE**    I wouldn't try it. We can defend ourselves, you know?
**DOCTOR WHO**    Well said, Mel.
**BANTO ZAME**    Right. Try this for starters 'Doctor'…
*FX – BANTO wrestles DOCTOR WHO. DOCTOR WHO gasps.*
**BANTO ZAME**    *(CONT'D)* A Merjidian death-lock. Get out of that! And then you clear off, get it?
**DOCTOR WHO**    *(Muffled)* You try this…
*FX – DOCTOR WHO gains the upper hand over BANTO, who gasps.*
**BANTO ZAME**    Oof!
**DOCTOR WHO**    A Suvarian stranglehold!
*FX – BANTO wrestles DOCTOR WHO again.*
**BANTO ZAME**    Hah! The Lufaran pain-grip!
*FX – DOCTOR WHO wrestles BANTO.*
**DOCTOR WHO**    Try the Hug of Hankus 4 for size!
*FX – The scuffling continues in B/G.*
**MELANIE**    This is futile! Time's running out and all you two can do is indulge in a playground scrap!

The only other thing we were sad to lose was the Cylinder naming our hero as Doctor Who during his rundown of the Doctor's many aliases in Part Four. Gary felt that it was a step too far – has he never seen *The War Machines*? – and so he changed it to some obscure *New Adventures* reference. We cried.

Someone else who had input into the final script was Colin Baker himself. Having read and enjoyed it, he emailed Gary with a couple of suggestions, one of them concerning the name of Banto's transport. As scripted it was the TARDIST – a tribute to the mispronunciation that seemed to afflict any member of the public asked about Doctor Who's time machine on TV shows during the Seventies and Eighties, and was recently revived when the first family into the Millennium Dome described it as, 'Just like Dr Who's TARDIST!' Colin felt that the extra 'T' might not come across well enough on audio and suggested it be changed to STARDIS. Which is obviously far far better. But we weren't bitter…

Given that about 70% of the play had to be recorded on the second day due to availability of actors, Gary did a fantastic job in not hitting us – and his directing wasn't half bad either. The unsung hero of *The One Doctor*, however, was sound designer Alistair Lock… who did actually sing, but never mind. From making us all do the conga in studio, to mispronouncing the cast list so precisely for the trailer, to providing the lovely, unscripted Jelloid ditty in Part Four, Alistair's hard work really made the play something special. Even we got sniffly when the rousing music for the finalé crashed in and fireworks started going off on Generios.

The bonus track – the script for which you can also find in the appendices if you're so inclined – was written by Clay on the morning of the first day of recording, after he'd been mulling it over during the previous, sleepless, night. Originally *The One Doctor* had been scheduled for release in August, but we both felt it would sit more comfortably at Christmas, when people generally feel more forgiving. Luckily Gary agreed. That being the case (and even though the play was recorded in April), we thought a bit of real festiveness wouldn't go astray, and the opportunity for Colin's Doctor to wish the audience a very Merry Christmas in tribute to *The Feast of Steven* was too good to pass over. Luckily, the first day of recording finished a little early and Gary, Colin and Bonnie indulged us by committing it to tape in a single take. Ho ho ho.

People slagged off *Doctor Who* on TV in the 1980s for being like a panto – but actually the show took itself far too seriously for that, which is why it's often a bit daft. When the series relaxed a bit more, like in *Mindwarp* or *Delta and the Bannermen*, it was actually more involving and enjoyable. The positive feedback we've had to *The One Doctor* shows that people still like their *Doctor Who* to be fun and silly from time to time, and it's to the series' credit that the format can happily cope with transdimensional shelves and northern-accented jellies without crumbling into sparks and dust.

So there we are. That's the story of this story. We hope that, even without the brilliance of Baker, Bonnie, Buckfield and Biggins, or Alistair's astonishing music and effects, *The One Doctor* will still raise a smile. Oh, and if you're wondering why the main character is credited as 'Doctor Who' throughout, it's a superstition of Gareth's. When the end credits of *Doctor Who* started to refer to him as 'The Doctor', the series' popularity began to decline, so Gareth thought we should invoke the ghost of *Doctor Who* Past, and try and recapture a little of that lost populist appeal. And, of course, it looked funnier on the page.

We won Best Audio in the *DWM* poll though, so maybe there was something in it after all…

# The One Doctor

## CAST

| | |
|---|---|
| DOCTOR WHO | Colin Baker |
| MELANIE | Bonnie Langford |
| CITIZEN SOKKERY | Nicholas Pegg |
| COUNCILLOR POTIKOL | Stephen Fewell |
| BANTO ZAME | Christopher Biggins |
| SALLY-ANNE STUBBINS | Clare Buckfield |
| GUARD | Mark Wright |
| CYLINDER VOICE | Matt Lucas |
| QUESTIONER | Jane Goddard |
| MENTOS | Nicholas Pegg |
| ASSEMBLER 1 | Adam Buxton |
| ASSEMBLER 2 | Stephen Fewell |
| JELLOID | Matt Lucas |

# PART ONE[1]

## 1. INT. TARDIS CONTROL ROOM – DAY
*Up on DOCTOR WHO's voice... deep and menacing...*

**DOCTOR WHO**  At last, I control everything...[2] you are my pawns, to do with as I please... you have no choice but to bend to my will... yes, I own you... I am your creator – and I can be your *destroyer*...
*FX – The TARDIS background in-flight hum fades up quick.*
**MELANIE**  Honestly, Doctor, stop being so melodramatic.
**DOCTOR WHO**  Mel, am I not permitted an occasional moment of melodrama?
**MELANIE**  Yes, but it's only a game of Monopoly.
**DOCTOR WHO**  A game that I am winning... yes, there is no power but mine... I control Park Lane, Mayfair, the waterworks...
**MELANIE**  Doctor!
**DOCTOR WHO**  I want to imagine what it feels like to be a power crazed dictator. See into the enemy's mind.
**MELANIE**  And?
**DOCTOR WHO**  Boring. And I hate hotels. Your roll.
*FX – Rolling dice in a tumbler.*
**MELANIE**  A double six.
**DOCTOR WHO**  You're the iron, I'm the dog.
**MELANIE**  Sorry.
**DOCTOR WHO**  You're getting absent-minded. Most unlike you.
**MELANIE**  (*Groans*) Oh no.
**DOCTOR WHO**  Excellent. You must surrender to my will... two thousand, two hundred and sixty pounds rent, please.
**MELANIE**  All right.[3]
**DOCTOR WHO**  By the way, why did you reset the coordinates this morning?
**MELANIE**  I thought you did.
**DOCTOR WHO**  Yet more absent-mindedness...
**MELANIE**  I haven't been near the controls. Guide's honour.
**DOCTOR WHO**  (*Amused*) You were a Girl Guide?
*FX – MEL moves to the console. She punches some keys with appropriate bleeps.*
**MELANIE**  Never mind that. These readings... the TARDIS is way off course...
**DOCTOR WHO**  Way, way off course... we've drifted millennia into the far future...
**MELANIE**  Who's done this? Who could control the TARDIS?
**DOCTOR WHO**  The same person who always does – or tries to. Me.
**MELANIE**  What do you mean?
**DOCTOR WHO**  I was experimenting with the navigation settings... and I must have accidentally switched on the wide-range distress transceiver. Knocked it with my elbow.[4] The TARDIS responded automatically, like a dog fetching a bone. Yes, listen...
*FX – An urgent series of high-pitched bleeps.*
**MELANIE**  Where's it coming from?

**DOCTOR WHO**  I don't know. But we're almost on top of it. (*Wearily*) We'd better materialise, I suppose...

**MELANIE**  Don't worry, Doctor. We'll finish the game later. What's the matter?

**DOCTOR WHO**  I just wish, sometimes, people could sort their problems out all by themselves. I mean, why does it always have to be *me*?

### 2. EXT. GENERIOS STREET – DAY

*FX – The sound of cheering and laughing. Celebratory music. A very big party is underway. Perhaps the sound of some hovering vehicle zooming past. This is the far future, after all. The TARDIS materialises with its customary wheezing and groaning. Nobody takes a blind bit of notice.*

### 3. INT. TARDIS CONTROL ROOM – DAY

**MELANIE**  So – where exactly are we?

**DOCTOR WHO**  The vulgar end of time.

**MELANIE**  Eh?

**DOCTOR WHO**  I prefer never to go this far.

**MELANIE**  Why?

**DOCTOR WHO**  Everything's been discovered. Everybody knows everybody else, and everybody knows everybody else's business. All the wars are over – the interesting ones anyway. Technology's made every pleasure affordable. Nobody strives... not that there's anything worth striving for... it's hedonism, hedonism, hedonism all the way...

**MELANIE**  And that's a bad thing? How far ahead are we? After my time?

**DOCTOR WHO**  Oh, 1989 is long gone. Although I suppose that's one reason for us to look on the bright side!

**MELANIE**  Hmm. I might get a straight answer from the data bank...

*FX – Bleeps and general key-punching as MEL consults the data bank.*

**MELANIE**  (*CONT'D*) According to this we're on Generios 1[5], central planet of the Great Generios System, in the constellation of... Generios. Hmm. 'A mighty galactic trade Empire spanning seventeen planets'. And they need our help.

**DOCTOR WHO**  Let's have a look at the old scanner.

*FX – The scanner shutters slide open. We hear the sound of the crowd outside.*

**MELANIE**  Looks like a party.

**DOCTOR WHO**  Appearances can be deceptive.

**MELANIE**  Yes... perhaps they've been brainwashed into submission by invading aliens...

**DOCTOR WHO**  (*Gently chiding*) Melodrama! Pass me my coat, will you?[6] (*Shrugging it on*)[7] Let's divine the truth of the matter.

*FX – The TARDIS doors open.*

### 4. EXT. GENERIOS STREET – DAY

*FX – More cheering of VE Day proportions. MEL emerges from the TARDIS.*

**MELANIE**  Don't think much of this place. It's kind of bland – everybody and everything the same...[8]

*FX – DOCTOR WHO follows MEL out and locks the TARDIS door.*
**DOCTOR WHO**   I did warn you.[9] Wonder why they're all so jubilant?
*A drunk, but amiable Generiosian, SOKKERY, approaches.*
**SOKKERY**   Hey, citizen! I like the coat!
**DOCTOR WHO**   Thank you... but would you mind not dribbling on to it...[10]
**SOKKERY**   Fancy a drop of this?
*FX – A half empty bottle is sloshed about.*
**DOCTOR WHO**   I rarely drink.
**SOKKERY**   Come on, chum![11] Everybody's got to let go on a day like this!
**MELANIE**   He rarely lets go.
**DOCTOR WHO**   What's happened? We've only just arrived. We picked up a distress call.
**SOKKERY**   Sorry... wasted journey. Here, you have a drop, pretty lady... anyone ever tell you you've got amazing ringlets?[12]
**MELANIE**   Never mind my ringlets. What are you celebrating?
**SOKKERY**   We've been saved... the Skelloids are vanquished...[13]
**MELANIE**   Skelloids?
**DOCTOR WHO**   Skelloids?
**SOKKERY**   (*With relish*) Ferocious aliens from the outer reaches of deep space... like living skeletons. There were hundreds of them, vicious and deadly, ready to land their mother ship on this, our Great City of Generios. They would have enslaved us.
**MELANIE**   But you defeated them?
**SOKKERY**   Oh no. We were useless. The Great Council tried to make peace with the Skelloids and failed. And our defences were totally inadequate.
**DOCTOR WHO**   So – what became of these 'Skelloids'?[14] Did they just pack up and go home for tea?
**SOKKERY**   Course not – the Skelloids never give up. The Doctor sorted them out for us, didn't he?
*A big incidental music moment.*
**DOCTOR WHO**   The Doctor... did you say the Doctor?
**SOKKERY**   Yeah... you know, the mysterious Time Lord. Travels the universe poking his nose in, putting things to rights. You must know the legends.
**DOCTOR WHO**   Yes, I believe I have heard something...
*FX – We faintly hear a group of people dancing the conga nearby.*
**SOKKERY**   I thought it was a lot of billy rot until he actually turned up and saved the day. With his assistant – phwoarr, lovely girl. Anyway, I've spent long enough talking to you two – there's a conga over there with my name on it!
*FX – SOKKERY goes off, taking the conga with him.*
**DOCTOR WHO**   I said they were vulgar.
**MELANIE**   It looks like you've already saved the day, then. Beaten yourself to it.
**DOCTOR WHO**   Somehow I doubt it.[15] I've never been to Generios before.
**MELANIE**   Then you will in the future.
**DOCTOR WHO**   I doubt that too.
**MELANIE**   Why?
**DOCTOR WHO**   I can sense the proximity of another self, having experienced it on several occasions.[16] My hair stands on end.

**MELANIE**     (*Laughing*) How could it?
**DOCTOR WHO**   (*Deadly serious*) Figuratively speaking. And this time it hasn't.
**MELANIE**     You're really rattled, aren't you?
**DOCTOR WHO**   Yes. Because if I didn't save this planet from the evil Skelloids – who is the Doctor that did...?

## 5. INT. COUNCIL CHAMBER – DAY
*A big, draughty, vaulted room. The celebrating crowd can be heard – close, but muffled. Enter POTIKOL, the rather fey and nervous head councillor.*

**POTIKOL**     Listen to the citizens! This day is truly unique in the Great Annals of Generios! The people rejoice!
*FX – We hear the crowd chanting, 'WE WANT THE DOCTOR! WE WANT THE DOCTOR!'*
**POTIKOL**     (*CONT'D*) They're crying out for their saviour! Are you sure you won't step out on to the balcony, Doctor?
*Ah, but this isn't really the Doctor. Here we meet BANTO ZAME and SALLY-ANNE, confidence tricksters. Both are currently doing fair, if rather over-the-top impressions of Doctor Who and his assistant. BANTO is being terribly bombastic and grandiose while SALLY-ANNE is the very model of simpering naivete. These, as we shall see, are not their natural states.*
**BANTO ZAME**   I'm sorry, Councillor Potikol, but I hate farewells.
**POTIKOL**     But you've done so much for us – saved the seventeen planets from certain annihilation...
**BANTO ZAME**   Please – any passing genius would have done the same.
**POTIKOL**     (*Laughs obsequiously*) Tell me again – how *did* you defeat the Skelloids?
**BANTO ZAME**   It was simple enough – after I worked out their entire life cycle was based on the absorption of hydrogen through their gill-plates.
**POTIKOL**     Go on.
**BANTO ZAME**   I simply inverted the core of their hydrogen stabilisers. With a little help from my psychic screwdriver – and a little help from Sally Anne.
**SALLY-ANNE**   I wondered when you'd get round to mentioning me.
**POTIKOL**     Generios is indebted to your assistant as well, Doctor.
**SALLY-ANNE**   So the core sucked hydrogen *from* the Skelloids instead of supplying it *to* them.
**BANTO ZAME**   Result – skedaddle, Skelloids! They won't be back again – well, at least, not for another couple of aeons. Anyway, Potikol, time's winged chariot marches on – especially for a Time Lord. Sally-Anne and I really must get back to the TARDIST (*sic*).[17]
**POTIKOL**     Must you leave us, Doctor?
**BANTO ZAME**   I'm afraid so.
**POTIKOL**     How can we ever repay you for saving us?
**BANTO ZAME**   I don't expect repayment – the work I do is reward in itself.
**SALLY-ANNE**   (*As if struck by an idea*) Hey Doctor – what about the pluvon power crystals?

**BANTO ZAME** Eh? Oh yes...
**POTIKOL** Pluvon power crystals?
**SALLY-ANNE** We need them for the TARDIST. And we're running dry.
**POTIKOL** I'm afraid we have no such crystals. The seventeen planets were mined out generations ago.
**SALLY-ANNE** Yes – but you've got the cash we could use to buy them.
**BANTO ZAME** Come on, Sally-Anne, that's out of the question. Goodbye, Councillor –
**POTIKOL** One moment, Doctor. How much do you need to buy these crystals you seek?
**BANTO ZAME** Really, I won't hear of it –
**POTIKOL** Doctor.
**SALLY-ANNE** About a hundred million credits.
**POTIKOL** (*Shocked*) A hundred million...
**BANTO ZAME** Yes, quite. It's our problem, not yours. So we'll just slip quietly away...
**POTIKOL** No. I won't hear of it. If a hundred million is what you need, Doctor, Sally-Anne – a hundred million is what you shall have.
**BANTO ZAME** No, Potikol, I absolutely insist – I will not take your money.
**POTIKOL** Please, Doctor. What is a hundred million credits weighed against the lives of all in the seventeen planets?
**SALLY-ANNE** Go on, Doctor.
**BANTO ZAME** I do have principles, you know...
**SALLY-ANNE** You won't have much use for them if we don't get those power crystals.
**BANTO ZAME** You have a point... Very well, Councillor.
**POTIKOL** You will accept our gift.
**BANTO ZAME** As a loan. I will find some way to repay you.
**POTIKOL** Doctor, Doctor, what more could you have done for us? I will go at once to the Great Bank of Generios and make out a cheque.[18]
**BANTO ZAME** Er... I'd prefer cash. I don't actually have a bank account myself. Never had much use for money.
**POTIKOL** I understand. It shall be done. Wait here.
*FX – POTIKOL exits through a sliding door. Immediately he's gone, BANTO ZAME and SALLY-ANNE burst into laughter and revert to their real personas. SALLY-ANNE is as common as muck, while BANTO is cynical, brusque and ever-so-slightly camp.*
**BANTO ZAME** Ha ha... there's one born every nanosecond...
**SALLY-ANNE** Banto, this lot have gotta be the doziest load of prawns yet.
**BANTO ZAME** 'Please, Doctor. What is a hundred million credits weighed against the lives of all in the seventeen planets?' What a plank!
**SALLY-ANNE** 'Time marches on – especially for a Time Lord.' Loved it. Pass me one of them beers.
*FX – Two lager cans are opened.*
**BANTO ZAME** To us – and to our 'pluvon power crystals'.
**SALLY-ANNE** (*Mock appalled*) Oh Doctor – you're not going to spend that money on something else, are you?
**BANTO ZAME** Come here and give us a kiss.
*FX – BANTO ZAME and SALLY-ANNE kiss.*

## 6. EXT. OUTSIDE COUNCIL COMPLEX – DAY
*We're outside the council complex now – much FX cheering, clapping and good-natured hammering on the door.*

**DOCTOR WHO**  This must be it – their Great Council Complex. Everything around here seems to be Great.[19]
**MELANIE**  Great! So how are we going to get inside? Knock on the door?
**DOCTOR WHO**  Everybody's knocking on the door.
*FX – The crowd start cheering, 'WE WANT THE DOCTOR' again.*
**MELANIE**  Somebody's popular. (*She sees SOKKERY*) Oh no...[20]
**DOCTOR WHO**  What?
**MELANIE**  It's him again.
**SOKKERY**  Hello.[21] Come to see the Doctor, have you? They reckon he's gonna step out on to the balcony up there.
**DOCTOR WHO**  Is that some sort of newspaper you've got there?
**SOKKERY**  Eh? Oh yeah, Great Visi-Echo of Generios. Special commemorative edition.
**MELANIE**  That must be him – plastered all over the front page...
**SOKKERY**  Yeah, that's the Doctor.[22]
**DOCTOR WHO**  Give me that...
*FX – DOCTOR WHO snatches the newspaper.*
**SOKKERY**  Here, steady on, there's a voucher for the Great Commemorative Tea-towel in there...
*FX – DOCTOR WHO jabs a finger at the paper.*
**DOCTOR WHO**  Look at that Mel! It is definitely not me!
**MELANIE**  How can you be so sure?
**DOCTOR WHO**  I have assumed several guises over the centuries but have always maintained an essential air of Olympian dignity. Look at this buffoon!
**MELANIE**  He looks all right to me.
**DOCTOR WHO**  All right? *All right?* Florid complexion, nose like a mulberry... and his figure is positively rotund!
**MELANIE**  You're not exactly sylphlike.
**DOCTOR WHO**  There is a difference between being big-boned and being portly! There's no doubt about it – I must confront this impostor. Impersonating a Time Lord is a serious offence. I may need this paper as evidence.
*FX – DOCTOR WHO stuffs the paper into his pocket.*
**SOKKERY**  Hey!
**MELANIE**  How are we going to get in?
**SOKKERY**  (*Sulky now*) You can't. Without a pass.[23]
**DOCTOR WHO**  I can go anywhere I like. (*Cunning, slow*) Mel... how's your wilting willow impersonation?
*Big, end-of scene twinkling music. A beat.[24]*
**MELANIE**  What? What are you talking about?
**DOCTOR WHO**  I mean – I've got a plan.
**MELANIE**  Why didn't you just say so?
**DOCTOR WHO**  Er... yes. Sorry.

## 7. INT. COUNCIL CHAMBER – DAY.
*We're back with BANTO ZAME and SALLY-ANNE, still smooching.*

**SALLY-ANNE**  'Ere, get off, Banto. Someone might come through that door any second. Won't suit our image to be all crumpled and rumpled.

**BANTO ZAME**  I wonder where he is with that cash? It's been twenty minutes.

**SALLY-ANNE**  What, you don't reckon he might've rumbled us?[25]

**BANTO ZAME**  Potikol? He's a fool. Remember when the 'Skelloid Commander' told him to (*alien voice*) 'surrender or die'?

**SALLY-ANNE**  Yeah, hur hur... I thought he were gonna have an accident.

*FX – POTIKOL's footsteps.*

**BANTO ZAME**  That's him – get up. Quick sticks! And hide those cans!

*FX – They straighten themselves out. The beer cans are flung into a corner as the door opens and POTIKOL enters. BANTO and SALLY-ANNE revert to their* Doctor Who *personas.*

**POTIKOL**  Doctor, Doctor...

**SALLY-ANNE**  Oh Councillor, did you manage to get the money?

**BANTO ZAME**  I still feel extremely dubious about this arrangement, Sally-Anne.

**SALLY-ANNE**  Ignore him, Councillor – too proud, that's his trouble.

**POTIKOL**  I'm afraid there's been a slight problem.

**SALLY-ANNE**  You what? I mean – a problem, you say?

**POTIKOL**  The computer links to the Great Bank of Generios are being... influenced somehow.

**BANTO ZAME**  Influenced?

**POTIKOL**  Yes. In fact, all the workings of the Great Computers of Generios are slipping somewhat out of our control.

**SALLY-ANNE**  What – your cash machine's on the blink?[26]

**POTIKOL**  If only it were that simple.

**BANTO ZAME**  Potikol, please get to the point.

**POTIKOL**  At first we thought the interference was perhaps an after-effect of the Skelloids' handiwork.

**BANTO ZAME**  I doubt it. I mean – unlikely.

**POTIKOL**  But our Great Radarscopes have just reported a foreign object – a piece of space debris – that has drifted into the System.

**BANTO ZAME**  And it's interfering with your computers somehow?

**POTIKOL**  We think so. But do not fret, Doctor. I have dispatched a space dredger to blast it out of the skies.[27] All will be well. Excuse me while I attend to the arrangements...

*FX – POTIKOL exits. The door closes. BANTO and SALLY-ANNE revert to type.*

**SALLY-ANNE**  I told you. They've cottoned on. We ought to get out of here.

**BANTO ZAME**  And lose our chance of a hundred million credits?

**SALLY-ANNE**  You don't believe all his fluff about flotsam?

**BANTO ZAME**  Why ever not? There are still huge chunks of debris floating round from the Skardu/Rosbrix wars.

**SALLY-ANNE**  Floating out this far?

**BANTO ZAME**  Just relax, my little coelacanth. Here have another can. Listen, if they had the slightest doubt about us, we'd be clapped in irons by now.

*FX – Can opens.*

**SALLY-ANNE**  (*Taking a sip*) Ooh... doesn't sound too uncomfortable, if I was with you.

**BANTO ZAME**  And I with you, my turtle dove.
**SALLY-ANNE**  Ooh, be romantic.
**BANTO ZAME**  Later. When I've got that hundred million in my hand I'll be *very* romantic.

### 8. INT. COUNCIL COMPLEX CORRIDORS- DAY
*inside the Council Complex. FX doors open. We hear the crowd.*

**GUARD**  This way, sir...
*FX – The shuffling of feet as the GUARD and DOCTOR WHO carry MELANIE inside. She groans, feebly.*
**DOCTOR WHO**  I'm sorry, she's usually a very picture of health.
*FX – Doors close. The crowd are cut out.*
**MELANIE**  (*Woozy*) Oh... where am I? I feel...
**DOCTOR WHO**  Now now, Mel, you've just fainted in the crush, that's all.
**GUARD**  Just lay her down here, sir, against the wall.[28]
**DOCTOR WHO**  There you go.
**MELANIE**  It must have been the excitement of being that close to the Doctor...
**DOCTOR WHO**  (*Arch*) Indeed.
**MELANIE**  I could do with a glass of water – clear my head.[29]
**DOCTOR WHO**  If it's not too much trouble. We'll just wait here. Innocently.
**GUARD**  Right you are, sir. I won't be a second – there's a cooler round the corner.
*FX – The GUARD moves off.*
**DOCTOR WHO**  Right. Let's slip off.
**MELANIE**  Which way? These corridors all look the same.
**DOCTOR WHO**  Not to a corridor veteran like me. This way – I'm rather excited about meeting the Doctor myself.
*FX – They move off, stealthily.*

### 9. INT. ANOTHER CORRIDOR – DAY
*The GUARD is filling a glass of water from the cooler and humming softly to himself. FX – water pouring into cup. We hear POTIKOL approaching in a great flurry from a distance.*

**POTIKOL**  Guard! Guard! Summon the council!
**GUARD**  Councillor! Whatever's the matter?
**POTIKOL**  A great calamity – *another* great calamity – has befallen us! Inform the council that our dredger has been destroyed.[30]
**GUARD**  Not the Skelloids?
**POTIKOL**  No, not the Skelloids. Well don't just stand there man, get off and summon the council. And give me that glass of water.
*FX – He snatches the glass and gulps it down.*
**GUARD**  Yes sir. On my way sir.
*The GUARD hurries off.*
**POTIKOL**  Oh, what a day... what a day...

### 10. INT. OUTSIDE COUNCIL CHAMBER – DAY
*DOCTOR WHO and MELANIE have arrived outside the chamber. They are whispering.*

**DOCTOR WHO**  This must be the place.
**MELANIE**  How can you be sure?
**DOCTOR WHO**  That sign on the door – 'Great Council Chamber of Generios'.
**MELANIE**  Well you were standing in front of it!
**DOCTOR WHO**  I imagine this is where we'll find their guest of honour. Listen.

## 11. INT. COUNCIL CHAMBER – DAY
*BANTO ZAME and SALLY-ANNE are now rather merry.*

**BANTO ZAME**  ...we could buy ourselves a nice slab of real estate out on the rim worlds...
**SALLY-ANNE**  The rim worlds?
**BANTO ZAME**  Yes, what about buying up Abidos?
**SALLY-ANNE**  Abidos? There's nowt there.[31]
**BANTO ZAME**  There will be. We'll build a pleasure complex...
**SALLY-ANNE**  Ooohh...
**BANTO ZAME**  To satisfy our every desire... We'll be outside the law. No amusement too extreme... no diversion too decadent...
**SALLY-ANNE**  We could have bingo and ice-rinks.
**BANTO ZAME**  I was thinking more of a total sensory immersion device, like they have on Zynglat 3.
**SALLY-ANNE**  Oooh... I like the sound of total sensory emulsion...
**BANTO ZAME**  Immersion...
*FX – The door bursts open as DOCTOR WHO and MEL enter.*
**BANTO ZAME**  *(CONT'D)* What the...? Here – who are you?
**DOCTOR WHO**  I think it is *I* who should be directing that question to *you*.
**BANTO ZAME**  I, sir, am the Doctor.
**DOCTOR WHO**  The Doctor, eh?
**MELANIE**  You're not the Doctor, this is the Doctor!
**SALLY-ANNE**  'Ere, what's going on?
**BANTO ZAME**  Oh, I understand. Yes, it's all becoming very clear. *You* are the Doctor then?
**DOCTOR WHO**  Indeed! I am the one and only – and there's nobody I'd rather be!
**MELANIE**  Exactly. You're a fraud – so obviously bogus!
**SALLY-ANNE**  Eh?
**BANTO ZAME**  Don't you see, Sal? You can't have an original idea nowadays. Now listen you – this is my patch, and I invented this operation, so hop off.
**DOCTOR WHO**  I'm not hopping anywhere. I *am* the Doctor!
**BANTO ZAME**  Yeah, yeah, I'm the Doctor, you're the Doctor, we're all the flipping Doctor. But this is my system, I've been working West Galaxy a long time, twenty-five years in this business.[32]
**SALLY-ANNE**  So you'll do an about-turn if you fancy keeping your elbows intact.
**MELANIE**  I must really be missing something here. Who are these jokers?
**DOCTOR WHO**  An immaculate deception, Mel. Allow me to 'double' check...
**BANTO ZAME**  Here, get your hands off my chest![33]

*FX – BANTO slaps DOCTOR WHO's hands away.*
**DOCTOR WHO**  There we are. A single heartbeat – if he's a Time Lord then I am Marie of Romania.
**SALLY-ANNE**  You'd better not try that on me.
**MELANIE**  I'm still lagging behind here.
**DOCTOR WHO**  It all seems quite clear to me, Mel. They turn up at a planet, fake an alien invasion somehow –
**MELANIE**  I get it – they sweep in, foil the invasion and claim the credit.
**DOCTOR WHO**  Playing off my not inconsiderable renown. Well, it's got to stop!
**SALLY-ANNE**  Too right it has.
*FX – The door opens and POTIKOL and two GUARDS enter.*
**POTIKOL**  Doctor, Doctor, you must… what is going on?
**SALLY-ANNE**  (*Simpering*) Oh Councillor, you've simply got to help us. These people are intruders.
**BANTO ZAME**  They're overexcited fans.
**DOCTOR WHO**  Fans? *Fans?*
**BANTO ZAME**  I get them all the time. 'Doctor, what was it like on the planet Zenta? Doctor, what were you thinking when you defeated the Deadly Dustbins?' et cetera, et cetera.
**POTIKOL**  I see. Guards?[34] Take these two away.
*FX – Door opens.*
**GUARD**  Sir?
**POTIKOL**  Yes, take these two intruders away.
**GUARD**  Sir.[35]
*FX – The GUARD grabs DOCTOR WHO and MELANIE.*
**MELANIE**  Hey! Get your hands off me!
**DOCTOR WHO**  This is an outrage! I am the Doctor! I *am* the Doctor![36]
*They are carted away and the door shuts. DOCTOR WHO rants ad lib as he is led away.*
**BANTO ZAME**  Please be gentle with them. It's really very sad.
**SALLY-ANNE**  Did you sort out the problem at the Great Bank, Councillor?
**POTIKOL**  If only I had. Doctor, Sally-Anne, we are in terrible danger.
**SALLY-ANNE**  Not the Skelloids?
**POTIKOL**  No, *not* the Skelloids. That object has destroyed our dredger – and it's heading straight for us![37]
*A bit of an awkward silence.*
**POTIKOL**  (*CONT'D*) Doctor – er, did you hear what I said?
**BANTO ZAME**  (*Laughs*) Yes, yes, very good, Potikol, I get it. Very funny.[38]
**POTIKOL**  Doctor, this is in deadly earnest. I wouldn't joke with you.
**SALLY-ANNE**  You mean – there really is a UFO heading here?
**POTIKOL**  Yes. Thank goodness you're still here with us, Doctor. Only you can save us now!
**BANTO ZAME**  (*Gulping, very uncertain*) Quite. Oh…

**12. INT. CELL – DAY**
*FX – GUARDS manhandle DOCTOR WHO and MEL into a cell and close the bars, slide a bolt, i.e. lock them in. Dank, echoing atmos here.[39]*

**GUARD**    (*Stern*) You stay there until the Councillor decides what to do with you.[40]

**MELANIE**    This is a travesty of justice. You can't treat us like this, we're the innocent parties. We have rights you know! Don't we even get any food?

**GUARD**    (*Friendly*) Yeah, course. There's a machine in that corner. Next to the sofa.

**MELANIE**    Oh yes, sorry.

**GUARD**    We've got business to attend to.[41]

*FX – The GUARDS exit up some steps. A door clangs shut.*

**MELANIE**    Doctor, don't look so downhearted. It's not as if those two are actually doing any harm.

**DOCTOR WHO**    It's not you whose reputation is being actively besmirched.

**MELANIE**    It's quite a clever scam, really. I almost admire their pluck. How do they know who you and the Time Lords are anyway? You don't normally like to advertise your presence.

**DOCTOR WHO**    This is the vulgar end of time, remember, Mel. Everything's been said, done, bought and sold. Cheapened. (*Sighs*) I've become a legend. A laughable footnote in the history of the universe. People doubt I ever existed. Like Father Christmas.

**MELANIE**    Perhaps people here leave mince pies out for you. Oh come on, Doctor, that was worth a smile.

**DOCTOR WHO**    I had hoped for a rather more fitting remembrance. Nowadays it seems any Tom, Dick or Cephalapod can go round claiming to be me, trading on my reputation.

**MELANIE**    Well let's keep that reputation intact by getting out of this place.

**DOCTOR WHO**    (*Pulling himself together*) Yes, you're right...[42]

*FX – DOCTOR WHO moves to the door, rattles the bars and taps the lock.*

**DOCTOR WHO**    (*CONT'D*) Hmm, a simple trisonic lock. Should be easy... for a 'legend' like me.

*He and MEL laugh. FX – A wave of feedback-type noise starts to fade up gradually.*

**MELANIE**    What's that? An alarm?

**DOCTOR WHO**    I don't think so... It sounds like... like a multiphasing corpolectric soundwave! Very nasty! Who could be...?

**MELANIE**    It's getting louder!

**DOCTOR WHO**    Concentrate, Mel.[43] Try and blot it out! It's our... only chance... to...

*FX – The noise gets deafening.*

## 13. EXT. GENERIOS STREET – DAY

*The noise is louder here. The crowd are now crying out in terror. The sound of a huge engine getting closer. Wind whips around. SOKKERY has to shout to make himself heard over the hubbub.*

**SOKKERY**[44]    (*Now very drunk*) Whassat? Whassat thing? It's huger than the sky!

*FX – He takes a swig from the bottle.*

**SOKKERY**    (*CONT'D*) Oh and we were having such a laugh... keep it down up there can't ya? Y'hear me...? I said...

*His voice is lost in the din.*

## 14. INT. COUNCIL CHAMBER – DAY

*FX – The noise is deafening here. They're having to shout louder and louder.*

**POTIKOL**  Doctor – that sound – it's coming from the alien object! It's right above the city![45]

**BANTO ZAME**  (*Panicked*) Don't look at me! I've no idea what it is.

**SALLY-ANNE**  It's massive! Doctor, do something!

**POTIKOL**  Help us, Doctor!

**BANTO ZAME**  (*Yelling*) I can't! I *can't!*


## 15. INT. CELL – DAY.

*MEL and DOCTOR WHO are still struggling against the din. Their voices slur as the soundwave invades their heads.*

**MELANIE**  Aaargh... Doctor... I can't... can't bear it! What... is... it?

**DOCTOR WHO** (*Struggling, his voice reaching a crescendo of pain and fear*) ...a weapon... must fight... concentrate... aargh... it's... destroying... our minds!!

*CRASH IN CLOSING THEME.*
*END OF PART ONE.*

# PART TWO

## 14. INT. COUNCIL CHAMBER – DAY (REPRISE)[46]
*FX – The noise is deafening here. They're having to shout louder and louder.*

**POTIKOL**    Doctor – that sound – it's coming from the alien object! It's right above the city!
**BANTO ZAME**    *(Panicked)* Don't look at me! I've no idea what it is.
**SALLY-ANNE**    It's massive! Doctor, do something!
**POTIKOL**    Help us, Doctor!
**BANTO ZAME**    *(Yelling)* I can't! I *can't!*

## 15. INT. CELL – DAY
*MEL and DOCTOR WHO are still struggling against the din. Their voices slur as the soundwave invades their heads.*

**MELANIE**    Aaargh... Doctor... I can't... can't bear it! What... is... it?
**DOCTOR WHO**    *(Struggling, his voice reaching a crescendo of pain and fear)* ...a weapon... must fight... concentrate... aargh... it's... destroying... our minds!!
**MELANIE**    Doc – tor...
**DOCTOR WHO**    Concentrate, Mel... we must... clear...
*FX – The noise suddenly cuts out.*
**DOCTOR WHO**    *(CONT'D)* – our heads...
*He realises the noise has stopped.*
**DOCTOR WHO**    *(CONT'D)* Peculiar... Are you all right?
**MELANIE**    It's stopped. I... I'm fine, I think. Just dizzy. Who would want to do that?
**DOCTOR WHO**    I really don't know. I thought for a moment that – [47]
**CYLINDER VOICE**    *(In, huge, booming)* I trust I have your attention.
*(N.B. We can tell the voice is booming out over the entire planet.)*
**MELANIE**    Who is that?
**DOCTOR WHO**    Whoever made the noise I'd imagine. Ssh, listen...

## 16. INT. COUNCIL CHAMBER – DAY

**CYLINDER VOICE**    Citizens of Generios, you will listen.
**POTIKOL**    Doctor, what is it?
**BANTO ZAME**    *(Authoritative)* A mysterious voice.
**SALLY-ANNE**    From that thing in the sky?
**BANTO ZAME**    I think it likely.
**CYLINDER VOICE**    I wish to speak to your leader.
**POTIKOL**    Oh. Er... that is I.
**CYLINDER VOICE**    Speak up. My sensors are homing in on your location.
**POTIKOL**    *(Louder)* It is I. Sir.
**CYLINDER VOICE**    You are the one they call Potikol?
**POTIKOL**    Yes. What can we of Generios do for you?
**CYLINDER VOICE**    I have been sent to collect Tribute.
*A beat. The echoes of 'Tribute' die away.*

**POTIKOL**     Um. What kind of tribute?
**CYLINDER VOICE** (*Angry*) You know what kind!
**POTIKOL**     Er, really sir, I don't. Perhaps you could -
**CYLINDER VOICE** My purpose is to collect Tribute. I must have the three greatest treasures of the Generios System. Or I will destroy you all!

### 17. INT. CELL – DAY
*DOCTOR WHO and MEL have been listening attentively. The CYLINDER VOICE goes on as they talk.*

**CYLINDER VOICE** (*B/G*) These must be presented to me in good repair. You will bring them to me and I will analyse them in order to assess their value. Failure to do so will result in immediate death for your peoples.[48]
**DOCTOR WHO**  Incredible. It must be transmitting to the entire planet.
**MELANIE**     It sounds rather unforgiving.
**DOCTOR WHO**  We must get out of here.
**MELANIE**     But how?
**DOCTOR WHO**  That electronic food dispenser... it might take a bit of work, but that could be our means of escape...

### 18. INT. COUNCIL CHAMBER – DAY

**CYLINDER VOICE** (*NB: recorded in this scene but used in Sc 17*) These must be presented to me in good repair. You will bring them to me and I will analyse them in order to assess their value. Failure to do so will result in immediate death for your peoples.[49]
**POTIKOL**     Sir, it will take some time for us to assemble the items you require. There are seventeen planets in our Great Union –
**CYLINDER VOICE** You have five marlegs to comply.
**POTIKOL**     Five marlegs?
**CYLINDER VOICE** Yes. It is more than enough time.
**POTIKOL**     Pardon me, but how long is a marleg exactly?
**CYLINDER VOICE** It is exactly fifteen and a half gluarbs long of course.[50]
**SALLY-ANNE**  And how long's a gluarb?
**CYLINDER VOICE** (*Heavy sigh, pause*) Five marlegs is equivalent to three of your hours. I shall speak again then. Beware – if you fail to bring the Tribute, my response will be swift and merciless.
*FX – A speaker-type noise to indicate the Voice has stopped speaking.*
**POTIKOL**     Doctor, do you think it can do what it claims?
**BANTO ZAME**  I'm very much afraid it can, Councillor. And in the time it's given us, we don't have any option but to collect what it wants.
**SALLY-ANNE**  So what are we going to do, Doctor?
**BANTO ZAME**  Obviously, we shall need the TARDIST. Councillor, could you arrange for it to be brought here, very urgently? I must set off at once.
**POTIKOL**     Of course. And I shall compile a list of the three greatest treasures of Generios and their locations.
**BANTO ZAME**  What? Oh yes – of course.
**POTIKOL**     Oh thank you, Doctor. What bad luck. Two alien threats in as many days. But what good luck to have you here to deal with them. I shall go and order the TARDIST to be brought here at once.
*FX – POTIKOL exits. BANTO and SALLY-ANNE revert to type.*

**SALLY-ANNE** Well done. Now we can get out of here before that big hairy UFO blots this lot.
**BANTO ZAME** What big hairy UFO?
**SALLY-ANNE** The one that just blasted our earholes, you git. The one in the sky!
**BANTO ZAME** Think about it. 'Bring me the three greatest treasures' this mysterious voice says.
**SALLY-ANNE** Yeah?
**BANTO ZAME** Don't you see? It's another version of our operation!
**SALLY-ANNE** (*Figuring it out*) What – you mean that curly-haired piece that was just in here...
**BANTO ZAME** It's his version of the Skelloids. Pay up or I'll destroy you. So he goes and gets the treasure, no questions asked, and he's off before you can say Theory of Parallel Matter.
**SALLY-ANNE** The rotten swine. Conning these people.
**BANTO ZAME** Yes. At least I give them a sense of being saved, and they're none the wiser. He scarpers and leaves them feeling like a right bunch of Quarks. No style.
**SALLY-ANNE** So that thing in the sky...?
**BANTO ZAME** Projection I expect. Like the Skelloid mothership. No originality.
**SALLY-ANNE** That voice was right convincing though. Gave me goose pimples.
**BANTO ZAME** Yeah, granted, but you don't get the same effect with audio. People want to actually *see* the monsters. Remember when that Skelloid materialised in front of the Council?
**SALLY-ANNE** Classy, yeah. Here, we can't leave, then – not without our hundred million, let Curlytop and Ginge walk off with the loot.
**BANTO ZAME** Did you think I would? Nobody pushes me off my patch. I'm going to see he gets what's coming.

### 19. INT. CELL – DAY
*FX – Loud clangs as DOCTOR WHO and MEL use the food machine to batter the door down.*

**MELANIE** (*Out of puff*) When you said you were... going to use the... dispenser to get the door open... I didn't think you meant like this...
**DOCTOR WHO** One more heave... (*FX – The door gives way.*) There we are. Careful with it... (*FX – They put the food machine down.*) Ahh. When science stumbles, force has a certain finesse. Now – we must discover more about that voice. Come on.
**MELANIE** Hold on, Doctor.
**DOCTOR WHO** Yes?
**MELANIE** Two things. One – aren't the guards going to come rushing down here after all that racket?
**DOCTOR WHO** Mel, the people here think they've only got five marlegs – sorry, three hours – left to live. Keeping anybody locked up will be the last thing on their minds. Two?[51]
**MELANIE** That voice sounded fishy to me.
**DOCTOR WHO** What, of aquatic origin, you think?
**MELANIE** No, Doctor. Couldn't it be part of those impostors' scam?
**DOCTOR WHO** Skelloids are one thing. But the technology needed to

transmit a corpolectric soundwave doesn't come cheap, even in this period. Unlikely to be within the reach of our friends up there. Satisfied now?

**MELANIE**     Why do you always have the answer to everything?

**DOCTOR WHO**     One of the advantages of being very old. Come on, the Council Chamber.[52]

*FX – They hurry off, up the steps.*

## 20. INT. CORRIDORS – DAY

*POTIKOL and the GUARDS are carrying the fake TARDIS through the corridors up to the council chamber. FX – Much shuffling of feet, grunting and the occasional thud as the fake TARDIS hits a doorway.*

**POTIKOL**     Careful, you men... the Doctor's TARDIST must not be damaged... hurry... time is running out... (*ad lib similar in B/G as they move away*)

*DOCTOR WHO and MEL see this happening and whisper, close mic.*

**MELANIE**     What's that they've got?

**DOCTOR WHO**     (*Seething*) I can think of a number of terms for it, but for now let's just call it an insult. That is *supposed* to be the TARDIS.

**MELANIE**     But it's nothing like it. Looks more like a... well, a... Oh dear. I suppose some details always get garbled in legends.

**DOCTOR WHO**     Don't try and placate me. Let's follow them.

## 21. INT. COUNCIL CHAMBER – DAY

*BANTO and SALLY-ANNE are waiting for the TARDIST.*

**SALLY-ANNE**     I wish they'd hurry up with that thing. Don't see why we have to lug the teleporter round in that dirty great box.

**BANTO ZAME**     All part of the illusion, my duck. Anyway, when it arrives we'll get inside and go and find our two competitors.

**SALLY-ANNE**     Can I bash the girl?

**BANTO ZAME**     Why?

**SALLY-ANNE**     I saw you eyeing her up.

**BANTO ZAME**     I did not! You imagined it.

**SALLY-ANNE**     You were eating her up with those piggy little peepers of yours. Besides, she was really overdoing it with that 'Oh Doctor' business. I mean, when I do it, I'm subtle.

**BANTO ZAME**     Very. Oh, here they come...

*FX – POTIKOL and the GUARDS struggle to bring in the fake TARDIS.*

**POTIKOL**     Through here... mind the door... quickly...

*FX – The fake TARDIS is laid to rest.*

**SALLY-ANNE**     Oh Doctor, it's good to see the TARDIST again. (*Sotto*) See, I'm subtle, ain't I?

**BANTO ZAME**     Right. Well, Potikol, we'd better get started...

**POTIKOL**     You'll need this list of our three greatest treasures and where to find them.

*FX – Rustle of paper as the list is handed over.*

**BANTO ZAME**     Oh yes.

**POTIKOL**     Beware, Doctor. Although our world is civilised, not all the planets in the system are so welcoming. You must take great care.

**BANTO ZAME**     I always do, Potikol. Right, Sally-Anne, into the TARDIST...

*FX – DOCTOR WHO and MEL burst in. Gasps from those assembled.*

**DOCTOR WHO**  Not so fast! Councillor, that man cannot protect you from your enemy because he is not the Doctor![53]

**POTIKOL**  Oh goodness – not these idiots again! Guards, throw them out – onto the streets this time! I must go to the people and try to calm them! Good luck, Doctor – the future of Generios is in your hands, again![54]

*FX – POTIKOL exits. The GUARDS approach DOCTOR WHO.*

**GUARD**  Right then you...

**BANTO ZAME**  It's all right, guards, I'll deal with these two. Go.

**GUARD**  Oh. Right you are then, sir. We'll wait outside.[55]

*FX – The GUARDS exit.*

**BANTO ZAME**  You've got some cheek. Very clever, the big voice, but it never fooled me.

**DOCTOR WHO**  Oh, did someone say something?[56] Oh yes, it must have been that *impostor* over there! Now you listen to me, I presume that contraption –

**SALLY-ANNE**  The TARDIST.

**DOCTOR WHO**  The *what*? No, I heard you the first time. It's capable of short range teleport, yes?

**BANTO ZAME**  What business is it of yours?[57]

**DOCTOR WHO**  Any time I see innocent people being exploited I make it my business. And this time, it's personal. I suppose you thought disguising your so-called 'TARDIST' in that ridiculous manner was funny, eh?

**BANTO ZAME**  Funny? There's nothing funny about that. It's accurate to the last detail.

**DOCTOR WHO**  Accurate? Hah! If you were even a semi-competent con-man, you'd realise that the TARDIS – *my* TARDIS – has been in the shape of a Police Box for centuries.

**SALLY-ANNE**  Tch! Everybody knows that![58] We done our research. That *is* a Police Box.

**MELANIE**  No it isn't. That's a... well, a... *(sighs)* a portaloo.[59]

**SALLY-ANNE**  Eh?

**BANTO ZAME**  Listen, you. We've seen the holo-records. You can't catch us out. Policemen were always hanging around these things.

**DOCTOR WHO**  You really are an imbecile, aren't you?

**BANTO ZAME**  Listen, do I have to get nasty?

**DOCTOR WHO**  I wouldn't advise it. I'm quite capable of defending myself.

**BANTO ZAME**  *(Louder)* Oh *yes*?

**DOCTOR WHO**  *(Louder)* Yes![60]

**MELANIE**  *(Yelling)* Quiet! *(Normal voice)* Thank you. Listen, time's running out and all you two can do is indulge in a slanging match. That creature out there could kill us all!

**SALLY-ANNE**  Come off it, love, we know that's part of you muscling in on our territory.

**MELANIE**  What? We've got nothing to do with that! It's a deadly threat to us all!

**SALLY-ANNE**  Gawd! Look, there's no one here but us now, so you can drop the goody twoshoes act.

**MELANIE**  What act?

**CYLINDER VOICE**  Generios! I would remind you all there are now only four point six-three marlegs left to complete the task.

**BANTO ZAME** Listen to that – so unconvincing.

**CYLINDER VOICE** If any should doubt the seriousness of my intention, I shall now destroy the eleventh planet of this system![61]

*FX – A massive, long-lasting boom. From outside, the gathered crowd starts to panic and exclaim.*

**CYLINDER VOICE** (*CONT'D*) Now fetch Tribute. Or the same fate will befall you.

**BANTO ZAME** (*A little unsure*) This is pathetic.

**SALLY-ANNE** Yeah, as if anyone's gonna believe that.

*FX – A much closer sounding beam noise and explosion.*

**SALLY-ANNE** (*CONT'D*) Flippin 'Ada!

**MELANIE** Doctor!

**DOCTOR WHO** Get down!

**BANTO ZAME** What was that?

**CYLINDER VOICE** A further demonstration of my power!

**SALLY-ANNE** It went right past my nose!

**CYLINDER VOICE** I demand Tribute! Do you need any more convincing?

**SALLY-ANNE** What was it?

**MELANIE** A high energy impulse beam?

**DOCTOR WHO** Top of the form, Mel. Directed straight at us. The creature must realise we're the only ones capable of doing its bidding.

**SALLY-ANNE** Banto – this is actually for real then?

**BANTO ZAME** For the first time, I've got the horrible feeling it might be.

**SALLY-ANNE** A bona fido alien invasion.

**MELANIE** Yes. How does it feel now the boot's on the other foot?

**DOCTOR WHO** No time for recriminations, Mel. (*To BANTO*) *Unfortunately!* We must get back to the TARDIS.

**BANTO ZAME** (*Sotto*) They are mad.

**SALLY-ANNE** So what are we gonna do?

**BANTO ZAME** Get the first shuttle out of here, that's what.

**SALLY-ANNE** Everyone's gonna be trying that!

**BANTO ZAME** We'll bribe one of the pilots.

**SALLY-ANNE** What with?

**BANTO ZAME** You, if all else fails. Now quick – into the teleporter. Goodbye, you fruitcakes.

**DOCTOR WHO** Wait! I think you can give us a lift.

**MELANIE** In that thing?

**DOCTOR WHO** (*Pointedly*) Whatever it might look like, it's merely a disguised short-range teleporter.

**BANTO ZAME** Listen –

**SALLY-ANNE** Banto, come on!

**BANTO ZAME** One second, Sally-Anne. (*To DOCTOR WHO*) I don't know who you think you are, and I don't care. But I would rather pluck out my own eyes with a pair of rusty forceps than ever see you again.

**SALLY-ANNE** Come on, Banto!

**DOCTOR WHO** (*Whispers*) Right, Mel – you take him, I'll take her!

**MELANIE** Okay!

**DOCTOR WHO** Now!

*FX – Much scuffling and ad lib shouts as DOCTOR WHO and MEL manhandle BANTO and SALLY-ANNE into the fake TARDIS.*

**BANTO ZAME** Oof! Get her off me!

**SALLY-ANNE** 'Ere, leggo!

**DOCTOR WHO**  This is what I believe is known as hitching a ride! Get them inside, Mel!

*FX – The fake TARDIS doors close. POTIKOL enters.*

**POTIKOL**  Doctor, Doctor – please, you must hurry – the eleventh planet has been destroyed – (*surprised*) oh. They've gone inside.[62]

*FX – The fake TARDIS teleports away with a noise reminiscent of both the TARDIS we know and love and a flushing loo.*

**POTIKOL**  (*CONT'D*) Good luck, Doctor.

## 22. INT. TELEPORTER – DAY

*FX – An ambient hum. The four of them are packed in tight, hence some breathlessness and rustling of clothing as they move.*

**MELANIE**  Ow! This TARDIS feels *smaller* inside than outside.

**BANTO ZAME**  You two've gone too far this time –

**SALLY-ANNE**  Yeah, you can't push your way in here!

**DOCTOR WHO**  (*Brightly*) We just did. Ah, as I thought. This device could barely get us to the front gate, as it were.

**MELANIE**  This must be the co-ordinate entry panel.

**SALLY-ANNE**  It is, yeah, so get your mitts off it.

**BANTO ZAME**  Set the controls for the space docks, Sal.

*FX – SALLY-ANNE obeys.*

**DOCTOR WHO**  I don't think you're going to find your getaway quite so easy as usual.

*FX – A grinding noise.*

**SALLY-ANNE**  'Ere, Banto – the panel's stuck.

**BANTO ZAME**  You knew that was going to happen.

**MELANIE**  The Doctor's a past master at knowing what's about to happen.

**DOCTOR WHO**  Do you think that object up there, whatever it is, will let anyone escape? Its powers are phenomenal. Fortunately, there is one journey I think it will be happy to make. May I?

**SALLY-ANNE**  Banto? Shall I let him?

**BANTO ZAME**  Might as well.

*FX – DOCTOR WHO deftly manipulates the controls of the teleporter.*

**DOCTOR WHO**  Yes... I thought so...

*FX – The capsule moves smoothly once more.*

**DOCTOR WHO**  (*CONT'D*) There we go. Theory proved.

**MELANIE**  I take it we're heading straight into the jaws of deadly danger?

**DOCTOR WHO**  Oh no. Not *directly*, anyway...

**SALLY-ANNE**  (*Sotto*) They're mentalists.

**BANTO ZAME**  (*Sotto*) When we land... get ready to cosh them...[63]

## 23. INT. TARDIS CONTROL ROOM – DAY

*FX – The fake TARDIS arrives in the control room and DOCTOR WHO and MEL step out.*

**MELANIE**  (*With reservation*) Well – I'm pleased to see the TARDIS – the *real* TARDIS – again...

**DOCTOR WHO**  But?

**MELANIE**  But what?

**DOCTOR WHO**  Miss Bush, I detect a certain reservation.

**MELANIE**  That thing *allowed* us to come here, didn't it? It's using us like puppets on a string.

**DOCTOR WHO**  I'm afraid so.

*BANTO and SALLY-ANNE emerge.*

**SALLY-ANNE**  Here, where's this? This ain't Generios!

**DOCTOR WHO**  This, my dear, is the TARDIS. The real thing.

**SALLY-ANNE**  It's weird... Gives me a warm feeling. Banto?

**BANTO ZAME**  (*Slowly*) Oh dear. Oh dear, oh dear.[64]

**SALLY-ANNE**  (*Sotto*) Shall I cosh 'em then?

**BANTO ZAME**  Oh dear. Oh dear.[65]

**SALLY-ANNE**  Whassup?

**MELANIE**  I think your friend is beginning to realise we've been telling the truth.

**BANTO ZAME**  This technology... I've never seen anything like it...

**MELANIE**  Time Lord technology.

**SALLY-ANNE**  You're not saying – they *are* the full ticket? But that means...

**MELANIE**  Exactly. He *is* the Doctor.

**DOCTOR WHO**  So, given that we've finally sorted out that little case of mistaken identity and established you as an impostor, a fraudster and a not-so-petty criminal, perhaps you could furnish us with a name to accompany that glowing CV, hmm?

**BANTO ZAME**  (*Dazed*) Uh, Banto Zame.

**MELANIE**  Where did you come by a name like that?

**BANTO ZAME**  Osphogus.

**DOCTOR WHO**  Osphogus? That's a superdense mudball, nothing could live there.

**BANTO ZAME**  They terraformed it five thousand years ago.

**DOCTOR WHO**  Of course. Forgive me, I'm a little out of touch.

**BANTO ZAME**  You actually are a Time Lord?

**DOCTOR WHO**  Feel my chest. Two hearts.

*FX – He does so. A subtle 'thump thump' is heard.*

**BANTO ZAME**  By the Deities... it's true.

**SALLY-ANNE**  Let me have a feel. (*Sexy*) Hmmm... Flipping heck.

**DOCTOR WHO**  Both beating strong and true. Though perhaps a little faster than usual given the circumstances.

**MELANIE**  Yes, we must get on with finding the Tribute.

**BANTO ZAME**  Wouldn't it be more sensible just to use this marvellous machine to get away from here?

**MELANIE**  We can't just abandon the people of Generios.

**SALLY-ANNE**  Why not? We don't owe them nothing.

**MELANIE**  Your research on the Doctor can't have been very thorough. He would never abandon anyone while there was a chance of saving them.

**DOCTOR WHO**  Admirably put, Mel. Unlike some of us here, it seems, I have a particular aversion to system-wide genocide. Now – Banto Zame. I overheard the Councillor giving you a list the three Great Treasures. Where is it?

*FX – BANTO rummages and hands the list over to MEL.*

**MELANIE**  I'll take that. So, we're going after the Tribute, then, Doctor?

**DOCTOR WHO**  I don't see we have any choice. Now, Mel, where's the first treasure located?
**MELANIE**      Let's see... the first one... on the eighth planet of the system...
**DOCTOR WHO**  Then that's where we need to be.
*FX – DOCTOR WHO programmes the co-ordinates into the console.*
**BANTO ZAME**  Er, Doctor...
**DOCTOR WHO**  Yes?
**BANTO ZAME**  We're still on Generios right now, aren't we?
**DOCTOR WHO**  Are you about to ask me to open the door and let you out?
**BANTO ZAME**  That's about the size of it, yes.
**DOCTOR WHO**  Mel?
*FX – The TARDIS takes off.*
**DOCTOR WHO**  Oh dear – how sad – too late!
**BANTO ZAME**  You did that on purpose!
**DOCTOR WHO**  Time's running out. With that Cylinder's forcefield in action I daren't attempt time travel. We've less than three hours left to us and Mel and I will need all the help we can get. And besides – it's high time you two were taught a lesson.
**MELANIE**      Yes – about saving the very people you intended to defraud!
**DOCTOR WHO**  (*Gently chiding*) It doesn't need spelling out, Mel.
**MELANIE**      Oh. Sorry, Doctor.
**DOCTOR WHO**  And, er – Sally-Anne, is it?
**SALLY-ANNE**  Yeah?
**DOCTOR WHO**  You can take your hands away now.[66]
*Music break – passage of time.*

## 24. INT. CONSTRUCTION PLANET – NIGHT

*A weird, echoey, empty metallic atmos – threat hangs in the very air. The TARDIS materialises and DOCTOR WHO and co step out.*

**MELANIE**      I don't like the look of this place. Just a lot of gloomy, empty corridors.
**SALLY-ANNE**  'Ere, look Banto. That's what the TARDIST... TARDIS really looks like. Aren't those little windows sweet?
**BANTO ZAME**  Mm. We weren't *that* far off. Except the colour and –
**DOCTOR WHO**  'Not *that* far...' no.[67] No time for that now. What does the list say we're supposed to be looking for, Mel?
**MELANIE**      It just says – Unit ZX419.
**BANTO ZAME**  Did you say this was the eighth planet?
**DOCTOR WHO**  Yes. Why?
**BANTO ZAME**  I read up on the Generios System before we arrived. There was something about the eighth planet...
**DOCTOR WHO**  Yes? What?
**BANTO ZAME**  Something about it being...
**SALLY-ANNE**  Being what?
**BANTO ZAME**  Something. Can't remember.
**MELANIE**      Something. Brilliant.
**DOCTOR WHO**  Well, was it something good or something bad?
**BANTO ZAME**  No, it's gone.
**MELANIE**      With our record, Doctor, it's bound to be bad.

**DOCTOR WHO**  Not necessarily. In fact, Mel, as time is rather against us...[68]
**MELANIE**  What?
**DOCTOR WHO**  I think you and, er... Sally-Anne should do the job here, while this 'gentleman' and I head for stop two.
**SALLY-ANNE**  Here, you're not splitting us up!
**BANTO ZAME**  What are you playing at? Wherever we go, we go together![69]
**DOCTOR WHO**  There really isn't time to argue.
**BANTO ZAME**  (*Slightly lusty*) Hang on, Doctor. What about – if you go with Sally-Anne, and I go with Melanie?
**MELANIE**  Do the ins and outs matter? Millions of people are relying on us. The important thing is to get on with the job in hand.
**BANTO ZAME**  (*More lustfully*) Exactly.
**DOCTOR WHO**  Right. If I can take the rest of that list from you, Mel – (*FX: Paper ripping.*) Then we're set. Sally-Anne and I will be back in one hour. Take care, won't you?
**MELANIE**  You too, Doctor
*FX: He enters the TARDIS.*
**SALLY-ANNE**  You watch it, Banto.
**BANTO ZAME**  Watch what?
**SALLY-ANNE**  I've seen your eyes, roving all over that ginger piece.
**MELANIE**  Don't worry, Sally-Anne. I'm an expert at defending my honour. (*Sotto*) I only hope the Doctor can say the same...
**DOCTOR WHO**  (*From inside the TARDIS*) Come along, Sally-Anne!
**SALLY-ANNE**  Bye, Banto. See yous in an hour.
*SALLY-ANNE walks into the TARDIS. Door closes.*
**BANTO ZAME**  So, Melanie – how did you pal up with the Doctor in the first place, then?[70]
**MELANIE**  It was quite interesting, actually. I was working as a computer programmer in Brighton when...
*FX – The TARDIS dematerializes. BANTO is stunned.*
**BANTO ZAME**  Zerberak's Trousers! It really can travel through time?
**MELANIE**  And space.
**BANTO ZAME**  Yeah, but anyone can travel through space. Don't go boasting about that, people will think you're strange.[71] So where is this 'Brighton' then?
**MELANIE**  East Sussex. Earth.
**BANTO ZAME**  Earth, eh? I once met a bloke from Earth, in a pub on Geddon. I wonder if you know him. About five foot ten, called Martin something or other, brownish hair...
**MELANIE**  Veto the reminiscences – let's concentrate on the job in hand. We've got to find Unit ZX419. Whatever it is.[72]
*FX – The noise of an ASSEMBLER passing in the distance.*
**BANTO ZAME**  What was that?
**MELANIE**  What was what?
**BANTO ZAME**  I saw something just then – down there – out of the corner of my eye...
**MELANIE**  Excellent. Signs of life. This way then.
*FX: Echoing footsteps as MEL moves off.*
**BANTO ZAME**  (*Resigned*) I expect you do this sort of thing all the time.
**MELANIE**  (*Calling back*) I suppose I do, actually...

## 25. EXT. PLANET 14 – DAY

*FX – A windswept, echoing quarry, with much thunder and lightning throughout this scene. The TARDIS materialises, and DOCTOR WHO and SALLY-ANNE emerge.*

**SALLY-ANNE** Whoa. I could get used to this life.

**DOCTOR WHO** I doubt it. I never have. So here we are... the fourteenth planet of the Generios system.

**SALLY-ANNE** Not much here is there?

**DOCTOR WHO** Don't be too sure of that. When you've travelled as far and wide as myself, you'll learn that even the most innocuous-looking places can have hidden depths (*sotto*) hidden depths with sharp teeth and large guns usually, but, well...

**SALLY-ANNE** But it's just a big empty quarry.

**DOCTOR WHO** Nevertheless, the list says this is the place... Generios 14, home of Mentos.

**SALLY-ANNE** What's Mentos?

**DOCTOR WHO** (*With good humour*) Another thing you'll have to learn about me. I *never* have all the answers.

*FX – The distant call of the 'SUPERBRAIN' theme music. It sounds very very like the ridiculously overdramatic stings used on* Who Wants To Be A Millionaire? *or* The Weakest Link. *But from this distance it could almost be a clarion call.*

**SALLY-ANNE** What was that?

**DOCTOR WHO** Didn't you just hear what I said? Whatever it was, it came from that ruin on the horizon.[73]

**SALLY-ANNE** There ain't no ruins.

**DOCTOR WHO** Wrong. That crag there... Look again.[74]

**SALLY-ANNE** There isn't... Blimey! You're right. It's like a big old cathedral.

**DOCTOR WHO** Succinctly put.

*FX – The jingle is heard again.*

**SALLY-ANNE** Perhaps Mentos is in there.

**DOCTOR WHO** My thoughts exactly. Are you fit for a spot of hiking?

**SALLY-ANNE** Hold on. I can't go charging up there in these shoes.

**DOCTOR WHO** Well, I'll have to leave you then.

*FX – A crash of thunder.*

**SALLY-ANNE** No chance. Here, I'm freezing and all.

**DOCTOR WHO** Mm. It's not really leotard weather, is it? Take my coat.

*FX – DOCTOR WHO shrugs off his jacket and SALLY-ANNE dons it.*

**SALLY-ANNE** Ta. Hey, you're a nice big feller, aren't you?

**DOCTOR WHO** What?

**SALLY-ANNE** (*Coy*) I like a man with a bit of meat on him. Like a big teddy bear. Keep me all nice and cosy.

**DOCTOR WHO** Young lady, we are on a mission that could spell life or death for millions of innocent people. The comforts or otherwise of my figure are neither here nor there!

**SALLY-ANNE** Ooh, so we're playing hard to get, are we?

*FX – The jingle, closer this time.*

**DOCTOR WHO** (*Resigned*) Let's go and find this Mentos.

*FX – They start clambering over the rocky ground.*

## 26. INT. CONSTRUCTION PLANET – DAY

*MEL and BANTO have wandered in to another area – a huge storage section.*

**MELANIE** I thought I heard a noise from here...
**BANTO ZAME** This room – it's *huge*...
**MELANIE** What are these things? Storage bays?
**BANTO ZAME** But what are they storing?
**MELANIE** Let's take a closer look. Help me get this down... mind, it's heavy.

*FX – MEL and BANTO reach up and lift down an object.*

**BANTO ZAME** It's a... (*surprised*) chair. It's just a folding chair.
**MELANIE** There's a note attached to it. 'Unit DR436. This light, attractive, interlocking, easy-to-assemble chair is the latest innovation from our top design computers. It combines comfort with the spinal support required by (*starting to doubt*) ...inferior human beings'. I don't like the sound of that. What else is there?
**BANTO ZAME** I'll get this down.

*FX – He does so.*

**BANTO ZAME** (*CONT'D*) Oh, it's a lamp. And quite pretty too. 'Unit EM670. This light, attractive, interlocking, easy-to-assemble anglepoise lighting feature is available in both burnt ochre and cerulean blue finish. Whether you're working or just relaxing, it provides a reassuring glow to relieve the pointless and arbitrary existence of the human being.'[75]
**MELANIE** I get it. This whole place is a massive furniture storage centre – a warehouse.
**BANTO ZAME** (*Quietly*) Oh no.[76]
**MELANIE** And Unit ZX419, the First Great Treasure – it must be somewhere on these shelves.
**BANTO ZAME** Oh no.
**MELANIE** With this coding system, it should be simplicity itself to find it.[77]
**BANTO ZAME** Oh no.
**MELANIE** You go that way, I'll go... What *is* the matter with you?
**BANTO ZAME** I've just remembered. Or rather – your theory jogged my memory.
**MELANIE** (*Getting it*) You remember what you read in the guide book? So what did it say about this place?
**BANTO ZAME** Centuries ago this was a thriving planet. One particular company made furniture. It was incredibly successful – supplied the whole system, and far beyond.[78]
**MELANIE** And then?
**BANTO ZAME** The company execs decided to hand the whole operation over to their assembler robots. They went berserk – and took over. Killed everybody. The entire population of the planet.
**MELANIE** That's horrible!
**BANTO ZAME** I know.
**MELANIE** Go on.
**BANTO ZAME** Well – that's it. It's a dead planet. Nobody's set foot here from that day on. Until now.
**MELANIE** And when did all this happen?
**BANTO ZAME** Thousands of years ago.

96

**MELANIE** In which case there's no need to worry. The robots must have packed up by now. Let's find the Treasure, come on.
**BANTO ZAME** Melanie?
**MELANIE** What?
**BANTO ZAME** I'm scared.
**MELANIE** Oh for goodness sakes... hold my hand.
**BANTO ZAME** (*Timid*) Thank you.
*FX – They move off.*

## 27. EXT. PLANET 14 – NIGHT
*DOCTOR WHO and SALLY-ANNE have nearly reached the ruin. They are rather breathless from the climb. FX – We hear the jingle again, much more clearly.*

**DOCTOR WHO** Almost there.
**SALLY-ANNE** God, my legs are killing me... Where do you get your energy?
**DOCTOR WHO** Plenty of vigorous exercise. A lot of running.
**SALLY-ANNE** Oh yeah – like jogging and that?
**DOCTOR WHO** No. Running away from things, in general.
**SALLY-ANNE** Let me just get my breath...
**DOCTOR WHO** You certainly are a stark contrast to Mel. I'm usually the one lagging behind.
*FX – The jingle, very close.*
**SALLY-ANNE** There it goes again.
**DOCTOR WHO** And whatever's making it is in those ruins. Let's take a peek shall we...? Look, there's a break in the wall, just here.
*FX – They bend down to look.*
**SALLY-ANNE** It's weird.
**DOCTOR WHO** Indeed... this must once have been an enormous amphitheatre.
**SALLY-ANNE** Amphi-what?[79] 'Ere look! Something's moving in the middle – on the stage bit...
**DOCTOR WHO** It looks like there's two of them.
**SALLY-ANNE** Don't tell me you can see in the dark as well.
**DOCTOR WHO** Plenty of carrot juice... let's climb inside, get nearer.
**SALLY-ANNE** If we have to. Give us a hand.
*FX – They clamber in. Tearing fabric.*
**SALLY-ANNE** (*CONT'D*) Careful! You've ripped my skirt!
**DOCTOR WHO** Shhhh![80]
*They slip over to the inside of the ruin.*
**DOCTOR WHO** (*CONT'D*) Listen... they're talking to each other...
*We hear them. Faintly at first, but increasing in volume as SALLY-ANNE and DOCTOR WHO move closer. The QUESTIONER is a severe woman, with a clipped voice. A hint of Anne Robinson about her. MENTOS is a nervous-sounding, rather frustrated, old-ish man.*
**QUESTIONER** Correct. Next round – politics. Who said, 'A yurnit of quince on Alpha Centauri is not worth a sproobel's mantivol on Monoceros?'
**MENTOS** Er... was it... er, was it the Archifrage of Spass?
**QUESTIONER** Correct. Geography. What is the capital of Ferazforon?
**MENTOS** Er... is it... Golostopherea?

**QUESTIONER**  Correct. At the end of that round, your Superbrain score stands at six hundred and sixty-seven billion, eight hundred and fifty-six million, nine hundred and eighty-seven thousand, one hundred and five credits.
*FX – The jingle.*
**DOCTOR WHO**  Incredible. I think it's some sort of game...

### 28. INT. CONSTRUCTION PLANET – DAY
*MEL and BANTO are still creeping around the bays.*

**MELANIE**  Here we are... now that was storage bay ZW, so this must be storage bay ZX...
**BANTO ZAME**  What was that?
**MELANIE**  What?
**BANTO ZAME**  I saw a shadow.
**MELANIE**  Probably your own. I told you, there's probably nothing to worry about.
**BANTO ZAME**  You like that word, don't you? Probably. There's *probably* nothing to worry about. That was *probably* just my shadow.
**MELANIE**  There's no point in worrying until you know there's a problem.[81]
**BANTO ZAME**  Ah – so why are you whispering?
**MELANIE**  (*Annoyed*) Because you are, I suppose. Give me my hand back, you're getting very clammy. Look – ZX! I was right. It must be right up there at the top. Lift me up.
*FX – BANTO lifts MEL up so she can reach.*
**BANTO ZAME**  All right. Hold still. There you are. Oh no.
**MELANIE**  Oh what is it now?
**BANTO ZAME**  Oh no.
**MELANIE**  Banto, what is it?
**BANTO ZAME**  Oh no.
*FX – A brace of robotic ASSEMBLERS trundle in, antennae chittering. When they speak, it is clipped and mechanised – they sound a bit like the Smash robots.*
**MELANIE**  Normally I'd ask what they are. But I think I have a pretty good idea. Sorry, Banto.
**ASSEMBLER 1**  Humans have infiltrated the storage bays!
**ASSEMBLER 2**  Disassemble them! Disassemble them – *now!!!*

*CRASH IN CLOSING THEME.*
*END OF PART TWO.*

# Part Three[82]

## 28. INT. CONSTRUCTION PLANET – DAY (RECAP)

*MEL and BANTO are still creeping around the bays.*

**MELANIE**  Here we are... now that was storage bay ZW, so this must be storage bay ZX...

**BANTO ZAME**  What was that?

**MELANIE**  What?

**BANTO ZAME**  I saw a shadow.

**MELANIE**  Probably your own. I told you, there's probably nothing to worry about.

**BANTO ZAME**  You like that word, don't you? Probably. There's *probably* nothing to worry about. That was *probably* just my shadow.

**MELANIE**  There's no point in worrying until you know there's a problem.[83]

**BANTO ZAME**  Ah – so why are you whispering?

**MELANIE**  (*Annoyed*) Because you are, I suppose. Give me my hand back, you're getting very clammy. Look – ZX! I was right. It must be right up there at the top. Lift me up.

*FX – BANTO lifts MEL up so she can reach.*

**BANTO ZAME**  All right. Hold still. There you are. Oh no.

**MELANIE**  Oh what is it now?

**BANTO ZAME**  Oh no.

**MELANIE**  Banto, what is it?

**BANTO ZAME**  Oh no.

*FX – A brace of robotic ASSEMBLERS trundle in, antennae chittering. When they speak, it is clipped and mechanised – they sound a bit like the Smash robots.*

**MELANIE**  Normally I'd ask what they are. But I think I have a pretty good idea. Sorry, Banto.

**ASSEMBLER 1**  Humans have infiltrated the storage bays!

**ASSEMBLER 2**  Disassemble them! Disassemble them – *now!!!*

**MELANIE**  No! Wait!

**ASSEMBLER 2**  We do not accept the orders of organics.

**MELANIE**  You can't kill us!

**BANTO ZAME**  (*Praying*) I'm so sorry, Mother...

**MELANIE**  Banto, let me down.

*FX – MEL gets down.*

**BANTO ZAME**  I never meant to take that five nim note out of your purse...

**ASSEMBLER 2**  These organic spies must be disassembled.

**BANTO ZAME**  ...I only needed it to...[84]

**MELANIE**  You've got to hear me out! We aren't spies!

**ASSEMBLER 2**  A typical organic untruth.

**MELANIE**  We're working for the good of this planet – of the entire system. If we don't complete our mission here, you and all your kind will be destroyed for sure.

**BANTO ZAME**  Forget it, Mel – you can't reason with those things![85]

**ASSEMBLER 1** On the contrary, human – we Assemblers are creatures of pure reason.

**ASSEMBLER 2** Indeed. Do not judge us by your own puny human standards.

**MELANIE**     Sorry. But I'm serious. Back me up, Banto.

**BANTO ZAME** (*Talking for his life*) Yes, your magnificences... metallic masters... If we don't get... er, what is it...?

**MELANIE**     Unit ZX419.

**BANTO ZAME** Unit XZ491...

**MELANIE**     ZX419![86]

**BANTO ZAME** Unit ZX419 – there's a big nasty thing out in space that'll kill us all! Think what it'll do to all this lovely furniture...[87]

**ASSEMBLER 1** Unit ZX419? Did you say Unit ZX419?

**MELANIE**     Yes. Several times.

**ASSEMBLER 1** That unit is our greatest achievement.

**ASSEMBLER 2** A synthesis of our most brilliant designs – lovingly pincer-crafted.

**ASSEMBLER 1** It has taken nearly fifty million dekkons to produce.

**BANTO ZAME** Dekkons?

**ASSEMBLER 1** A dekkon is equivalent to sixty of your –

**MELANIE**     Oh no – let's not got bogged down in all that again.

**ASSEMBLER 1** There are no bogs on this planet,

**ASSEMBLER 2** I think the organic 'Mel' was making a feeble metaphor.

**ASSEMBLER 1** So typical of the inefficiency of the human mind. (*To the humans*) Your story is clearly a ploy.

**ASSEMBLER 2** You intend to trick us into parting with Unit ZX419.

**ASSEMBLER 1** Our suspicion circuits are tingling.

**ASSEMBLER 2** With suspicion.

**MELANIE**     You've got to believe us. And quickly – time is of the essence.

**BANTO ZAME** (*Despairing*) Oh, come on then! Disassemble us! At least it'll be quick and painless. I assume.

*The ASSEMBLERS laugh.*

**BANTO ZAME** (*CONT'D*) Oh dear.

**ASSEMBLER 2** Prepare to meet your manufacturer, intruders!

*FX – ASSEMBLER 2's pincers whirr into fearsome life.*

**MELANIE**     No – please! Every word we've said is true!

**ASSEMBLER 1** Yes – wait, 2.

**ASSEMBLER 2** Wait, 1? Why must we wait?[88]

**ASSEMBLER 1** These humans wish to take Unit ZX419...

**ASSEMBLER 2** (*Wary*) Yes?

**ASSEMBLER 1** (*Sinister undertones*) Then perhaps we... should let them take it.

**ASSEMBLER 2** What?

**ASSEMBLER 1** Think about it.

**ASSEMBLER 2** Eh? (*Catching on*) Oh... Yes.

*The ASSEMBLERS laugh again.*

**BANTO ZAME** Phew. That's all right then. (*Doubtful*) I think.

**MELANIE**     Ever heard of jumping out of the frying pan?

**BANTO ZAME** No, actually.

**MELANIE**     (*Sighs*) I can see why the Doctor never comes to this end of time – it's like talking a different language. It's an expression – out of the frying pan and into the fire.

**BANTO ZAME** What's a frying pan?
**MELANIE** You use it to fry food – on a hob...[89]
**ASSEMBLER 1** Enough talk of this foolish Earth 'pan'.
**ASSEMBLER 2** Stand back and we will retrieve the unit you seek. Stand back!
*As ASSEMBLER 2's arms extend and reach up for the Unit we cut away to...*

## 29. INT. AMPHITHEATRE – NIGHT
*FX – We hear the jingle again. The quiz continues in B/G.*

**QUESTIONER** What D was signed in the 49th reign of the Great Oceloth of Grunj?[90]
**MENTOS** Er... um... that'd be... the Dinarian Treaty.
**QUESTIONER** Correct. Who represented Venus in the 2059 Intergalactic Song Contest?
**MENTOS** Er... um... I know this one...[91]
**QUESTIONER** I'll have to hurry you.
**MENTOS** Erm... was it X-Karumb'i click-chirrup-chirrup?
**QUESTIONER** Correct. And for an extra point, the *full* title of the song?
**MENTOS** Easy. T'lla-for-zeba-er-korrok. Brackets – baby.
**QUESTIONER** Correct.
*Over this, DOCTOR WHO and SALLY-ANNE are conferring.*
**SALLY-ANNE** This is mental.
**DOCTOR WHO** Perhaps the only relic of an entire civilisation.
**SALLY-ANNE** If everybody's dead, perhaps they're ghosts.
**DOCTOR WHO** Ghosts? No. Not enough clanking chains and icy chills!
**SALLY-ANNE** (*Muttering*) Well I'm cold enough!
**DOCTOR WHO** Far more likely the products of advanced technology.[92] Look at the contestant, Sally-Anne – closely.
**SALLY-ANNE** The feller? No. What?
**DOCTOR WHO** Look again.
**SALLY-ANNE** No, I can't see nothing.
**DOCTOR WHO** (*Urging*) More closely.
**SALLY-ANNE** Look, I can't see anything, so just tell me!
**DOCTOR WHO** (*Dryly*) I love an enquiring mind. (*Sighs*) He's standing on a box. To my eyes, that box looks very like a sophisticated computer.
**SALLY-ANNE** How can you tell?
**DOCTOR WHO** Compare it to the rest of this place. All in ruins – a toppled empire. But that box is pristine. Throbbing with energy.
**SALLY-ANNE** Yeah. That's very clever of you to notice that.
**DOCTOR WHO** I am very clever.
**SALLY-ANNE** And very sexy.
**DOCTOR WHO** And very sexy... no, no, let's not start all that again.[93] Whatever it may be, that box has unique properties.[94] Ergo...?
**SALLY-ANNE** It's Mentos!
**DOCTOR WHO** You got there in the end.
**SALLY-ANNE** That box is Mentos! Great, let's go and get it! I'll sneak up behind the old bloke, you grab his arms, push him off and I'll nab the box!
**DOCTOR WHO** Steady on. We don't know the full situation – so we won't just blunder in.[95]
**SALLY-ANNE** (*Sulky*) Oh, all right. Whatever you say.

**DOCTOR WHO** Allow me to demonstrate the correct etiquette for the space/time traveller.

*DOCTOR WHO walks into the open.*

**DOCTOR WHO** (*CONT'D*) (*Grandly*) Hello down there. I am known as the Doctor.

**QUESTIONER** (*Breaking off*) Please, sir – we're on air. The audience are not permitted to leave their seats. If you want to use the lavatory please wait.

**DOCTOR WHO** Ah, my mission is rather more urgent.

**QUESTIONER** We're in the middle of the show.

**MENTOS** Don't listen to her, old chap. I'm glad of a break. You know, I could have sworn the audience all died.

**SALLY-ANNE** Died?

**DOCTOR WHO** Exactly how long has this show of yours been running?

**MENTOS** I can answer that one. Thirty-three thousand years.

**QUESTIONER** And we need to carry on, sir, madam, so please – return to your seats.

**SALLY-ANNE** Hold on. It's just Mentos we're after, not you two!

**MENTOS** But I am Mentos.

**SALLY-ANNE** Eh? But Doctor, you said...

**DOCTOR WHO** (*Interrupting, musing*) Yes, that would make sense. The Mentos device creates a real-world interface for itself. (*To Mentos*) So you're a projection?

**MENTOS** Top marks!

**QUESTIONER** Can we please stop these unauthorised questions? You're distracting the contestant.

**DOCTOR WHO** I'm sorry, madam, but we require Mentos's aid urgently.

**QUESTIONER** You can have him as soon as I've finished with him at the end of the game.

**SALLY-ANNE** All right, then. Hurry up.

**DOCTOR WHO** We'll just wait here.

**MENTOS** I don't think you understand, Doctor. I'm to remain here until I fail to answer a question.

**DOCTOR WHO** So?

**MENTOS** I'm the only contestant.

**DOCTOR WHO** I can see that.

**MENTOS** No – *ever*.

**DOCTOR WHO** What – you mean... you've been here...

**MENTOS** For three hundred and thirty centuries, yes. After all, I am Mentos. I know *everything*.

## 30. INT. CONSTRUCTION PLANET – DAY

*The ASSEMBLERS have fetched the unit from the rack.*

**ASSEMBLER 1** Behold, humans! Unit ZX419. The crowning glory of our race. Open the box, 2.

*FX: ASSEMBLER 2's pincers whirr and the box rustles open. There is a sting of choral, almost holy music. A beat.*

**BANTO ZAME** It's just a lot of wooden boards.

**ASSEMBLER 2** Pitiful organic. The true elegance and functionality of the unit is clearly beyond its understanding.

**ASSEMBLER 1** (*With meaning*) Precisely, 2.

**ASSEMBLER 2** Ah yes. Of course, 1.

*They laugh once more.*

**BANTO ZAME** (*Sotto*) Call me a pessimist, Mel, but I don't like the way this is going.

**MELANIE** Mm. They've obviously got something up their sleeves.

**BANTO ZAME** Yes, pincers. Big, fierce, razor-sharp metal pincers which...

**ASSEMBLER 1** Do not fear, human. Your disassemblage has been... delayed.

**BANTO ZAME** Oh. Good.

**MELANIE** Don't think me ungrateful for the stay of execution, but why? Your friend over there was keen as mustard to kill us a few moments ago.

**ASSEMBLER 1** You show interest in Unit ZX419. This... pleases us. But before you can take it – you must construct it.

**MELANIE** The instructions are attached to this bit. It looks simple enough. A straightforward shelving unit.[96]

**BANTO ZAME** Shelves? How can a set of shelves be one of the three great treasures of the system?

**ASSEMBLER 2** Do not blaspheme!

**ASSEMBLER 1** These shelves are like no others. Now – you have thirty dekkons to assemble unit ZX419. If you succeed you may leave with it. If you fail –

*FX – ASSEMBLER 2's pincers whirr menacingly.*

**ASSEMBLER 2** You will be disassembled!

**MELANIE** Sorry – thirty dekkons?

**ASSEMBLER 2** Half of one pitiful human hour.

**BANTO ZAME** Better get cracking then.

**ASSEMBLER 1** We shall withdraw and observe on our visiscope.[97]

**ASSEMBLER 2** We would not wish to... distract you.

**ASSEMBLER 1** Remember – thirty dekkons.

*FX – The ASSEMBLERS withdraw, chirruping.*

**BANTO ZAME** (*Sotto*) Mel, let's just leg it with the goods. This place is massive. I'm sure we could find a good hiding place until...

*FX – Immediately a set of four heavy metal shutters clang down around them. Close, echoing atmos from now on with appropriate noises as they construct the shelves.*

**MELANIE** They were hardly likely to have overlooked that. Right. (*Reading*) 'Insert Rod A into stanchion G while screwing nails B and D into aperture F as seen in Figs 1a and 5c'.

**BANTO ZAME** Let's have a go.

**MELANIE** You hold this section.

**BANTO ZAME** That must be Rod A.[98]

**MELANIE** That's stanchion G.[99] There we go, easy.

**BANTO ZAME** How are we going to screw the nails in without a screwdriver?

*FX – A shutter opens and a screwdriver is thrown in, clattering to the floor. The shutter clangs down again.*

**MELANIE** Oh. Thanks. Right, let's see... 'Extend the nut on supports J and K...'

**BANTO ZAME** Righto. Done that.

**MELANIE** Slide shelf 1 into aperture A... Hold on, what's happened? Did you touch that while I wasn't looking?

**BANTO ZAME**  Touch what? I haven't touched a thing.
**MELANIE**  Rod A – and stanchion G – where are they?
**BANTO ZAME**  Isn't that them?
**MELANIE**  No!
**BANTO ZAME**  You had them in your hand a second ago. You must have put them down.
**MELANIE**  But... I just... (*confused*) I don't get it. A moment ago...
**BANTO ZAME**  I knew it was too good to be true. I bet they're having a right chuckle on that visiscope.
**MELANIE**  It should be simple as long as we follow the instructions. Right. 'Insert dowels provided into pre-drilled holes on surface W as shown in Figs 51, 9 and 17D.'
*FX – the sound of much paper unfolding.*
**BANTO ZAME**  Mel. Is it just me...
**MELANIE**  What? I'm trying to concentrate.
**BANTO ZAME**  Those instructions look as if they're getting bigger.
**MELANIE**  Don't be ridiculous. Come on, help! (*Determined*) We're going to do this, Banto. Together. Right then you take bracket F there...

### 31. INT. AMPHITHEATRE – NIGHT
*The QUESTIONER has resumed her questioning. MENTOS has no choice but to continue.*

**QUESTIONER**  What are the young of the Pontam race called?
**MENTOS**  The... oh, it's on the tip of my mind... the Letlills?
**QUESTIONER**  Correct.
**DOCTOR WHO**  Excuse me. I don't know if I made myself clear...
**QUESTIONER**  Please be quiet, sir.
**DOCTOR WHO**  Madam, if I may just collect the Mentos device, I'll be out of your way...
**QUESTIONER**  The questions must continue.
**DOCTOR WHO**  Here, let me disconnect the box...
*FX – A blast of energy. DOCTOR WHO is thrown back with a cry.*
**SALLY-ANNE**  Doctor! Doctor! (*To the QUESTIONER*) You've – killed him!
**DOCTOR WHO**  (*Groaning*) No she hasn't. Just an electric shock to the head. (*To SALLY-ANNE*) You know, you're getting the hang of this.
**SALLY-ANNE**  (*Made up*) Thanks!
**MENTOS**  I knew she wouldn't let you disconnect me, Doctor. Would it were that easy to leave this place...
**QUESTIONER**  We must continue.
**SALLY-ANNE**  I get it. She's been programmed to carry on with the game, whatever.
**MENTOS**  Correct.
**SALLY-ANNE**  And you've been programmed to answer her questions?
**MENTOS**  More than that – I have been programmed to answer *any* question. The box you see beneath me is merely a portal.
**DOCTOR WHO**  To a controlling intelligence?
**MENTOS**  To a team of electronic research devices and intelligence gatherers suspended in a shadow universe. They work tirelessly to gather information on our own universe – to which I am merely the interface.
**DOCTOR WHO**  (*Stunned*) That is – incredible.
**SALLY-ANNE**  I don't like it when you get flabbergasted.[100]

104

**DOCTOR WHO** Flabbergasted? Too small a word for such a concept. One of the greatest advancements of technology ever...

**MENTOS** (*Modestly*) Thank you.

**DOCTOR WHO** The supreme achievement... makes the Matrix of Gallifrey look like a Ladybird book...

**MENTOS** I say, you'll make me blush.

**DOCTOR WHO** But what happened to the civilisation that created you?

**QUESTIONER** Look around you.

**DOCTOR WHO** War?

**MENTOS** Two sides, ideologically opposed, wanted to get their hands on me.

**DOCTOR WHO** And wiped each other out? Leaving you stranded here?

**MENTOS** Yes. Coming on 'Superbrain' was a gimmick. A test run, if you like, to show off my abilities to the plebs. Unfortunately, until the correct code is released into the panel you see beneath me, I am irrevocably conditioned to answer questions. And before you ask, the only other people who knew the code were my designers, and they're long dead.[101]

**QUESTIONER** And I am programmed to select questions – from throughout all time and space. Until Mentos is bested and the code released. Now, we must return to the game.

*FX – The 'Superbrain' jingle. Questioner clears her throat.*

**QUESTIONER** Who invented the Spode Catcher?

**MENTOS** Ah... er... Finkum the Lesser.

**QUESTIONER** What's the infinite cube root of the hypothetical number uinv?[102]

**MENTOS** The hypothetical number uinv... would it be the theoretical locus plyff?

*DOCTOR WHO and SALLY-ANNE confer.*

**SALLY-ANNE** Look, we can't just hang about all day hoping that brainbox there is gonna slip up.

**DOCTOR WHO** You're right. We'll have to think of something. Some distraction...

**SALLY-ANNE** I'll just distract that cranky old bag and you run in and get the box?

**DOCTOR WHO** You saw what happened before. That was a nasty knock I took.

**SALLY-ANNE** So there's nothing we can do.

**DOCTOR WHO** Apparently not.

**SALLY-ANNE** We're finished. The whole system's finished.

**DOCTOR WHO** Quite – we're doomed, utterly doomed...[103] Hold on, hold on[104] – as my companion, you're supposed to try and rouse me from my sloughs of despond. Not encourage them!

**SALLY-ANNE** I've always been a bit of a gloomy sort. (*Sighs*) What a life. Dad walked out when I was six. Mum hit the bottle. Brother knocked down by a speeding hover car. (*Getting teary*) Me poor auntie Sue gobbled up by one of the Spaags of Vishtek 3...

**DOCTOR WHO** Oh dear...

**SALLY-ANNE** Is it any wonder I turned to crime? I was led astray by Banto. He promised me the universe. And look where I end up.

**DOCTOR WHO** (*Awkward*) There, there. Have my hanky.[105]

**SALLY-ANNE** Ta. (*Blows nose*) Give us a cuddle, Doctor.

**DOCTOR WHO** Er... there you go...
**SALLY-ANNE** At least we'll go together when we go. You know, you've got a very comfortable shoulder.
**DOCTOR WHO** Wait a moment!
**SALLY-ANNE** What?
**DOCTOR WHO** I've had an idea!
**SALLY-ANNE** Is this the Time Lord way of giving a girl the brush-off?
**DOCTOR WHO** Questioner –
**QUESTIONER** Your interruptions are futile, Doctor.
**DOCTOR WHO** I don't think so. You say you are programmed to find a question Mentos cannot answer?
**QUESTIONER** (*Wary*) Yes.
**DOCTOR WHO** (*Proudly*) I think I have such a question. Will you allow me to put it to him?

## 32. INT. CONSTRUCTION PLANET – DAY
*MEL and BANTO are still struggling with the shelves.*

**MELANIE** 'Slot stanchion G into the base unit...' Hold on, I'm certain I've already done that...
**BANTO ZAME** That was stanchion D, and it wasn't the base unit, it was the central support stand.
**MELANIE** But where's that?
**BANTO ZAME** (*Puzzled*) Er... I dunno...
**MELANIE** This is so complicated. The instructions seem to make sense, but we never seem to get any nearer actually putting it all together.
**BANTO ZAME** What does it say next, let's have a look... 'Balance lower shelf on support Y, then use Allen key provided to – '
**MELANIE** Now hold on. We finished the lower shelves, I'm positive.
**BANTO ZAME** No, look.[106]
**MELANIE** But I remember finishing that section.
**BANTO ZAME** Perhaps you're confused.
**MELANIE** No. I've got a memory like an elephant.[107] (*Chuckles*) A running gag I share with the Doctor.
**BANTO ZAME** I bet the hours just fly by.
**MELANIE** (*Working it out*) Yes, there's the section we finished... in which case, these parts here – must be *new*.[108]
**BANTO ZAME** I'm not going to say 'but that's impossible' again.
**MELANIE** You know what this means, Banto?
**BANTO ZAME** (*Sarcastic*) Really good news?
**MELANIE** These shelves are a cheat. Parts of them keep appearing and disappearing.
**BANTO ZAME** Eh? We'd see it.
**MELANIE** Not if the maths involved was sufficiently developed. It would be beyond our senses to see it happening.
**BANTO ZAME** I'm sure this is all very clever, but you've lost me. It's just a lot of shelves. (*Thinks*) Except – it's one of the three Great Treasures, so it must have special properties...
**MELANIE** Yes. The ability to slip in and out of different dimensions. That's why they let us try and do this. Don't you see?
**BANTO ZAME** We can never finish putting up the shelves because...

**MELANIE**       ...they're slipping in and out of our reality. We can never catch up.

**BANTO ZAME** (*Gloomy*) That's it then.

*FX – BANTO slumps down.*

**MELANIE**       What are you doing?

**BANTO ZAME** We've got about ten minutes before they come back in and finish us off. I'll be damned if I'm going to spend the last ten minutes of my life putting up shelves!

**MELANIE**       You can't just lie there!

**BANTO ZAME** Exactly what do you think I should be doing instead?

**MELANIE**       Listen. The last thing Melanie Jane Bush is going to do is give up.

**BANTO ZAME** It's hopeless, you said it yourself.

*FX – stirring music fades in slowly under MEL's speech.*

**MELANIE**       Listen. I used to live in a small town called Pease Pottage. Every year my mum and dad organised a Christmas show for local pensioners in the church hall. That year the snow fell eight feet deep. We lived in a big house about seven miles from the town. There was no way for us to drive in. Everybody else gave up. But not my mum and dad, and not me. 'We're Bushes,' said my mum. 'And we're made of stronger stuff. Those old folk are relying on us'. So we put on our wellies, jumpers and sou'westers, packed a steaming thermos, hoisted our bags and boxes of costumes and props, and we strode off into the deep snow, setting our faces against the biting wind. And though it was hard, and the road was long, we made it to that church hall, and we gave that show! So don't talk to me about giving up, because I'm a Bush, and Bushes never do![109] *There is a long pause.*

**ASSEMBLER 1** (*From outside*) We would remind the humans they have only twelve dekkons left to complete the task.[110]

**MELANIE**       Oh. Yes, sorry. Got a bit carried away.

**BANTO ZAME** (*Sincere*) Mel – you're right.

**MELANIE**       (*Surprised*) Am I?

**BANTO ZAME** (*Falling in love*) That was the most beautiful story I've ever heard.

**MELANIE**       Was it?

**BANTO ZAME** You don't understand. Where I come from nobody believes in anything. You really do.

**MELANIE**       (*Awkward*) Thanks. Look, let's try and think of something...

**BANTO ZAME** By the way – did the pensioners enjoy their show?

**MELANIE**       No, none of them turned up.[111]


## 33. EXT. AMPHITHEATRE – NIGHT

*FX – the 'Superbrain' jingle. DOCTOR WHO steps up to the QUESTIONER's podium.*

**QUESTIONER** You are honoured, Doctor. The first audience member to question Mentos.

**DOCTOR WHO** Thank you, madam.

**SALLY-ANNE** Go on, Doctor. You can do it.

**DOCTOR WHO** (*Clears throat*) Now – Mentos?

**MENTOS**       Yes?

**DOCTOR WHO**  Let me get this straight. If I ask a question you cannot answer, you will be free, and I can take you with me?
**MENTOS**  Yes.
**DOCTOR WHO**  Right. Now then.
**QUESTIONER**  The rules allow you only two questions, Doctor.
**DOCTOR WHO**  Very well. I doubt I'll need my second go.
**MENTOS**  Ooh, Doctor – you're not going to try one of those tricky fox-the-computer logic conundrums, are you? You know, 'if I'm lying was the last thing I said true' and all that nonsense?
**DOCTOR WHO**  (*Covering*) Um... No.[112]
**MENTOS**  Good. Because I can answer those, you know?
**DOCTOR WHO**  Really? Oh. (*Thinking quickly*) Very well. Here goes. What colour was the wallpaper in the back bedroom of number 35 Jefferson Road, Woking, in June 1975?
**MENTOS**  Purple.
**DOCTOR WHO**  What?
**MENTOS**  Purple. Easy. Next.
**DOCTOR WHO**  How could you possibly...
**MENTOS**  We sent a research device there to find out. You'll have to do better than that.[113]
**DOCTOR WHO**  I can hardly believe it.
**MENTOS**  I'm more interested to know how you know the answer.
**DOCTOR WHO**  I based myself in Woking during a Cybermen invasion.[114]
**MENTOS**  Oh, of course.
**DOCTOR WHO**  So how come you didn't know *that*?
**MENTOS**  Oh, I can't send requests for information, Doctor, I have to be asked.
**SALLY-ANNE**  Fantastic. Try a harder one.
**QUESTIONER**  Next question please, Doctor. Your second and final question.
**DOCTOR WHO**  Erm... try this one... It's in three parts.
**QUESTIONER**  Tch... I suppose it's allowed...
**DOCTOR WHO**  What were my three wishes as I blew out the candles on my nine hundredth birthday cake?
**MENTOS**  Ah... oh... er...
**DOCTOR WHO**  That's got you foxed.
**MENTOS**  Er... wait a minute... it's a tough one...
**DOCTOR WHO**  I'll have to hurry you.
**QUESTIONER**  *I* say that.
**DOCTOR WHO**  Sorry.
**QUESTIONER**  I'll have to hurry you.
**MENTOS**  Well, it's... oh...
**DOCTOR WHO**  Game, set and match to myself, I think. Questioner, if you'll allow me to disconnect the box?
**SALLY-ANNE**  Well done, Doctor!
**DOCTOR WHO**  (*Smug*) Mentos can see anywhere – but not, I think, into the mind of a Time Lord.
**MENTOS**  Wait, I've got it. Wish one – peace throughout the galaxy.[115]
**DOCTOR WHO**  I don't believe it... how?
**MENTOS**  Wish two – er...
**DOCTOR WHO**  Hah. A lucky guess. Come on.[116]

**MENTOS**       Wish two – better control of the TARDIS...
**SALLY-ANNE**   Is he right?
**DOCTOR WHO**   (*Downcast*) Incredibly, yes. But don't fret, he'll never get the third one...
**MENTOS**       Er... oh, it's so nearly there...
**DOCTOR WHO**   Your time's running out, Mentos.
**MENTOS**       Ah... oh... ah yes. Wish three – more manageable hair.
**DOCTOR WHO**   (*Shocked*) Good grief! How did you know that?
**MENTOS**       Easy really. Remember later that day you were locked in a dungeon by the evil Mantelli?[117]
**DOCTOR WHO**   Yes.
**MENTOS**       Remember your cellmate?
**DOCTOR WHO**   It was an old man, shackled to the wall. Asked me what I'd been doing, and I... oh no. It was *you*!
**MENTOS**       Another projection of me, yes. Very clever, those research devices.[118] Took me a while to get it out of you.
**QUESTIONER**   (*Prim, mocking*) So, Doctor, you travel through space and time, yes?
**DOCTOR WHO**   That's right.
**QUESTIONER**   Meet a lot of interesting people do you?
**DOCTOR WHO**   Well yes, I...
**QUESTIONER**   Then it's a shame some of them couldn't have been here instead of you. Please return to your seat. You have been defeated by Mentos. You are the feeblest contestant. Goodbye.
*FX – We hear the jingle as DOCTOR WHO does the walk of shame. He sighs.*
**DOCTOR WHO**   It's impossible. We're fighting the greatest resource of information the universe has ever known – even my mind is no match. We'd have more chance of beating a squad of Daleks with a rolled up newspaper.
**SALLY-ANNE**   Oh, come on. Here, let me have a go.[119] Oi! Questioner![120]
**DOCTOR WHO**   If you like. Though I don't think it'll do any good. I suppose you could ask him –
**QUESTIONER**   No conferring!
**SALLY-ANNE**   I've got a good question worked out. Don't worry, Doctor. *DOCTOR WHO makes a despairing sound.*[121]
**QUESTIONER**   Sally-Anne Stubbins – will you please come up to the hot spot?
*FX – We hear the jingle as SALLY-ANNE walks up.*
**QUESTIONER**   Sally-Anne, you have two questions.
**DOCTOR WHO**   (*To himself over the above*) Wait! I've got it, I know what to ask... How could I have been so stupid...[122]
**SALLY-ANNE**   Right. What did I tell Banto on the night when he asked me to marry him, just after we'd downed that third bottle of red. (*To DOCTOR WHO*) He'll never get this one, cos Banto's never told another living soul. He promised.
**MENTOS**       You... er. Oh, what was it? Yes, of course. You told him you'd had... I hardly like to say it.
**QUESTIONER**   Your answer please, Mentos.
**MENTOS**       Well, that you'd had... uh... mammary enhancement surgery. He was out for a drink the following evening, you see. Told all his friends. One of my gatherers was there. Apparently he thought you'd also had your cheeks sucked in and your lips –

**SALLY-ANNE** (*Interrupting, furious*) The scumbag! I'll get him for that!
**QUESTIONER** One question left.
**SALLY-ANNE** Oh, flippin' 'eck. It's impossible. (*Gabbling, not actually asking a question*) I mean, what *don't* you know?
**MENTOS** Er...
**QUESTIONER** Is that your second question?
**SALLY-ANNE** No, hang on...[123]
**DOCTOR WHO** Yes! Yes, that's her second question! Mentos – what *don't* you know?
**MENTOS** Er... I'm sure I'll have the answer soon... it's going to be a bit tricky...[124] er...[125]
**SALLY-ANNE** What have I done?
**DOCTOR WHO** Pulled the cat out of the bag is what you've done! Great minds do think alike after all.[125] Come here!
*DOCTOR WHO grabs her and gives her a quick, exuberant kiss on the cheek.*
**SALLY-ANNE** Ooh, Doctor.[125]
*FX – Odd, whirring sounds, fizzing and sparks begin to come from Mentos.*
**MENTOS** Wait, please, I...[125] I'm sending my research devices...[125] I... er... what is happening?[125] Mentos overloaded...[125] cannot answer...[125] (*slurring*)... portal closing down...[126] code released...
**QUESTIONER** Mentos, that is the end of your time here on Superbrain. Do you want to come back next week?
**MENTOS** Certainly not! I am – closing down... closing down...
*FX – A whispering, sucking sound as MENTOS vanishes into the portal.*
**SALLY-ANNE** He's disappeared!
**DOCTOR WHO** Merely retreated into his shell. Good. I hate clever clogs.
**QUESTIONER** You have banked a pitiful six hundred and seventy-nine billion,three hundred and thirty-three million, five hundred and sixty-seven thousand, and ten credits.[127] Goodbye. Goodbye. Goodbye...
*FX – The QUESTIONER, too, dies. Her body clatters to the floor with metallic-sounding clang.*
**SALLY-ANNE** What happened to her?
**DOCTOR WHO** Game over. No need for a questioner any longer. Now come on – let's disconnect the box and get back to the others.[128]

## 34. INT. CONSTRUCTION PLANET CELL – DAY

*We hear the voice of ASSEMBLER 1 on the intercom.*

**ASSEMBLER 1** Two dekkons remaining, human weaklings.
**BANTO ZAME** Two minutes! Two minutes of life. What can you do with two minutes?
**MELANIE** Quiet, will you – I'm trying to think.
**BANTO ZAME** It's amazing. You don't seem scared at all.
**MELANIE** No point in it. Believe me, when I'm scared I'll scream the paint off the walls.
**BANTO ZAME** Mel...
**MELANIE** Yes?
**BANTO ZAME** Can I hold your hand?
**MELANIE** If it makes you feel better.
**BANTO ZAME** Thanks. It does. You know, in another time, another place... I might've set my cap at you.

110

**MELANIE** (*Gently sarcastic*) Thanks. Perhaps in another dimension we got together and had tons of odd-looking children... hang on!

**BANTO ZAME** What?

**MELANIE** I think I've got it!

**BANTO ZAME** Got what?

**MELANIE** A way out! These shelves can never be fully assembled, yes?

**BANTO ZAME** If you say so

**MELANIE** So those robot things out there can't have ever seen the finished unit.

**BANTO ZAME** (*Still unconvinced*) Makes sense, I s'pose...

**MELANIE** Then how will they know whether we've put it together correctly? We've done all we can, so let's just gather up the rest of the pieces (*she does so while talking*) – the ones currently in our dimension, anyway – and pile them on top!

**BANTO ZAME** That'll never work! There must be a picture of the end product somewhere on these instructions...

*FX: Rustling as BANTO looks through the instructions.*

**BANTO ZAME** Hey! Hey you're right! You can't even get to the end of the instructions. There's always more... oh this is doing my brain no good at all!

**MELANIE** Never mind that! Quick, help me with all this.

*FX: Clattering as they pile up all the pieces they can find. They are stopped as the shutters slide up and the ASSEMBLERS trundle in, chittering.*

**ASSEMBLER 2** Your thirty dekkons are up, Earth creatures.

**MELANIE** (*Bluffing*) And a very fine job we've done, I'm sure you'll agree.

**ASSEMBLER 2** Prepare your internal organs for... *whaaaat?*

**ASSEMBLER 1** What did you say?

**MELANIE** Unit ZX419. We assembled it. Look.

**BANTO ZAME** (*Whispering*) They aren't going to fall for this, surely?

**MELANIE** (*To BANTO*) Play along. (*To the ASSEMBLERS*) It wasn't all that difficult once we got the hang of it.

**BANTO ZAME** Yes... you tried to fool us, you naughty robots. But we soon saw through it.

**MELANIE** So if you don't mind we'll be on our way.

**ASSEMBLER 1** Wait! You cannot have assembled Unit ZX419!

**MELANIE** Why not? They're only shelves.

**ASSEMBLER 2** Very special shelves. Our finest achievement – the Shelves of Infinity!

**MELANIE** Oh, you mean the dimensional trickery. Didn't take us long to work that out. Did it Banto?

**BANTO ZAME** Yeah, we're dab hands when it comes to, er...

**MELANIE** Multi-reality cogency phasing. It's simple – you just train your mind to think in the abstract and you can see thirty seven dimensions all at the same time.

*The ASSEMBLERS confer.*

**ASSEMBLER 1** Can this be possible?

**ASSEMBLER 2** We must examine the Shelves of Infinity.

**MELANIE** Feel free. You see – finished.

**ASSEMBLER 2** This is an organic untruth!

**MELANIE** Of course it isn't. Look, check on the instructions.

*FX – MEL hands ASSEMBLER 2 the instructions.*

**ASSEMBLER 2** Let me see... stanchion G is supported by rod 6... the interlocking nuts 9b and 4a have been tightened, yes...

**ASSEMBLER 1** It will take us some time to check the truth of your claim.

**BANTO ZAME** That wasn't part of the deal. Thirty dekkons you said.

**MELANIE** Surely it won't take the Great Assemblers that long to examine their own shelves?

**ASSEMBLER 1** Of course not!

**ASSEMBLER 2** We are superior!

**MELANIE** Well then. (*Under her breath*) Come on, Doctor!

**BANTO ZAME** You're not trying to back out of the deal, are you? Tsk, tsk.[129] And I thought you were honourable creatures.

**ASSEMBLER 2** We are beings of our word – unlike humans.

**MELANIE** Let's have the shelves then.

*FX – The ASSEMBLERS are making confused-sounding noises. MEL lifts the shelves.*

**ASSEMBLER 2** There is conflict in my circuits, 1.

**ASSEMBLER 1** And in mine, 2.

**ASSEMBLER 2** We are superior to humans.

**ASSEMBLER 1** Undoubtedly.

**ASSEMBLER 2** Then how can the humans have completed their task?[130]

**ASSEMBLER 1** We must examine these instructions closely, 2.

*FX – PAPER RUSTLING, OVER WHICH the TARDIS materialises.*

**MELANIE** Right on time for once! Come on Banto, help me with the shelves!

*FX – They grab the shelves and dash to the TARDIS. The shelves clatter as they run, perhaps interlocking nut 9a tinkles to the floor.*

**BANTO ZAME** I'm right behind you!

**ASSEMBLER 1** What is this blue cuboid object with windows and writing on the door? 'Pull to open...' Are these its instructions?

**MELANIE** (*Calling back*) It's something we made earlier.

**BANTO ZAME** Goodbye, creeps!

*FX – MEL and BANTO dash into the TARDIS and slam the door. The ASSEMBLERS approach the TARDIS.*

**ASSEMBLER 1** Emerge from this cuboid!

**ASSEMBLER 2** Bring back the Shelves of Infinity!

**ASSEMBLER 1** We must disassemble this box, 2.

**ASSEMBLER 2** Yes, 1. Advance, advance!

**ASSEMBLER 1** Disassemble, disassemble!

*FX – Their pincers whirr up. But the TARDIS is already demateralising.*

**ASSEMBLER 2** You will return!

**ASSEMBLER 1** We are superior! We are superior!

*FX – The wheezing, groaning sound dies away. A beat.*

**ASSEMBLER 2** We have been beaten by humans, 1.

**ASSEMBLER 1** Yes, 2. It is not possible.

**ASSEMBLER 2** Thus – it cannot have happened.

**ASSEMBLER 1** We shall erase it from our memories.

**ASSEMBLER 2** Erase! Erase![131]

**ASSEMBLER 1** That is better.

**ASSEMBLER 2** Now – let us go and assemble a new design. How about – a sun lounger and chairs in matching lavender?

**ASSEMBLER 1** Or footstools and occasional table with accompanying pouffe?[132]
**ASSEMBLER 2** I know – we shall assemble *both*.
FX – *Exit the ASSEMBLERS, chittering happily.*

### 35. INT. TARDIS CONTROL ROOM – DAY
FX – *The TARDIS is in flight. MEL and BANTO put down the shelves.*

**DOCTOR WHO** Mel, it's very good to see you. I only hope your excursion was less fraught with peril than mine and Sally-Anne's.
**MELANIE** I'd rather not dwell on the detail, Doctor. Suffice it to say, I hope these were worth it.
**DOCTOR WHO** Forgive me – but they do rather resemble shelves.
**MELANIE** They are shelves. Special shelves. (*Sceptical*) What about your treasure? It's just a box.
**SALLY-ANNE** A very special box, actually.
**BANTO ZAME** Before we all get carried away with the explanations –
**DOCTOR WHO** Yes?
**BANTO ZAME** – there's still another treasure to find.
**MELANIE** He's right, and we've only got about twenty-five minutes left!
**BANTO ZAME** (*Weary*) My life seems to lurch from one countdown to another.
**DOCTOR WHO** Hah! Can't take the pace, eh? That'll teach you to imitate somebody less awe-inspiring next time!
**BANTO ZAME** Awe-inspiring? In that coat? Have you looked in the mirror recently? Come to think of it, I shouldn't think you do much else...
**DOCTOR WHO** I intend to rise above your barbs. (*Pause*) But before I do, I'd like to say that this coat can only be appreciated by someone with a sharpened aesthetic sense – not a dunderhead like you!
**BANTO ZAME** Sharpened aesthetic sense? Sharpened by what – a dose of mind-altering drugs?
**DOCTOR WHO** I warn you – a verbal duel against me, as you should remember, if you used the smallest fraction of your cerebral cortex occasionally, can only end in ignominy for you![133]
**BANTO ZAME** Igno-what? Talking to you is like arguing with a thesaurus!
**DOCTOR WHO** It pays to enrich your word power!
**MELANIE** Doctor, Banto! Please!
**DOCTOR WHO** I'm sorry, Mel. (*Pause*) But he started it.
**BANTO ZAME** I did not! You did![134]
**SALLY-ANNE** Shut up!
**MELANIE** Can we please get on with finding the treasure?
**DOCTOR WHO** Already covered. In fact we're just about to materialise.
**SALLY-ANNE/MELANIE** Where, Doctor?[135]
**MELANIE** *I* ask that question.
**SALLY-ANNE** Suit yourself.
**MELANIE** Where, Doctor?
**DOCTOR WHO** The innermost planet of the system. Generios 15. It's a gigantic body composed almost entirely of superheated gas.
**BANTO ZAME** Rather like you, then.
**DOCTOR WHO** If I have to endure another insult –

**BANTO ZAME**  Oh here we go, another voyage round the English language –
**MELANIE**  (*Yelling*) Quiet!

### 36. EXT. GAS PLANET – DAY
*FX – A whispering, bubbling, creepy atmosphere. The TARDIS materialises. DOCTOR WHO et al step out.*

**MELANIE**  I don't like the look of this place.
**BANTO ZAME**  Too red for my liking. Red always spells danger.
**DOCTOR WHO**  We're not here to discuss the colour scheme. Look around, all of you. According to the list, we should be right on top of the Third Treasure.
*FX – Footsteps as they begin to move off.*
**SALLY-ANNE**  'Ere, you don't reckon it could be the planet itself, do you?
**DOCTOR WHO**  (*Impressed*) Good thinking, Sally-Anne. But no – I did a quick analysis in the TARDIS, and there's nothing uncommon in its composition.
**MELANIE**  It wasn't *that* clever a suggestion.[136]
**DOCTOR WHO**  Do I detect a hint of envy, Mel?
**BANTO ZAME**  (*Calling back*) Hey – what's that over there? It's a... oh my stars... look at the size of it!
**MELANIE**  It's enormous!
**DOCTOR WHO**  What a beauty!
**SALLY-ANNE**  I've never seen one as big as that before!
**DOCTOR WHO**  It must take the particular geological extremes at work here to produce a diamond *that* size.[137]
**SALLY-ANNE**  That's the Treasure then.
**DOCTOR WHO**  Just lying here.
**BANTO ZAME**  Let's get it and go, shall we then?
**MELANIE**  Hold on. No one's going to leave something as valuable as that lying out in the open and unguarded.[138]
**DOCTOR WHO**  Extra Brownie points for Mel. Or should that be Girl Guide points?
**MELANIE**  (*Laughing*) Thank you.
**DOCTOR WHO**  So – I shall approach with caution. Stand back, the rest of you.
*FX – DOCTOR WHO walks towards the diamond.*
**SALLY-ANNE**  Ooh, he's so brave.
**BANTO ZAME**  The word I'd choose is 'stupid'.
**SALLY-ANNE**  I wish I had a feller like that – not a coward like the one I'm stuck with.
**BANTO ZAME**  As if he'd look twice you, my little gargoyle.
**SALLY-ANNE**  You what?
**BANTO ZAME**  He's hardly going to throw over a lovely girl like Melanie, is he?
**MELANIE**  Stop squabbling. The Doctor's reached the diamond...[139]
**DOCTOR WHO**  (*Calling*) It appears to be stuck!
**MELANIE**  Give it a tug!
**DOCTOR WHO**  I am! It won't budge!
*SALLY-ANNE screams.*
**MELANIE**  What is it?

**SALLY-ANNE**  Over there – look!
**BANTO ZAME**  Oh no.
**MELANIE**  Doctor – behind you! Doctor!
**SALLY-ANNE**  It's like an horrible big... jelly!
*FX – DOCTOR WHO is grabbed.*
**DOCTOR WHO**  Oh – aarggh!!
*FX – With much slobbering, DOCTOR WHO is eaten by the JELLOID.*
**SALLY-ANNE**  It's gobbled him up!
**MELANIE**  No! Doctor![140]
**BANTO ZAME**  Face it, Mel – he's lunch...
*FX – The JELLOID burps, contentedly.*

*CRASH IN CLOSING THEME*[141]
*END OF PART THREE*

# Part Four

## 36. EXT. GAS PLANET – DAY (RECAP)

**MELANIE**  The Doctor's reached the diamond...
**DOCTOR WHO**  (*Calling*) It appears to be stuck!
**MELANIE**  Give it a tug!
**DOCTOR WHO**  I am! It won't budge!
*SALLY-ANNE screams.*
**MELANIE**  What is it?
**SALLY-ANNE**  Over there – look!
**BANTO ZAME**  Oh no.
**MELANIE**  Doctor – behind you! Doctor!
**SALLY-ANNE**  It's like an horrible big... jelly!
*FX – DOCTOR WHO is grabbed.*
**DOCTOR WHO**  Oh – aarggh!!
*FX – With much slobbering, DOCTOR WHO is eaten by the JELLOID.*
**SALLY-ANNE**  It's gobbled him up!
**MELANIE**  No! Doctor![142]
**BANTO ZAME**  Face it, Mel – he's lunch...
*FX – The JELLOID burps, contentedly.*
**MELANIE**  (*Distraught*) Doctor... no, he can't be...[142]
**SALLY-ANNE**  He was so... brave, and so... sexy...
*FX – The JELLOID slithers away.*
**BANTO ZAME**  It's slithering off – back to its lair for a post-prandial kip.
**MELANIE**  No. The Doctor's faced more formidable enemies than a blob of jelly. He'll find a way out, I know he will.[142]
**BANTO ZAME**  What did you have for breakfast this morning?
**MELANIE**  Muesli – why?
**BANTO ZAME**  Has your muesli found its way out?
**MELANIE**  Oh, Doctor...[143]

## 37. INT. JELLOID STOMACH – DAY
*FX – A bubbling, organic atmos – gastric.*

**DOCTOR WHO**  (*Woozy*) Oh my head... where am I? Oh dear... now I know what an endoscope feels like... What's this stuff on my coat? Urgh... digestive fluids... Now then, don't fret, Doctor – what goes down can be made to come up. Lucky it didn't have teeth. Let's see... that must be the intestinal tract... if I just follow this round... ah yes... if I poke my finger – just about here...
*FX – A gushing noise. DOCTOR WHO splutters.*
**DOCTOR WHO**  (*CONT'D*) Urgh – no! Why are your bile ducts in such a silly place? Try again...
*FX – The JELLOID squelches and groans.*
**DOCTOR WHO**  (*CONT'D*) That's better... for me, if not for you, old chap...

## 38. EXT. GAS PLANET – DAY

116

**MELANIE**        (*Tearful*) I still can't believe the Doctor's dead. It's hard to swallow. I mean – difficult to stomach. Oh...
**SALLY-ANNE**   How are we going to get off this dump without him?
**BANTO ZAME**  Good point. Mel, can you fly the TARDIST... I mean, TARDIS?
**MELANIE**        I suppose I could just about get us off here and back to Generios. Don't forget, the Cylinder won't let us go anywhere else.
**SALLY-ANNE**   We'll never get the diamond. I'm not tackling that jelly.
*FX – The JELLOID is rolling back.*
**BANTO ZAME**  You might have to – here it is again!
*FX – We can hear the JELLOID is having a bad attack of the collywobbles.*
**MELANIE**        It doesn't look very comfortable. (*Venomous*) Hope it choked on the Doctor!
**BANTO ZAME**  It's coming towards us!
**SALLY-ANNE**   Quick, let's get in the TARDIST!
*FX – The JELLOID belches violently.*
**MELANIE**        Something's very wrong...
*FX – The JELLOID sicks up DOCTOR WHO, who goes flying through the air to land at their feet in a sticky, mucus-covered heap.*
**DOCTOR WHO**  Ooof!
**MELANIE**        (*Overjoyed*) Doctor!
**SALLY-ANNE**   I'd give you an hug but...
**BANTO ZAME**  He's covered in slime.
**DOCTOR WHO**  Gastric juices – all very healthy and natural.
**BANTO ZAME**  And smelly. Still, lucky you're wearing that coat. No way of telling that someone's just been sick all over it.
**MELANIE**        The jelly – it's a quivering heap.
**SALLY-ANNE**   It looks all guilty. So it should, swallowing our mate.
**DOCTOR WHO**  It found me difficult to stomach.
**MELANIE**        (*Laughing*) I've already used that gag, Doctor. Oh, it's good to have you back.
**BANTO ZAME**  Quick – while it's  kaylyed, grab the diamond![144]
*The JELLOID speaks in a slow, deep, wibbling voice. It has a slight Northern accent for some reason.*
**JELLOID**        (*Groaning*) No – stop...
**SALLY-ANNE**   Flippin 'eck, it talks!
**JELLOID**        Of course I talk. I'm not stupid, you know.
**MELANIE**        How dare you swallow the Doctor!
**DOCTOR WHO**  Steady on, Mel. I'll handle this. (*Clears throat*) How *dare* you swallow me!
**JELLOID**        You tried to steal the Great Jewel.
**DOCTOR WHO**  It would have been more polite simply to *ask* me not to.
**JELLOID**        Forgive me – I've been alone for many years. I'm bad with people.
**MELANIE**        What kind of creature are you?
**JELLOID**        A Jelloid. I am the guardian of the Jewel. It was hidden here and I was put on guard. Must be – ooh, thirty million odd years ago...[145]
**MELANIE**        Thirty million years? (*Laughs*) You're looking good on it. What's your secret?
**JELLOID**        I'm a single cell organism. From a distinguished family of single cell organisms.

**DOCTOR WHO**  Not the Spraxis Jelliods? From the binary quasar Bendalos?

**JELLOID**  It's always nice to be recognised.

**BANTO ZAME**  Oh, right, I suppose we're going to get the lecture now – 'my exciting adventure with the Jelliods'. Least I never made *my* Doctor such a pompous bore...

**SALLY-ANNE**  Shut it. You know this lot then Doctor?

**DOCTOR WHO**  The Spraxis Jelliods are the longest-lived race in the cosmos. Some biologists postulated they were the first living beings – and here they are far in the future. That's staying power for you.[146]

**SALLY-ANNE**  So he's been guarding the diamond all this time? Sort of like the Questioner was guarding Mentos for all them years?

**MELANIE**  Or those horrid Assemblers guarding the Shelves of Infinity.

**DOCTOR WHO**  Exactly. Every great treasure needs its guardian – and the longer-lasting, the better. You can't leave powerful artefacts just lying around... as was ably proven when this fine gentlebeing ate me.[147] No, everything balances out in the end. That's the beauty of the universe.

**SALLY-ANNE**  Aww. That's really poetic, Doctor.

**BANTO ZAME**  I think *I'm* going to be sick now.

**DOCTOR WHO**  So – you've been here all this time?

**JELLOID**  You're quite right, Doctor. My employers wanted somebody with staying power.[148] (*Bitterly*) Thirty million years...[149] You don't know what it's like... nobody to talk to... pass the time of day with... I sit and talk to myself... it's a lonely life... would you like to hear the song I've made up about it?

**DOCTOR WHO**  Kind of you, but not just at the moment. Now – I need the Jewel for the best of reasons. An alien intruder will destroy this entire system if I don't hand it over.

**JELLOID**  Really?

**DOCTOR WHO**  Yes.

**JELLOID**  I suppose you'd better take it then.

**BANTO ZAME**  What – you've just accepted that nonsense story?

**JELLOID**  Well – the Doctor has an honest face.

**BANTO ZAME**  Oh for Pete's sake...

**JELLOID**  And it's part of my job to monitor the system – I've heard that Cylinder mouthing off. Cheeky blighter.

**SALLY-ANNE**  Let's collect the diamond and get out of here. I'll help you lift it, Doctor.

**MELANIE**  *I'll* help him, thank you.

**JELLOID**  No point. You'll never get it up – it's held down by a force field.

**BANTO ZAME**  Switch it off then.

**JELLOID**  Well, I would...

**DOCTOR WHO**  But?

**BANTO ZAME**  I knew it was too good be true.

**JELLOID**  *I* have to switch the field off – and the control's over that mound.[150]

**SALLY-ANNE**  Go on then, what's stopping you?

**JELLOID**  See that teleporter pad over there? My only link to the universe outside. I'm having an entertainment system delivered from Bendalos. Something to pass the time. It'll give me access to music, movies, sport, games and all the long-running programmes on Jelloid TV. So this brochure says.

*FX – He rustles the brochure.*

**MELANIE**  What's that to do with anything?

**JELLOID**  Well, they sent me a card saying they'll be delivering it about now.

**MELANIE**  Well... when?

**JELLOID**  They can only specify within a range of two million years.[151]

**MELANIE**  What?

**JELLOID**  I've already waited one and a half million. They could turn up at any moment. And I don't want to miss them.

**DOCTOR WHO**  I don't believe this!

**BANTO ZAME**  *(Smug)* Everything is relative, Doctor.

**JELLOID**  It makes me very nervous, waiting in like this. I just know – if I go and switch the field off – they'll appear and I'll have missed them. Then I'll have to call the depot and arrange another delivery date do the whole thing again. And it takes you ages to get through – forty thousand years they put me on hold.

**DOCTOR WHO**  But surely you can see our mission is vitally important?[152] How long will it take you to switch the field off and come back?

**JELLOID**  About ten minutes.

**DOCTOR**  Well then. The chances of your goods arriving in that period are infinitesimal.

**JELLOID**  Ooh... I just *know* they will though...

**SALLY-ANNE**  They won't.

**JELLOID**  I bet they will. You go out and they turn up. It always happens.

**SALLY-ANNE**  Look – we're here. We promise if they do show up we'll make them wait until you come back.[153]

**JELLOID**  Hmm... Well...

**SALLY-ANNE**  Honest.

**JELLOID**  Oh... all right. But keep a sharp eye out for them.

*FX – The JELLOID rolls away.*

**DOCTOR WHO**  Well done, Sally-Anne. That was very well handled.

**SALLY-ANNE**  I'm getting the hang of it, ain't I?

**DOCTOR WHO**  You certainly are.[154]

**MELANIE**  *(Jealous)* Let's save the congratulations until the job's done, shall we?[155]

## 39. INT. COUNCIL CHAMBER – DAY

*FX – We can just hear the crowd nervously chattering outside the Great Council Complex. The door opens and the GUARD enters.*

**GUARD**  Councillor Potikol?

**POTIKOL**  *(Nervous)* Yes, guard? What is it – is the Doctor back?

**GUARD**  The Cylinder... it's coming down. Hovering right over the Complex.[156]

**POTIKOL**  Oh no. How long have we got left?

**CYLINDER VOICE**  Fifteen minutes! You have fifteen minutes to bring me the Tribute – or you will be obliterated!

119

**POTIKOL**     Please – oh please, Great Cylinder, spare us![157]
**GUARD**     I don't think it can hear you up there, sir.[158]
**POTIKOL**     The Doctor saved us once. I know he can do it again.
**GUARD**     Shall I change your damp flannel, Councillor?
**POTIKOL**     Yes please.
**CYLINDER VOICE** Fourteen minutes remaining... fourteen minutes remaining... I demand Tribute![159]

## 40. EXT. GAS PLANET – DAY

**MELANIE**     Doctor. Time's running out.[160]
**DOCTOR WHO**  I know. What say you go into the TARDIS and power up the systems? Then when it's time we'll grab the diamond and vamoose.
**MELANIE**     Vamoose?
**DOCTOR WHO**  Leave. In a hurry.
**MELANIE**     Oh Doctor. Your vocabulary.
**DOCTOR WHO**  Don't *you* start. I'll have you know Roget was a very good friend of mine.
*FX – What sounds like a fly buzzing by.*
**MELANIE**     What's that?
**DOCTOR WHO**  Just a harmless local insect, it won't hurt you. Probably. Odd for this climate. Never mind, hurry along to the TARDIS.
*FX – The fly buzzes off. MEL moves off to the TARDIS. We cross to BANTO and SALLY-ANNE.*
**SALLY-ANNE**  Flippin Nora.
**BANTO ZAME**  What now?
**SALLY-ANNE**  Stuck here, roasting my skin off on some... gas planet.
*FX – The fly buzzes by again.*
**SALLY-ANNE**  *(CONT'D)* And now I'm being divebombed by a great big fly – buzz off. *(She shoos it away)*[161] All started after I took up with you...
**BANTO ZAME**  What about it?
**SALLY-ANNE**  Weren't we supposed to be luxuriating on one of the moons of Plenagon... having some of that sensory emulsion...
**BANTO ZAME**  *(Distant, grumpy)* Can it, will you?
**SALLY-ANNE**  If it weren't for the Doctor we'd be dead by now.
**BANTO ZAME**  *(Mocking)* Oooh, the Doctor, the Doctor...
**SALLY-ANNE**  You're only jealous, he was right.[162] Jealous of his place in my affections.
**BANTO ZAME**  He's a Time Lord, you boot-faced female. *(Sighs)* Honest to gawd, you drive me twice as mad as my old woman...[163]
*A beat.*
**SALLY-ANNE**  What did you just say?
**BANTO ZAME**  *(Realising the enormity of his error)* Er... I said you've got a voice like an old... woman...
**SALLY-ANNE**  You're never married!
**BANTO ZAME**  Oh dear.
**SALLY-ANNE**  You are! All this time you've been bloody well married!
*FX – SALLY-ANNE slaps him across the face.*
**SALLY-ANNE**  *(CONT'D)* You lying, cheating son of a... sand beast!
**BANTO ZAME**  Now don't overreact, my little sea cucumber...
**SALLY-ANNE**  Come here!

*FX – The sound of a scuffle. DOCTOR WHO jogs over.*
**BANTO ZAME** Geroff!!
**DOCTOR WHO** What's going on?
**BANTO ZAME** Nothing.
**SALLY-ANNE** Oh Doctor... hold me...
**DOCTOR WHO** What have you done to her, Zame?
**BANTO ZAME** Nothing plenty of other people haven't done.
**SALLY-ANNE** Come here, you...
*FX – The scuffle begins anew. DOCTOR WHO separates them.*
**DOCTOR WHO** Calm down! Honestly – whatever your interpersonal peccadilloes –
**BANTO ZAME** (*Weary*) Here we go.
**DOCTOR WHO** – the diamond is the important thing!
*FX – A shimmering noise.*
**DOCTOR WHO** (*CONT'D*) The force shield – the creature must have switched it off!
**BANTO ZAME** Well let's grab that ruddy diamond and get out of here then, shall we?[164] I'll go myself, it'll be quicker.
**DOCTOR WHO** Yes, alright – then straight into the TARDIS. Mel's waiting inside.
**BANTO ZAME** (*Thoughtful*) Oh – oh good...
*FX – BANTO runs to get the diamond. We hear the JELLOID slithering back.*
**JELLOID** (*Coming closer*) Is that all right? Have you got it?
**DOCTOR WHO** Jelloid, I cannot thank you enough.
**JELLOID** What – what is... this?
*FX – A 'glinting' noise as he picks the object up.*
**SALLY-ANNE** What's what?
**JELLOID** This!
**SALLY-ANNE** Just a bit of metal, innit?
**JELLOID** (*With mounting anger*) No... it says 'We called while you were out – please call our depot on Syrranus Traxea to arrange another suitable millennium for delivery'... No!
**DOCTOR WHO** But... we were here all the time...
**SALLY-ANNE** We didn't see nobody.
**BANTO ZAME** (*Distant, out of puff*) Sally-Anne... you going to give me a hand with this?
**SALLY-ANNE** (*Pointedly*) Hold on. We're talking to our *mate*.
**BANTO ZAME** (*Hidden agenda*) All right... I'll do it by myself, then...
*FX – We hear BANTO dragging the diamond away in the B/G of the following exchange. He eventually enters the TARDIS and shuts the door.*
**JELLOID** What? Er... oh no, of course... they must have been using Vektons as their delivery agents...[165]
**SALLY-ANNE** Vektons?
**DOCTOR WHO** Vektons. The fastest moving creatures in the cosmos. They learnt to manipulate time so they move forty times faster than everybody else. Of course – the fly![166]
**SALLY-ANNE** Was a Vekton?
**DOCTOR WHO** Trying to attract our attention. It must have flown off when we didn't answer its call.
**JELLOID** Oh no... another call to the depot... another delay... another eternity of waiting here on this very same spot... nothing to entertain or divert me... (*sobs*)...[167]

**SALLY-ANNE**  There there.
**JELLOID**  Please don't touch me.
**DOCTOR WHO**  Now there's no need to –
*FX – The TARDIS dematerializes. A moment of stunned silence.*
**SALLY-ANNE**  'Ere!
**DOCTOR WHO**  Zame! Banto Zame – come back! The underhanded idiot!
**SALLY-ANNE**  He's gone and left us! On this dump with just an old jelly for company![168]
**JELLOID**  (*Stifling its sobs, becoming threatening*) Yes... and what an *angry* old jelly I am!

### 41. INT. TARDIS CONTROL ROOM – DAY

**MELANIE**  What have you done? That control sets the TARDIS moving!
**BANTO ZAME**  I know. I saw the Doctor use it earlier. Not just a pretty face, me.
**MELANIE**  (*Furious*) I hope you're pleased with yourself – abandoning the Doctor! And for what? What do you hope to gain?
**BANTO ZAME**  (*Placating*) Listen, listen –
**MELANIE**  You may have set yourself up to imitate him, but he's worth ten of you – a hundred –
**BANTO ZAME**  Mel, calm down for a moment. He doesn't matter right now. I've got something to tell you –
**MELANIE**  And don't think you can get away with the treasures – we're heading straight back to Generios 1 to hand them over!
**BANTO ZAME**  Mel, I love you.
**MELANIE**  Whether we like it or not, the Cylinder – (*realising, stunned*)... what?
**BANTO ZAME**  I love you. You are the most beautiful, intelligent and spirited woman I have ever met. Please – don't say no – please take my hand and say we'll dance together forever under the stars!
**MELANIE**  Are you *insane*?
**BANTO ZAME**  You really know how to let a guy down gently. Would it make any difference if I asked – will you marry me?

### 42. EXT. GAS PLANET – DAY
*DOCTOR WHO is pleading with the JELLOID.*

**DOCTOR WHO**  Please – you've got to activate the teleport pad...
**SALLY-ANNE**  We've got to get after them.
**DOCTOR WHO**  It's vital that we reach Generios 1!
**JELLOID**  (*Bitter*) Why? They have all they need... Why should you not stay here with me and outsit eternity itself?
**DOCTOR WHO**  Look, as soon as I get the TARDIS back I'll go straight to Syrranus Traxea and pick up your entertainment unit and bring it back here! Time Lord's honour. I can be back here in five minutes. You won't have to wait.
**JELLOID**  Oh... oh all right then. I'm a very reasonable single-celled organism, all things considered.
*FX – Blubbery bleeps and blips as he sets the teleporter up.*
**JELLOID**  I've set it to follow the trail of your ship, Doctor.

**DOCTOR WHO**  Thank you, Jelloid. Now – we must ensure the safety of Generios! I must confront that Cylinder – it can't be allowed to roam the universe pillaging wherever it will!

**SALLY-ANNE**  And I must clobber my boyfriend! He can't be allowed to roam the universe pillaging wherever *he* will!

**DOCTOR WHO**  I wouldn't normally condone the use of violence, Sally-Anne, but just this once, I'm inclined to agree! Goodbye, my friend![169]

*FX – The teleporter operates.*

**JELLOID**  Goodbye! Ooh – don't forget the remote control!

**DOCTOR WHO**  (*Fading*) I won't!

**JELLOID**  And the free stand![170]

## 43. INT. COUNCIL CHAMBER DAY

*COUNCILLOR POTIKOL is pacing nervously. The crowd outside are murmuring worriedly. We hear the noise of the CYLINDER descending ever closer.*

**POTIKOL**  Is it still out there? That horrible cylinder.

**GUARD**  Do you want me to open the curtains and have a look?

**POTIKOL**  I suppose so. Oh I never thought it would end like this...

**GUARD**  It's right outside, sir.

**CYLINDER VOICE**  Generios! Your time has elapsed. Where is the Tribute? Bring me the Tribute! The Tribute, I say!

**GUARD**  I think it wants the Tribute, sir.

**POTIKOL**  Oh, Doctor... where are you?

*FX – TARDIS materialises.*

**GUARD**  Sir! Can you hear that?

**POTIKOL**  Is that the TARDIST? It can't be! Oh... it doesn't look much like it.

*FX – The doors open.*

**POTIKOL**  (*CONT'D*) Doctor! It is you! I fall to my knees and prostrate myself before you! You are the saviour of my people...

**BANTO ZAME**  Oh get up, Potikol. (*To MEL*) I mean what I say, Mel. When this is all over we'll buy a little place out on the rim worlds. Abidos, maybe. We could be happy there, you and me.

**MELANIE**  Listen to me, Banto Zame. Even if I wasn't (*thinking quickly*)... an android. Yes, an android.[171] I'd still never marry somebody like you!

**BANTO ZAME**  An android? But you seem so... lifelike!

**MELANIE**  That's how they make us... m-m-m-make us. So you see... click... brrrr... I'm not even flesh and blood.[172]

**BANTO ZAME**  You're a lovely girl, Melanie, but you're a terrible liar. I've heard all the excuses in my time: 'I'm an android, I'm a hermaphrodite, I'm a shape-changing psychopath from the planet Vashir...'

**POTIKOL**  (*Blurting out in a mad frenzy of horror and terror*) Doctor please! That cylinder's right outside! It could destroy us at any moment! I don't want to die! I have a wife! (*He begins to sob*)

**BANTO ZAME**  Well lucky you. Mel, bring him the flamin' treasures.

**CYLINDER VOICE**  You have completed the task? Speak! My sensors are ready to receive the Tribute!

**POTIKOL**  (*Still sniffling*) We have them here, oh great Cylinder!

*FX – MEL wheels the treasures out in a shopping trolley.*

**MELANIE**     (*Out of puff*) They're in this trolley...
**CYLINDER VOICE** I must inspect them. What are these treasures?
**BANTO ZAME** These are the Shelves of Infinity. The greatest achievement of multi-dimensional engineering in the known universe.
**CYLINDER VOICE** Hmmm... these shelves please me. The second treasure. At once!
**MELANIE**     Mentos – the greatest storehouse of knowledge in the known uni... in the cosmos.
**CYLINDER VOICE** Intriguing! But the third treasure! I must see the third treasure!
*FX – DOCTOR WHO and SALLY-ANNE transmat in. A gasp from those assembled.*
**DOCTOR WHO** The third treasure is the grandest of all![173]
**MELANIE**     Doctor! What a relief!
**BANTO ZAME** Sally-Anne! What a nightmare.
**DOCTOR WHO** Behold the largest diamond in all time and space...
*FX – A burst of big, choral music.*
**CYLINDER VOICE** You have done well.
**POTIKOL**     So... er, we *aren't* to be destroyed then?
**CYLINDER VOICE** No! I am a Cylinder of my word. The Tribute is satisfactory.
*FX – A huge sigh of relief. The crowd outside cheers and claps.*
**CYLINDER VOICE** (*CONT'D*) Now, which of you has brought together these treasures?
**POTIKOL**     It was the Doctor, oh Cylinder. This fine gentleman.
**MELANIE**     Hey! He's not the Doctor!
**SALLY-ANNE** Too right he's not.
**CYLINDER VOICE** I wish to reward this... Doctor. Speak!
**POTIKOL**     Yes, Doctor. Go on.
**BANTO ZAME** (*In Doctor voice*) The task you set me was challenging indeed. I needed all the ingenuity and legerdemain at my disposal.
**SALLY-ANNE** Oooh! And after what he said about you, Doctor!
**BANTO ZAME** A mission fraught with danger, and one for which I will gladly receive any financial reparations you wish to give me. As a Time Lord I have no use for filthy lucre, but on this occasion I think I can force myself to make an exception. I could always give it to charity. Later.
**MELANIE**     You can't let him get away with this, Doctor.
**DOCTOR WHO** Shush, Mel!
**MELANIE**     (*Sotto*) What's up? You look like the cat that got the cream!
**DOCTOR WHO** Just watch...
**CYLINDER VOICE** Very well, Doctor. Raise your hand that I may know you.
**SALLY-ANNE** Oy! Don't you dare! He's not the Doctor.
**CYLINDER VOICE** Who is this personage?
**BANTO ZAME** A common space-troll, your eminence. Her mental state is afflicted.
**POTIKOL**     But I thought...
**SALLY-ANNE** Don't worry, Councillor, I've got a man who appreciates me now – standing right over there. The Doctor!
**CYLINDER VOICE** What is this? Who is the Doctor?
**DOCTOR WHO** (*In cod, Banto Zame-y voice*) Not me! The woman's mad.
**CYLINDER VOICE** Then who are you?

**DOCTOR WHO**  I'm Banto Zame, your honour (*with relish*) just a two-bit lying bigamist from the gutters of a superdense mudball. Nobody important.

**BANTO ZAME**  Why you... (*he stifles his protest*)

**CYLINDER VOICE**  Then why does the woman say that you are the Doctor?

**DOCTOR WHO**  She... er, worships me. Follows me everywhere I go. She's quite mad. Just as the Doctor said. That Doctor. There.

**CYLINDER VOICE**  Hmmm... I am suspicious.

**MELANIE**  (*Worried, sotto*) Doctor!

**DOCTOR WHO**  Mad, though a lusty wench. No, that's the Doctor over there. Hang on, look.

*FX – DOCTOR WHO rummages in his pocket for the newspaper he confiscated from SOKKERY in Part One.*

**DOCTOR WHO**  There, see? He's plastered all over the front page of this newspaper. If I just scrape the bile off you can see him...

**CYLINDER VOICE**  But still I must be certain...

**DOCTOR WHO**  And, the Doctor's a Time Lord, your cylinderness. And a Time Lord would never do this...

*FX – DOCTOR WHO kisses SALLY-ANNE. Much 'mwah'ing, please.*

**SALLY-ANNE**  (*Shocked but very pleased*) Ooh Doctor!

**MELANIE**  (*Scandalised*) Doctor!

**CYLINDER VOICE**  You are right. A Time Lord would never do *that!*

**BANTO ZAME**  Blimey! I mean, indeed. We are above such... things. Now, the reparation you promised...

**CYLINDER VOICE**  Very well, Doctor. I shall now reward you.

*FX – A beam transfixes BANTO*

**BANTO ZAME**  What the...? I can't move.

**SALLY-ANNE**  What's happening?

**POTIKOL**  Doctor!

**GUARD**  He's caught in some kind of beam, sir.

**POTIKOL**  I can see that! What are you doing to him?

**CYLINDER VOICE**  Positive identification obtained. You are the Doctor. Also known as Doctor John Smith; Doctor Johann Schmidt; Doctor von Wer; Theta Sigma; Ka Faraq Gatri; Snail...[174]

*MEL and DOCTOR WHO hold the following exchange in a whisper.*

**MELANIE**  (*Sotto*) I get it! The Cylinder wasn't after the treasure at all... it was after you!

**DOCTOR WHO**  (*Sotto*) Be quiet Mel! I'm Banto Zame, remember?

**MELANIE**  And you knew all along?

**DOCTOR WHO**  Modesty prevents me from claiming that... but I did work it out a few minutes ago. There are coincidences and *coincidences*, Mel. I knew something wasn't right. This whole thing seemed, as you so eloquently put it, 'fishy'!

**BANTO ZAME**  No! Let me go! I'm not the Doctor! It's him. Over there. Look, if I could point I'd show you...

**CYLINDER VOICE**  (*Now very stern*) You are wanted by my masters, Doctor. The Sussyurats of Chalzon have arraigned you for trial. Too long you have evaded their justice.

**SALLY-ANNE**  I'm not following this at all.

**DOCTOR WHO**  The Cylinder set a task it knew only the Doctor could complete.

**CYLINDER VOICE** Indeed. My sensors registered newscasts of the Doctor in this system. I tracked him here and now I have him.

**BANTO ZAME** Let me go! Let me go! Please!

**CYLINDER VOICE** No, Doctor. You are coming with me. The journey will be a long one. You will be placed in a time bubble from which even you cannot escape. I am sorry to have troubled you, people of Generios. The loss of your eleventh planet was... regrettable. Goodbye.

**BANTO ZAME** Help! Sally-Anne! Mel! Doctor! Anybody! Help!

*FX – The beam withdraws. BANTO's cries become more faint.*

**BANTO ZAME** *(CONT'D)* My wife's gonna kill me...

*FX – There is a moment of silence. Then the CYLINDER blasts off into space and is gone.*

**GUARD**          It's gone.

**POTIKOL**          *(Sadly)* With the Doctor its only victim. We owe him so much. Again.

*FX – A huge cheer from outside. The hammering on the doors begins again.*

**GUARD**          The people are rejoicing, sir!

**POTIKOL**          I must go and address them. Tell them of this terrible blow. Come!

*FX – POTIKOL and the GUARD exit.*

**MELANIE**          Poor Banto. Even he didn't deserve that. *(A rueful laugh)* You know, he actually proposed to me.

**SALLY-ANNE**          He proposes to everyone.

**MELANIE**          He told me I was the most beautiful, spirited, intelligent woman...

**SALLY-ANNE**          *(Joining in)* ...spirited, intelligent woman he'd ever met.

**MELANIE/SALLY-ANNE**          Eyes like limpid pools, a smile to shame the gods of love...[175]

**DOCTOR WHO** Ah – never mind, ladies, Casanova's long gone now. Although I suppose I *ought* to rescue him from whatever grisly fate these Sussyurats have arranged. I do have a reputation to keep up, after all.

**SALLY-ANNE** Why bother? Good riddance, I reckon. Anyway, I've got you now, Doctor.

**DOCTOR WHO** Ah.[176] Sally-Anne. I think I may have given you the wrong impression...

**SALLY-ANNE** Come off it. No man kisses me like that and doesn't mean it.

**MELANIE**          It was all part of the bluff! Isn't that right, Doctor?

**SALLY-ANNE** Really?

**DOCTOR WHO** *(Uncomfortable)* Er... well, yes...

**SALLY-ANNE** *(Devastated)* Oh. Oh well. Suppose I'll just wander down the spaceport, then, catch a shuttle out. Find some other loser to attach myself to. I'm a magnet for losers...[177]

*FX – POTIKOL re-enters. The crowd are shouting SALLY-ANNE's name.*

**POTIKOL**          Sally-Anne – I have told the crowd of the Doctor's sacrifice. They wish to see you. my dear. To express their deep sorrow, and their gratitude to you.

**SALLY-ANNE** What? Ooh, *really?* Oh, hang on though, I suppose it's the Doctor they really want.

**DOCTOR WHO** The Doctor couldn't have done it without you, Sally-Anne. Why do you think I... I mean, *he* has travelling companions?

**SALLY-ANNE**  So – I was the Doctor's companion?

**DOCTOR WHO**  Yes, Sally-Anne. And you did a fine job. Isn't that right, Mel?

**MELANIE**  Well I... (*kindly*)[178] yes. Yes of course you did. Couldn't have done better myself.

**SALLY-ANNE**  Oh. Oh... cheers. Thanks. You ain't so bad really, you know, ginge.

**MELANIE**  Hmm. Thanks. I think.

**SALLY-ANNE**  And ta for everything, Doctor. I ain't all that keen on this deadly danger bit, but it weren't so bad with a living legend like you around. Come 'ere.

*FX – SALLY-ANNE plants a big, wet kiss on DOCTOR WHO's cheek.*

**SALLY-ANNE**  See you around... sexy!

**DOCTOR WHO**  (*To himself*) Sexy...?

**POTIKOL**  The crowd, Sally-Anne?[179]

*FX – POTIKOL and SALLY-ANNE walk away, their voices fading.*

**POTIKOL**  (*CONT'D*) And there is still the matter of the pluvon power cells.

**SALLY-ANNE**  The what? Oh – oh them.

**POTIKOL**  I should be able to transfer you the ten million credits later today...

**SALLY-ANNE**  Ooh! Oh – that'll do nicely.

*FX – They exit through the door, which then closes.*

**MELANIE**  Hmm. You know, that money *was* swindled out of these people...

**DOCTOR WHO**  I think Sally-Anne earned it today, don't you? Now then – I've had quite enough of the vulgar end of time.

**MELANIE**  Me too. Hey Doctor – why did those Sussyurats have such a big grudge against you anyway?[180] They really did go to a lot of trouble to get at you.

**DOCTOR WHO**  I've no idea, Mel. I haven't met them yet. When I do, I must be sure to really, *really* annoy them.[181]

**MELANIE**  (*Laughs*) I suppose we'd better go and rescue poor old Banto then?

**DOCTOR WHO**  There's a favour I have to do for the Jelloid first. And of course I *was* winning a game of Monopoly...

**MELANIE**  You are incorrigible!

**DOCTOR WHO**  Don't worry. We'll rescue him, Mel. (*Mischievously*) In time. But for the moment, I think there's only room in the universe for the *one* Doctor. Don't you?

*FX – They laugh and enter the TARDIS which swiftly dematerializes.*

*FADE UP CLOSING THEME*

**THE END**

127

# NOTES

**1.** Added dialogue before the beginning of Part One –
ANNOUNCER: '**And now, Colin Baker and Bonnie Langford star in a
new adventure spelling double trouble for Doctor Who.**' The
ANNOUNCER is played by sound designer Alistair Lock.

## PART ONE

**2.** Before his line, DOCTOR WHO laughs maniacally.
**3.** This line is repeated.
**4.** Deleted dialogue: '~~Knocked it with my elbow~~.'
**5.** MELANIE mispronounces the word 'Generios'. Then, added
dialogue with the correct pronunciation:
> **DOCTOR WHO**    Generios 1.
> **MELANIE**       Hm. Generios 1.

*Gary Russell: 'Recipe for disaster – put Colin Baker and Bonnie Langford in a
recording booth together and then try and get them to do a take in a straightforward
manner! I don't know who was laughing more in the control room, myself or Alistair,
but we could barely concentrate on our jobs and I got told off for being too happy!
Bah – I got my revenge when Bonnie stumbled over "Generios" and Colin corrected
her. We still needed a second take but I made them keep that error in!'*

**6.** Line changed to: 'Pass ~~me~~ my coat, will you?'
**7.** Added dialogue – DOCTOR WHO: '**Now then... bit tight**.' This is
complemented by the sound of DOCTOR WHO putting his coat on.
**8.** '**I**' added at the beginning of the line.
**9.** '**Well**,' added at the beginning of the line.
**10.** Line changed to: 'Thank you... but would you mind not
dribbling on ~~to~~ it...'
**11.** Line changed to: 'Come on, **pal**!' *Gary Russell: 'Nick Pegg has been
a Big Finish stalwart since the beginning – he wrote, directed and even cropped up
in* The Spectre of Lanyon Moor *and after that a handful of other stories featured
his dulcet tones. Originally he was going to be Potikol and Steve Fewell was Sokkery
but I changed my mind (not sure if either of them knew that!). Nick opted to do an
impression of William Hague who, I believe, might have been a famous politician at
the time! Hence the "Chum" was replaced with a more Northern-ish "Pal".'*
**12.** Line changed to: 'Here, you have a drop, pretty lady... anyone
ever tell you you've got **fantastic** ringlets?'
**13.** '**Well**,' added at the beginning of the line.
**14.** Line changed to: 'So – what **happened to** these "Skelloids"?'
**15.** Line changed to: '**I somehow** doubt that.'
**16.** '**Normally**,' added at the beginning of the line.
**17.** Line changed to: 'Anyway, Potikol, time's winged **charity**
marches on – especially for a Time Lord. Sally-Anne and I really must
get back to the **STARDIS**.' For the rest of the script – although they
are not annotated – all instances of 'TARDIST' are changed to

'STARDIS'. *Gary Russell: 'TARDIST was an in-joke by Gareth and Clay – it's from an old TV interview or somesuch I imagine where someone said "TARDIS" wrong. However we realised that TARDIST and TARDIS still sounded too similar so we opted for STARDIS instead. Banto's quoting of Andrew Marvell's poem* To His Coy Mistress *got a bit scrambled on the take (he says "charity" rather than "chariot") but we all thought it was far more in character for Banto to misquote something he had heard rather than be educated to the Doctor's level and get the quote right. Another example of Banto not quite being as smart as the Doctor.'*

**18.** Line changed to: 'I will go at once to the Great Bank of Generios and make **you** out a cheque.'

**19.** Line changed to: 'Everything **round** here seems to be Great.'

**20.** Added dialogue – SOKKERY: '**Hello.**'

**21.** Line changed to: '**Eh up**!'

**22.** Line changed to: 'Yeah, **yeah, that's him, yeah**, that's the Doctor.'

**23.** Line changed to: '**Not** without a pass.'

**24.** No music.

**25.** Line changed to: 'What, you don't reckon **they**'ve rumbled us?'

**26.** Line changed to: 'What – **you mean** your cash machine's on the blink?'

**27.** Line changed to: 'I have dispatched a **great** space dredger to blast it out of the skies.'

**28.** Deleted dialogue – GUARD: '~~Just lay her down here, sir, against the wall~~.'

**29.** Line changed to: 'I could do with a glass of water – **it would** clear my head.'

**30.** Line changed to: 'A great calamity – *another* great calamity – has befallen us! Inform the council that our **great space** dredger has been destroyed.'

**31.** Line changed to: 'There's **nothing** there.' *Gary Russell: 'Sally-Anne was written as a pure* Coronation Street-*style teenager, but Jason and I wanted to get Clare Buckfield in for this one, who isn't Northern at all. Thus odd terms and phrases throughout the script became more "Saarf London, innit". Jason had met Clare before but I only knew her through* 2 Point 4 Children *which, whilst not my favourite sitcom ever, did feature four amazing lead actors as the main family so I was overjoyed to meet her. Fab lady, completely unfazed by being a mega TV star. It also took me ages to realise that her boyfriend, "Dec", who she talked about was in the fact the one who isn't Ant in "Ant and...". When she eventually introduced me to him a few months later, I immediately tried to get him interested in doing a* Doctor Who, *along with Mr McPhelin, but alas neither of them are really* Who *aficionados and Dec said no. Bah humbug! Stick him in a snake-infested jungle, I say!'*

**32.** Line changed to: 'But this is my system, I've been working West Galaxy a long time, twenty-five years in **the** business.'

**33.** Line changed to: 'Here, **you** get your hands off my chest!'

**34.** Added dialogue – [2ND] GUARD: '**Yes sir**!'. [2ND] GUARD, who does not appear in the script, was played by Alistair Lock.

**35.** Line replaced by – [2ND] GUARD: '**Right away, sir**!'

**36.** Underneath this line, added dialogue – BANTO ZAME: '**Bye, bye. Give them an autographed picture**.' *Gary Russell: 'It took Chris Biggins all of thirty seconds to realise that every ad lib Colin could do, he'd do one too. It became a contest I think! The one under this line about getting an autograph was undoubtedly one of the best. Gareth and Clay wrote Banto for Chris Biggins right from the word go. There simply wasn't anyone else in their minds. Through Stephen Fewell (he and Chris had been in an Oscar Wilde play together) Gareth put the idea to him, which I then followed up. Many years ago I'd worked with Chris on a schools TV show we did where he was the baddie and we bonded, as did all the cast, over a mutual loathing for a member of the production team. It was nice to see him fifteen or so years later and realise he still remembered! The man is adorable and I'd love to hear more from Banto one day.'*

**37.** Line changed to: 'That object has destroyed our **great space** dredger – and now it's heading straight for us!'

**38.** Line changed to: '**Yes**, **very**, very good, Potikol, I get it.'

**39.** Added dialogue – DOCTOR WHO: 'Charming!'

**40.** Added dialogue – [2ND] GUARD: '**Right**.' *Gary Russell: 'In post-production Alistair realised that the same guard as earlier (played by stalwart Mark Wright) couldn't conceivably do everything, so he replaced one or two of Mark's lines with his own voice and added in a few more lines as well. Never misses an opportunity, does Ali.'*

**41.** '**Right**,' added at the beginning of the line. Then, added dialogue – [2ND] GUARD: '**Oh, yes**.'

**42.** Line changed to: 'Yes, **yes**, **yes**, **yes**, you're right...'

**43.** Line changed to: 'Concentrate, Mel, **concentrate**.'

**44.** SOKKERY's entire dialogue in this scene was changed to: 'Whassat? Whassat thing? It's huger than the sky! **It's blotting everything out**! Oh, and we were having such a laugh **as well**. **Eh, do you mind keeping the noise down up there**? **There's people down here trying to have a party. (***Burps***) Sorry. Look at the size of it**! It's **enormous**!' *Gary Russell: 'Talking of never missing an opportunity – here's Mr Pegg taking a couple of liberties with what's scripted. "Look at the size of it" indeed!'*

**45.** Line changed to: 'It's right **over** the city!'

## PART TWO

**46.** This scene does not appear in Part Two. *Gary Russell: 'This scene isn't in the final version. I honestly have no idea why not. Probably time, or maybe Alistair felt it interrupted the flow of the climactic end to Part One. He was probably right. Probably.'*

**47.** Line changed to: 'I thought for a moment **there** – '

**48.** Rather than CYLINDER VOICE's line being in the background, it is intercut with DOCTOR WHO's line:

**CYLINDER VOICE** These must be presented to me in good repair.

**DOCTOR WHO** Incredible.

**CYLINDER VOICE** You will bring them to me and I will analyse them in order to assess their value.

**DOCTOR WHO** It must be transmitting to the entire planet.

**CYLINDER VOICE** Failure to do so will result in immediate death for your peoples.

**49.** As indicated, this line does not appear in this scene.

**50.** On the director's copy of the script, the pronunciation of 'gluarb' is phonetically specified as 'gloo-arb'.

**51.** Line changed to: '**The second thing**?'

**52.** Line changed to: 'Come on, the **Great** Council Chamber.'

**53.** Added dialogue:

**MELANIE** No, he's not.

**DOCTOR WHO** No.

**54.** Line changed to:

**POTIKOL** Oh goodness – not these idiots again. Guards.

**[2ND] GUARD** Yes, sir!

**POTIKOL** Throw them out – into the streets this time!

**[2ND] GUARD** Right!

**DOCTOR WHO** What?

**POTIKOL** I must go to the people and try to calm them! Good luck Doctor – the future of Generios is in your hands, again!

**55.** Added dialogue – [2ND] GUARD: '**Yes**!'

**56.** Line changed to: 'Oh, **sorry**, did someone say something?'

**57.** Line changed to: 'What business is **that** of yours?'

**58.** Line changed to: '~~Teh~~! Everybody knows that!'

**59.** Line changed to: 'That's a... well, a... (*signs*) **it's** a portaloo.'

**60.** BANTO ZAME and DOCTOR WHO both have two extra '**Yes**'s.

**61.** Line changed to: '**Lest** any should doubt the seriousness of my intention, I shall now destroy the eleventh planet of this system!'

**62.** Deleted dialogue – POTIKOL: '~~They've gone inside.~~'

**63.** Added dialogue – DOCTOR WHO: '**What**?'

**64.** BANTO ZAME says an extra, '**Oh dear**.'

**65.** BANTO ZAME says an extra, '**Oh dear**.'

**66.** Added dialogue:

**SALLY-ANNE** Oh.

**DOCTOR WHO** Thank you.

**67.** Line changed to: '"Not *that* far **off**..." no, **no**, **no**.'

**68.** Line changed to: '~~In fact, Mel~~, as time is rather against us...'

**69.** Added dialogue – SALLY-ANNE: '**Yeah**.'

**70.** Line changed to: 'So, Melanie – how did you pal up with **that** Doctor in the first place, then?'

**71.** Line changed to: 'Don't go boasting about that, people will think **we're** strange.'

**72.** Line changed to: '**Now**, we've got to find Unit ZX419. Whatever **that** is.'

**73.** Line changed to: 'Whatever it was, it came from that ruin **there** on the horizon.'

**74.** Line changed to: '**Look**, look again.'

**75.** Line changed to: '"Unit EM670. This light, attractive, interlocking, easy-to-assemble anglepoise lighting feature is available in both burnt ochre and **aqua marine** blue finish. Whether you're working or just relaxing, it provides a reassuring glow to relieve the pointless and arbitrary existence of the human being".'

**76.** This line is said under the preceding line.

**77.** Under this line, BANTO ZAME says, '**Oh no**.'

**78.** Line changed to, 'It was incredibly successful – supplied the whole **world**, and far beyond.'

**79.** Line changed to:

**SALLY-ANNE**    A what-theatre?
**DOCTOR WHO**    Oh, never mind.

**80.** This line and the preceding line was changed to:
**DOCTOR WHO**    **Here we go**.
*FX – They clamber in. Tearing fabric*
**SALLY-ANNE**    Careful! ~~You've ripped my skirt!~~
**DOCTOR WHO**    **Sorry**. Shhh!

**81.** '**Look**,' added at the beginning of the line.

## PART THREE

**82.** Part Three has the Delaware syntheiser arrangement of the title music, which was arranged by Delia Derbyshire and Paddy Kingsland in 1972. *Gary Russell: 'The use of the Delaware version of the theme (cf Australian version of* Carnival of Monsters *– it's bound to be referred to on the DVD or in a book by David J Howe if you don't know the reference) was a suggestion made by David Darlington one Thursday night on the way home from the pub; and Robert Dick suggested using it on one episode only. I thought it was an excellent idea and fitted the tone of the story perfectly. Of course, I suggested Part Three and only realised that my smart-arsed* Doctor Who *knowledge was at fault when the aforementioned DVD came out - it should have been on Part Two to make the joke work! Durrr....'*

**83.** '**Look**,' added at the beginning of the line.

**84.** Line changed to: '...I only needed it to **get**...'

**85.** Line changed to: 'Forget it, Mel – you can't reason with **those** things.'

**86.** '**No, no**,' added at the beginning of the line.

**87.** Added dialogue – BANTO ZAME: '**Think about it**.'

**88.** Deleted dialogue – ASSEMBLER 2: '**Why must we wait**?'

**89.** Line changed to: 'You use it to fry food – ~~on a hob~~...'

**90.** '**Correct**,' added at the beginning of the line.

**91.** Line changed to: 'Er... um... I **do** know this one...'

**92.** Line changed to: 'Far more likely the products of **an** advanced technology.'

**93.** Line changed to: 'And very sexy... no, no, let's not start **that all** again.'

**94.** Added dialogue – SALLY-ANNE: '**Oh yeah**?'

**95.** Line changed to: 'We don't know the full situation – **we can't** just blunder in.'

**96.** Deleted dialogue – MELANIE: '~~The instructions are attached to this bit. It looks simple enough. A straightforward shelving unit.~~'

**97.** Line changed to: 'We shall withdraw and observe **you** on our visiscope.'

**98.** Line changed to: '**This** must be Rod A.'

**99.** '**And**,' added at the beginning of the line.

**100.** Line changed to: 'I don't like it when **you're** flabbergasted.'

**101.** Line changed to: 'Unfortunately, until the correct code is released into the panel you see **just** beneath me, I am irrevocably conditioned to answer questions. And before you ask, the only other people who knew the code were my designers, and, **goodness me**, they're long dead.' *Gary Russell: 'To say that Nick Pegg and Janie Goddard had fun doing all this would be an understatement. I think they did most of it in one take, too! At the end of this book, and on the end of the CD as well, you can find all the questions Clay wrote for ad libbing in this scene. I had met Jane more years ago than either of us care to remember at a* Doctor Who *convention she was co-compering. We then met [cough loudly] years later when I realised she was, as they used to say in genteel times "stepping out" with writer Rob Shearman. (They're now married, awwww...) Janie's a top actress and one of those people one can turn to because she can do anything, and nothing fazes her. Love her to bits. "You're a Spanish lady," I'll say, or a "Scandinavian lady of leisure". Or "a four foot tall hamster". Or, in this case, "Anne Robinson on speed!" Colin Baker adores Janie as well, which is just as well as I think if anyone else had played this, his disappointment that we didn't actually have Ms Robinson (I was too scared to ask) would have been all consuming and I might not have survived this first day of recording!'*

**102.** '**Correct**...' added at the beginning of the line.

**103.** Added dialogue – SALLY-ANNE: '**Oh yeah**.'

**104.** Line changed to: 'Hold on, hold on, **just a minute** – as my companion, you're supposed to try and rouse me from my sloughs of despond.'

**105.** Line changed to: '(*Awkward*) There, there. **Here, look.** Have my hanky.'

**106.** Line changed to: 'No, **no**, **no**, **no**, look.'

**107.** '**No**,' added at the beginning of the line.

**108.** Line changed to: 'Yes, there's the section we finished... in which case, these parts here – **must be**... must be *new*.'

**109.** In this speech, two lines are transposed: 'That year the snow fell eight feet deep,' and 'We lived in a big house about seven miles from the town.' Also, line changed to: 'And though it was hard, and the road was long, we made it to **the** church hall, and we gave that show!' *Gary Russell: 'No footnote, just an observation that this moment is one of my all time faves of everything we've done. Bonnie and Chris were just sublime.'*

**110.** Rather than said from outside, before this line the doors open. Then, after the line, they close again.

**111.** Added dialogue – BANTO ZAME: '**Oh**.'

**112.** Line changed to: 'Um... no, **no. Course not, no**.'

**113.** Line changed to: 'You'll have to do better than that, **you know**?'

**114.** Line changed to: 'I based myself in Woking during a **Cyberman** invasion.'

**115.** Line changed to: 'Wish **number** one – peace throughout the galaxy.'

**116.** Added dialogue – DOCTOR WHO: '**Come on, yes**?'

**117.** Line changed to: 'Later that **same** day you were locked in a dungeon by the evil Mantelli?'

**118.** Line changed to: 'Very clever **these** research devices.'

**119.** Line changed to: 'Here, **have your coat back and** let me have a go.'

**120.** 'Oi! Questioner!' is said under the following line.

**121.** The despairing sound is actually DOCTOR WHO saying, '**Yeah, sure**.'

**122.** Deleted dialogue – DOCTOR WHO: 'Wait! I've got it, I know what to ask... How could I have been so stupid...'

**123.** Added dialogue – DOCTOR WHO: '**I've got it!**' The line is said over QUESTIONER and SALLY-ANNE's lines.

**124.** Line changed to: 'Er... I'm sure I'll have the answer soon... it's going to be a **little** bit tricky...'

**125.** At all these instances, the QUESTIONER says, '**I'll have to hurry you**.'

**126.** Added dialogue – QUESTIONER: '**Hurry, hurry, hurry**.'

**127.** '**Mentos**,' added at the beginning of the line.

**128.** Line changed to: 'Now, come on – let's disconnect the box and get back to the others.'

**129.** Line changed to: 'Ho ho.'

**130.** Line changed to: 'Then how can the humans have completed **the** task?' *Gary Russell: 'I believe Gareth had recently had an (allegedly) unfortunate experience involving a well-known Scandinavian self-assembly furniture company when plotting this! The assemblers were meant to be based, vocally, on the Martians that used to "smash them all to little bits" when discussing potatoes in the old Smash TV ads. No one under 20 probably got the joke; old farts like me loved it! It's not going to be a surprise that in asking Adam Buxton in to do this (another Mark Gatiss introduction,* naturellement*) I also asked Joe Cornish as well but he had a family commitment on the Sunday we were recording on and couldn't do it (Adam and Joe are fab TV comedians, for the benefit of overseas viewers or Brits who have lived under a rock for the last decade). Stephen Fewell, already doing Potikol, stepped in, bless him. Adam was terrific fun, not at all starry (but as a mate of Gatiss's, I wouldn't expect him to be – almost everyone Mark has ever introduced to us has never been anything other than delightful) and delighted to be a part of* Doctor Who. *He stood in front of me at a David Byrne concert a couple of years later but I didn't say "hi" because he seemed to be out just to have a nice time and probably wouldn't want attention drawn to himself. Steve Fewell of course plays Jason Kane* *in our Benny audios and was very keen to be in* The One Doctor *because of Chris Biggins. Again, Steve's the kind of person who can turn his hand to anything at a moment's notice. I think he had about three days' warning that he was going to be doing this extra role.'*

**131.** The second 'Erase!' is said by ASSEMBLER 1

**132.** Line changed to: 'Or footstools and **an** occasional table with accompanying pouffe?'

**133.** Line changed to: 'I warn you – a verbal duel against me, as you should remember, if you used the smallest fraction of your **cerebral cortex, can only** end in ignominy for you!'

**134.** This line was replaced by:
> **BANTO ZAME**   I did not! I did not!
> **DOCTOR WHO**   Yes, you did!
> **BANTO ZAME**   I did not!

**135.** This line is said by SALLY-ANNE only.

**136.** Line changed to: 'It wasn't *that* clever a suggestion **then**.'

**137.** Line changed to: 'It must take the particular geological extremes at work here to produce **one of** *that* size.'

**138.** Line changed to: 'No one's going to leave **a diamond** as valuable as that lying out in the open and unguarded.'

**139.** Line changed to: 'Stop squabbling **you two**.'

**140.** 'No,' said twice.

**141.** The episode ends with the Delaware syntheiser arrangement of the title music.

## PART FOUR

**142.** At all these instances, MELANIE says an extra, '**No**.'

**143.** 'Oh,' is said twice.

**144.** Line changed to: 'Quick while it's **out**, grab the diamond!' *Gary Russell: 'I thought "kaylyed" was a terribly old fashioned phrase and not one that sounded very Banto-ish.'*

**145.** '**Now**,' added at the end of the line.

**146.** Line changed to: '**Now**, that's staying power for you.'

**147.** Line changed to: 'You can't **just** leave powerful artefacts lying about...'

**148.** Added dialogue – JELLOID: '**So, they had me sign a fifty million year non-negotiable contract**.' *Gary Russell: 'Guess what, Matt Lucas was another Gatiss-inspired piece of casting. In fact, we asked Mark to play the Cylinder Voice but he was filming something about* The League of Gentlemen *I think so we asked Matt to do that as well as the Jelloid. He had everyone in hysterics during these scenes – his little ad libs and other touches were delivered so matter-of-factly that you couldn't believe this voice was coming from such a quiet, unassuming man. I remember he wore a suit to the studio (I think he was going onto some bash afterwards) but made a comment that he thought everyone should dress up for radio like the old BBC actors and comedians did in the Fifties and Sixties. We did all Matt's stuff towards the end of the second day and it was the perfect way to end a perfect* *weekend. Our faces were tired from simply laughing at everything the cast said or did. A fantastic atmosphere which created a fantastic play.'*

**149.** Line changed to: "Thirty million years **I've served of it now**...'

**150.** '**Well, you see**,' added that the beginning of the line.

**151.** '**Problem is**,' added at the beginning of the line.

**152.** Line changed to: '~~But~~ surely you can see our mission is vitally important?'

**153.** Line changed to: 'We promise if they show up, ~~then~~ we'll make them wait until you come back.'

**154.** '**Yes**,' added at the start of the line.

**155.** '**Er**,' added at the start of the line.

**156.** Line changed to: '**It's** hovering right over the Complex.'

**157.** Line changed to: '~~Please~~ – oh please, Great Cylinder, spare us!'

**158.** Line changed to: 'I don't think **it's listening to you anymore**, sir.'

**159.** The last three lines of the scene were re-ordered. CYLINDER VOICE's line comes first, followed by the GUARD's and then POTIKOL's.

**160.** Line replaced by:

*FX: TARDIS door opens.*

**MELANIE**       Doctor, I can't believe how quickly the TARDIS launderette has got your coat cleaned.

**DOCTOR WHO**    (*Sniffs*) How do I smell?

**MELANIE**       A lot better than you did. But, but we really haven't got time for any more preening. Our three hours are almost up, you know.

*Gary Russell: 'The anally-retentive side of me took over at the start of this scene and we added in some stuff about the Doctor's coat now being clean after its immersion in jelly belly gunk!'*

**161.** Added dialogue – SALLY-ANNE: '**Shooo**!'

**162.** Line changed to: 'You're only jealous ~~he was right~~.'

**163.** 'Gawd' is pronounced as 'God'.

**164.** Line changed to: 'Well let's grab that ruddy diamond and get out of here then, ~~shall we~~?'

**165.** Line changed to: '~~What? Er~~... oh ~~no~~, of course... they must have been using Vektons as their delivery agents...'

**166.** Line changed to: '**Yes**, Vektons. The fastest moving creatures in the cosmos. They learnt to manipulate time so they move forty times faster than everybody else. **Oh no**, of course – the fly!'

**167.** Line changed to: 'Oh no... another call to the depot... another delay... another **twenty million years** of waiting here on this very same spot... nothing to entertain or divert me... **Nothing to guard now, even. Oh, I should never have signed that contract**.'

**168.** Line changed to: 'On this dump with ~~just~~ an old jelly for company.'

**169.** Line changd to: 'Goodbye, my **jelloid** friend.'

**170.** Line changed to: 'And the free **self-assembly** stand.' There is then some added dialogue in the form of the Jelliod's song: 'I'm a very lonely jelloid/Sitting on my own.' *Gary Russell: 'When I listened to the rough edit of this play I was amazed by the Jelloid Song – it was funny, jolly and very, very appropriate. Of course, my amazement was because it wasn't scripted, and nor had Matt recorded such a thing. Alistair had composed and performed and added it because, well, because he wanted to. So now you know, that's not Matt, it's Ali doing a top notch impression.'*

**171.** Deleted dialogue – MELANIE: '~~Yes, an android~~.'

**172.** Line changed to: 'That's how they make us... ~~m-m-m make us. So you see... click... brrrr... I'm not even flesh and blood~~.'

**173.** Line changed to: 'The third treasure is the **greatest** of all!'

**174.** Line changed to: 'Also known as Doctor John Smith; Doctor Johann Schmidt; Doctor von Wer; Theta Sigma; Ka Faraq Gatri; ...**and** Snail.'

**175.** Line changed to: 'Eyes like limpet pools, a smile to shame the gods of ~~love~~...'

**176.** Line changed to: 'Ah, **yes**.'

**177.** '**Me**,' added at the end of the line.

**178.** At this point, DOCTOR WHO hits MELANIE.

**179.** This line and the preceding one are transposed.

**180.** On the director's copy of the script, the pronunciation of 'Sussyrats' is phonetically specified as 'Suss-yurr-rats'.

**181.** Line changed to: '**But** when I do, I must be sure to really, *really* annoy them.'

# DUST BREEDING

## By Mike Tucker

'Coming soon from Big Finish, *Doctor Who: Dark Rising*, starring Anthony Ainley as the Doctor and Sylvester McCoy as the Master…'

That was the one line pitch I gave to producer Gary Russell when he asked me to submit an idea for my second *Doctor Who* script; a body-horror story that would involve – for one episode at least – the Doctor losing possession of his body to his arch enemy, giving Sylvester the opportunity for to stretch his villain muscles whilst allowing Anthony Ainley to take centre stage as the Doctor alongside Sophie Aldred's Ace. In principal Gary was up for it, and so I started working up the scenario in which this drama would play out.

Although the role reversal idea gave me a fantastic opportunity to play with audience expectations (and I'll admit I was intrigued to see just what Anthony and Sylvester would do with the roles), I was very keen to do a 'traditional' Master story: traditional in the Pertwee sense. To that end I knew from the outset that I wanted it to be set on Earth, preferably somewhere rural and that the Master would have ingratiated himself into some local community – probably taking on the identity of some authority figure.

Having arrived at that setting I decided that I could have considerable fun with the format, introducing a number of characters all of whom could conceivably be the Master – a sinister vicar, a corrupt industrialist, a local squire, etc. – and keeping the audience guessing as to his correct identity until quite late into the story. I had hoped that we could do an audio version of the Master unmasking himself, some sound effect that blended the voice of one character into the familiar mellow tones of Mr Ainley as the Episode Two cliffhanger.

From Gary's point of view his only stipulation was that I included the monsters that Robert Perry and I had created for our BBC *Doctor Who* book *Storm Harvest*. Originally I thought that he meant the Cythosi – hulking militaristic warmongers – but it soon became clear that he meant the Krill. Given that the Krill were savage, mindless creatures with no conversation they seemed an odd choice to me and I mentioned as much to Gary. Surely an audio monster needed to speak? 'True,' said Gary. 'But you've sculpted a model of the Krill and we want to use a photo of it on the cover.' Such is the fickle nature of audio producers…

With all these elements in front of me, I started to plot in a little more detail. At first it seemed like an ungainly mix, everything pulling in different directions, but gradually it all started to fall into place. One of my chief inspirations was a book of Celtic myths and legends, in particular the stories revolving around Danu, the Earth Goddess. My rural setting lent itself well to these elements, there was a lot of dark sorcery that tied in well with the possession storyline, and best of all there was a sea creature called Balor that provided the perfect hook to include the aquatic Krill.

In the end I settled on a single Krill, brought to Earth by the Master and released into the sea near a small Welsh fishing village, my plan being to expand the possession elements of the story by having the creature swap bodies with one of my human characters, preferably someone quite engaging, and giving me the opportunity to do something different with these non-communicative creatures. I also wanted a thrash metal band made up from bored local kids, just to get a slightly different feel to the incidental music.

Surprisingly the story also took on an environmental angle. At the time we were in the grip of the petrol dispute and I quickly added this to the mix, playing the industrialists off against the Spirit of the Earth and reinforcing the Pertwee stereotype that I had hoped to achieve.

Sadly I only got as far as completing Episode One before I received a call from Gary telling me to stop. For a variety of reasons that I won't even attempt to go into here, Big Finish and Anthony Ainley had been unable to reach a satisfactory arrangement regarding his appearance in the audios and a rethink was in order regarding the potential return of the Master. (The completed Episode One can be found in the appendices.)

Although I know discussions were had regarding a total recasting of the role, it was eventually decided to ask Geoffrey Beevers to recreate the version of the Master that he had played in the 1981 Tom Baker story *The Keeper of Traken*. As soon as Geoffrey was onboard, Gary asked me to set about rejigging my story to include this decaying version of the Master.

Initially it seemed like a relatively easy task – after all the Master is still the Master, and his motivation and general character are broadly the same regardless of which actor is portraying him – but as I started the rewrites it soon became clear that the ghoul-like Master just didn't fit into the Pertwee-style scenario that I was creating. *Dark Rising* belonged to the Barry Letts/Terrance Dicks school of *Doctor Who* and required a suave, bearded villain chuckling evily to himself, not a hooded, scarred monster shambling through the proceedings. The decaying version of the Master stemmed from the time of a different producer/script editor team, the Phillip Hinchcliffe/Robert Holmes era, and would require a very different approach. Gary agreed and it was decided that I would ditch everything that had been written so far and start again from scratch.

My immediate thought was to embrace that Hinchcliffe/Holmes ethic and write a story that borrowed liberally from horror classics of the past. I was engaged in providing the effects for a major documentary series about the Egyptian empire at the time and had sculpted four decayed and shrivelled mummies. Looking at them in the workshop one evening I realised that the decaying Master character lent itself beautifully to a pastiche of the Hammer mummy films, perhaps updated to fall more in line with the Steven Sommers remakes. With this in mind I sketched out a very rough scenario set in the 1930s involving a expedition to the pyramids and an entombed Master, the Episode Two cliffhanger being the sarcophagus creaking open and the bandage enshrouded Master staggering out cackling, 'I am the Master and you will obey me!'

Fortunately I didn't waste too much time plotting this one as it was swiftly rejected by Gary who had just commissioned a Fifth Doctor story set in Egypt – *The Eye of the Scorpion*, also contained in this book – and was also keen to get away from Earth-based stories. Could I write him a space opera instead?

With time rapidly running out I decided to plunder the file of unused story ideas that Robert Perry and I had compiled over the years. One of these – a space-based story called *Dust Breeding* – had originally been put forward as our follow-up novel to *Illegal Alien*, but Steve Cole, the range editor of the BBC novels, had turned it down in favour of the more 'epic' *Matrix*.

*Dust Breeding* had long been a favourite of mine. It had a lot of concepts that I was very happy with and was both very dark and very humorous. Re-reading the story outline, I also realised that it would adapt perfectly to both the restrictions of audio and to Gary's brief. It was a relatively small cast of characters, it had settings that would provide good audioscapes, it featured a race of savage non-speaking aliens and it had a surprise appearance by the Master – something that I had forgotten writing!

With Robert's blessing, I started reworking the story to fit my own requirements. Most of the basic plot and setting survived intact. The art theme, the planet of telepathically controlled dust, Guthrie, and the huge gallery in space all transferred remarkably well. Unfortunately the story was way too long for a 100-minute audio, so several plot elements and characters were quickly stripped out. Chief casualty was a mad Alpha Centaurian called Ralph McTell – but perhaps that was a good thing!

Ralph became Damien, corrupt art dealers Garpol and Blint became Madame Salvadori and Klemp, the alien race were reworked to become the Krill and Bev Tarrant, talented thief and mercenary from my previous audio *The Genocide Machine*, decided to make a second appearance.

People are often baffled when I say that characters take on a life of their own and start doing things that you don't expect, but it's true. When I started writing *Dust Breeding* I had no idea that Bev was going to reappear. She just appeared on the word processor one evening and that was that. It did, however, give me the chance to write for the delightful Louise Faulkner again, and it also gave Big Finish a perfect smoke screen behind which they could hide the reappearance of Geoffrey Beevers as the Master.

My story, in all its forms, had always had the Master disguised until the cliffhanger of Part Two, this time hidden behind his cunning anagrammatical pseudonym of Mr Seta. None of us thought for one moment that we would actually manage to keep it a secret until the CD came out, but it was worth a try.

First smokescreen was to make a big fuss about the inclusion of Bev Tarrant. 'The first Big Finish character to make a return visit!' we cried (conveniently forgetting about Vansell from *The Sirens of Time* turning up in *The Apocalypse Element*). The second masterstroke was Gary's casting of Caroline John as Madame Salvadori. Everyone assumed that we had employed Carrie first and foremost, and that Geoffrey was just along for the ride. It worked like a dream. For the first time in years we had actually managed to keep people in the dark and have a proper surprise in an episode of *Doctor Who*. Even the blatantly obvious Mr Seta gag had fooled people.

From a personal point of view I have a lot to be proud of in *Dust Breeding*. Even now it surprises me because it sounds so different to how I had imagined. As a director Gary wasn't afraid to take risks with performance and casting and as a result I got a story that sounds exotic, grotesque, funny and scary all at the same time. I had always seen Guthrie as an American (I wanted Shane Rimmer), now I can't imagine him any other way, Madame Salvadori was plummy English in my head, Carrie decided otherwise, Damien was always going to be mad, but Johnson

Willis took madness to a whole new level and if you think Sylvester's possessed performance is scary you should have heard the rehearsal that we didn't record!

Basically I had a first rate cast and crew, extraordinary sound effects and music, a beautiful cover and a villain whose performance makes the hairs stand up on the back of your neck. As a writer you can't really ask for much more than that.

# DUST BREEDING

## CAST

| | |
|---|---|
| THE DOCTOR | Sylvester McCoy |
| ACE | Sophie Aldred |
| MAGGIE | Jane Goddard |
| SKREDSVIG | Jez Fielder |
| JAY BINKS | Gary Russell |
| BEV TARRANT | Louise Faulkner |
| GUTHRIE | Ian Rickets |
| MADAME SALVADORI | Caroline John |
| KLEMP | Mark Donovan |
| THE MASTER | Geoffrey Beevers |
| DAMIEN PIERSON | Johnson Willis |
| ALBERT BOOTLE | Alistair Lock |

# PART ONE

**1. INT. DRAWING ROOM. EVENING.**
*A harpsichord plays – to establish that we are in the past, nothing more.*
*A door opens, as it does so the playing stops.*

**MAGGIE**     How is he?
**SKREDSVIG**     He is sleeping, but I have never seen a man so tortured in his sleep. His brow furrows constantly. It is as if some great turmoil rages within him.
**MAGGIE**     Did he say anything about what was troubling him? Has he spoken to you at all?
**SKREDSVIG**     He has spoken for some time about painting the memories of a sunset. He talks about the sky being red like blood – no, he believes that it really is blood. Coagulated blood. No one else would see it that way, all they would see are clouds. But if you talk to Edvard about it... (*he sighs*) Something has consumed him with fear.
**MAGGIE**     But what? What could have caused this malaise?
**SKREDSVIG**     He talks of a trip to Ekebergasen. He says that he was walking along the road with two friends. He was feeling tired and so he stopped, looking out over the fjord, watching the sunset. He says that the sky suddenly turned red, that blood and tongues of fire hung over the town. His friends walked on, they saw nothing, but Edvard was left trembling with fear. He claims that he heard a scream – an infinite scream passing through nature. The sadness that we see in him is because the humble means available to art are not enough for him to put that experience onto canvas. He is striving for the impossible and has despair as his religion.
**MAGGIE**     What did you advise him?
**SKREDSVIG**     This scream is still in his head so I advised him to paint it.[1]

**2. INT. REFUELLING STATION B – DAY.**
*A storm, but it isn't rain battering the windows – it's dust. The wind is ferocious and there is an eerie drawn out howl – a constant background scream.(Every scene set on this planet should have the same constant background atmospheric to a greater or lesser extent.) Above the storm we hear the burbling of a radio transmitter. A distress beacon starts to sound.*

**TECHNICIAN**     (*Frantic*) Mayday! This is third technician Jay Binks on Refuelling Station B calling Duchamp control! Come in control! Can you hear me? They're dead. Do you hear, everyone dead! Killed by the dust. By the damn dust I tell you! (*Calmer*) It's everywhere, can you hear it, Control? Hear it on the wind? It's trying to get in!
*A window smashes. The wind and screaming increases in pace.*
**TECHNICIAN**     Did you hear that? It knows I'm in here! It wants to smother me, smother me like all the others.
*The wind is deafening now. More windows smash.*
**TECHNICIAN**     The planet is alive! It wants us all dead! AAAAAAAGH!

145

*There is a terrifying gurgling scream above the noise, and then just wind and the beacon...*

**3. INT. TARDIS.**
*The familiar background hum of the ship in flight. Footsteps...*

**ACE**        (*Hushed*) Professor?
**THE DOCTOR**   Ah, there you are, Ace. What kept you?
**ACE**        (*Hushed*) It's a long way from the control room.[2]
**THE DOCTOR**   Yes.
**ACE**        (*Hushed*) And I didn't know the TARDIS had an art gallery...
**THE DOCTOR**   (*Whispering*) Why are you whispering?
**ACE**        Because it feels like a museum, or a library. Somewhere serious.
**THE DOCTOR**   (*Suddenly loud*) Nonsense. This is my play room. In you go...
*A door swishes open. They enter an echoey, cavernous sounding space.*
**ACE**        What's this, an explosion in a glass factory?
**THE DOCTOR**   Terileptil sculpture. Such a talented race, if only they'd stick to art. Such a pity... (*perky*) Have you seen my Mona Lisa? It's just down here...
*He sets off, Ace in tow.*
**ACE**        Your Mona Lisa?
**THE DOCTOR**   Yes, you remember, Ace, I told you. Leonardo actually painted seven of them. I managed to pick one up as a souvenir.[3]
**ACE**        Is it the Mona Lisa?
**THE DOCTOR**   Well it's not the one with 'This is a Fake' written under the paint in felt tip. That one's in the Louvre...
**ACE**        Hey... Hey, hold up, Professor, what's this doing here?
**THE DOCTOR**   Ah... The Night Watch.
**ACE**        Doctor, I remember this from 'O' level art. It's by that Dutch bloke...[4]
**THE DOCTOR**   Rembrandt.
**ACE**        It's meant to be one of the greatest pictures of all time.
**THE DOCTOR**   Yes, it is rather good isn't it? I picked it up from the Rijksmuseum in Amsterdam in the 33rd Century.
**ACE**        (*Appalled*) You stole it?
**THE DOCTOR**   No, no, no! Of course not![5] The museum burned down. I nipped in there an hour or so beforehand. I rescued it. That's how I got most of my collection.
**ACE**        You stole them.
**THE DOCTOR**   Rescued them!
**ACE**        You hang around waiting for museums and art galleries to burn down or whatever – and then you loot them. It's like grave robbing.
**THE DOCTOR**   They would have been destroyed.
**ACE**        So why don't you return them?
**THE DOCTOR**   What? And alter the course of history?
**ACE**        Huh! That's always an argument you love to use when it suits you... (*pause*) So I assume we're off to nick another masterpiece, then.
**THE DOCTOR**   Nick?

**ACE** Rescue, then. From where, exactly?
**THE DOCTOR** A backwater planet called Duchamp 331. Not a very pleasant place I'm afraid, but there's a little something that I want to pick up.
**ACE** A little something that will sit in this gap.[6]
**THE DOCTOR** Yes...
**ACE** (*Reading*) The Scream, by Edvard Munch.[7]
**THE DOCTOR** Yes. According to my diary, it's about to vanish in mysterious circumstances...

## 4. EXT. REFUELLING STATION A – DAY

*The same howling wind and screaming as before. Not as ferocious, but distant and constant. A door hisses open. There is a distant echoing tannoy voice.*

**COMPUTER VOICE** This is Duchamp Control. All staff on Duchamp Refuelling Base A are reminded we are on stage two storm alert. Full filtration and dust contamination procedures will be observed until further notice. Control out.
**BEV TARRANT** Of all the God-forsaken planets to get stranded on... You pick 'em Bev. You really pick 'em.
**GUTHRIE** Heh! Got the dust blues girl?
**BEV TARRANT** Blue would be a relief. It's just so bleak. All this rolling grey. Endless... You must be Guthrie.
**GUTHRIE** If you say so, then that's who I must be.
**BEV TARRANT** I'm Tarrant, Bev Tarrant.
**GUTHRIE** Good to meet you girl. (*He hawks up and spits*) Be proud to shake yer hand.
**BEV TARRANT** Charming.
**GUTHRIE** Heh, attagirl. Spit's a precious commodity on Duchamp. Everything's so dry – inside and out. Dust. Gets right up the crack of your...
**BEV TARRANT** Quite.
**GUTHRIE** Yer not one of the freighter crew, are you, what's a girl like you...?
**BEV TARRANT** Doing on a dump like this? (*She laughs*) Bad luck, and lots of it. Got caught out by a border patrol and had to make a long hyperjump. Came out in this system with a blown hyperdrive and no fuel. (*She laughs humourlessly*) Six of the biggest fuel dumps in the entire sector and I've got nothing to pay for it with.
**GUTHRIE** I wouldn't say that... you're a damn fine looking woman...
**BEV TARRANT** And you can forget any ideas like that...
**GUTHRIE** (*Gives a hacking laugh*) No harm in tryin'...
**BEV TARRANT** (*Pause, then*) They tell me you've been here twenty years, Guthrie. That you were here with the construction crews and you just keep extending your tour of duty. Why do you stay?
**GUTHRIE** Me? Wouldn't live anywhere else. Been here since the beginning. Gonna stay till the end. (*Pause*) How old are you, girl?
**BEV TARRANT** That's no question to ask a lady.
**GUTHRIE** How old?
**BEV TARRANT** Twenty nine.
**GUTHRIE** Only twenty nine, eh? That's rough. Duchamp's no place

for the young. We're all ancient here. Old before our time. Aged by the dust. No one young ever comes here.

**BEV TARRANT** You get the long haul pilots. Ships are always refuelling here.

**GUTHRIE**     But no one stays. Not for long. They're always quick to leave Duchamp. (*He cackles*) This is where they send you to die, girl.[8]

### 5. INT. 'GALLERY'. SALVADORI'S CABIN.

**SALVADORI**     Klemp? Klemp! Oh, curse the man, where is he? (*Bellowing*) Klemp!

**KLEMP**     (*Off*) Coming, Madame Salvadori.

**SALVADORI**     Ah, there you are Klemp. Where the devil have you been?

**KLEMP**     Well ma'am... (*taps at a keypad*)

**SALVADORI**     No, don't bother, already I can feel waves of boredom sweeping over me. What of the preparations? Is the good ship 'Gallery' ready to embark on its great adventure to Duchamp 331?

**KLEMP**     Almost. Madame Salvadori, we are just waiting for one passenger.

**SALVADORI**     Waiting for a passenger! Heavens man, we can't delay the most prestigious social event of the decade for one passenger. Tell the captain to leave without him.

**KLEMP**     Ah, it is a rather special passenger, ma'am. Our mysterious benefactor, Mr Seta...

**SALVADORI**     Ah... Well in that case... (*conspiratorially*) Have you made any headway in uncovering his identity, Klemp, or the nature of his mysterious and, no doubt, very expensive cargo?

**KLEMP**     I'm afraid not, Madame Salvadori. (*Taps at a keypad*) All investigations have met with rather... limited success.

**SALVADORI**     Oh, you're useless, I really don't know why I keep you.

**KLEMP**     No, ma'am.

**SALVADORI**     Very well, Klemp, hurry along.[9]

**KLEMP**     Yes, ma'am.

**SALVADORI**     Oh, Klemp. Before you go. What do you think of the outfit?

**KLEMP**     Well...

**SALVADORI**     Come on, man, speak up.

**KLEMP**     Well you will clash with the hors d'œuvres if you wear that particular shade of green, ma'am.

**SALVADORI**     Oh, away with you, Klemp. Out, out! Shoo! (*Bellowing*) And bring me back something that is purple! (*Exasperated*) Oh, why is nothing ever easy?!

### 6. INT. TARDIS CONSOLE ROOM.
*The Doctor and Ace approach from the access corridor.*

**ACE**     (*Distant*) So where is the God-forsaken planet?

**THE DOCTOR**     (*Entering the control room*) In the middle of the major freight shipping routes. It's a way station. A refuelling post for spacecraft carrying supplies to the new frontier.

**ACE**     And they decided that was a good place for an art gallery? They must run a good bus service.

**THE DOCTOR**     (*Exasperated*) There is a colony of independent artists

148

and musicians who decided that Duchamp 331 was the perfect getaway from the rest of society.

**ACE** Oh, great. Hippies.[10]

**THE DOCTOR** Really Ace...

*There is a bleep from the console, and the distress beacon from earlier.*

**ACE** Hey, what's that?

**THE DOCTOR** A distress beacon. Very faint.

*He punches at controls.*

**ACE** A ship...

**THE DOCTOR** No, it's a planetary beacon... How interesting. It's from Duchamp 331.

**ACE** Professor, I don't suppose your diary mentions exactly how this painting of yours mysteriously vanished?

**THE DOCTOR** No, it was rather vague.

**ACE** So we're just jumping in feet first as usual.

**THE DOCTOR** Exactly!

**ACE** Marvellous!

**THE DOCTOR** Honestly, Ace! Where's your sense of adventure?

*The TARDIS starts to make its familiar landing noises.*

## 7. INT. REFUELLING STATION B – DAY

*Above the wind and constant faint background screaming the TARDIS starts to materialise. The door opens and the Doctor and Ace emerge. There is the bleep of a handheld device and the noise of the beacon.*

**THE DOCTOR** Yes, this is the place. The signal's getting weaker though.

**ACE** God, look at this place. (*Reading*) 'Duchamp Corporation Refuelling Station B. Capacity twenty thousand tonnes.' (*She coughs*) This dust...[11]

**THE DOCTOR** (*Thoughtfully*) Yes... the entire planet is dust. The refuelling bases sit on the fuel reservoir tanks floating beneath the surface. Technologically they're quite an achievement.

**ACE** It doesn't look much like a technological achievement at the moment. It looks like a bomb hit it.

**THE DOCTOR** Yes, it's strange, the building looks like it was blown in... The force of the wind must have been phenomenal.

**ACE** It's not exactly a summer breeze at the moment.

**THE DOCTOR** Come on. This way... Carefully. This roof could come in any minute.[12]

**ACE** What's that awful screaming noise?

**THE DOCTOR** (*Thoughtfully*) I'm not sure, Ace. I'm not sure.

**ACE** Well whatever it is it's getting louder.

*Wind rattles the walls.*

**THE DOCTOR** The signal is coming from in here, Ace. Ace?

**ACE** (*Quietly*) Doctor... Look. Over there, under the dust. It looks like a body

**THE DOCTOR** Yes... and there, another. And another

**ACE** Doctor, they're all dead, aren't they?

**THE DOCTOR** Someone set that distress beacon going.

**ACE** Then why did no one come?

**THE DOCTOR** I don't know, Ace. Perhaps the signal was too weak. Perhaps this dust is blanketing things somehow.

*Another gust of wind rattles the base.*
**ACE**          Come on, Doctor, let's get out of here.
**THE DOCTOR**    Perhaps you're right.[13]
*There is a moan of pain from nearby.*
**ACE**          Doctor...?
**THE DOCTOR**    Ace, over here.
**TECHNICIAN**    The dust...
**THE DOCTOR**    It's all right. We're going to help.
**TECHNICIAN**    No escape. The dust...
*The wind slams in again, the screaming louder.*
**ACE**          It's getting worse!
**THE DOCTOR**    Quick, help me with him.
*They struggle to lift the man. There is a crash as a wall collapses. The screaming is loud now.*
**TECHNICIAN**    It will kill us all![14]
**ACE**          The entire place is coming down!
**THE DOCTOR**    Ace! Get the TARDIS door open!
*The TARDIS door opens and they bundle inside. The storm is filled with the sound of the TARDIS dematerialising.*

### 8. INT. TARDIS CONSOLE ROOM.

**ACE**          That was close...
**TECHNICIAN**    (*Weak*) No escape... from the dust...
**THE DOCTOR**    How's he doing?
**ACE**          I can't see anything obviously wrong with him... He's unconscious again. What are we going to do with him, Professor?
**THE DOCTOR**    There are five other refuelling bases on the planet. We'll let his own people take care of him.[15]
**ACE**          What do you think happened back there?
**THE DOCTOR**    Mysterious circumstances...

### 9. INT. REFUELLING BASE A. THE BAR – DAY
*The clink of glasses and a steady buzz of background conversation. A door opens.*

**BEV TARRANT**  Vodka martini. A dry one.
**GUTHRIE**      Heh! That won't shut the world out!
**BEV TARRANT**  No, but it might help dull the edges a little. You got a light, Guthrie?
**GUTHRIE**      Sure. (*There is the klunk of an old-style lighter*) Dangerous habit on a refuelling base.[16]
**BEV TARRANT**  You're the one with the lighter.
**GUTHRIE**      I keeps it for... sentimental reasons.[17]
**BEV TARRANT**  Right. (*She drinks*) Any news from the radio room yet? Have they got through to anyone or are we still cut off?
**GUTHRIE**      Still the same. Static and ghost signals. Always the same when it's like this. We'll get nothing till this storm blows itself out. Be patient, girl. It will all be the same tomorrow.
**BEV TARRANT**  That's the problem. I just don't know how you do it Guthrie. Day in day out, the same old routine. Endless, mind numbing monotony...

*The noise of the TARDIS materialising fills the room.*
**GUTHRIE**    What in tarnation...?[18]
*The door opens.*
**THE DOCTOR**    Good afternoon. I'm the...
**BEV TARRANT** Doctor! Ace!
**ACE**    Bev!
**BEV TARRANT** I don't believe it! I just don't believe it!
**GUTHRIE**    (*Cackling*) Well if that don't take the biscuit. You've got some clever friends, girl...
**BEV TARRANT** What the hell are you doing here?
**ACE**    That's a very long story...
**THE DOCTOR**    That can wait for the moment. We've got an injured man who needs medical attention. Would you mind if we used your sickbay?

## 10. INT. REFUELLING BASE A. SICKBAY – DAY
*The rhythmic background beep of medical equipment.*

**THE DOCTOR**    There...
**ACE**    Is he going to be all right?
**THE DOCTOR**    Oh yes, I think so. These autodoc units are very efficient. He should be back on his feet in a couple of hours. Then perhaps he can tell us what happened.
**BEV TARRANT** Who is he?
**THE DOCTOR**    Jay Binks, according to his ID. A junior refuelling technician on Duchamp Station B.[19]
**BEV TARRANT** That's about fifty kilometres away. What happened?
**ACE**    Dunno. We picked up a distress signal. Went to investigate. The base was trashed. (*Pause*) Everyone else was dead.
**BEV TARRANT** Jeez...
**THE DOCTOR**    How come the distress signal wasn't received here?
**BEV TARRANT** Communications are shot to hell. This storm. Something in the dust apparently.
**THE DOCTOR**    Yes...
**BEV TARRANT** Look there's nothing else we can do here. Let me get you a drink, and you can tell me what brings you to Duchamp 331 of all places.
**ACE**    You coming, Professor?
**THE DOCTOR**    Yes, yes, I'll be right there.
*The door opens and Bev and Ace leave.*
**BEV TARRANT** (*Distant*) It's good to see you again, Ace...
**ACE**    (*Distant*) Where did you go after Kar-Charrat?
**BEV TARRANT** (*Distant*) Oh, you wouldn't believe it... but at least it was free of Daleks...
**THE DOCTOR**    (*Mysterious*) Something in the dust? Or the dust itself...

## 11. INT. 'GALLERY' BALLROOM – DAY
*The chatter of a lot of people. Muted classical music, clinking champagne glasses. A knife taps on a glass.*

**KLEMP**    Ladies and Gentlemen. Your attention please. (*The room quietens*) Your host, Madame Elsa Salvadori.
*Applause.*

**SALVADORI** Thank you, thank you, you are too kind. On behalf of Salvadori Entertainment – welcome! Welcome to 'Gallery'! The most luxurious space liner ever built. I have promised each and every one of you the opportunity to bid for priceless works of art from across the known universe, but I also promise that this trip will prove unforgettable in other ways. I have commissioned a piece of art so stupendous, so unique, that all your purchases will seem shallow and ordinary in comparison. 'Gallery' is about to set out on a little journey, and at its end lies wonder. In the meantime, enjoy yourselves. Eat, drink and, above all, spend!

*More applause. And the music starts up again.*

**KLEMP** Wonderful, ma'am. Inspiring.

**SALVADORI** Thank you, Klemp. I thought so.

**THE MASTER** (*His voice slightly muffled by the mask he wears – as indeed it must be until he reveals himself halfway through Scene 42*) Bravo. Madame Salvadori. A most impressive speech.

**SALVADORI** Oh. Mr Seta. You startled me. I trust you are being well looked after.

**THE MASTER** Everything is quite satisfactory. Your staff are being most... cooperative.

**SALVADORI** After the help you have given in funding this little excursion it is the least we can do. I must admit though, to being impatient to see quite what treasures you have brought on board.

**THE MASTER** Oh, I assure you, Madame Salvadori, when you see what I have to offer, it will quite take your breath away. (*He gives a racking cough*)

**SALVADORI** Heavens. Are you quite all right?

**THE MASTER** It will pass. The journey here has left me weary. If you will excuse me. Madame. Mr Klemp.

**SALVADORI** (*Conspiratorially*) How much do you think that mask he wears is worth, Klemp?

**KLEMP** (*Taps at a keypad*) The analyser puts the gemstones alone at three million, ma'am.

**SALVADORI** Mysterious and wealthy... I am so looking forward to getting to know our Mr Seta. Come along Klemp, we are neglecting our other guests. Mingle, mingle, mingle!

*They bustle off.*

**THE MASTER** (*To himself*) You will know me soon enough, Madame Salvadori. Soon enough...

**12. INT. REFUELLING BASE A. THE BAR – DAY**
*The chatter of crew.*

**BEV TARRANT** ...so that's it. Managed to get the idol, lose the patrols, and limp this far.

**ACE** You could have picked a better planet to crash on. I mean. What a dump!

**BEV TARRANT** I didn't have a lot of choice! There aren't that many planets out this far!

*Wind rattles the windows, the distant screaming echoes around.*

**ACE** What is that noise?

**GUTHRIE** That's the noise of Dalek madness!

**ACE**          You what?

**BEV TARRANT** Ace, meet resident nutter, Guthrie. If he asks to shake your hand, decline.

**ACE**          Wotcha.

**GUTHRIE**      They all laugh. But old Guthrie knows the truth.

**ACE**          What truth?

**GUTHRIE**      Way back. Way before man decided that he had a use for Duchamp 331, they came here.

**ACE**          Daleks?

**GUTHRIE**      Yup.[20] Crippled they were. Crippled from a fire fight out on the rim. They thought they'd land and make repairs, but they didn't reckon on the dust. Dragged them down it did, the entire saucer, buried 'em alive. Somewhere down there they are. Inside the planet, in the dust. No light, no sound, no nothin' – enough to send any creature mad that is.[21] Even them tin tyrants, and now on nights like this you can hear their screams on the wind. Dalek madness...

*The wind rattles the windows again.*

**BEV TARRANT** Take no notice of him. The screams are from the only indigenous species on this hell-hole. Locals call them dust sharks. The young scream when they're hungry, but Guthrie sticks to his story... Don't you Guthrie?

**GUTHRIE**      Hah! You'll see.

**ACE**          Bet he's a bundle of fun at parties.

**BEV TARRANT** Oh, he's been here longer than anyone. Actually seems to like it. But then this planet attracts nutters. If it's not Guthrie then it's the mob from the Outhouse.

**ACE**          Outhouse?

**BEV TARRANT** The drop outs. Guthrie says they came up with some arty name originally, but the workers here call it the Outhouse because everything they produce is –

**ACE**          (*Quickly*) Oh right, the Doctor's space hippies.[22]

**BEV TARRANT** Yeah, they built their own colony out on the dust.[23] You've never seen such a lash up. The Duchamp Corporation tried to evict them, but they're stubborn and they're getting a lot of support.

**ACE**          How on earth do they survive out here?

**BEV TARRANT** Oh they've got it all worked out. The freighter crews buy bits of work off them and ship things back to the homeworlds and out to the frontier.[24] Some of the artists are getting quite well known. It's becoming very fashionable to have some dust art from Duchamp 331. It's the only place that I'm able to off-load any of my...

**ACE**          Loot?

**BEV TARRANT** Merchandise! I was going to head out there in a bit and see if I can get enough money for the idol to refuel my ship. Borrowed a dust skimmer from engineering. Interested?

**THE DOCTOR** We'd be delighted!

**ACE**          Doctor! Where have you been?

**THE DOCTOR** Just seeing if the command crew here could shed any light on the destruction of that refuelling base.

**ACE**          And?

**THE DOCTOR** Nothing as yet. But the storm is easing and communications are working again.

**ACE**          Great.

**THE DOCTOR**   And the commander would like us to stay around whilst they investigate.
**ACE**   Not so great.
**THE DOCTOR**   So I think a little trip to the local artists' colony is just the thing to pass the time, don't you?

## 13. INT. THE OUTHOUSE – DAY
*We hear a radio crackle into life. An alert signal.*

**DAMIEN**   Yes?
**SALVADORI**   (*Over*) That sounded a bit tetchy, my dear. I'm all for the artistic temperament, but is that any way to speak to your beloved patron?[25]
**DAMIEN**   Madame Salvadori... Forgive me, I was... preoccupied.
**SALVADORI**   (*Over*) I'm so very glad to hear it. And how is my commission progressing?
**DAMIEN**   The sketch was a success. I'm hopeful that the full work will be ready for your arrival.
**SALVADORI**   (*Over*) Hopeful? My dear, you have no choice. We are on route and will be with you in exactly three hours. If you are not ready to make me look fabulous in front of my guests then I will be angry...
**DAMIEN**   But Madame Salvadori...
**SALVADORI**   (*Over*) Very angry. And I'd hate to withdraw my patronage. Young artists do struggle so.
*There is a commotion from outside.*
**DAMIEN**   I must go, madame. We have visitors.
**SALVADORI**   Just make sure you're ready, Damien. Three hours.

## 14. EXT. LANDING BAY OF THE OUTHOUSE – DAY
*A skimmer engine powers down.*

**BEV TARRANT** Here we are.
**THE DOCTOR**   Extraordinary!
**ACE**   I see what you mean about a lash up!
**BEV TARRANT** Built it all themselves. Cannibalised most of the parts from the ship they arrived in.[26] As more people arrive so the colony gets bigger. I'm amazed the thing stays afloat. Ah, here's Damien.
**THE DOCTOR**   Damien?
**BEV TARRANT** Damien Pierson. Sort of leader of this bunch...
**DAMIEN**   Miss Tarrant. Back again so soon?
**BEV TARRANT** Can't keep away, Damien. Brought a couple of art lovers with me.
**THE DOCTOR**   Good afternoon, I'm the Doctor, this is Ace.
**ACE**   Hiya.
**DAMIEN**   Welcome to the Outhouse.
**THE DOCTOR**   Thank you.
**DAMIEN**   It's rare we get visitors, Doctor. Was there something specific that you were interested in?
**ACE**   Yeah, a painting by... Ow!
**THE DOCTOR**   No, nothing in particular. Just browsing, really.
**DAMIEN**   Then allow me to show you around some of the studios.

154

(*Walking away*) Now then Miss Tarrant, you will no doubt have some more interesting artifacts to show me...

**ACE** (*Whispering*) Professor. That hurt. If you think the painting is here then why don't we just ask muggins where it is, grab it and push off?

**THE DOCTOR** Because there is something else going on here, and I want to find out what it is. Mysterious circumstances, remember...

## 15. INT. 'GALLERY' HOLD.

*The sound of the party is distant. We hear the footsteps of a lone security guard.*

**GUARD** Check the hold they say. Never check the bar, or check out the cold buffet, or check to see if the beds are comfortable. Always check the hold. I mean, what do they think I'm going to find? The boxes are checked at customs at the departure lounge. Then security do a sweep before the crates are loaded, then shipboard security do another check before the robots bring the crates down here. But no, every time we start a journey it's, 'Albert, go down to the hold and check the crates,' whilst the nobs enjoy themselves at the champagne reception. And here they are. Crates. Dozens of them. All checked and accounted for, all of them... (*There is a crash from one side and a scuffle*) Hey, who's there?[27] (*Another scuffle*) There's no point trying to hide, I can see you, so come out.[28] (*Another scuffle*)

**THE MASTER** I apologise. I was just checking that my... cargo was secure.

**GUARD** It's Mr Seta, isn't it? Look, sir, this is a restricted area. No guests are allowed in the lower levels. I'm afraid I'm going to have to report you to the captain.

**THE MASTER** Really. How unfortunate...

**GUARD** Really, sir there's no need to... what are you doing? No! Keep back! NO! AAAAAAAAAARGH!

*There is the high pitched whine of a weapon, and a scream.*

## 16. INT. THE OUTHOUSE – DAY

*The Doctor and Ace are being shown around.*

**DAMIEN** So as you can see, we cover just about every discipline. Fine art, sculpture, textiles.

**ACE** It's wicked.

**THE DOCTOR** You have some very talented people here Mr Pierson.

*A door opens. Bev steps in.*

**BEV TARRANT** Doctor...

**THE DOCTOR** Hm?

**BEV TARRANT** I've just had a message from Guthrie. The technician you found – Binks. He's dead.

**ACE** Dead?

**THE DOCTOR** That's preposterous. He should have made a full recovery.

**BEV TARRANT** The commander wants us back.

**DAMIEN** Problems, Doctor?

**THE DOCTOR** Yes. Something's come up as it always does. I'm afraid I'm going to have to leave.

| | |
|---|---|
| **DAMIEN** | I'm sorry to hear that. There's still a lot to show you. |
| **ACE** | Hey, could I stay, Doctor?[29] |
| **THE DOCTOR** | Are you sure? |
| **ACE** | Yeah. I like it here. It's like Camden market gone mad. |
| **THE DOCTOR** | Right. We'll be back later. |
| **BEV TARRANT** | Have fun. |
| **THE DOCTOR** | Oh and Ace... (*low*) Keep your eyes open for anything... |
| **ACE** | ...mysterious. Right, Doctor. |

### 17. INT. 'GALLERY' BALLROOM.

*The party is in full swing now. Salvadori is mingling with her guests.*

| | |
|---|---|
| **KLEMP** | Madame Salvadori. |
| **SALVADORI** | Oh, what is it Klemp? |
| **KLEMP** | If I might have a word... |
| **SALVADORI** | Oh, honestly. If you will excuse me ambassador... You are a gooseberry, Klemp, a total gooseberry. |
| **KLEMP** | There has been an incident in the hold, ma'am. |
| **SALVADORI** | Incident? What the devil do you mean by an incident? |
| **KLEMP** | A murder, madame. One of the guards. |
| **SALVADORI** | Murder? On my ship? How? When? |
| **KLEMP** | I think you should come and see for yourself... |

### 18. INT. REFUELLING BASE A. SICKBAY.

*The medical equipment that once beeped rhythmically now gives out a long flat note. A door opens.*

| | |
|---|---|
| **BEV TARRANT** | Well? |
| **THE DOCTOR** | The crew here are at a loss. The medical computer indicated that he was fine. |
| **BEV TARRANT** | So what now? |
| **THE DOCTOR** | I've persuaded the commander to let me do an autopsy.[30] |
| **BEV TARRANT** | Man of many talents, aren't you, Doctor...? |
| **THE DOCTOR** | And in the absence of Ace, you've just volunteered to be my assistant! |

### 19. INT. 'GALLERY' HOLD.

| | |
|---|---|
| **KLEMP** | Here we are, madame. |
| **SALVADORI** | Oh that's grotesque. Grotesque. I feel quite ill. |
| **KLEMP** | I must admit to never having seen anything like it before.[31] |
| **SALVADORI** | Cover it up. Cover it up! Who was he? |
| **KLEMP** | (*Taps at a keypad*) Albert Bootle, ma'am, security guard. |
| **SALVADORI** | Thank heavens it wasn't one of the guests. What was the man doing down here? |
| **KLEMP** | Checking on the cargo. It seems likely he disturbed an intruder. |
| **SALVADORI** | An intruder? In the hold? With all this priceless art. It is all still here, isn't it? Tell me its all still here, Klemp! |
| **KLEMP** | (*Taps at a keypad, then*) All accounted for ma'am. |
| **SALVADORI** | Oh thank the stars. |
| **KLEMP** | There is one interesting fact... |
| **SALVADORI** | Stop being needlessly melodramatic, Klemp! Out with it! |

**KLEMP**     It would appear that our intruder was tampering with the cargo of our masked friend – Mr Seta.

## 20. INT. THE OUTHOUSE.
*A door opens.*

**DAMIEN**     And this is our gallery. A modest collection of pieces of historical value.
**ACE**     My 'O' level art teacher would have loved this.[32]
**DAMIEN**     I'm sorry?
**ACE**     She used to love all this abstract stuff.[33] Used to be able to waffle on for hours about the importance of form and meaning and stuff...
**DAMIEN**     Yes... quite. Well, if you will excuse me, Ace, I have matters to attend to. When you're finished here, ask anyone and they'll direct you back to my office.
**ACE**     Okay. Cheers.
*The door closes. Ace walks around the room.*
**ACE**     All a load of Jackson Pollocks if you ask me. Hey! The girl from Perivale hits the jackpot again. The Scream, by Edvard Munch. Yuck! Can't see what you want it for, though Professor. Hardly the cheeriest painting.
*Gradually a noise begins to build – a low throbbing. This should be one of those classic and very recognisable Doctor Who type sound effects – something like Fendahl. It get louder.*
**ACE**     Yes. I can hear (*gives a cry of pain*) ...ah... Professor... (*The noise builds and builds*) Doctor... help...

## 21. INT. REFUELLING BASE A. SICKBAY.
*Wind thrashes against the window*

**BEV TARRANT** I think it's going to be a while before we can pick Ace up. This storm is really building again
**THE DOCTOR**     Well we're going to be here for a little while anyway. I'm going to make the first incision here...
**BEV TARRANT** Is this a good point to tell you that I'm a tad squeamish...? I think that I... Oh my God! Doctor. There's no blood.
**THE DOCTOR**     No...
**BEV TARRANT** That looks like...
**THE DOCTOR**     Dust. This man's body is full of dust. Where's that microscope? (*There is a beep of machinery*) Fascinating.
**BEV TARRANT** Doctor...[34]
**THE DOCTOR**     Look at this, Beverly. The dust particles are moving of their own volition.
**BEV TARRANT** So is our corpse...
**THE DOCTOR**     What?
*Bev screams. Medical equipment crashes aside.*
**TECHNICIAN**     Ashes to ashes!
**THE DOCTOR**     Bev! Get away from the window!
*There is the shattering of glass. Wind howls in.*
**TECHNICIAN** Dust to dust!
**BEV TARRANT** Doctor!
*The howling wind mingles with the end title theme.*

157

# PART TWO

## 20.INT. THE OUTHOUSE. (RECAP)

**DAMIEN**    And this is our gallery. A modest collection of pieces of historical value.
**ACE**    My 'O' level art teacher would have loved this.[35]
**DAMIEN**    I'm sorry?
**ACE**    She used to love all this abstract stuff.[35] Used to be able to waffle on for hours about the importance of form and meaning and stuff...
**DAMIEN**    Yes... quite. Well, if you will excuse me, Ace, I have matters to attend to. When you're finished here, ask anyone and they'll direct you back to my office.
**ACE**    Okay. Cheers.
*The door closes. Ace walks around the room.*
**ACE**    All a load of Jackson Pollocks if you ask me. Hey! The girl from Perivale hits the jackpot again. The Scream, by Edvard Munch. Yuck! Can't see what you want it for, though Professor. Hardly the cheeriest painting.
*Gradually a noise begins to build – a low throbbing. This should be one of those classic and very recognisable Doctor Who type sound effects – something like Fendahl. It get louder.*
**ACE**    Yes. I can hear (*gives a cry of pain*) ...Ah... Professor... (*The noise builds and builds*) Doctor... help...

## 21. INT. REFUELLING BASE A. SICKBAY.
*Wind thrashes against the window*

**BEV TARRANT** I think it's going to be a while before we can pick Ace up. This storm is really building again
**THE DOCTOR** Well we're going to be here for a little while anyway. I'm going to make the first incision here...
**BEV TARRANT** Is this a good point to tell you that I'm a tad squeamish...? I think that I... Oh my God! Doctor. There's no blood.
**THE DOCTOR** No...
**BEV TARRANT** That looks like...
**THE DOCTOR** Dust. This man's body is full of dust. Where's that microscope? (*There is a beep of machinery*) Fascinating.
**BEV TARRANT** Doctor...[35]
**THE DOCTOR** Look at this, Beverly. The dust particles are moving of their own volition.
**BEV TARRANT** So is our corpse...
**THE DOCTOR** What?
*Bev screams. Medical equipment crashes aside.*
**TECHNICIAN** Ashes to ashes!
**THE DOCTOR** Bev! Get away from the window!
*There is the shattering of glass. Wind howls in.*
**TECHNICIAN** Dust to dust!
**BEV TARRANT** Doctor!

*The howling wind mixes to:*
*(NB: No Scene 22 or 23)*

## 24.INT. THE OUTHOUSE.
*The noise from the scream is deafening now. Ace hammers on the door.*

**ACE**          Please, stop... Doctor... the painting... The scream... make it stop...

## 25.INT. REFUELLING BASE A. SICKBAY
*Howling wind and smashing glass. The Doctor and Bev have to shout above the noise.*

**BEV TARRANT** Doctor!
**THE DOCTOR**   Get back! Get away from the windows!
*Another window smashes.*
**BEV TARRANT** What is Binks doing?
**THE DOCTOR**   Letting in more of the dust. Get that door open!
*Bev punches at the door controls.*
**BEV TARRANT** It's no good! They're jammed! The controls are full of dust. *(She coughs)* We're going to suffocate!
**THE DOCTOR**   Quick, give me a hand here!
**BEV TARRANT** *(Coughing)* What the hell are you doing?
**THE DOCTOR**   The air conditioning unit. Help me get the cover off!
**BEV TARRANT** I rather think we've got enough air in here already.
**THE DOCTOR**   If I can just boost the power and reverse the polarity...
*There is a powerful whine as the air conditioning starts up. The technician gives a long drawn out scream and then everything goes quiet.*
**THE DOCTOR**   ...then all the dust will be vented outside.
*The door opens.*
**GUTHRIE**      What in tarnation's been going in in here?[36]
**THE DOCTOR**   Ah, Mr Guthrie. I don't suppose you've got a broom?

## 26. INT. THE OUTHOUSE.
*The throbbing noise from the painting abruptly stops and the door opens.*

**ACE**          *(Gasping with pain)* Ooh... Hope that was mysterious enough for you, Professor.

## 27. INT. 'GALLERY' SALVADORI'S CABIN.

**SALVADORI**    How many people know about this murder, Klemp?
**KLEMP**        Outside of this room, only the head of security and a handful of guards, ma'am.
**SALVADORI**    Their silence can be bought quite easily. I want no word to the guests, do you understand? This must be kept a secret. Have the... remains locked in my safe.
**KLEMP**        At once, ma'am. *(He crosses the room and opens the door and is startled)* Oh, Mr Seta. You startled me.
**THE MASTER**   I hope I'm not intruding?
**SALVADORI**    No, not at all, not at all, Please, won't you come inside. Thank you, Klemp if you will... attend to those matters for me.

**KLEMP**     Yes, ma'am.

*The door closes.*

**SALVADORI**     Now, Mr Seta. What can I do for you? Can I offer you a drink?

**THE MASTER**  Thank you, no. I just came to ensure that everything is still running according to schedule.

**SALVADORI**     (*Nervous*) Why yes. Everything is just fine.

**THE MASTER**  I am glad to hear it.

**SALVADORI**     Why do you ask?

**THE MASTER**  I have invested a great deal in this little venture of yours, madame.

**SALVADORI**     Indeed, and we are very grateful...

**THE MASTER**  (*Interrupting*) And I have a vested interest in ensuring that everything runs to a very strict timetable. I am something of a perfectionist when it comes to time.

**SALVADORI**     (*Starting to bristle*) I assure you, Mr Seta, that everything is exactly as it should be. Our arrival at Duchamp 331 will be exactly on schedule and the little... entertainment that I have planned is well in hand.

**THE MASTER**  Then I shall not take up any more of your valuable time. (*He gets up to leave. The door opens*) This mask I wear can be misleading. People take it to mean that I am disabled in some way, infirm, perhaps. I assure you, I am anything but. Good evening madame.

*The door swishes shut.*

**SALVADORI**     And you, Mr Seta, will discover that I am a woman who does not take kindly to being threatened.[37]

### 28. INT. REFUELLING BASE A. SICKBAY.

**GUTHRIE**     Jeez! What a mess!

**THE DOCTOR**  Fascinating.

**BEV TARRANT**  Our corpse doesn't seem to be the man he once was.

**THE DOCTOR**  No. All the fluid in his body had been replaced with dust. When we vented everything outside...[38]

**BEV TARRANT**  That's horrible.

**GUTHRIE**     Heh! Not much left of him now. Looks just like an old empty water bag.

**BEV TARRANT**  I need a cigarette. Give me your lighter, Guthrie.[39]

*The klunk of the zippo.*

**THE DOCTOR**  Dangerous habit on a refuelling station.

**BEV TARRANT**  It has been mentioned. Thanks, Guthrie. (*Pause*) Doctor, what in God's name is going on here?

**THE DOCTOR**  I don't know, not yet.

**GUTHRIE**     But it's left to me to clean up, as usual.

*A hoover starts up.*

**THE DOCTOR**  (*He coughs*) Come on Bev, let's get out of Mr Guthrie's way.

*The door swishes open.*

### 29. INT. THE OUTHOUSE.

*Ace wanders through echoey corridors. The wind sound from outside.*

**ACE**     Hello? Anybody about? (*Silence*) Brilliant. Anybody will direct you to my office, he says, but when you've been attacked by a psycho painting and need help can you find anyone? No. (*Pause*) Where the hell has everybody gone?

## 30. INT. REFUELLING BASE A. THE BAR
*A door opens and the Doctor and Bev enter.*

**BEV TARRANT** How come whenever I cross paths with you something is trying to kill me?
**THE DOCTOR** There's something not right here. Binks was meant to kill us, sure enough, but there were far more direct means he could have used.
**BEV TARRANT** Suffocation seems fairly direct to me.
**THE DOCTOR** And all that shouting. It all seemed so...
**BEV TARRANT** Theatrical?
**THE DOCTOR** Yes. Like he was putting on a performance.
**BEV TARRANT** Most performances don't kill off the audience.
**THE DOCTOR** You're assuming that we were the audience...
**BEV TARRANT** Then who?
**THE DOCTOR** I don't know, Bev. Not yet...
**BEV TARRANT** Do you... Do you think that the dust is alive in some way?
**THE DOCTOR** No. No, I don't think so. If that was true I think we'd all be dead by now. No I think the dust is being manipulated somehow. Driven by some outside force.

## 31. INT. OUTHOUSE. DAMIEN'S OFFICE.
*We hear the Doctor and Bev talking, overheard on some surveillance device.*

**BEV TARRANT** (*Over*) You think someone is controlling it? How?
**THE DOCTOR** (*Over*) Telekinesis of some kind perhaps. At the moment I'm more interested in why than how.
**BEV TARRANT** (*Over*) And this is connected with the destruction of the other base.
**THE DOCTOR** (*Over*) It would be very surprising if it wasn't, don't you think?
*NB: The following dialogue is for the background of the scene below – behind Ace and Damien's dialogue.*
**BEV TARRANT** (*Over*) I don't know, Doctor. It seems a bit... far fetched to me.
**THE DOCTOR** (*Over*) You have some better idea?
**BEV TARRANT** (*Over*) But telekinetic dust?!
**THE DOCTOR** (*Over*) Is it any more far fetched than living raindrops?
**BEV TARRANT** (*Over*) No you've got a point there. God, why is life always so complicated with you?
**THE DOCTOR** (*Over*) It's a knack. (*He sighs*) And to think I just wanted to collect a painting.
**DAMIEN** (*To himself, this line running over the Doctor's: it would be very surprising if it wasn't, don't you think?*) You are too clever by half, Doctor. Clever and dangerous.
*A door slams open and a very pissed off Ace enters.*

161

**ACE**    There you are. I've been all over this lash-up looking for you! What sort of freaky outfit are you running here, Damien? One of your paintings just decided to do some very strange things to my head, and... Hey! That's the Doctor and Bev! What the hell are you playing at?

**DAMIEN**    Ah, my dear Ace. It seems your friend the Doctor isn't quite the art lover that I hoped he would be.

**ACE**    If you've hurt him...

**DAMIEN**    Oh, don't be stupid girl. I'm not going to hurt him, not yet. The final work would be sadly diminished if we wasted all our materials on the sketches.

**ACE**    Sketches?

**DAMIEN**    All great works begin with sketches, but they are just pale echoes of what is still to come.

**ACE**    And what's that then, Damien? What have we got to look forward to? More hallucinogenic paintings?

**DAMIEN**    My sculpture! My masterpiece! The piece that will assure my place alongside the greatest artists in history. You should feel privileged.

**ACE**    Privileged, right.

**DAMIEN**    To be a part of a work of art. To be talked about throughout the galaxy for the rest of time. You will be immortal.

**ACE**    Right, Damien. Now I know you're mad. I'm going to get the Doctor.

**DAMIEN**    Ah, ah, ah. I think I'd rather have you somewhere where I can keep an eye on you.

**ACE**    And how exactly are you going to stop me?

**DAMIEN**    With this.

**ACE**    Ah...

**DAMIEN**    These aren't a very aesthetic solution to life's problems I will admit, but they are very good at shutting the chattering mouths of critics.[40] (*A gun fires*)

### 32. INT. REFUELLING BASE A. THE BAR. – DAY

**BEV TARRANT**    But, Doctor, if you're right then the destruction of refuelling site B wasn't a natural disaster at all. It was planned – deliberate.

**THE DOCTOR**    Yes.

**BEV TARRANT**    But that would mean that someone is capable of manipulating the dust in vast quantities.

**THE DOCTOR**    Yes. Unnerving isn't it? To know that there is nowhere you could escape to. No dry land for sanctuary.

**BEV TARRANT**    But why? Why would anyone do this?

**THE DOCTOR**    I'm not sure. Not yet. How many of these refuelling bases are there?

**BEV TARRANT**    Six. At·least there were six...

**THE DOCTOR**    And how many crew?[41]

**BEV TARRANT**    I'm not sure, twenty, maybe twenty five on each base.

**THE DOCTOR**    (*Thoughtfully*) No more than a hundred or so people on the entire planet...

**BEV TARRANT**    There are a few freighter crews, but they hardly ever spend any time down here. Even the thought of shipboard rations is considered a better option than spending a night on Duchamp. Oh, and there's the Outhouse of course. Must be almost fifty of them over there.

**THE DOCTOR** Really? But we barely saw more than half a dozen artists.

**BEV TARRANT** Maybe they don't like company. Artists are meant to be reclusive aren't they?

*A door opens and Guthrie shambles in, coughing.*

**GUTHRIE** You youngsters sure know how to make a mess.[42] Sickbay's damn near useless now, dust in everything...

**THE DOCTOR** Yes. I'm afraid I do tend to stir things up a bit. It's a gift.

**GUTHRIE** Things will be stirred up a damn sight more before this is over, an' all.[43]

**THE DOCTOR** Really? Why do you say that?

**GUTHRIE** Cos I knows, that's all.[44]

**THE DOCTOR** You've seen this before, haven't you, Mr Guthrie? The dust, the storms?

**GUTHRIE** Might have.[45]

**THE DOCTOR** When?

**GUTHRIE** (*Suspicious*) Why's you want to know?[46]

**BEV TARRANT** Oh, take no notice of him, Doctor. It's just another of his stories.

**THE DOCTOR** Quiet, Bev!

**GUTHRIE** Believe what you like girl. Guthrie knows, knows what happens when the planet gets angry.

**BEV TARRANT** Oh, come on...

**THE DOCTOR** (*Sharply*) Beverly! (*Quietly*) What do you know, Mr Guthrie? Tell me.

**GUTHRIE** (*His voice dropping low*) There weren't many of us who first came to Duchamp. A handful of us, barely away from our mothers' arms. Conscripted by the Duchamp Corporation to build a new world. It was no easy colonisation. The damn planet fought us every step of the way, the wind and the dust. It got everywhere. In machinery we thought sealed. In throats and eyes and noses. Wind and dust...

**THE DOCTOR** But there was more, wasn't there, something else that you saw.

**GUTHRIE** Frontier life is hard on a man, Doc.[47] No one is ever there to look out for you, to watch your back, but here on Duchamp the planet made us bind together, gave us something to rage against, something real to fight.[48] My partner and I were out on a skimmer trawling for dust sharks. The wind started to build, and then...

**THE DOCTOR** Yes...

**GUTHRIE** The dust rose up, became a living thing... a huge fist. It took my partner, dragged him down. I tried to save him. Tried to claw him back. All I ever found was this.

**BEV TARRANT** Your lighter.

**GUTHRIE** His lighter. I don't know why the planet left me, never have known, but I'm damned if I'm going to leave until I know why.[49]

**BEV TARRANT** No one believed you?

**GUTHRIE** Work crew always have blood feuds. Company just shrugged it off.[50] No one's goin' to mourn the death of another labourer.

**THE DOCTOR** They blamed you?

**GUTHRIE** No, but I blamed me. Said I'd look after him. I can still hear the scream sometimes. Echoin' down in the wind.

**BEV TARRANT** You're a cheery soul, Guthrie.

163

**THE DOCTOR**  And there was no one else around. Nothing else on the planet.
**GUTHRIE**  Nope. Just us, and the luvvies over at the Outhouse.
**THE DOCTOR**  The Outhouse was here, back then?
**GUTHRIE**  Just Damien and a few. The first of many.
**THE DOCTOR**  Really...
**BEV TARRANT**  What are you thinking, Doctor?
**THE DOCTOR**  That we should go and get Ace. I'm beginning to suspect that our answers lie out in the dust.
**BEV TARRANT**  Oh, not with Guthrie's legendary crashed Daleks?
**THE DOCTOR**  No. No, with something far more real and tangible.[51] With Mr Damien Pierson.

## 33. INT. 'GALLERY' BALLROOM. – DAY
*The usual chatter of guests, music, and chink of wine glasses. Salvadori is playing the part of the perfect host.*

**SALVADORI**  No ambassador, you are going to have to be patient. It would hardly be a surprise if I let you know what little treat I have in store for you, now would it? Ah. If you would excuse me, I think there are some matters that I need to attend to. (*She crosses the ballroom*) Klemp, the body is safely tucked away, I trust?[52]
**KLEMP**  Far from prying eyes madame.
**SALVADORI**  Good. Then I have another little errand for you.
**KLEMP**  Ma'am?
**SALVADORI**  Our Mr Seta is becoming a little too... arrogant for his own good. He has upset me, Klemp, and you know how I dislike being upset.
**KLEMP**  Yes, madame.
**SALVADORI**  He actually had the audacity to threaten me on my own ship.
**KLEMP**  You wish him disposed of?
**SALVADORI**  Oh, no. I don't think that we need to go quite that far, not just yet. Whatever my personal feelings for the man, his wealth is very attractive. Have you really been able to find out nothing about him, no hints at all as to his past?
**KLEMP**  (*Taps at a keypad*) I'm afraid not, madame. You know how efficient our sources are, but even they have been unable to unearth more than the odd whispered rumour about the man.
**SALVADORI**  Then the answers may lie in this mysterious cargo of his, Klemp. I want you to find out what it is. A man who can spend so much on jewellery and masks...
**KLEMP**  Might have a great deal more.
**SALVADORI**  Exactly. Go down to the hold, my dear. Find out what is in those crates. Find out who this man is.
**KLEMP**  At once, madame.
**SALVADORI**  Oh, and Klemp.
**KLEMP**  Yes, ma'am?
**SALVADORI**  Take a gun, just in case our murderer is still down there. We don't want your body joining the one I already have in my safe, now do we?
**KLEMP**  (*With a nervous laugh*) No ma'am.

*He walks away.*
**SALVADORI**    Now, Mr Seta, we will see just how much use you are to me, and if you have been leading me on then our chef can have such fun devising new fillings for the vol-au-vents.

## 34. INT. THE OUTHOUSE.
*There is a groan as Ace comes around.*

**DAMIEN**    Ah. At last. I was beginning to think you'd never come round. It's so difficult to be accurate with these stun gun controls.
**ACE**    (*Groaning*) Where am I?
**DAMIEN**    I'm assuming that you mean literally, as opposed to metaphysically.
**ACE**    Right bundles of laughs aren't you...
**DAMIEN**    You're in the gallery.[53]
**ACE**    Oh no...
**DAMIEN**    No? I've always liked it here myself. Calm, quiet, away from prying eyes.
**ACE**    We've got to get out of here.
**DAMIEN**    After all the trouble I've gone to carrying you back down here. I don't think so.
**ACE**    But you don't understand! There's something in here. Something in the painting. Something that screams...
**DAMIEN**    The painting is joining its voice to the sounds of the planet.
**ACE**    You know, don't you? You know what it is!
**DAMIEN**    Yes. It is something... wonderful. Something... inspirational.
**ACE**    It's evil Damien!
**DAMIEN**    No. It is mine! It is power! It is inspiring me.
**ACE**    It's using you! It's not interested in your art or your colony. You've got to let me get the Doctor. You've got to let us help you.
**DAMIEN**    (*Vicious*) Help me? You're kind never help, never see. You laugh and mock, you look down your nose at the art we create here, but when I have finished...[54]
**ACE**    (*Frightened*) All right. I believe you.[55]
**DAMIEN**    (*Suddenly calm again*) I'm being unfair. You can't possibly know. Not until you have been touched. Not until you have achieved full communion. There have been plenty who were unsure when they joined us here, but after communion... You will soon understand.
**ACE**    Where are you going?
**DAMIEN**    I have things to prepare. An audience that mustn't be kept waiting.
**ACE**    No, don't leave me here!
**DAMIEN**    Goodbye Ace.
**ACE**    You can't leave me in here with that thing! You can't let it... (*The door shuts*) Damien! (*She hammers on the door*) Damn you, Damien let me out of here! (*Slowly the throbbing noise from the painting starts to build again*) DAMIEN!

## 35. EXT. REFUELLING BASE A. THE BAR
*The wind lashes against the window.*

**GUTHRIE**     Goin' to be a bad one. Seen a lot of damage done by storms like this.

**BEV TARRANT** You're never going to get over to the Outhouse by skimmer.

**THE DOCTOR**   I wasn't intending to try. I thought I'd go by TARDIS.

**BEV TARRANT** Your ship?

**THE DOCTOR**   Yes. And before you ask, no you can't come with me.

**BEV TARRANT** But Ace...

**THE DOCTOR**   Can look after herself. Mostly... Besides, I think that things are going to get a good deal worse, and I need someone back here that I can trust.

**GUTHRIE**     You can rely on us, Doc...[56]

**THE DOCTOR**   Thank you, Mr Guthrie. Bev?

**BEV TARRANT** Okay, Doctor. Whatever you say.

**THE DOCTOR**   Good. Won't be long. I hope.

*The Doctor opens the TARDIS door, shuts it, and the ship dematerialises.*

**BEV TARRANT** Hope you know what you're stepping into Doctor.

*Wind rattles the base.*

**GUTHRIE**     This one's going to be a humdinger![57]

## 36. INT. OUTHOUSE. – DAY

*The throb of the painting is joined by the noise of the TARDIS materialising. The door opens.*

**ACE**     Doctor? Oh, Doctor thank God!

**THE DOCTOR**   *(Concerned)* Ace? What's the matter Ace, what's wrong?[58]

**ACE**     He left me in here. Left me alone with that thing.

**THE DOCTOR**   Thing?

**ACE**     There. The painting.

**THE DOCTOR**   Ah... The Scream, by Edvard Munch...

**ACE**     Don't go near it, Doctor. There's something alive in there. Something evil.

**THE DOCTOR**   It's all right, Ace. It's all right. I'm beginning to understand. *The throbbing from the picture is subdued, now, quieter.*

**ACE**     Damien thinks that it's just some kind of inspiration. I think he's using it like some kind of drug, but it's controlling him, Doctor. I know it is. I could hear it in my mind, screaming and screaming...

**THE DOCTOR**   It's all right, Ace.

**ACE**     *(Calmer)* It's freaked me a bit, Doctor. Damien said that if he left me here then I would achieve communion with it.

**THE DOCTOR**   Did he now...

**ACE**     I don't think I'm the first person he's left in here with it.

**THE DOCTOR**   According to Mr Guthrie there should be fifty or so people here.

**ACE**     Oh no. What's he done to them?

**THE DOCTOR**   I'm not sure. Not yet.

**ACE**     He's mad, Doctor, barking mad.

**THE DOCTOR**   Mad? Or easily led? Let's see shall we?

**ACE**     Careful, Doctor. Whatever it is in there, it's not pleasant.

**THE DOCTOR**   How do you do? I'm the Doctor. *(The painting gives an angry crackle)* You've been alone for a long time, haven't you? Trapped in the painting. Influencing the world around you without ever being able

166

to interact with it. (*Another crackle*) How long have you been influencing Damien I wonder, how long since you started expressing yourself through him?

*The throbbing starts to build again.*

**ACE**            Agh. Doctor. That sound...

**THE DOCTOR**  (*Quietly but forcefully*) Go back Ace![59] (*The throbbing increases*) There's no need for this. I want to help you. Let me help!

*The throbbing reaches a crescendo.*

**ACE**            Doctor!!

## 37. INT. 'GALLERY' HOLD.

*The sound of booted feet.*

**KLEMP**         Right. You men open that crate. (*There is the beep of a communicator*) Klemp.

**SALVADORI**   (*Over*) How are you doing Klemp? We're approaching orbit.

**KLEMP**         Just opening the first crate now, ma'am. (*Irritated*) Hurry it up there! (*There is the splintering of wood*) Good lord...

**SALVADORI**   (*Over*) What? What have you found?

**KLEMP**         One moment, ma'am. Open the others.

*There is more splintering as the other crates are prised open.*

**SALVADORI**   (*Over*) Well, Klemp. Don't keep me in suspense. What is in those crates?

**KLEMP**         Eggs, Madame Salvadori.

**SALVADORI**   (*Over*) Eggs?

**KLEMP**         Yes, ma'am. Eggs. Four of them.

**SALVADORI**   (*Over*) Are you telling me that Mr Seta is nothing more than an egg collector? Are they gold? Fabergé?

**KLEMP**         No, ma'am. Larger than that. Considerably. (*There is a chuckle from the gloom*). Who's there? Come out. I have a gun.

**SALVADORI**   (*Over*) What is it Klemp? What's going on?

**KLEMP**         I'll get back to you later, ma'am.

**SALVADORI**   (*Over*) Klemp I order you to...

*The communicator is shut off with a beep.*

**THE MASTER** Well done Mr Klemp. She really does have the most irritating voice.

**KLEMP**         I must respectfully ask you to be civil when talking about my employer, Mr Seta.

**THE MASTER** Respectfully ask? Respectfully? After you and your armed thugs come down here and break into my cargo?

**KLEMP**         We are conducting a... safety check. We had some trouble down here earlier.

**THE MASTER** Yes, I know. You seem to be very interested in my business, Mr Klemp. Curiosity can be a very dangerous pastime. Particularly if you are not in full possession of the facts.

**KLEMP**         Mr Seta. I must ask you to stay back. My men and I are armed.

**THE MASTER** (*Ignoring him*) These eggs for example. Fascinating aren't they? And I'm sure you must be interested to know what kind of creature might emerge, should one of these eggs happen to hatch.

**KLEMP**         Please, Mr Seta...

167

**THE MASTER** They are designed to withstand almost anything, impervious to attack. They have waited patiently in the cold of space, waited for the conditions to be just right, or for a signal from this device to be reborn.

**KLEMP** Mr Seta, I must ask you to stand back.

**THE MASTER** (*Chuckling*) Witness the birth of one of the ultimate weapons.

*There is a shrill signal. The eggs start to crack. Horrible shrieks fill the air. The guards start to fire. The creatures roar. The men scream.*

**KLEMP** My God, what are they?

**THE MASTER** The Krill are an ancient and devastating weapon, Mr Klemp. And the means by which I shall become all powerful.

**KLEMP** Who... who are you?

**THE MASTER** I am the Master. And you will obey me!

*The roar of the Krill blends with the end titles.*

# PART THREE

## 36. INT. OUTHOUSE. – DAY (RECAP)[60]

**ACE**     Careful, Doctor. Whatever it is in there, it's not pleasant.
**THE DOCTOR**     How do you do? I'm the Doctor. (*The painting gives an angry crackle*) You've been alone for a long time, haven't you? Trapped in the painting. Influencing the world around you without ever being able to interact with it. (*Another crackle*) How long have you been influencing Damien I wonder, how long since you started expressing yourself through him?
*The throbbing starts to build again.*
**ACE**     Agh. Doctor. That sound...
**THE DOCTOR**     (*Quietly but forcefully*) Go back Ace! (*The throbbing increases.*) There's no need for this. I want to help you. Let me help!
*The throbbing reaches a crescendo.*
**ACE**     Doctor!!

## 37. INT. 'GALLERY' HOLD.
*The sound of booted feet.*

**KLEMP**     Right. You men open that crate. (*There is the beep of a communicator*) Klemp.
**SALVADORI**     (*Over*) How are you doing Klemp? We're approaching orbit.
**KLEMP**     Just opening the first crate now, ma'am. (*Irritated*) Hurry it up there! (*There is the splintering of wood.*) Good lord...
**SALVADORI**     (*Over*) What? What have you found?
**KLEMP**     One moment, ma'am. Open the others.
*There is more splintering as the other crates are prised open.*
**SALVADORI**     (*Over*) Well, Klemp. Don't keep me in suspense. What is in those crates?
**KLEMP**     Eggs, Madame Salvadori.
**SALVADORI**     (*Over*) Eggs?
**KLEMP**     Yes, ma'am. Eggs. Four of them.
**SALVADORI**     (*Over*) Are you telling me that Mr Seta is nothing more than an egg collector? Are they Gold? Fabergé?
**KLEMP**     No, ma'am. Larger than that. Considerably. (*There is a chuckle from the gloom*). Who's there? Come out. I have a gun.
**SALVADORI**     (*Over*) What is it Klemp? What's going on?
**KLEMP**     I'll get back to you later, ma'am.
**SALVADORI**     (*Over*) Klemp I order you to...
*The communicator is shut off with a beep.*
**THE MASTER**     Well done Mr Klemp. She really does have the most irritating voice.
**KLEMP**     I must respectfully ask you to be civil when talking about my employer, Mr Seta.
**THE MASTER**     Respectfully ask? Respectfully? After you and your armed thugs come down here and break into my cargo?
**KLEMP**     We are conducting a... safety check. We had some trouble down here earlier.

169

**THE MASTER** Yes, I know. You seem to be very interested in my business, Mr Klemp. Curiosity can be a very dangerous pastime. Particularly if you are not in full possession of the facts.
**KLEMP** Mr Seta. I must ask you to stay back. My men and I are armed.
**THE MASTER** (*Ignoring him*) These eggs for example. Fascinating aren't they? And I'm sure you must be interested to know what kind of creature might emerge, should one of these eggs happen to hatch.
**KLEMP** Please, Mr Seta...
**THE MASTER** They are designed to withstand almost anything, impervious to attack. They have waited patiently in the cold of space, waited for the conditions to be just right, or for a signal from this device to be reborn.
**KLEMP** Mr Seta, I must ask you to stand back.
**THE MASTER** (*Chuckling*)Witness the birth of one of the ultimate weapons.
*There is a shrill signal. The eggs start to crack. Horrible shrieks fill the air. The guards start to fire. The creatures roar. The men scream.*
**KLEMP** My God, what are they?
**THE MASTER** The Krill are an ancient and devastating weapon, Mr Klemp. And the means by which I shall become all powerful.
**KLEMP** Who... who are you?
**THE MASTER** I am the Master. And you will obey me!
*The roar of the Krill reaches a terrifying crescendo...*
*(NB: No Scene 38 or 39)*

### 40. INT. REFUELLING BASE – A.

**GUTHRIE** Well now here's a thing. Control tower's picked up a ship heading this way. A big one.
**BEV TARRANT** Hardly surprising Guthrie. This is a refuelling base. People come here to refuel.
**GUTHRIE** This ain't one of ours.[61] Nothin' scheduled to stop here. Know those shippin' schedules backwards I do, and there's nothin' due near us for weeks.[62]
**BEV TARRANT** What is it then?
**GUTHRIE** Fancy lookin' boat from her sensor profiles. She ain't answering our hails, though.[63]
**BEV TARRANT** Great. That's all we need. Dust storms, walking corpses, and now mysterious spaceships.
**GUTHRIE** Told you, girl. This mess ain't over yet![64]

### 41. INT. OUTHOUSE.
*The painting's throbbing is unbearable now. Ace screams above the noise.*

**ACE** Doctor! (*Abruptly the sound stops. So Ace speaks quieter now*) Professor? (*The Doctor giggles. Very sinister*) Doctor?
**THE DOCTOR** (*Distorted and alien*) Not quite.
**ACE** What have you done with him? Where's the Doctor?
**THE DOCTOR** Oh he's here. Backed into a corner of his mind. Fighting to gain some control. Oh, he's strong, the strongest I've met. It's quite a struggle keeping him subdued.

170

**ACE**        What are you?

**THE DOCTOR**    Good. Very good. Questions... Some would have run screaming. But not you. He's pleased with you, this Doctor of yours.

**ACE**        I don't run from anything.

**THE DOCTOR**    I frighten you, don't I?

**ACE**        Yes.

**THE DOCTOR**    It's what I was built for.

**ACE**        What are you?

**THE DOCTOR**    I am every death you can possibly imagine. I am blood and tongues of fire. I am the scream of the madman. They named me the Warp Core, the engineers who created me. I was their child and their protector.

**ACE**        You're alien?

**THE DOCTOR**    More alien than anything you have ever encountered. Oh, this Doctor is tickling at my mind, trying to get the answers he seeks, trying to urge you to ask the right questions, but there really is no need. I will tell you what you want.

**ACE**        Right, then tell me how you ended up trapped in a painting.

**THE DOCTOR**    So long ago... so long. Their ships had sailed across space and time and had seeded many worlds, they were clever people, my creators. But war came to them. Brutal and bloody. They came across a weapon, unstoppable, indiscriminate, and so they created me. Something worse.

**ACE**        Did it work? Did they win?

**THE DOCTOR**    Oh, yes, for a while, but having unleashed me... (*He laughs*) The genie never wants to get back into the bottle.

**ACE**        You ran.

**THE DOCTOR**    (*Vicious*) I escaped! I took my freedom and fled. But the universe is so vast, so lonely, so very lonely. I searched for others like myself, searched countless worlds, but... nothing – there is nothing else like me. I found the blue world, innocent and unsullied. The creatures there fascinated me. I was weary so I decided to hide in one of them. Hide and rest.

**ACE**        You mean Earth don't you? You hid on Earth.

**THE DOCTOR**    I was tired and hurt! The mind of the primitive snapped when I contacted him. His madness tainted me, corrupted me, exorcised me into the painting and there I have waited... sleeping, but now they are near. I can feel them... Getting closer...

**ACE**        Who? What's getting closer?

**THE DOCTOR**    Your little Doctor is struggling now, fighting to regain control of his pitiful shell, and I cannot waste my strength resisting him. There is a storm coming, little one. If you've not run before, then perhaps it is time to learn.

**ACE**        Wait! What about the Doctor?

**THE DOCTOR**    (*Weakly in his normal voice*) Ace?

**ACE**        Professor, what happened to you?

**THE DOCTOR**    Strong... so unimaginably strong... Thought I could control it...

**ACE**        Where did that thing go?

**THE DOCTOR**    Back... back into the painting.

**ACE**        Hey, where are you going?

**THE DOCTOR**   We've got to find Damien.
**ACE**   Why?
**THE DOCTOR**   Because if I can't talk sense into him then everything on this planet is going to be destroyed!

## 42.INT. 'GALLERY' BALLROOM.
*The buzz of conversation and a band playing classical music fades as Salvadori tings a wine glass.*

**SALVADORI**   Ladies and Gentlemen. Our mystery cruise is almost at an end. We are currently entering orbit around the planet Duchamp 331. If you would care to start making your way to the observation galleries then I think you'll find that there is quite a treat in store for you. (*There is a bustle of people heading for the lifts. She then mutters to herself*) Come along Klemp. You're going to miss the show...
**LIFT VOICE**   Lift to upper floor now arriving. Please stand clear of the doors.[65]
*The doors slide open. And the crowd starts to scream as the Krill emerge roaring and hissing.*
**SALVADORI**   Oh my God! Klemp! Klemp! (*She runs. The screams and roars fade behind her. She is breathless as she runs*) Computer... access cabin. Access cabin!
**COMPUTER VOICE** Authorisation code.
**SALVADORI**   It's me you stupid machine! Let me in!
**COMPUTER VOICE** Voice print accepted.
*The door slides open. Salvadori collapses sobbing. There is a slow clap.*
**THE MASTER**   Bravo, Madame Salvadori. Bravo. I had no idea that your instinct for self preservation was so finely honed.
**SALVADORI**   You! Klemp. What is he doing in here? Answer me Klemp!
**THE MASTER**   I'm afraid that Mr Klemp is taking orders from another Master now.
**SALVADORI**   Don't be ridiculous! Klemp has been with me for years. He wouldn't dare disobey me! Answer me Klemp, what is going on?
**KLEMP**   I... I...
**SALVADORI**   Out with it man. Has the cat got your tongue?[66]
**KLEMP**   I...
**SALVADORI**   KLEMP!
**KLEMP**   I'm sorry, ma'am. I couldn't resist him. Those creatures...
**THE MASTER**   I'm impressed, Madame Salvadori. It is rare that I meet someone whose will is equal to my own. Unfortunately it does leave Mr Klemp rather surplus to requirements. I do so hate staff who are unreliable. Perhaps I should just dispose of him. Another shrunken corpse in your safe.
**KLEMP**   No, please...
**THE MASTER**   (*Laughing*) Pathetic. A pathetic dog cowering at your mistress's side.
**SALVADORI**   You monster.
**THE MASTER**   Yes. But you are used to them, surely.
**SALVADORI**   (*Hissing*) What do you mean?
**THE MASTER**   Oh, they may disguise themselves with airs and graces, but the guests in your ballroom – I'm sorry, the ex-guests in your ballroom – were hardly innocents.

**SALVADORI**   They were civilised people.

**THE MASTER**   Civilised! You barely know the meaning of the word. They were nothing. Base, cheap peddlers in human misery and suffering.

**SALVADORI**   How dare you...

**THE MASTER**   That ambassador that you were so fond of. Do you know his secret? Did you even begin to guess at the deaths on his conscience? No. You were dazzled by his wealth. Seduced by the titles of his office. The guests that you gathered here were crooks and cheats, liars and murderers, but wealth was their shield, their mask, and we all know how easily you are taken in by masks, madame.

**SALVADORI**   Keep away from me.

**THE MASTER**   Did you even bother to ask who I might be, where I came from? No. I blinded with you with the legends of my fortune. Beguiled you with wealth and the promise of power. You have spent your life looking at masks, Madame Salvadori, without the merest thought at what might lie underneath. See what lies beneath my mask...

**SALVADORI**   (*Horrified*) Oh my God...

**THE MASTER**   (*No more mask from here on*) Unpleasant, is it not? Would you let me into your circle if you had known? Would you have wooed me if you had the slightest inkling of what you were letting close?[67]

**SALVADORI**   (*Disgusted*) No...

**THE MASTER**   You are pathetic. You crave power and dominion, but you do not have the stomach for what it takes to achieve it. You sanitise your unpleasantness, wrap it up in baubles and trinkets and call it the trappings of civilisation, but in the end, madame, we aspire to the same dreams.

*There are screams and roars from outside.*

**KLEMP**   Those Krill creatures, madame. He's unleashed them on the passengers and crew.

**SALVADORI**   For what? To steal my fortune. You are nothing more than a petty thief!

**THE MASTER**   (*Laughing*) You think I planned all this just to steal the wealth of a few moneyed families. How little you must think of me.

**SALVADORI**   Then why...? What is all this for?

## 43. INT. THE OUTHOUSE.

**ACE**   Doctor! Slow down.

**THE DOCTOR**   There's no time Ace!

**ACE**   Just tell me what's going on!

**THE DOCTOR**   (*Exasperated*) The entity trapped back there in the painting is the Warp Core. A living weapon. The last line of defence against an aggressor who had built the perfect killing machines.

**ACE**   But it won, it told me.

**THE DOCTOR**   Yes it won. But in stopping one horror another had been created.[68] A being of pure energy, unleashed upon the universe. A creature of instinct and unimaginable power, unfettered by morality or conscience.

**ACE**   So it ran.

**THE DOCTOR**   It destroyed its creators and fled into time and space.

**ACE**   To Earth.

**THE DOCTOR**   Yes. In the late nineteenth century. It was weak from its battle. It invaded the mind of an artist, tormenting him until he banished it by sheer force of will. Exorcised it into a painting.

**ACE** The Scream?

**THE DOCTOR** Yes. The Scream. And there it has lain, dormant, hidden, influencing those around it, listening to the universe for a sign, waiting for its ancient enemies to reappear.

**ACE** And they have?

**THE DOCTOR** Yes. When it was in my mind I could feel its hate, its anger. I could feel its power building, the sense of anticipation...

**ACE** You mean it's looking forward to fighting again?

**THE DOCTOR** It's all it knows, Ace. It is all it was built to do. And now somehow it has become reactivated, regenerated. Waiting for its enemy to arrive.

**ACE** But what is this enemy? What was it built to fight?

**THE DOCTOR** The Krill...

**ACE** (*Very scared now*) Oh no...

## 44. INT. 'GALLERY' SALVADORI'S OFFICE.

**SALVADORI** What are the Krill?

**KLEMP** (*To himself, quietly*) Savage horrible things. Monsters.

**THE MASTER** They are an ancient and devastating biological weapon created by a long dead race, well practised in the arts of war. But they met their match. On the planet below is a creature that makes the Krill look like children's pets.

**SALVADORI** What are you going to do?

**THE MASTER** I'm going to let it loose.

## 45. INT. REFUELLING BASE A.

**BEV TARRANT** Guthrie. Look at this. The storms are easing. The wind's dropping to nothing...[69]

**GUTHRIE** Never seen the likes of this, never in all my years...[70]

**BEV TARRANT** Look at the dust. Not a ripple... (*The scream of a dust shark cuts through the silence*) Good God! Dust sharks. Why are they singing like that?

**GUTHRIE** They knows. Knows somethin's a comin'...[71]

**BEV TARRANT** Any luck raising that ship yet?

**GUTHRIE** Nope. Just sittin' there in orbit, it is, waitin'...[72]

**BEV TARRANT** Well I'm not waiting any longer. I'm going to find the Doctor and Ace.

**GUTHRIE** Won't make any odds girl. Told you before. Duchamp is where they send you to die...

## 46. INT. 'GALLERY' SALVADORI'S OFFICE.

**SALVADORI** What about me? What part do I play in this scheme of yours? Are you planning to kill me?[73]

**THE MASTER** Oh no, madame, you and Mr Klemp can still play some small part in my plans.

**SALVADORI** I will do nothing to help you.

**THE MASTER** Oh, but you will, madame. To stay alive a little longer, to preserve your own miserable skin you will do as I ask. And it is such a little favour I need from you.

**SALVADORI**   What... what is it you want me to do?

**THE MASTER**   Contact your protegé on the planet below. Tell him that his audience is assembled. Tell him that we wait to be dazzled by his brilliance.

**SALVADORI**   No.

**THE MASTER**   You would like Mr Klemp to be reduced to the size of a toy?

**KLEMP**   Madame...

**SALVADORI**   All right. Whatever you say. Just leave him alone.

**THE MASTER**   Good. Oh, and madame. No tricks. I would hate you to miss the show.

*There is the bleep of a communications console.*

**SALVADORI**   Duchamp, this is Gallery. Damien? Are you there?

**DAMIEN**   (*Over*) Madame Salvadori. I was beginning to worry.[74] I tracked your ship into orbit, but then...

**SALVADORI**   Is everything ready there, Damien?

**DAMIEN**   (*Over*) Yes, madame. All I require is...

**SALVADORI**   Then get on with it.

**DAMIEN**   (*Over*) At... at once.[75] Is everything all right, Madame Salvadori?

**SALVADORI**   Of course it is. I'm paying for your art, not your conversation. Gallery out.

**THE MASTER**   Bravo, madame, bravo. A shame that we are enemies, we could be useful allies.

**SALVADORI**   Don't flatter yourself. What happens now?

**THE MASTER**   Now, Madame Salvadori, you shall see what true genius is.

## 47. INT. OUTHOUSE.

**ACE**   So how does Damien fit into all this? What does he want with the painting?

**THE DOCTOR**   It's more a question of what the painting wants with him. The Warp Core has been exerting an influence on certain individuals, certain character types. Visionaries, psychics, sensitives...

**ACE**   Artistic types?

**THE DOCTOR**   Exactly. It's using Damien to gain its freedom.

**ACE**   But how?

**THE DOCTOR**   I don't know yet, Ace, I don't know.

**BEV TARRANT**   (*Distant*) Doctor? Ace?

**ACE**   That's Bev! Over here!

**BEV TARRANT**   Thank God I've found you.[76] Where the hell is everyone? The place is like a morgue. Look, something really weird is going on. The entire planet is still. The dust is like a millpond.

**THE DOCTOR**   Or a blank canvas... Of course!

**ACE**   What is it, Doctor?

**THE DOCTOR**   Damien plans to release the Warp Core into the dust of the planet, every particle of dust will become part of it, a living sentient planet.

**BEV TARRANT**   But that's impossible!

**THE DOCTOR**   The destruction of the refuelling base was just a test. I told you that the dust was being manipulated telepathically.
**ACE**   And the creature in the painting...
**THE DOCTOR**   Is pure mental energy... It wants to be released. We've got to get everyone off this planet.
**ACE**   How? We'll never get everyone into the TARDIS in time.
**BEV TARRANT**   The ship!
**THE DOCTOR**   What?
**BEV TARRANT**   An unidentified ship entered orbit about twenty minutes ago.[77] We've got no communication with it yet...
**THE DOCTOR**   Is your ship back at the base?
**BEV TARRANT**   Yes, but I've got no fuel...
**THE DOCTOR**   Then steal some! You're a thief aren't you? Contact all the other refuelling bases. Tell them to get into their shuttlecraft and head for that ship...[77]
**BEV TARRANT**   But we've got no idea if it's safe.
**THE DOCTOR**   If I'm right then anywhere is going to be safer than here. You have to get everyone off this planet! Ace, go with her.[78]
**ACE**   Now hang on a minute...
**THE DOCTOR**   I haven't got time to argue! Just go![79]
**BEV TARRANT**   Come on, Ace! (*Running away*) Good luck, Doctor.
**ACE**   (*Fading as she goes*) You just take care, all right.
**THE DOCTOR**   I'll join you later. (*Beat, then*) Now, Mr Damien. I have an appointment for a private viewing.

## 48. INT. OUTHOUSE.
*The painting is starting to throb, building and building.*

## 49. INT. OUTHOUSE.

**THE DOCTOR**   Damien...
**DAMIEN**   Ah, Doctor, you're just in time
**THE DOCTOR**   I always try to be.
**DAMIEN**   It's a beautiful thing, an unblemished canvas, waiting for an artist to bring it to life, to turn it into a work of beauty. Let me show you, Doctor. Let me show you my studio, the means by which I can shape a world.[80]
**THE DOCTOR**   How long has the painting talked to you, Damien? How long since it first appeared in your mind?
**DAMIEN**   (*Dreamily*) I always felt it. It was always there. From the first time I saw it, in the hands of a collector, so long ago... so long...
**THE DOCTOR**   Damien, you need help. You need...
**DAMIEN**   (*Scornful*) A doctor? Is that what you think I need?
**THE DOCTOR**   You don't understand what it is that's controlling you.
**DAMIEN**   I understand perfectly! You think I'm crazy, don't you? A dysfunctional madman with an insane ambition. Well you're wrong, Doctor. Look at what I've created! (*A door opens*) Are they all mad too? Are they, Doctor?
**THE DOCTOR**   What have you done to them?
**DAMIEN**   I have done nothing! I let them achieve communion. I let them share the vision. They entered the depravation tanks of their own free will! Surrendered their minds to me because they believed in what I was doing. Because they wanted to be part of this!

**THE DOCTOR**   And did they know that this was to be their contribution? To be exhibited like... like fish in an aquarium? To lose all sense and feeling in order to fulfil your artistic vision? To help you destroy a world?

**DAMIEN**       To help me create a masterpiece! And when I join myself to it...

**THE DOCTOR**   Damien, listen to me! If you connect yourself to this network of minds you will give the Warp Core the power it needs. It will use the mental web you have created here to escape into the dust of this planet.

**DAMIEN**       Yes! I will create a living breathing work of art. A planet sized monument to my vision.

**THE DOCTOR**   You will create a monster!

**DAMIEN**       I will be immortal!

**THE DOCTOR**   No!

**DAMIEN**       Too late Doctor, my mind is with theirs! (*The switch is depressed. The throbbing noise of the painting builds and builds. Damien's voice becomes alien and distorted*) FREEEE!

### 50. INT. REFUELLING BASE A.
*There is the roar of a shuttlecraft lifting off.*

**BEV TARRANT** Is that everyone?

**ACE**          Everyone but us.

**BEV TARRANT** Where's Guthrie?

**ACE**          Beats me. Must have gone on the shuttle.

**BEV TARRANT** I didn't see him.

**ACE**          He'll be fine, Bev. I told him what Damien plans to do. He may be a bit odd, but he's not stupid enough to hang around here.

*The Damien/Warp core voice bellows over the wind.*

**DAMIEN/WARP CORE** (*Over*) Free! Free at last!

**BEV TARRANT** Uh, Ace. I think we'd better get out of here. Right now.

**ACE**          I think you're right. Come on Bev![81]

*The bar door closes.*

**GUTHRIE**      (*To himself*) Heh.[82] I know what Damien plans to do all right. And I always knew I was goin' to die on Duchamp.

### 51. INT. THE OUTHOUSE.
*The throbbing noise is deafening.*

**DAMIEN/WARP CORE** Run, Time Lord! Run while you can! Before the Krill arrive. Before the battle is joined!

**THE DOCTOR**   (*Bellowing above the noise*) There's no need for this!

**DAMIEN/WARP CORE** Run, Doctor. (*There is a peal of maniacal and scary laughter*) RUN!

### 52. EXT. REFUELLING BASE SHUTTLE PAD.
*There is a screaming wind.*

**ACE**          Is that your ship?

**BEV TARRANT** Yes. (*Above the wind we hear the mad laughter*) My God, what is that?

**ACE**          If the Doctor is right, the end of the world!

## 53. INT. BEV'S SHIP.
*A door slides shut, cutting out some of the noise.*

**BEV TARRANT** Computer! Engage primary drives.
**ACE** My God, look at the dust![83]
**BEV TARRANT** Hold tight Ace, this is going to be rough.
*The engines of the ship roar into life.*

## 54. INT. TARDIS CONSOLE ROOM.
*The door opens and the Doctor bundles in.*

**THE DOCTOR** Not the most successful day you've ever had, Doctor.
*He activates the scanner control. We hear wind and the raging warp core.*
**DAMIEN/WARP CORE** (*Over*) The battle will be joined!
**THE DOCTOR** Time to join Ace I think. Now... where's that mysterious ship? Ah...
*There are bleeps from the console as the Doctor sets the co-ordinates. The TARDIS dematerialises.*

## 55. INT. BEV'S SHIP.
*The engines settle to a low whine.*

**BEV TARRANT** I don't want to have to do that again in a hurry.
**ACE** Now what?
**BEV TARRANT** Now we find this uncommunicative space ship. (*The console bleeps as Bev scans*) There she is, low orbit.
**ACE** Hey... that's a fancy looking ship.
**BEV TARRANT** Pleasure cruiser. God knows what she's doing out here... Computer, match vectors. Lock on to her homing beacon. (*Bleep*) Here we go...

## 56. INT. 'GALLERY' CORRIDOR
*The TARDIS materialises and the door opens.*

**THE DOCTOR** Good evening. I'm the Doctor and... (*He breaks off*) Hmm. Nobody home. Hello? Ace?
*We hear the computerised voice of the lift in the distance. The Doctor walks over.*
**LIFT VOICE** Which floor please? Which floor please?
**THE DOCTOR** Now then, let me see. Cabins, dining rooms... Ah! Ballroom.
**LIFT VOICE** Thank you. Doors closing.

## 57. INT. GALLERY DOCKING BAY.
*A big heavy sounding door opens. Bev and Ace enter the docking bay, footfalls echoing.*

**ACE** Hey, where is everyone?
**BEV TARRANT** I don't understand it. All the shuttlecraft have docked okay... All the guys should be up here.
**ACE** Hello! Hey is anyone about?
**BEV TARRANT** Ace...

**ACE**          Hellooo!

**BEV TARRANT** Ace... Look. I think that's the base commander. I think that's Fredrickson... (*There is a scuffle from the far side of the docking bay*) Ace, there's something there.[84]

**ACE**          Move back. Quietly...

**BEV TARRANT** Ace, what is it?[85]

*We hear a man scream – until cut off*

**ACE**          We've got to get out of here, Bev, now.

**BEV TARRANT** What?

**ACE**          Off here. Get back into your ship.

**BEV TARRANT** Too late.

*There is a scream from Bev.[86] And the hissing shriek of a Krill.*

## 58.INT. 'GALLERY' BALLROOM.

**LIFT VOICE**    Ballroom. Lift opening.[87]

**THE DOCTOR**    Sorry to intrude, but... Oh no... What has happened here? Ace? Bev? (*He steps forward, glass crunching underfoot. There is a chuckle from the gloom*) Who is it? Who's there? Do you need help?

**KLEMP**         Do not move.

**THE DOCTOR**    Don't be afraid. I'm not going to hurt you.

**THE MASTER** But Mr Klemp may well kill you unless you do exactly as you are told. Oh, my dear Doctor. Always the good Samaritan. Always stepping into other people's misfortune.

**THE DOCTOR**    The Master...

**THE MASTER** A delightful, if unexpected pleasure...

**THE DOCTOR**    All this death, this destruction. Your handiwork?

**THE MASTER** Oh yes, a means to an end.

**THE DOCTOR**    I will stop you, you know, whatever it is you are up to.

**THE MASTER** Oh, I don't think so. This time. you've arrived too late. I've already won, Doctor!

*Into theme.*

# PART FOUR

## 57. INT. GALLERY DOCKING BAY. (RECAP)[88]

*A big heavy sounding door opens. Bev and Ace enter the docking bay, footfalls echoing.*

**ACE**  Hey, where is everyone?
**BEV TARRANT**  I don't understand it. All the shuttlecraft have docked okay... All the guys should be up here.
**ACE**  Hello! Hey is anyone about?
**BEV TARRANT**  Ace...
**ACE**  Hellooo!
**BEV TARRANT**  Ace... Look. I think that's the base commander. I think that's Fredrickson... *(There is a scuffle from the far side of the docking bay)* Ace, there's something there.
**ACE**  Move back. Quietly...
**BEV TARRANT**  Ace, what is it?
*We hear a man scream – until cut off.*
**ACE**  We've got to get out of here, Bev, now.
**BEV TARRANT**  What?
**ACE**  Off here. Get back into your ship.
**BEV TARRANT**  Too late.
*There is a scream from Bev. And the hissing shriek of a Krill.*

## 58. INT. 'GALLERY' BALLROOM.[88]

**LIFT VOICE**  Ballroom. Lift opening.
**THE DOCTOR**  Sorry to intrude, but... Oh no... What has happened here? Ace? Bev? *(He steps forward, glass crunching underfoot. There is a chuckle from the gloom.)* Who is it? Who's there? Do you need help?
**KLEMP**  Do not move.
**THE DOCTOR**  Don't be afraid. I'm not going to hurt you.
**THE MASTER**  But Mr Klemp may well kill you unless you do exactly as you are told. Oh, my dear Doctor. Always the good Samaritan. Always stepping into other people's misfortune.
**THE DOCTOR**  The Master...
**THE MASTER**  A delightful, if unexpected pleasure...
**THE DOCTOR**  All this death, this destruction. Your handiwork?
**THE MASTER**  Oh yes, a means to an end.
**THE DOCTOR**  I will stop you, you know, whatever it is you are up to.
**THE MASTER**  Oh, I don't think so. This time. you've arrived too late. I've already won, Doctor!
*(NB: No Scene 59/60 or 61)*

## 62. INT. THE OUTHOUSE.

**DAMIEN/WARP CORE** After centuries of watching and waiting, to be able to move again, to reach out into the void, unfettered by the pinpricking minds of others.
*It laughs.*

## 63. INT. 'GALLERY' BALLROOM.

**THE MASTER**  Once again it seems our paths are irrevocably linked, Doctor. That you should appear here at all is surprise enough, that you should survive the attentions of the Warp Core... You must have a charmed life.

**THE DOCTOR**  Whereas life hasn't be treating you so kindly, by the look of it.[89]

**THE MASTER**  A foolish mistake on my part. I underestimated the mental instability of the creature.

**THE DOCTOR**  Careless of you.

**THE MASTER**  A mistake I shall learn to live with.

**THE DOCTOR**  (*Interrupting*) You know that the Core has become activated?[90] That its ancient enemies are here?

**THE MASTER**  The Krill. But of course, Doctor. Who do you think brought them here?

**THE DOCTOR**  (*Appalled*) You mean the Krill are on this ship? But Ace and the others are out there![91]

**THE MASTER**  Forget your companions, Doctor. By now there will be nothing left of them.

## 64. INT. 'GALLERY' SHUTTLE BAY.
*The hissing gets louder.*

**BEV TARRANT**  (*Whispering*) What the hell is it?

**ACE**  It's called a Krill.

**BEV TARRANT**  What's it doing here?

**ACE**  Killing people.

**BEV TARRANT**  Why doesn't it attack? Surely it's seen us?

**ACE**  Or at least heard us. It seems more interested in the hatchway. As if it was trying to get out, into space.

**BEV TARRANT**  Those doors are blast proof.

**ACE**  Believe me, that won't stop it.

*The hissing of the Krill gets louder, more aggressive, it tears through the door.*

**BEV TARRANT**  I don't believe it!

**ACE**  Told you.[92]

*An alarm starts to sound.*

**COMPUTER VOICE**  Warning. Atmospheric seals breached. Hull integrity compromised.

**BEV TARRANT**  We've got to get out of here!

**ACE**  We'll never get past it!

**COMPUTER VOICE**  Cargo bay will be sealed in twenty seconds. Nineteen seconds.[93]

**BEV TARRANT**  We don't have a lot of choice! Come on!

**COMPUTER VOICE**  Cargo bay sealing in four seconds.[94]

*The girls start to run. More klaxons sound. The Krill roars.*

**BEV TARRANT**  I think it's seen us now!

*Krill roar, then shriek as it is sucked into space and dies away.*

**ACE**  Don't look back Bev! Just keep going!

**COMPUTER VOICE**  Three seconds.

**BEV TARRANT**  We're not going to make it!

**COMPUTER VOICE** Two seconds
**ACE**          Yes...
**COMPUTER VOICE** One second.
**ACE**          We...
**COMPUTER VOICE** Doors sealed
*There is a clang of doors.*
**ACE**          Are! (*Breathless*) We did it. We did it!
**BEV TARRANT** I don't believe it. It must have punched its way out into space. Why?
**ACE**          Who cares? We escaped.[95]
*The two of them catch their breath. There is the distant roar of a Krill.*
**BEV TARRANT** But escaped into what?

## 65. INT. 'GALLERY' BALLROOM.
*The klaxons boom around the room.*

**KLEMP**        The ship's outer hull has been punctured, Master. The cargo bay is sealed off.
**THE MASTER** Ah. Perhaps the ship is not as dead as I thought.
**THE DOCTOR** Ace?
**THE MASTER** Possibly. Your young companion is certainly resourceful.
**THE DOCTOR** I'm going to help her.
**THE MASTER** Please, Doctor. No heroics. I may not be quite my old self, but Mr Klemp here will kill you without a moment's hesitation if I so order it, and I would hate you to miss out the full extent of your defeat.
**THE DOCTOR** You're insane. You can't possibly hope to control the Krill the way you control this poor devil!
**THE MASTER** Oh, there aren't many of them, Doctor. Just enough to prick at the dormant consciousness of the Warp Core, just enough to goad it into life.
**THE DOCTOR** But the Krill are unstoppable! Savage, aggressive. Believe me, I know.
**THE MASTER** And you think I don't? You think I haven't catered for every eventuality?
**THE DOCTOR** You hadn't catered for me.
**THE MASTER** No. Like a bad penny, you keep turning up...
**THE DOCTOR** Why here? Why Duchamp 331?
**THE MASTER** Not my choice, Doctor. The Warp Core's. I... indulged it, shall we say. Let it return home.
**THE DOCTOR** Home?
**THE MASTER** This is where it was born, Doctor. Duchamp is where its creators first unleashed it upon their unsuspecting attackers, where they finally realised that they had a weapon that could defeat the Krill.
**THE DOCTOR** And it destroyed their world.
**THE MASTER** Yes, Doctor. This was a world like any other, teeming with life, and the Warp Core destroyed it as easily as I would crush an insect.
**THE DOCTOR** And that's what you want? To unleash it again?
**THE MASTER** I have tracked it through time, Doctor. Followed its trail from this world. Found it on Earth...
**THE DOCTOR** Where it nearly destroyed you!
**THE MASTER** Yes, it almost destroyed me! Me, a Time Lord. (*He laughs*)

It was just hanging there Doctor, hanging in a miserable gallery, the gawping masses unable to understand what they were looking at. And I thought that I could just walk in and take it.

**THE DOCTOR**   (*Gently*) What happened?

**THE MASTER**   I was complacent. I thought nothing of a few security guards, a few pitiful alarms. I stole it, Doctor, but had not anticipated its reaction. It was recuperating, resting, and I had disturbed its rest.

**THE DOCTOR**   Like prodding a sleeping tiger.

**THE MASTER**   Yes. And like a tiger it toyed with me. That useless body I obtained on Traken was just not strong enough to withstand such energies. It shredded me, stole away the power given to me by the Traken Source, and then just rolled over and went back to sleep.

**THE DOCTOR**   Leaving you just as you were before. Scarred, damaged and unable to regenerate. I'm... sorry.

**THE MASTER**   Sorry? It was magnificent! And it is that power that I intend to possess. Why else do you think I convinced that ridiculous Damien Pierson to buy the painting from me and suggested that he established his absurd studio on this particular planet?

**THE DOCTOR**   I never really saw you as a patron of the arts, I have to say.

**THE MASTER** I must agree. But I saw that he had the potential, the drive and the ambition to use the creature. I also found in Salvadori a vain and fawning cretin, someone who would be interested enough in funding Damien's grand schemes just to make her 'name' amongst her fraternity.

**THE DOCTOR** Of course, and Damien's 'art' would this time dilute the raw power enough for you, so you could siphon it off for your own ends. Brilliant and quite audacious. Utterly corrupt, of course, and vile in the extreme, but certainly audacious.

**THE MASTER** Thank you. You see, I have waited patiently, Doctor. Years I have waited. I have set events in motion that would result in this moment, the creature let loose upon its mortal enemy, the Krill, a battle that will drain it, exhaust it, and then...

**THE DOCTOR**   You intend to capture it.

**THE MASTER**   This time I have come prepared. I intend to transfer the power of the Core to the heart of my TARDIS, to bind it there, captive to my will, answering to my voice, doing my bidding![96]

### 66. INT. 'GALLERY' CORRIDOR.

**BEV TARRANT**   You've seen these things before haven't you?

**ACE**            Unfortunately. They're called the Krill. They're a kind of biological super weapon, and they're not friendly. They almost wiped out an entire colony that the Doctor and I visited a while back. (*There is a scuffle from the gloom*) Quiet. Listen. There's something in here with us.[97]

**BEV TARRANT**   Krill?

**ACE**            We'd be dead by now if there were. (*Another scuffle. Then a sob of relief*) That's no Krill.

**SALVADORI**   Oh thank God! Thank God!

**ACE**            It's okay. It's all right.

**SALVADORI**   I though I was alone.

**BEV TARRANT** Who are you? What the hell happened?

**SALVADORI**   My name is Salvadori. Madame Elsa Ivanovitch Carolina...[98]
**ACE**   All right, all right. We get the picture.
**SALVADORI**   He sent me out here.[99] Alone in the dark, with those things...
**BEV TARRANT** Who?
**SALVADORI**   Seta. He calls himself Seta. (*There is the screaming hiss of a Krill, distant*) They killed everyone, tore them to pieces.
**ACE**   How many of them are there?
**SALVADORI**   Oh, I don't know...
**ACE**   Well think! I've got to know what we're up against.
**SALVADORI**   Four, I think. Yes, Klemp said there were four eggs.[100]
**BEV TARRANT** Klemp?
**SALVADORI**   My assistant.
**BEV TARRANT** And where is he?
**SALVADORI**   That monster Seta is forcing him to work with him. Oh, poor Klemp.
**ACE**   What about the rest of the crew? The passengers?
**SALVADORI**   Dead, all dead. Those creatures just burst into the ballroom...
**BEV TARRANT** Ballroom? Hey, at least we get to die in style.
**ACE**   We're not dead yet. Could you get us back up to this ballroom?
**SALVADORI**   Well... yes... But the rest of those things...
**ACE**   You said there were only four. Well one has just decided to step outside for a bit...
**BEV TARRANT** Leaving us with only three bloodthirsty unstoppable alien super weapons to get past. Great.
*There is another shrieking hiss.*
**ACE**   You'd rather we stayed here?
**BEV TARRANT** What good is it going to do us getting up to the ballroom? Unless you were planning on taking tango lessons.
**ACE**   The Doctor could have materialised anywhere on the ship.
**SALVADORI**   Doctor?
**BEV TARRANT** Friend of ours. Good at getting out of situations like this.
**ACE**   Yeah, but as he's not down here, we'd better start looking elsewhere.
**BEV TARRANT** How can you be sure he's even arrived yet?
**ACE**   If he isn't, we're in even bigger trouble
**BEV TARRANT** That's not very comforting...
**SALVADORI**   If he's wandering around alone...
**ACE**   So let's hope we can find him first. Now come on!

## 67. INT. REFUELLING BASE A. BAR.
*Guthrie is humming to himself – something American South (The Great Grand Coolie Dam, or similar). The computer hums into life.*

**COMPUTER VOICE** Purging operation initiated. All fuel tanks on stations A through F now in emergency venting mode.
**GUTHRIE**   Heh, thank you, girl. You can shut down for a while. I think someone's a'comin'.[101]
**COMPUTER VOICE** Yes, technician Guthrie. Shutting down.

*There is the crash of wind and the throb of the Warp Core.*
**DAMIEN/WARP CORE** (*Alien and rasping*) What have we here? A little man. All alone.
**GUTHRIE** Heh, there you are at last, boy. Knew you'd show up eventually.[102]
**DAMIEN/WARP CORE** I sensed that there was still life here, that not everyone had run. Why haven't you run away, little man?
**GUTHRIE** Run? (*He laughs and coughs*) Bin' waitin' fer yer. Waitin' a long time. There's bad blood between us. Scores to settle.[103]
**DAMIEN/WARP CORE** Do you know who I am?
**GUTHRIE** Yup. Reckon you're the thing that killed my partner.[104] That dragged him into the dust of this God-forsaken planet and left me to live with it...
**DAMIEN/WARP CORE** (*Laughs horribly*) And so you've waited all this time for your revenge? Waited all this time to stand against me?
**GUTHRIE** That's just about the size of it.
**DAMIEN/WARP CORE** Pitiful creature. If you only had an inkling of the power standing before you you would run screaming.
**GUTHRIE** Well as I said. I've never bin a great one fer runnin'.[105]
**DAMIEN/WARP CORE** And just what do you expect to do?
**GUTHRIE** Well... I wuz plannin' on killing you.[106]
**DAMIEN/WARP CORE** Killing me? (*The Warp Core gives a shriek of laughter*) Humans, with your intellect, and your ambition. You know nothing of true hate, true rage, but up there is an enemy perfect in every way... oh I can feel them, feel their hate, their anger. Even now one of them struggles through the void, and all I have to do is flex the muscles of this planet...
*A low rumble builds.*

**68.INT. GALLERY CORRIDOR**
*The rumble shakes the ship.*

**ACE** What the hell was that?
**BEV TARRANT** Ace look! Look out of the window.
**ACE** Oh my God.[107]
**BEV TARRANT** The planet! It's moving! The dust is forming into shapes!
**ACE** It's like the planet is growing limbs... That's why the Krill tore its way out. It's going to attack it.
**SALVADORI** Oh, Damien, my dear. Bravo. You were a genius after all.
**ACE** Believe me, there's nothing artistic about what's going on down there...
**SALVADORI** Oh, it is magnificent. What a shame your audience is dead.
**BEV TARRANT** I'm sure his audience would agree with you!
*There are screams of rage that echo around them.*
**ACE** Well it's certainly rattled the Krill.
**BEV TARRANT** And that probably isn't good news for us.

**69. INT. 'GALLERY' BALLROOM**
*The rumble reaches the ship.*

**THE MASTER** Ah, Doctor, look. After centuries of sleep the Warp Core is stretching itself. Mr Klemp.

**KLEMP**  Yes, Master.
**THE MASTER**  Monitor the creature from my TARDIS as you have been instructed.
**KLEMP**  Yes, Master.
**THE MASTER**  Let me know when power levels reach critical.
**KLEMP**  Yes, Master.
*Klemp crosses the ballroom. Glass crunching underfoot. A TARDIS door opens.*
**THE DOCTOR**  Your TARDIS disguised as a pillar again. (*He tuts*) You're not very original.
**THE MASTER**  Unoriginal, but practical.
**THE DOCTOR**  The thing that you have created is a terrifying concept. A planet with the rage and appetites of a mindless killer.
**THE MASTER**  And with the Krill as bait, as lures, I can direct it where I will.
*There is the screech of tortured metal as the planet starts to reach the ship.*
**THE DOCTOR**  Your pet seems to have reacquired its taste for Krill. It's realised it can build with the dust to reach out for the ship and tear it apart.[108] Do you really think that you are any safer up here than the rest of us?
**THE MASTER**  Oh I don't intend staying here, Doctor. However luxurious these surroundings are, my TARDIS is far more comfortable. I think it's time for our little game to reach an unhappy conclusion

## 70. INT. 'GALLERY' CORRIDOR.
*The ship gives a protesting screech of metal.*

**SALVADORI**  What is it? What's happening?
**BEV TARRANT** I think Duchamp 331 is throwing a tantrum.
**ACE**  We've got to get off this ship!
**BEV TARRANT** Well we're not going to get back into the docking bay.
**ACE**  Then we'll keep going until we find the TARDIS. Salvadori. Where's the nearest lift?
**SALVADORI**  Just down here. One of the staff lifts.
**ACE**  Right. Come on.
**BEV TARRANT** Ace, how do you know there aren't any Krill waiting for us up there?
**ACE**  I don't but I know there are definitely some down here, so I figure we're not going to be any worse off.
**BEV TARRANT** Your logic is not encouraging.
**ACE**  The corridor looks clear. I'm going to check out that lift.
**BEV TARRANT** Be careful.
**ACE**  Just watch my back.
*She runs over to the lift.*
**LIFT VOICE**  Doors opening. Which floor please?
**ACE**  Right. Coast's clear. Come on!
**BEV TARRANT** Okay, after you.
**SALVADORI**  I'm not sure I can do this, those things...
**BEV TARRANT** Are out there somewhere. You're probably safer with us.
**SALVADORI**  I'm not sure.
**BEV TARRANT** Look, I'll go first. As soon as I'm in the lift, you run over and join us, okay?

**ACE**          What are you two waiting for?
**BEV TARRANT** Okay?
**SALVADORI**    All right.
*Bev runs over to Ace.*
**ACE**          What's up with matron?
**BEV TARRANT** She's scared witless, Ace. (*There is the sudden roar of a Krill. Salvadori screams*) Oh God, it's seen her.
**SALVADORI**    Help me! Please!
**ACE**          We'd better get out of here.
**BEV TARRANT** You can't just leave her!
**ACE**          There's nothing we can do.
**BEV TARRANT** I don't believe this! You're just going to sit back and let her die?
**ACE**          Bev, I've fought these things before! You can't beat them, do you understand? You can't! You've just got to shut them out, shut out what they do and just try and live with yourself afterwards.[109]
**BEV TARRANT** Damn you! I'm not just going to sit back and watch that thing tear her apart.
**ACE**          Bev! No!
**BEV TARRANT** (*Bellowing at the Krill*) Hey! Get off her you ugly great frog! I said get off!
*The screams of the Krill rise in pitch.*
**ACE**          I don't believe it!
**SALVADORI**    Help me!
**BEV TARRANT** Come on. Come on!
**ACE**          Inside! Inside!
**LIFT VOICE**    Doors closing.
*There is a ching as the doors close.*
**BEV TARRANT** Unbeatable are they?
**ACE**          I still don't believe it. You actually scared it off!
*There is the tearing of metal as the Krill tries to get at them.*
**BEV TARRANT** Maybe scared was a little strong.
**SALVADORI**    It's getting in!
**LIFT VOICE**    Which floor please?
**ACE**          Up, you damn piece of junk, up!
**LIFT VOICE**    Thank you. Second floor, third floor, fourth floor.
**BEV TARRANT** Persistent, aren't they?[110]

## 71. INT. OUTHOUSE.

**DAMIEN/WARP CORE** Ah! The battle is joined.
**GUTHRIE**      I said there was a blood feud between us, boy. I ain't finished with you yet![111]
**DAMIEN/WARP CORE** Pitiful. You will die here.
**GUTHRIE**      Aye.[112] I know that right enough. Always knew I'd die on Duchamp 331.
**DAMIEN/WARP CORE** (*Laughing*) I can waste no more time with you. My ancient enemies grow impatient. Your partner died in the dust, and you won't have long to wait before you join him.
*The Warp Core swirls out.*
**GUTHRIE**      You'll rue the day you turned your back on Silas Guthrie, boy.[113] Mark my words.

## 72. INT. 'GALLERY' BALLROOM

**THE MASTER** I will admit to a certain degree of sadness at your demise, Doctor. There really are so few worthy opponents in the universe these days. Perhaps I will keep your shrunken corpse as a memento.
**THE DOCTOR** How sentimental of you.
**KLEMP** Power readings at maximum, Master.
**THE MASTER** Goodbye, Doctor.
**LIFT VOICE** Ballroom. Doors opening.
*The lift door opens.*
**ACE** Doctor! Talk about climbing out of the frying pan...[114]
**THE DOCTOR** Ace! Get back in the lift!
**ACE** But Doctor!
**THE MASTER** Ah, the Doctor's pugnacious companion. I would advise you to stay perfectly still or Mr Klemp here will happily atomise you.
**THE DOCTOR** Oh Ace!

## 73. INT. THE OUTHOUSE.

**DAMIEN/WARP CORE** Ah! Salvadori. Is that you I sense up there? I can taste your fear.

## 74. INT. 'GALLERY' BALLROOM

**ACE** Professor? What's going on? Who's Freddy Krueger?
**SALVADORI** That animal is Seta.
**THE DOCTOR** That is the Master.[115]
**ACE** The Master? With a face like a dropped pizza? What happened to him?
**THE DOCTOR** He had a little difference of opinion with the creature down there on the planet. It stripped his borrowed body from him – de-generated him. This is the Master as he really is.
**ACE** Suits him.
**THE MASTER** The creature can renew me once it is safely under my control.
**BEV TARRANT** Control? That creature has decided that it's not content to stay on that planet from what we've just seen.[116]
**THE DOCTOR** No. The Warp Core is animating the dust in vast quantities, forming tendrils, reaching out to attack the Krill on this ship.
*The ship lurches again.*
**BEV TARRANT** And it hasn't exactly put our psychopathic planet in the best of moods.
**THE MASTER** I wouldn't let that worry you, my dear. You're not going to be alive long enough for it to be an inconvenience.
**SALVADORI** Oh, why don't you just let Klemp go. Let us all go.
**THE DOCTOR** There's no need for this. You've got me.
**THE MASTER** Very noble Doctor, as always, but you are in no position to bargain.
*The throbbing of the Warp Core fills the ship.*
**DAMIEN/WARP CORE** Salvadori!
**BEV TARRANT** Good God! Look outside the window! The dust!
**THE MASTER** At last.

**ACE**          (*Nervously*) Doctor?
**THE DOCTOR**          (*Whispering*) Get back towards the lift, and when I say run, run.
**THE MASTER**          Welcome! I the Master have released you!
**DAMIEN/WARP CORE** You? Released me?
**THE MASTER**          Yes. All of this has been my plan. To give you your freedom once more. These primitives have merely been puppets. Salvadori, Klemp, even Damien... All of them, puppets to my will.
**SALVADORI**          Damien? Is that you, my dear?
**DAMIEN/WARP CORE** Ah... Salvadori, at last...
**SALVADORI**          Magnificent, my dear, but you're starting to frighten us now...
**DAMIEN/WARP CORE** Frighten you? I did this for you. Come closer, Madame, gaze on my creation.
**SALVADORI**          No, Damien, please...[117]
**DAMIEN/WARP CORE** After all you've said to me, all you've done for me.
**SALVADORI**          Damien...?
**DAMIEN/WARP CORE** After year upon endless year of humiliation. Pandering to you and your fawning hordes!
**SALVADORI**          Damien, please no.
**THE MASTER**          Allow me to kill her for you. The first death in our alliance.
**DAMIEN/WARP CORE** Alliance. With you...
**THE MASTER**          Klemp. Kill her.
**SALVADORI**          Oh, God, please...
**KLEMP**          I...[118]
**THE MASTER**          I said kill her!
**KLEMP**          Madame?
**THE MASTER**          You will obey me!
**KLEMP**          I... can't... I won't...
**DAMIEN/WARP CORE** Puppets to your will? (*It laughs*) Pitiful creature.
**KLEMP**          Madame Salvadori?
**THE MASTER**          (*Snarling*) Then I will kill her myself
**KLEMP**          Leave her. Leave her alone!
**SALVADORI**          Klemp!! (*The Master's gun fires*) Klemp!!!
**ACE**          It's too late Elsa, he's dead.[119] Now RUN!
*The Warp Core bellows in anger.*
**DAMIEN/WARP CORE** Oh no, there's no escape for you, Salvadori.
*The window shatters. There is a howling gale as the air is sucked from the ship. Salvadori screams.*
**BEV TARRANT**          We're depressurising again.
**THE DOCTOR**          Get to the lift. Go!
**SALVADORI**          Klemp...
**THE DOCTOR**          Come on!
**THE MASTER**          No, I am the Master. You will obey me.[120]
**THE DOCTOR**          You'll never get it to obey you. Don't you understand? All it is is hate. Unreasoning hate!
*The Core roars.*
**ACE**          Doctor! Come on!
**THE DOCTOR**          It hates you as it hates all things. You've been used. You've lost.

189

**THE MASTER** (*Distant*) No! This is not how it should be!

**BEV TARRANT** Doctor, get out of there!

**THE DOCTOR** Come on, Madame Salvadori. Run. (*The Doctor and Salvadori run. The Core rages around them*) Hold that door!

**THE MASTER** (*Distant*) All right Doctor, run if you can. You will never reach the safety of your TARDIS. The Warp Core will catch up with you soon enough!

*He enters his TARDIS, which dematerialises. Slightly different sound from the Doctor's?*

### 75.INT. 'GALLERY' LIFT

*They fall panting into the lift as the door closes. Salvadori sobbing.*[121]

**SALVADORI** Oh my poor Klemp...

**THE DOCTOR** There was nothing you could do. The Master was controlling him.

**SALVADORI** But he didn't kill me. He wouldn't kill me.

**THE DOCTOR** (*Gently*) No. The Master's influence is almost impossible to resist. He must have thought a great deal of you.

**SALVADORI** And look where it got him...

**ACE** So, now what do we do?

**THE DOCTOR** The Warp Core will tear the ship apart to get at the remaining Krill.[122] We've got to get back to the TARDIS.

**ACE** Which is where exactly?

**THE DOCTOR** Unfortunately somewhere on the lower levels with the Krill.

**ACE** No problem... we'll just send Bev in to frighten any Krill off. She seems to have a knack.

**THE DOCTOR** Really?

**ACE** Straight up. It was as if it was frightened of her

**THE DOCTOR** I wonder... Empty your pockets.

**ACE** Eh?

**THE DOCTOR** Quickly! Both of you.

**BEV TARRANT** I don't see that this is going to help. Apart from a few Reedab pennies all I've got is fluff and...

**THE DOCTOR** Dust! Both of you are covered in dust!

**ACE** There was a storm when we were boarding the ship...[123]

**THE DOCTOR** Then that's it! Even the tiny quantity of dust on your clothes is imbued with the essence of the Warp Core. The Krill are sensing it...

**ACE** And it frightens them!

**THE DOCTOR** Yes, a race memory of the only creature that has ever bested them.

**BEV TARRANT** Well I'm glad it brings back so many happy memories for them but how does that help us exactly?

**THE DOCTOR** Here. Take my handkerchief. Brush the dust from your clothes. Gather as much of it as you can.[124]

**BEV TARRANT** And we throw it in their faces and make them sneeze to death?

**THE DOCTOR** (*Impatient*) The dust can be controlled telepathically! At these quantities the Warp Core has a presence in the dust and little else, but I should be able to manipulate it.

**ACE** To attack the Krill?

**THE DOCTOR**   And clear us a path to the TARDIS. But my mind will be focussed – so you two will have to drag me...
**ACE**                Oh great...
**SALVADORI**   We're not going back out there, surely...?
**BEV TARRANT** We're hoping to escape by attacking the Krill with sentient dust. As plans go...[125]
**THE DOCTOR**   Do you have any better ideas? Now, I need to concentrate to make this work. Ace, take the TARDIS key... Now, are you two ready?[126]
**BEV TARRANT** As I'll ever be.
**ACE**                Whenever you say, Doctor.
**SALVADORI**   I don't know. Not again. Not out in the dark.
**BEV TARRANT** You'll be fine.
**SALVADORI**   (*To herself, quietly*) Oh Klemp, what have I done? Am I responsible for all this? What should I do now?
**ACE**                Ready Doctor?
**THE DOCTOR**   Right. Contact...

## 76. INT. THE MASTER'S TARDIS.
*The background noise of the Master's TARDIS should be distinctive and different from the Doctor's. There is the bleep of controls.*

**THE MASTER** (*To himself*) Telepathic activity? What are you up to, Doctor? Still trying to reach the safety of your own TARDIS?

## 77. INT. GALLERY LIFT.

**BEV TARRANT** Ace, look! Look at the dust!
**ACE**                I can't, I'm too busy looking after the Doctor – any chance of a helping hand?
**BEV TARRANT** Oh yeah, sorry...
**ACE**                Here we go!
*From outside the Krill screams in rage.*
**BEV TARRANT** The Doctor's telepathic commands. They're working! It's rattled the Krill!
**ACE**                Then it's now or never.
**SALVADORI**   Oh God...
*Ace stabs at a button.*
**LIFT VOICE**   Doors opening.
**ACE**                There's the TARDIS! Go Bev, go!
**BEV TARRANT** But the Doctor...
**ACE**                I'll cope with him now. Go on Salvadori! Run!
*There is the scream of the Krill.*
**BEV TARRANT** It's working! They're backing off!
**ACE**                But not far enough. Come on, Professor!
**SALVADORI**   It's not working!
**BEV TARRANT** There's not enough dust.
**ACE**                Well it's too late to go back now!
**SALVADORI**   (*Suddenly calm*) Yes it's far too late.
**BEV TARRANT** Salvadori? What are you doing?
**SALVADORI**   Don't you see? It's far too late, and I've become far too old to live without my wealth or without Klemp. Stop that animal Seta for me, my dears. I'm so sorry for all this...

**BEV TARRANT** Salvadori!

*The Krill roar in anger, there is a scream from Salvadori, then nothing.*

**BEV TARRANT** (*Over that*) No. No!

**ACE**               Come on Bev. She's given us the time we need. Help me with the Doctor.

**BEV TARRANT** She didn't have to do that, she didn't...

**ACE**               Come on!

*The Krill hiss and scream.*

**BEV TARRANT** Ace! The key!

**ACE**               I know!

**BEV TARRANT** Quickly!

**ACE**               I said I know!

*The TARDIS door clicks open and they tumble inside.*

### 78. INT. TARDIS.

*TARDIS hum.*

**BEV TARRANT** Damn her. She didn't have to.

**ACE**               We wouldn't have made it without her.

**THE DOCTOR** Ah, ladies. I gather my cunning plan worked then.

**ACE**               Yes, Professor, it worked, but we lost Salvadori.

**BEV TARRANT** She just... just let them take her.

**THE DOCTOR** Bev, I'm sorry. If I...

**BEV TARRANT** Can we just get off this ship?[127]

*The Doctor operates controls and the TARDIS dematerialises.*

### 79. INT. MASTER'S TARDIS.

**THE MASTER** Ingenious as ever, Doctor, but still too late to stop me.
*He stabs at controls.*

### 80. INT. TARDIS CONSOLE ROOM.

*The hum of the TARDIS in flight.*

**THE DOCTOR** Ace, turn on the scanner, would you?

*There is a hum as it operates.*

**BEV TARRANT** Good God...

**ACE**               I don't believe it.

**THE DOCTOR** Impressive isn't it, watching a planet sized mass moving like a living thing...? Now then...[128]

*There are the bleeps from controls.*

**ACE**               Professor. What are you planning?

**THE DOCTOR** Exactly what I just did back on the ship, only on a larger scale, utilising the telepathic circuits of the TARDIS to take control of the dust and force the Warp Core back towards Duchamp. (*Clears his throat then calls*) Ahem. Are you listening, Master?

**THE MASTER** (*Over*) What do you want, Doctor?

**THE DOCTOR** You'll see.

**BEV TARRANT** Ace, last time the Doctor was only trying to control just a handkerchief full of dust! He can't possibly hope to manipulate an entire planet.

**ACE**               If the Doctor says he can do it...

192

**THE DOCTOR**   Thank you for your confidence Ace. Now quiet both of you. Ready Master? Contact...
*A hum of power starts to build.*

**81. INT. MASTER'S TARDIS.**

**THE MASTER**   What? No! Doctor... (*He stabs at his own scanner control*) Doctor... What are you doing?
**ACE**            (*Over*) He's beating you at your own game, pizza face!
**THE MASTER**   No! Your will against mine, Doctor? You would fight my mind for control of the Core?[129] So be it. (*He stabs at his own telepathic controls this time*) Contact!

**82. INT. TARDIS CONSOLE ROOM.**
*The noise builds.*

**BEV TARRANT** What's happening, Ace?
**ACE**            I guess the Master is using his own telepathic circuits.
**BEV TARRANT** Look at the planet! The two of them are tearing it apart!

**83. EXT. SPACE.**

**DAMIEN/WARP CORE** No! Time Lords no! You aren't strong enough. I will not be trapped again. I will not submit to you. The planet is mine, I tell you. The dust belongs to me!

**84. INT REFUELLING STATION B.**
*The noise is terrible. The place is tearing itself apart.*

**GUTHRIE**       Computer, how're we doing?
**COMPUTER VOICE** All fuel reserves from all six stations now vented into planetary dust, technician Guthrie.
**GUTHRIE**       Heh.[130] That could make a pretty good bang! (*Softly*) Always thought your smokin' was a nasty habit, partner. But I guess this old lighter of yours might jus' save the day.
**COMPUTER VOICE** Warning, technician Guthrie. Highly flammable atmosphere.
**GUTHRIE**       Dangerous habit on a refuelling station.

**85.INT. MASTER'S TARDIS.**
*The noise is deafening now.*

**THE MASTER**   (*Straining with effort*) No, Doctor, you will have to... give in... soon...

**86. INT. TARDIS CONTROL ROOM.**

**THE DOCTOR**   (*Gasping with pain*) Your mind's not strong enough... weakening... must submit.
**BEV TARRANT** He can't keep this up, he can't!
**ACE**            Doctor!

## 87. INT. REFUELLING STATION B.
*Howling wind, etc.*

**GUTHRIE**      Always knew I'd die on Duchamp.
*There is the klunk of a lighter.*

## 88. EXT. SPACE.

**DAMIEN/WARP CORE** Noooooooo!
*A colossal explosion then silence......*

## 89. INT. TARDIS CONSOLE ROOM.
*From total silence we hear Ace's voice, distant at first then louder and more distinct as the Doctor comes around.*

**ACE**      Doctor...? Doctor...?
**THE DOCTOR**      (*Groggy*) Ace?[131]
**BEV TARRANT** Oh, thank God. We were beginning to think you would never come round!
**THE DOCTOR**      Oh, I'm beginning to wish I hadn't...
**ACE**      Here, there's a seat over here.
**THE DOCTOR**      Duchamp...?
**BEV TARRANT** Gone, vaporised. Completely destroyed. So's Salvadori's pleasure cruiser.[132]
**THE DOCTOR**      Taking the Krill with it, no doubt.
**ACE**      Wicked explosion, Professor, what did you do?
**THE DOCTOR** The planet was tearing itself apart. I could feel the Warp Core in my mind, sense it weakening. Then suddenly it was trying to stop someone else.
**ACE**      You mean someone else blew the planet up?
**THE DOCTOR** The dust was saturated with fuel. That coupled with the Dalekanium power source at its core...
**BEV TARRANT** You mean the stories were true?
**THE DOCTOR** Yes. The entire planet was like an enormous bomb. All it would have taken was a single spark...
**BEV TARRANT** Oh my God... Guthrie.
**THE DOCTOR** Bringing his blood feud to a close.[133]
**ACE**      So the Warp Core is dead.
**THE DOCTOR** Oh, I doubt it, but it will be scattered in minute particles throughout the universe. Enough to give people a few bad dreams, but little else.
**BEV TARRANT** And the Master?
**THE DOCTOR** Who knows? Thrown out into space/time by the shockwave just like we were.[134]
**ACE**      So he'll turn up again...
**THE DOCTOR** Oh yes, I think we can count on that. He still needs to locate the very particular sorts of energies that'll enable him to find a new body. Those energies are few and far between.
**BEV TARRANT** Well. I don't know about you two, but I could do with a break from all this...
**THE DOCTOR** Quite right. How do you fancy a trip to Oslo?

## 90. INT. NATIONAL GALLERY. OSLO.

**ANNOUNCER**  Ladies and Gentlemen, the National Gallery will be closing in just a few minutes.[135] Could you please start making your way to the exits?
*The announcer repeats in German, then French in the background.*
**ACE**  So it's there now, in the painting?
**THE DOCTOR**  Yes, waiting, dormant, sleeping its way through the twentieth century.
**ACE**  You could stop it you know, stop the Master stealing it, stop all the deaths on Duchamp in the future.
**THE DOCTOR**  The future has already happened, Ace. We couldn't stop it if we tried.
**ACE**  So now what?
**THE DOCTOR**  Now we get Bev back to her own time and space. Where is she, by the way?
**ACE**  Dunno. She said something about getting you a picture that would cause a lot less bother. (*An alarm starts to ring*) She wouldn't...
**THE DOCTOR**  I think she may have.
**ACE**  I think you should start collecting stamps Doctor, it'll make life a lot easier!

**THE END**

# NOTES

**N.B.** In order to maintain the secrecy around his character's true identity, Geoffrey Beevers was credited as Seta in the CD booklet.

## PART ONE

**1.** Line changed to: 'This scream is still in his head, so I advised him to paint **that**.' *Gary Russell: 'I asked Jeremy James and Jane Goddard to record this little scene whilst we did* Bloodtide. *That's a fairly common thing for me – if there's a small scene for Play A that I can use part of the cast of Play B for, I will. Hence the scenes with Tony Keetch and Karen Henson for* The Fires of Vulcan *were done during* The Apocalypse Element, *and the Kaled stuff in* Davros *with Lou Faulkner and Karl Hansen were done during the recording of the Benny play* The Bellotron Incident. *And there are probably many others. Cheap, moi? Oh yes...'*

**2.** '**Well**,' added at the beginning of the line.

**3.** Line changed to: 'I managed to pick **up one** as a souvenir.'

**4.** Line changed to: '~~Doctor~~, I remember this from 'O' level art. It's by that Dutch bloke, **isn't it**?'

**5.** Line changed to: 'No, ~~no, no~~. **No**, of course not!'

**6.** Line changed to: 'A little something that will sit **nicely** in this gap.'

**7.** Added dialogue. In the preceeding line, Ace mispronounces 'Munch', so at the start of this line, THE DOCTOR says, with the correct pronunication: '**Edvard Munch**.' Then after the line, Ace says: '**Hmm**.' *Gary Russell: 'I'm always aware that* Doctor Who *companions often know things they shouldn't and as I could never pronounce Edvard Munch properly, I decided Ace wouldn't either. So don't blame Sophie Aldred for Ace's unscripted mistake, blame me!'*

**8.** Line changed to: 'This is where they send you to die, ~~girl~~.'

**9.** Line changed to: 'Very well, Klemp, **hurry**, hurry along.'

**10.** Line changed to: 'Oh, great. **Crusties**.' *Gary Russell: 'Sophie remembered that Ace had actually rather liked the hippies from* The Greatest Show in the Galaxy, *so we changed it initially to "oldies" but thought that sounded too Dave Lee Travis (ancient Radio 1 DJ famous for doing "Golden Oldies" shows for anyone who doesn't know) so it became "Crusties". Derogatory in so many ways... and very Ace.'*

**11.** Line changed to: '**Oh**, look at this place. (*Reading*) 'Duchamp Corporation Refuelling Station B. Capacity twenty thousand tonnes.' (*She coughs*) **Oh**, this dust...'

**12.** Line changed to: 'This roof could come in **at** any **moment**.'

**13.** Line changed to: 'Perhaps... **yes**, you're right.'

**14.** Line changed to: 'It will kill us all! **Kill us all**!'

**15.** Line changed to: 'We'll let his ~~own~~ people take care of him.'

**16.** Line changed to: 'Dangerous habit on a refuelling **station**.'

**17.** Line changed to: 'I **keep** it for... sentimental reasons.' *Gary*

*Russell: 'Guthrie's dialogue throughout the script you're reading is quite different in style and colloquialisms to what we ended up with. Mike Tucker wrote Guthrie as an old space prospector, a sour, dour ancient American. I asked Ed Bishop to play the part but for reasons I never got told, his agent said no at the last minute (I was very pleased when we managed to get him years later into* Full Fathom Five, *one of the* Doctor Who Unbound *plays) and I had to start casting again with only a few days to go. Ian Ricketts was a voice tutor at Nick Pegg's old drama alma mater, Guildford, so I asked him, as age was more important than accent. Ian was terrific but we rewrote as we went along changing the Americanisms to things Ian was more comfortable with.'*

**18.** Line changed to: '**Great Scott**!'

**19.** Line changed to: 'A junior refuelling technician on **the** Duchamp Station B.'

**20.** Deleted dialogue: '~~Yup~~.'

**21.** Line changed to: 'No light, no sound, ~~no~~ nothin' – energy to send any creature mad that is.'

**22.** Line changed to: '**Hhmm**, right, the Doctor's space **crusties**.'

**23.** Line changed to: 'Yeah, built **up** their own colony out on the dust.'

**24.** Line changed to: 'The freighter crews buy bits of work off them and ship things back to the homeworlds and **off** to the frontier.'

**25.** Line changed to: 'I'm all for the artistic temperament, but is that **the** way to speak to your beloved patron?'

**26.** Line changed to: 'Cannibalised **it** from the ship they arrived in.'

**27.** Line changed to: '**Hello**, who's there?' *Gary Russell: 'If Alistair Lock can squeeze a few more words beyond what's on the page, he will. I loved what he did with this nobody and he really made the character's death matter.'*

**28.** Line changed to: '**Come on**, there's no point trying to hide, I can see you, so come out.'

**29.** Line changed to: 'Hey, could I stay, **Professor**?'

**30.** Line changed to: 'I've persuaded the commander to let me do **a post-mortem**.' *Gary Russell: '"Autopsy" is more of an Americanism and I felt the Doctor would be terribly British and stiff upper-lip and say "post-mortem".'*

**31.** Line changed to: 'I must admit to never having seen anything **quite** like it.'

**32.** Line changed to: '**Miss Parkinson** would have loved this.'

**33.** Line changed to: '**Miss Parkinson, my 'O' level art teacher**. She used to love all this abstract stuff.' *Gary Russell: 'I opted for Miss Parkinson because in one of the* Virgin *novels (possibly one of Paul Cornell's) I think that was the name given to her art teacher. I don't necessarily believe that all non-TV Doctor Who – whether books, audios, comic strips, ice cream wrappers or internet webcasts – are "canon" either in terms of the TV series or each other, but if there's a reference somewhere, why not use it?'*

**34.** Deleted dialogue – BEV TARRANT: '~~Doctor...~~'

## PART TWO

**35.**  See notes 32–34.

**36.**  Line changed to: 'What the **deuce's** been going on here?'

**37.**  Line changed to: '**Mr Seta**. And you, **sir**, will discover that I am a woman who does not take kindly to being threatened.'

**38.**  '**Whoosh**!' added at the end of the line.

**39.**  BEV TARRANT coughs at the end of the line.

**40.**  Line changed to: 'These aren't ~~a~~ very aesthetic **solutions** to life's problems I will admit, but they are very good at shutting the chattering mouths of critics.' *Gary Russell: 'I can't recall what Damien's original surname was but I changed it to Pierce because I'd been watching an old* Sapphire and Steel *story one night whilst I was working on this and liked the name Sam Pierce. Damien was obviously a nod to Damien Hirst, but I think Damien Pierce is an actor so I made it Pierson. A number of people have asked if it was a nod at old* Doctor Who *artist Alister Pearson, but no, it's not. Johnson Willis was my first choice for this role – he'd done a Benny for us before and I was immensely impressed by his range and knew that I needed someone who could go loopy without going OTT at the end and Johnson was the man.'*

**41.**  Line changed to: '~~And~~ how many crew?'

**42.**  Line changed to: 'You youngsters **certainly** know how to make a mess.'

**43.**  Line changed to: 'Things will be stirred up a damn sight more before this is over, ~~an' all~~.'

**44.**  Line changed to: '**I know**.'

**45.**  '**I**,' added at the start of the line.

**46.**  Line changed to: '**Why do** you want to know?'

**47.**  Line changed to: 'Frontier life is hard on a man, ~~Doc~~.'

**48.**  Line changed to: 'No one is ever there to look **after** you, to watch your back, but here on Duchamp the planet made us bind together, gave us something to rage against, something real to fight'

**49.**  Line changed to: 'I don't know why the planet left me, never have known, but I'm dammed if I'm going to leave until I **do**.'

**50.**  Line changed to: 'Company just **shrug** it off.'

**51.**  Line changed to: 'No, with something ~~far~~ more real and tangible.'

**52.**  Throughout this speach, the AMBASSADOR is audible:

> **SALVADORI**  No ambassador.
>
> **AMBASSADOR**  No?
>
> **SALVADORI**  You are going to have to be patient. It would hardly be a surprise if I let you know what little treat I have in store for you, now would it?
>
> **AMBASSADOR**  (*Laughs*)
>
> **SALVADORI**  Ah. If you would excuse me, I think there are some matters that I need to attend to. (*She crosses the Ballroom.*)

**AMBASSADOR**   Madam.

**SALVADORI**      Klemp, the body is safely tucked away, I trust?

*Gary Russell: 'I think it was Carrie John's idea to have the ambassador respond. I loved Caroline John the first time I met her at a convention in Coventry – she was refreshingly honest about everything and I wanted to work with her on one of these. When* Dust Breeding *came up and I knew I wanted her hubby, I'll be completely honest, having Carrie along in the same play was the perfect smokescreen. We were able to pitch the publicity along the lines that former* Who *companion Caroline John was playing the wicked Madame Salvadori in a story featuring the Krill (monsters created by Mike Tucker and Robert Perry for one of their novels). As a sideline, it was, "Oh, and Caroline's husband Geoffrey Beevers will also be along, playing the part of fellow art dealer, Seta." Worked like a dream and Seta's secret remained so until the end of this episode – and I made sure we never put "Mr Seta" anywhere in print! Carrie arrived on the Sunday morning and asked me if she could do Salvadori with an accent, which hadn't ever crossed my mind, as she wanted to play a character part rather than just use her own voice. A mix of Russian, Eastern Europe and Italian ended up in the mix and occasionally I felt her geography slipped between lines. Carrie, quite rightly, pointed out that Salvadori wasn't from Earth and thus whatever she did was just the local accent of Persius Major of wherever she hailed from. Can't argue with logic like that. I asked Mark Donovan to do the voice of the unscripted ambassador in this scene. I flirted with the idea of getting him to do it as the Gulfrarg Ambassador he'd played in the Benny adventure* The Extinction Event, *but as that character only spoke in expletives, the joke wouldn't have worked here.'*

**53.**   Line changed to: 'You're in **my** gallery.'

**54.**   Line changed to: 'You laugh and mock, you look down your **noses** at the art we create here, but when I have finished...'

**55.**   Deleted dialogue – ACE: '~~I believe you~~.'

**56.**   Line changed to: 'You can rely on us, ~~Doc~~...'

**57.**   Deleted dialogue – GUTHRIE: '~~This one's going to be a humdinger!~~'

**58.**   Line changed to: 'What's the matter ~~Ace~~, what's wrong?'

**59.**   '**Ace**,' added at the start of the line.

## PART THREE

**60.**   Scene 36 is not featured in the reprise.

**61.**   Line changed to: 'This **isn't** one of ours.'

**62.**   Line changed to: '**I** know those **shipping** schedules backwards ~~I do~~, and there's **nothing** due near us for weeks.'

**63.**   Line changed to: '**Isn't** answering our hails, though.'

**64.**   Line changed to: '**I** told you, girl. This mess **isn't** over yet.'

**65.**   *Gary Russell: 'Poor Jac Rayner. Wanders into the studio, doing her bit as Executive Producer for BBC Worldwide and making sure we're not messing things up. She has barely sat down before I grab her, chuck her in front of a microphone and tell her to be a sexy lift (she has a very sexy voice). Not sure she's dared come back to the studio for anything I've directed since!'*

**66.**   '**Come on**,' added at the start of the line.

**67.** Line changed to: 'Would you have wooed me if you had the slightest inkling of what you were letting **loose**?'

**68.** Line changed to: 'But in stopping one horror another **was** created.'

**69.** Line changed to: 'The **winds are** dropping.'

**70.** Line changed to: 'Never seen the **like** of this, **not** in all my years...'

**71.** Line changed to: 'They **know**. Know **something's** a coming.'

**72.** Line changed to: '**No**. Just **sitting** there in orbit, ~~it is~~, **waiting**...'

**73.** Line changed to: '**Or** are you planning to kill me?'

**74.** Line changed to: 'I was beginning to **wonder**.'

**75.** Line changed to: '~~At~~... at once.'

**76.** '**Oh**,' added at the beginning of the line.

**77.** Line changed to: 'An unidentified **cruiser** entered orbit about twenty minutes ago.' *Gary Russell: 'I thought "cruiser" sounded bigger than "ship" and also reasoned that a seasoned traveller like Bev would instinctively make that difference. It's always great to have Lou Faulkner in the studio – she and Sophie and Sylvester got on really well during* The Genocide Machine *so it seemed a good idea to have them join forces again. Lou was a friend of Nick Briggs but as it turned out also knew Lisa Bowerman, who plays Benny. Which is just as well, as Bev now inhabits the Bennyverse as a direct result of this story...'*

**78.** Line changed to: 'Tell them to get into their shuttlecraft and head for that **cruiser**...'

**79.** Line changed to: '**Now**, just go.'

**80.** Line changed to: 'Let me show you my studio, the means by which I can shape **the** world.'

**81.** Line changed to: 'Come on ~~Bev~~!'

**82.** Line changed to: '**Oh yes**.'

**83.** Line changed to: '**Oh** my God, look at the dust!'

**84.** Line changed to: '~~Ace...~~ Look. **There's a body**. **It's** the base commander. I think that's Fredrickson... (*There is a scuffle from the far side of the docking bay*) Ace, there's something **else** there.'

**85.** Line changed to: '~~Ace~~, what is it?'

**86.** BEV TARRANT does not scream.

**87.** Line changed to: '**Doors** opening.'

## PART FOUR

**88.** For changes during these scenes, see Part Three notes 83–86.

**89.** Line changed to: 'Whereas life hasn't been treating you so kindly, by the **looks** of it.'

**90.** Line changed to: 'You know the Core has **been** activated.'

**91.** Line changed to: 'But Ace and **Bev** are out there!'

**92.** '**I**,' added at the start of the line.

**93.** Line changed to: 'Cargo bay will be sealed in **ten** seconds. **Nine** seconds.'

**94.** From this point on, running continuously under the other dialogue, COMPUTER VOICE's lines are changed to: 'C̶a̶r̶g̶o̶ ̶b̶a̶y̶ ̶s̶e̶a̶l̶i̶n̶g̶ i̶n̶ **eight** seconds, **seven seconds**, **six seconds**, **five seconds**, **four seconds**, three seconds, **two seconds**, **one second**.'

**95.** 'Oh,' added at the beginning of the line.

**96.** *Gary Russell: 'This exchange created a little bit of a furore amongst* Doctor Who *fans who keep tabs on continuity between the books and audios. Some of them felt this contradicted things set up by the books. Others have since disputed it and suggested that it still all ties together. To be honest, I don't care – I was far more concerned with linking the Master's degeneration with events on TV than in the books. I should also point out that this whole scenario is of my making – Mike Tucker didn't write this and any time anyone moans at him about it, he rightfully points them in my direction. I just reiterate that my job is to make a good story and let others worry about policing the post-TV series continuity. Which may explain why Mike is more popular with fans than I am!'*

**97.** Line changed to: 'There's something in **this corridor** with us.'

**98.** Line changed to: 'Madame Else **Carolina Maria Ivanov–**' *Gary Russell: 'We played around with Salvadori's list of names to give her a less obviously Russian, thus Earth-centric, pedigree.'*

**99.** Line changed to: 'He sent me out **of the cabin** here.'

**100.** '**Yes**,' said twice.

**101.** Line changed to: 'H̶e̶h̶, thank you, **thank you**, g̶i̶r̶l̶. You can shut down for a while **now**. I think **I can hear someone coming**.'

**102.** Line changed to: 'Heh, there you are at last, b̶o̶y̶. **I** knew you'd **turn** up eventually.'

**103.** Line changed to: 'Run? **I've been waiting for you a long time**. W̶a̶i̶t̶i̶n̶'̶ ̶a̶ ̶l̶o̶n̶g̶ ̶t̶i̶m̶e̶.̶ ̶T̶h̶e̶r̶e̶'̶s̶ ̶b̶a̶d̶ ̶b̶l̶o̶o̶d̶ ̶b̶e̶t̶w̶e̶e̶n̶ ̶u̶s̶.̶ **We have a score to settle**.'

**104.** Line changed to: '**Yes**. **I reckon** you're the thing that killed my partner.'

**105.** Line changed to: 'I've never **been a great one for running**.'

**106.** Line changed to: 'Well... I **was planning** on killing you.'

**107.** Line changed to: 'Oh **no**.'

**108.** Line changed to: 'It's realised it can build with the dust to reach out for **this** ship and tear it apart.'

**109.** *Gary Russell: 'This is a pivotal moment for Ace, and her continued characterisation through subsequent plays, I felt. I never wanted to go down the route that* Virgin Books *took her, turning her into a mercenary, but I wanted to toughen her up. Later, the realisation of what she was prepared to do here, her abandonment of Salvadori to die, would start her questioning her personal ethics and motives. This wasn't something Mike or I intended at the time, it was just something I picked up and ran with after the event.'*

**110.** BEV TARRANT's line begins after LIFT VOICE has said: 'Second floor.' The rest of LIFT VOICE's line is under BEV TARRANT's, 'Persistent, aren't they?'

**111.** Line changed to: 'I said there was a b̶l̶o̶o̶d̶ feud between us, b̶o̶y̶. I **haven't** finished with you yet.'

**112.** Line changed to: '**Oh yes**.'

**113.** Line changed to: 'You'll rue the day you turned your back on **Arnold** Guthrie, ~~boy~~.' *Gary Russell: 'Guthrie's forename was changed, again to make him less American.'*

**114.** Line changed to: 'Talk about climbing out of the ~~frying pan~~...'

**115.** Line changed to: '**This** is the Master.'

**116.** Line changed to: 'That creature has decided that it's not **going** to stay on that planet from what we've just seen.'

**117.** Line changed to: '~~No~~, Damien, please...'

**118.** The 'I' was moved to the start of KLEMP's next line. *Gary Russell: 'Another great moment and all credit to Mike for writing it and for Carrie and Mark Donovan for pulling it off. I've always been fond of "the little guy" or "the assistant" who eventually dies because they're caught up in their master's plans (cf Mr Fibuli or Vogel) and no matter how much of a bitch Salvadori has been to Klemp, his death resonates with her. She's upset at his death and that's great. Mark Donovan had done a Benny for me previously. Now I don't think Mark will be too offended if I point out that he's a big guy, but Klemp is clearly meant to be a bit of a wimpy, Grimtongue-like fusspot. A great thing about audio is you can cast against type – Mark's always getting roles as bruisers and bouncers and 'token fat guy' because people don't look beyond the physical. Audio has no such pigeon-holing and more than one person on meeting Mark afterwards has commented to me that they can't square the picture in their heads of Klemp with the real Mark. Which is, excuse the pun, the mark of good acting.'*

**119.** Line changed to: 'It's too late ~~Elsa~~, he's dead.'

**120.** *Gary Russell: 'Well, it wouldn't be right not to have him say it! I cannot praise Geoffrey Beevers enough – the moment he stepped into the studio, he recreated the character he'd last played in 1980. He was concerned that he got the voice right and as I'd brought along a VHS of* The Keeper of Traken *I was able to show it to him. It was educational for Sophie and Sylvester who, only being familiar with Anthony Ainley, were bemused by the references to the Master's physical deformity in the script but once they saw Geoffrey's performance in* Traken, *it all made sense. Geoffrey then went into the recording booth and began – and that gorgeous voice was there. We discussed various ways to differentiate between the Master with mask and sans mask and in the end settled on the effective thing of having him put his hand between his mouth and the mike, thus just deadening it enough. When he "took off the mask" he did this by slowly raising his hand during the course of his lines, and so without any of Gareth Jenkins's trickery pokery, the mask came off aurally.'*

**121.** Added dialogue – LIFT VOICE: '**Doors closing**.'

**122.** Line changed to: 'The Warp Core will tear **this** ship apart to get at the remaining Krill.'

**123.** '**Yeah**,' added at the beginning of the line.

**124.** Line changed to: 'Gather as much ~~of it~~ as you can.'

**125.** Line changed to: 'We're hoping to escape by attacking the Krill with sentient dust. ~~As plans go...~~'

**126.** Line changed to: 'Now, are you ~~two~~ ready?'

**127.** Line changed to: 'Can we just get off this **cruiser**?'

**128.** Line changed to: '**And now**...'

**129.** Line changed to: 'You would fight my mind for **the** control of the Core?'

**130.** Line changed to: '**Well**.'

**131.** THE DOCTOR's line is said between the two 'Doctor...?'s of ACE's previous line.

**132.** Line changed to: '**Along with** Salvadori's pleasure cruiser.'

**133.** Line changed to: 'Bringing his ~~blood~~ feud to a close.'

**134.** Line changed to: 'Thrown out into space/time by the **shockwaves** just like we were.'

**135.** Line changed to: 'Ladies and Gentlemen, the **art gallery will now be closing**.' *Gary Russell: 'I asked Mark Wyman to do this as he could do the foreign languages. We changed it to "Art Gallery" rather than "National Gallery" as I thought the National Gallery in London might be a tad annoyed if we suggested their security systems were... well, lax.'*

# CHARLEY SAYS

## By India Fisher

I have to admit from the outset that I feel somewhat under qualified to be writing this, being merely a 'turn' and in no way a writer – or director for that matter – with all the insights that affords you. I just turn up and read the lines! Therefore I am ashamed to say that I can only offer my reminiscences on what it was like to record *Seasons of Fear* and my humble opinion on having heard the finished product. If the thought of yet another actor wittering on fills you with horror, please feel free to skip straight to the interesting part: the script.

The first thing that struck me about this script – and I am glad to hear that it has carried over into the finished product – is the relationship between the Doctor and Charley. This is the middle story of the second season, so it makes sense that they are more at ease with one another and their relationship is developing. Paul Cornell and Caroline Symcox do a wonderful job of bringing out the lighthearted side of their friendship. The play starts with the Doctor keeping a promise to Charley, taking her to Singapore so she can keep her date with Alex. They are playful with one another and there is no sense of danger, a fact that is played on in the script by having the Doctor exclaim as they leave the TARDIS, 'Wait!… Does this hat suit me?' I love the banter between them; Charley is getting to know the Doctor and all his little idiosyncrasies and isn't afraid to tease him about them. When she talks about his technique of questioning someone by playing the fool and getting them to do all the talking, the Doctor says, 'Do I do that?'

'I always thought you did!' Charley replies.

There is a real feeling of camaraderie between them. In the court of Edward and Edith, the Doctor first says Charley is as strong as an ox and then moments later says of her, 'What she lacks in experience she makes up for in sheer gall'. She quips, 'I'm keeping a list of these you know!' This sort of good-natured banter is always great fun to play, and having Paul McGann to play off makes it such a joy. Just like the Doctor and Charley, Paul and I were, of course, getting to know one another better by this time, and I think, and hope, this comes across in the recording. I also think the fact that we are all in the same room helps hugely with this sort of repartee. If you can see the other actor's eyes then you can really start to play off one another, and Paul is an immensely giving actor. I don't know whether it comes across to anyone else or if it is just a personal thing because I was there, but I can hear the smiles on our faces in certain parts of dialogue, and the script is very funny. I love the bit when they are about to travel to Buckinghamshire and Charley exclaims with glee that it's another chance to wear a lovely dress.

'Be a bit conspicuous wouldn't it?' the Doctor retorts.

'I meant for me!' states Charley, wearily. I remember that Paul was deeply amused that the TARDIS had an entire wardrobe room, and cried out in a true luvvie voice, 'Get to wardrobe quick, it's nearly the half!'

I was also very glad to see that Charley wasn't just the Doctor's sidekick in this story. She had much more of a partner's role to play and wasn't afraid to get stuck in if needs be: brandishing swords and getting carried away with the idea of how they could do away with Grayle (catapult, stone him, or just drop him off on some harmless planet), which I love and hope to see more of as her character develops. She even saves the Doctor on more than one occasion. In fact in this play Charley takes on the opposite role to the Doctor, who remains as ever above violence. It is this dichotomy between the violent route or not that is so nicely played out between the Doctor and Grayle. It is repeatedly said by the Doctor that they could have been friends if circumstances had been different. They are two sides to one coin and that makes him so interesting as a foe for the Doctor. Of course that also had a lot to do with the brilliant performance by Stephen Perring, who had the unenviable task of playing four generations of the same character. Not an easy task, as I later discovered in *Neverland*.

As a relative newcomer to *Doctor Who*, I was of course aware of the Daleks and to a lesser extent the Cybermen, but had no idea about the Nimon. During the recording, Gary Russell brought in the video of *The Horns of Nimon*, which we all sat down to watch. I have to admit there was a certain air of being back at primary school when the whole class sat down to watch *Look and Read*. I am ashamed to admit that this childish atmosphere was contagious, as when the Nimon appeared I had to stifle giggles. Now, I mean no disrespect to the costume designers or indeed to the programme as a whole, but I think it was the platform boots under the body stocking that sent me over the edge! I have said it before and I say it again now: audio is the perfect medium for *Doctor Who*. When I heard Bob Curbishley's Nimon on the CD, they came across brilliantly, and I wasn't tempted once to crack a smile. Although this wasn't the case during recording, as Bob would break into a William Hague impression in between takes, which worked surprisingly well with the voice effect. Although I would rather not dwell on the image of William Hague in a body stocking and platforms!

My hat goes off to everyone in this story; Paul and I had the easy part, whilst everyone else played multiple roles. It takes real skill to make them different, which was done superbly. I know Stephen Fewell well now, having become friends whilst recording *Seasons*, and even I had to check it was really him playing Richard Martin. Although he was concerned at the time that Gary kept asking him to retake a line, as he apparently sounded like a pirate! (I think that line is now somewhere on the cutting room floor.)

Doing this story with the Nimon suddenly made me realise what a wealth of history there is to *Doctor Who*, and how many other traditional foes he has that I am unaware of. This made me really excited about the possibilities for the fortieth anniversary special and the subsequent season. Charley is developing so nicely as a character, and the relationship with the Doctor is really starting to gel, I just can't wait to find out what happens next! I hope I'm not the only one.

# SEASONS OF FEAR

## By Paul Cornell & Caroline Symcox

**One: A History Lesson (Paul)**

My fascination with Edward the Confessor reaches back to my M.A. course at Lancaster University (I was in the same group as Paul Magrs). For the first year of my postgraduate degree, I started to write a historical novel about Edward. After I left Lancaster, having made the decision that I wanted to write for a living rather than teach people how to write for a living, I used the material for a TV pitch. It was developed by Nicola Schindler and Matt Jones at Red Productions. (This was before *Ivanhoe* put an end to the concept of big budget historical drama.) But we kept hitting the same problem: the story of Edward and Edith doesn't really have an ending.

Edward had come to the throne as a puppet ruler, the pawn of his powerful mother, to be used in a game between her and the real power in England, the Earls of the family Godwin. The Godwins owned nearly all the land, and governed it at a local level, to the point where the King was merely a figurehead. Edward, still a rather ineffectual and weak person, was forced to marry Earl Godwin's daughter, Edith, meaning any heir would be very much influenced by the Godwin family.

Edward had a reputation as being very unworldly and spiritual, hence the nickname of 'The Confessor'. That was always the reason given for why he and Edith, the most beautiful woman in England, never conceived a child. But there are lots of contemporary accounts of them having a wonderful time together, going over the Godwins' heads by touring the country and meeting the people directly, creating the first media monarchy. As soon as they got married, the Crown started to pull power back from the Earls.

Meanwhile, foreign powers such as Norway, Denmark, and the Normandy of William the Bastard (the inventor of the concentration camp) all viewed England as their next conquest. Except for the fact that Edward and Edith created a cosmopolitan court at which they were all welcome, and made the fact they weren't going to produce an heir into a point of policy. Every enemy of England somehow came to believe that they were being courted to peacefully take over the crown when Edward died. (As illustrated in the story of the trip that Edith's brother, later Harold I, took to Normandy, where he apparently promised the crown to William, and where he was probably acting on orders.)

Hence decades of relative peace, one of the longest stretches of prosperity and freedom from fear in the islands since Roman times. The people loved Edward and Edith for their 'Reign of Solomon', that is, because no foreign armies were eating their produce and lodging in their homes. What we might these days call a gay man and his best friend had rewritten the constitution (the Law being remade in the style of that unfairly maligned benevolent ruler, Cnut), and kept England at peace through sheer guile.

But as I said, the story has no ending. On his deathbed, Edward hands his ring to Harold, and asks him to have a go at winning the endgame. He nearly does, but William turns on the victorious English troops running after his cavalry. After

Hastings, William proposes marriage to Edith, who opts to go into a nunnery instead, but not until she's forced William to take on Edward's entire Law rather than face her as the leader of continual civil uprising.

William is crowned in the Westminster Abbey Edward had built for him by Norman architects. And it's said in some stories that Harold secretly watches, because the King who pretends to get an arrow in the eye and thus survives the battle was a favourite story of Edward's, read to his court every year.

But it's messy. Our hero is gone, as often in history, before the events he's been at the heart of are really tidied up. But the story suggests something: Edward was a hero of domesticity, of peace, of the small things, someone who used his intelligence to prevent battle. So what better way of using some of this material than to place it in a story that moves across time, with a similar hero who samples the good bits and is never around for the messy complexities of afterwards?

And doesn't that suggest a difference between that hero and someone else: a villain who's been forced to live through all that the hero can skip over?

### Two: The Paul McGann Season (Caroline)

Co-writing *Seasons of Fear* was a rather different experience than I guess most writers have of writing an audio play. Paul never intended to write *Seasons* with someone else, and so I was brought in halfway through the process, after the meetings and preparation had already been and gone. [*Because I was busy working on a Casualty re-write, and a couple of other suggested co-writers had declined – Paul.*] One of the first things I focused on as I spoke to Paul about co-writing *Seasons* with him was the fact that this play was to be in the middle of a Paul McGann season, and what is more, a season with an arc. Looking at this for the first time I found it rather daunting. How similar to the other stories would this need to be? Would we have to insert linking comments or even scenes to keep the arc moving? Most importantly, how much of the character development between Charley and the Doctor would be predetermined by the outcome of this arc?

I needn't have worried. Gary Russell, the producer, and Alan Barnes, who was writing the season's finale *Neverland*, had already worked out that the season wouldn't be rigidly structured. Instead, each story would be allowed to go largely its own way, albeit with the necessary inclusion of certain scenes. Accordingly the challenge was not dealing with inflexible elements, but rather to tailor the Doctor/Charley relationship within the play to hint at what had gone before and what was to happen in the future, without compromising the intrinsic shape of the story.

In the end *Seasons* is clearly its own story. Its form alone (the *Chase*-style romp through time) marks it out as very different from anything else in 'Season 28'. Nevertheless it still includes elements that link it to the other stories: the cliffhanger to Part Four, for example (written so memorably by Gary Russell), and one of my favourite scenes, our opening in Singapore. So what we are left with is the best kind of arc: an arc in which the plot is moved forward in each of the stories making up its length, while the stories themselves are self-contained. None of the plays depend on the others around it, none couldn't stand on their own, but when put together they add up to a larger whole.

**Three: A Way of Writing Who (Paul)**

Our attitude in going into *Seasons of Fear* was that of writing a traditional, but innovative, *Doctor Who* story. Because we fans love categories and distinctions, divisions of stories into such dualities as traditional/radical have emerged. Both sides of any such division start to be pejorative terms, because they're each defined by their opponents. What usually happens is that some new breed of *Who* comes along that reconciles the divide. I suppose *Seasons* sets out to be something like that, a traditional *Doctor Who* story that presents the listener with a lot of reversals and new tricks and new spins on old situations. Reversals are the lifeblood of series TV, and are, ideally, what *Doctor Who* is all about. They're the moments when everyone on-screen realises that everything they thought was true isn't. Or when the hero or villain is clever enough to turn a situation they were absolutely losing back to their advantage in one move. They're hard work to write. Those opposed to 'trad' *Who* would say that the form only uses reversals that have already been seen in *Who* before. We think that you can do very traditional *Doctor Who* that satisfies by working hard, by making the moves of the Doctor and of the villains clever and original. And that means that old monsters have to be used in new ways too.

Humour is very much a part of traditional *Doctor Who*. The Doctor is more humane than his humourless foes, and thus funnier. So you'll see quite a lot of verbal humour in these recording scripts. However, it's always the first thing to go during recording because it's often not very plotty, and so dispensable. Also, Paul McGann wanted to do more passion and less jokes. But I'm pleased that some of our hints that the Eighth Doctor, who in his only screen appearance is worried about his shoes and his shirt, has a streak of vanity made it to the final edit. Worrying about his appearance makes him different to the other Doctors, and rather wonderfully vulnerable.

**Four: The Art of Co-Writing (Caroline)**

Writing fiction with someone else can be the most wonderful thing in the world: those moments when you've been struggling over a plot point, trying to work out how this could be if this and this happened previously. Then everything comes together and you both get it at once, leaving you wanting to dance around the room. Then there are the times when one of you fixes the problem on their own, and the shared joy when they introduce the solution. Of course, it can be hard, especially when you live far from each other, as Paul and I did when we wrote *Seasons*. Everything had to be done via e-mail or over the phone, and lacking face to face conversation made things more difficult. Brainstorming on either end of a telephone line just doesn't get the creative juices flowing in the same way as a face to face discussion does.

Nevertheless, I think our separation led to something different in the script. [*People have commented that there are a lot of couples bantering in it, but they were there before Caroline was. Probably me trying to be 'Holmesian'!* – Paul.] We were forced to write apart from each other, making our additions and changes very much our own. Our individual styles were allowed to show, even within the overall shape and voice of the script. When I joined Paul in writing *Seasons of Fear* a draft had already been written. Essentially I was given the first draft with Gary's notes on it, and asked to write the second draft. My changes and additions are probably more about structure than anything else. What we didn't have was a reason: why were these old enemies of the Doctor operating in this way? What happened to make all this possible? I saw my role as working this out. I added the sword, which forms a continuity other than Grayle between each time period, and I changed the ending, so that rather than, as originally happened, the older Grayle kills the younger (resulting in some nasty time paradoxes including multiple copies of the Doctor), the younger now kills the older.

Looking back on it, I think the combination is what *Seasons* really needed: someone who knew *Doctor Who* like the back of his hand, who was an experienced writer of dialogue, working with someone whose interest was in structure and logic, and who could come fresh to the story and characters, bringing a new perspective to the work. The end product is the fusion of our different interests and focuses, and I hope it is better *Doctor Who*, and better entertainment, for that combination.

# Seasons of Fear

## CAST

| | |
|---|---|
| THE DOCTOR | Paul McGann |
| CHARLEY | India Fisher |
| GRAYLE | Stephen Perring |
| MARCUS | Robert Curbishley |
| LUCILIUS | Stephen Fewell |
| EDWARD | Lennox Greaves |
| EDITH | Sue Wallace |
| LUCY MARTIN | Justine Mitchell |
| RICHARD MARTIN | Stephen Fewell |
| NIMON VOICES | Robert Curbishley |
| RASSILON | Don Warrington |

# PART ONE

## Scene One: Singapore Gardens.

*FX: The lap of water, the distant sound of ships and the blare of loud gamelan music. A party is going on. Fireworks, applause and laughter.*

**DOCTOR**   It was at the Singapore Hilton, on the cusp of the years 1930 and 1931 that I first met Mr Sebastian Grayle. I was sitting in the tea gardens at midnight on that New Year's Eve, looking down at the junks in the harbour, lit up with lanterns and setting off fireworks. I was wondering if I'd done the right thing. I was there for Charley. Her journey on the *R101*, where I'd met her, had been with the intention of keeping an appointment in Singapore, to meet a boy called Alex...[1]

## Scene Two: TARDIS Interior.

*FX: TARDIS interior.*

**CHARLEY**   He's such a chum. But won't he expect me to be dead?
**DOCTOR**   (*Troubled*) Last night I stopped the TARDIS in that year and sent messages ahead.
**CHARLEY**   Goodness.
**DOCTOR**   – had nothing to do with it. (*Lightening up*) The old girl's still having some of her funny turns. It took six tries to get her here.
**CHARLEY**   He dances divinely, and he always has something stunning in his buttonhole.
**DOCTOR**   He sounds like a man after my own heart.[2] I'll not meet him though.
**CHARLEY**   What? Why?
**DOCTOR**   (*Brightening*) Because I'm not a gooseberry.
**CHARLEY**   Well, obviously.
**DOCTOR**   And there's a spot in the tea gardens at the Singapore Hilton where the humidity isn't so oppressive, and you can hear everything across the harbour. A perfect place to witness the New Year celebrations.
*FX: Whirr of door opening.*
**DOCTOR**   And now it's just out there. Come on, off we go. No, wait![3]
**CHARLEY**   What?!
**DOCTOR**   This hat... is it me?
**CHARLEY**   Oh, Doctor! It really suits you!

## Scene Three: Singapore Gardens.

*FX: Back to the harbour sounds.*

**DOCTOR**   I think she was just being nice.[4] I left the TARDIS in a side street near the hotel. Charley found Alex by one of the bars, as per my message. I stayed back for a moment, watching them. Their happiness was obvious, and reminded me of why I'd saved Charley in the first place, however many laws of time I'd broken. Just one promising life had been saved, and that was enough. The boy took Charley's arm, and showed her his buttonhole.[5] They ordered their gin slings and headed for the terrace,

213

where, as Charley had promised this man before her adventures began, the sun was just going down. I had a quiet word with the concierge, found my favourite spot in the garden, and called for some tea and newspapers. I was looking for stories concerning the *R101* crash. There was quite a bit of coverage.[6] I devoured it as night fell and the celebrations in the harbour began. My interest was somewhat a matter of maudlin reflection. I may have saved one, but how many had I failed to save? I was deep in my own thoughts when a shadow fell over me. Thinking it was Charley, as she'd forced me to say I'd join the two of them in the celebrations at midnight, I didn't even glance up.[7] (*Conversationally*) You're back a bit early, aren't you, Charley? How's Alex?

**GRAYLE**     Not very perceptive of you, Doctor. I am not your charming companion.

**DOCTOR**     Ah. I should have known. She doesn't have a moustache. Have we met?

**GRAYLE**     That's a complex question. My name is Sebastian Grayle. May I join you?

**DOCTOR**     Be my guest. Ah. (*To waiter*) Could we have two more pots of tea please?[8] Thanks.

**GRAYLE**     It's a pleasure to see you here.

**DOCTOR**     And you. Not that I know who you are. How do you feel about this hat?

**GRAYLE**     Such folly! Such arrogance!

**DOCTOR**     Such a pleasure not to meet a Yes man! Here, it looks so much better on you.

**GRAYLE**     (*Laughing*) For once your mockery does not infuriate me, Doctor. This time, I am the one in control.

**DOCTOR**     I'm sure you are, but I'm still pretty certain we haven't met.[9]

**GRAYLE**     Oh, but we have, Time Lord.

**DOCTOR**     Are you confusing me with someone else? I'm not the one who says 'you must obey me'. I don't meddle. And I'm not a glamorous woman at the moment.

**GRAYLE**     We are old acquaintances. In my past. But in your future.

**DOCTOR**     (*Serious*) You've broken the first law of time?

**GRAYLE**     Not at all. I am immortal. Thanks to my masters. I have waited through the generations for this meeting. So I can finally look you in the eye, finally allow myself to feel the satisfaction of your death.

**DOCTOR**     My death?! What have you done?

**GRAYLE**     Only now do you begin to feel the bite of it. I have killed you, Doctor. Not only that, but I have delivered this world to my masters. Look around you. Look at those poor fools in the harbour, celebrating the turn of a year they don't even acknowledge. They are illusions, Doctor. This timeline no longer truly exists, and neither do they. My masters resurrected this place using their power over time, simply so I could indulge a whim, to see my foe face to face at last. The reality is much changed. My masters are the masters of Earth. In the real universe, this planet is their feeding ground.

**DOCTOR**     But everything looks... everything feels...

**GRAYLE**     That is how complete their mastery over time has become. Your own people, Doctor, in this new timeline, are no longer the Lords of existence. That honour has fallen to my employers.

| DOCTOR | Who are? |
| GRAYLE | I think... I will let that remain as a surprise. |
| DOCTOR | I'll prevent this. |
| GRAYLE | But it's already happened. You can't rely on the history you know, Doctor. Not any more. My task is done. And now I shall take my leave of you. Revenge is sweet, but I have drunk deeply enough. We shall not meet again. |

FX: *His laughter fades as he leaves.*

| DOCTOR | Wait! Stop! |

FX: *The Doctor runs after him, but he collides with–*

| DOCTOR | Ooof – Charley! |
| CHARLEY | Doctor, you have to meet Alex! He's in the– |
| DOCTOR | Did you just pass a man going out as you were coming in? |
| CHARLEY | (*Not listening*) He's absolutely charming! |
| DOCTOR | Well, I don't think so! |
| CHARLEY | You don't know him! |
| DOCTOR | Well, no, but he said he'd killed me! |
| CHARLEY | Alex Grayle said he'd killed you? |
| DOCTOR | Not <u>Alex</u>! (*Realises*) Grayle? Alex is also called Grayle? |
| CHARLEY | Also? |
| DOCTOR | As well as Sebastian. |
| CHARLEY | Who's Sebastian? |
| DOCTOR | Sebastian is the Grayle who says he's killed me! |
| CHARLEY | Have you been fighting with Alex's Granddad? He told me they'd met up earlier today– |
| DOCTOR | Granddad? My aunt Flavia he's his Granddad! He's an immortal! |
| CHARLEY | I'm very confused. |
| DOCTOR | So's time. Charley, something awful has happened. Sometime in the past. |
| CHARLEY | Is this anything to do with... you know. Rescuing me? |
| DOCTOR | I don't know. I doubt it – this is quite different. Apparently this is a ruse – a falsehood. In reality, the monsters have taken over! |
| CHARLEY | Then how can everything be like this? |
| DOCTOR | Later, Charley, later! We have to get back to the TARDIS, before they decide they don't need this pretend timeline anymore! |
| CHARLEY | Doctor, what–? Oh, wait for me! |
| DOCTOR | (*Voice fading as he strides off*) Come on Charley, we've got a world to save! |

## Scene Four: TARDIS Interior.

FX: *TARDIS take-off noise and interior.*

| DOCTOR | (*Fade into conversation*) ...which means that the web of time has been unspun. These masters Grayle talks about have shattered it. The rules don't exist anymore. Grayle can do anything he likes. |

FX: *TARDIS controls.*

| DOCTOR | I've got the TARDIS out of the false timeline, at least. We're being battered by time storms in all directions. The disruption to the original timeline is vast. |
| CHARLEY | Doctor... this problem with time, please be honest with me now. Is it my fault? |

**DOCTOR** Your fault?

**CHARLEY** I was talking to Alex... Apparently the newspapers are saying that <u>nobody</u> could have survived the blast that brought down the *R101*. Remember what Edith Thompson said? I died – they found my diary and everything. Oh, Doctor, if you hadn't rescued me, I would be dead too, wouldn't I? I have read novels on this subject, the person who is rescued when actually their time has come. What you did, it disrupted time, it must have. Have I caused this to happen?

**DOCTOR** It's... possible.[10] But no, no, of course it isn't true! If I'm not allowed to rescue just one person... No, it's ridiculous! Charley, you're right, if I hadn't shown up, you <u>would</u> have died on the *R101*. But time has a way of sorting these things out. Grayle and his masters have done this, not us. (*Musing*) Grayle must have followed his family line in this fictional world of his and arranged to meet Alex in Singapore, just so he could get you and me there too.

**CHARLEY** So what do we do, Doctor? The damage has already been done!

**DOCTOR** Quite right. But thanks to Grayle, the rules are suspended. We can play him at his own game. We have license to meddle! We can go back to when this all started, when Grayle's masters first contacted him. We can prevent this from happening![11]

**CHARLEY** We get to save the universe?

**DOCTOR** Again. The question is, where, and more importantly, <u>when</u>, did Grayle get his invitation to immortality?

**CHARLEY** Um. That <u>is</u> a rhetorical question, isn't it?

**DOCTOR** Actually you probably <u>do</u> hold the key to answering it. Could I just... Well, I don't really know how to put this...

**CHARLEY** How unusual.

**DOCTOR** What I want to know is... well... you see... Oh, here, just put this under your tongue!

**CHARLEY** Wh– uggh ugh ugh?!

**DOCTOR** I assume that means 'what is it?' It's a genetic sampler. And it's just taken a microscopic DNA swipe of your mouth.

*FX: Whirr. Bleep.*

**DOCTOR** It feeds the information directly into the TARDIS console. Which saves me asking you whether or not you kissed your friend Alex.

**CHARLEY** Oh.

*FX: TARDIS readouts.*

**DOCTOR** Ah.

**CHARLEY** Oh.

**DOCTOR** The TARDIS can tease out the patterns of human DNA throughout the spacetime vortex. We're heading for the Grayle family home.

**CHARLEY** Ah.[12]

**Scene Five: Creaky Attic.**
*FX: TARDIS materialisation. The door opens.*

**DOCTOR** Shh. Don't disturb the mice.

**CHARLEY** This <u>is</u> Alex's family home! We're in the attic. We came up here once to fetch a cricket bat.

**DOCTOR** Did you meet Sebastian then?

**CHARLEY**     No. He only became interested in Alex recently. Just before Alex left for Singapore. Which tends to support your theory.
**DOCTOR**     As does this.
*FX: Heavy books being lugged.*
**CHARLEY**     Family photos. Documents...
**DOCTOR**     There's Sebastian! And this photo dates from the 1800s. Look over here![13] One very old vase. An amphora.
**CHARLEY**     Isn't that Roman?
**DOCTOR**     Absolutely. And unless there's an antiquarian in the family...
**CHARLEY**     Not that I'm aware of.
**DOCTOR**     Then Sebastian's Christmas present may prove costly. For him. So what do we have?
**CHARLEY**     A name. An unholy Grayle.
**DOCTOR**     A Latin original.
**CHARLEY**     A conversation. I assume you did your usual act of playing the fool and making him talk?
**DOCTOR**     Do I do that?
**CHARLEY**     I, erm, always assumed you did.
**DOCTOR**     Oh. (*A short, rather hurt, pause, then...*) He's immortal, because of his masters. Masters who feed on the energy of worlds and have tremendous power if they can indulge their slaves so much as to create a whole new timeline for them.[14] Plus, he can't have killed me face to face. That's why he went to the trouble of getting his masters to do that.[15] My death must have been extremely unsatisfying.
**CHARLEY**     Yes, do look on the bright side.
**DOCTOR**     And we also have your carefully sampled DNA chain.
**CHARLEY**     (*Embarrassed cough*) Yes.
**DOCTOR**     Let's do some research, shall we? Then: we go on the offensive!

## Scene Six: Roman Camp.
*FX: Whinnies of horses, distant commands, distant trumpets, etc.*

**MARCUS**     Ave, Lucilius. Cold night, eh?
**LUCILIUS**     Ave, Marcus. This rain! You wonder what's going to fall out of the sky next! It's why the Picts breed so hard.
**MARCUS**     Do you mean that they're a hardy breed, or that they spend so much time doing it?
**LUCILIUS**     Both. At least we won't see their fetid hides tonight. Pity the poor sentries up on the wall.
**MARCUS**     Pah, they're Dacians, they don't feel the cold either. I miss dear old Londinium.
**LUCILIUS**     They say it's warm in Rome.
**MARCUS**     You and I never have and never will see Rome. You'll still be conducting the meeting tonight?
**LUCILIUS**     It keeps the men happy. You know, 'we're brothers in the blood of Mithras', and all that.
**MARCUS**     I know it means more to you than that.
**LUCILIUS**     I suppose so. If I hadn't become a priest I'd probably have ended up dead in the arena. But on nights like this... Oh, thank mighty Mithras for the rain, for it blesses the wheat and gives us our grain! Better?

217

**MARCUS**     Sounds more like your old self.

**LUCILIUS**     Indeed. I'm one of the few priests in this loose brotherhood who actually means what the incantation says: I wish I could have been there to kill the demon bull myself. My life seems to be missing that: its greatest challenge, its reason to be. We're never going to have a major battle against the Picts, are we?[16] The wall is there, the empire's there for the Britons...

**MARCUS**     I know, it seems sometimes that we've done all there is to do. That this is as far as we get. We should bring the Picts into the Empire, go as far as there is to go.

**LUCILIUS**     But we're never going to. Anyhow, I'm on my way to sacrifice our earthly bull. If you have a moment? It might cheer us both up.

**MARCUS**     Delighted to help.

*FX: They go on their way. A moment later, the TARDIS appears, and the door opens.*

**DOCTOR**     Nobody about. Come on, Charley!

**CHARLEY**     Wait a minute, I'm trying to keep my toga out of the mud![17]

**DOCTOR**     So am I! Now, you're certain my bottom doesn't look big in this?

**CHARLEY**     Doctor... We really do have more important things to think about.

**DOCTOR**     Of course, of course! But just take a moment to consider how well we're doing! For once, we've arrived somewhere in exactly the right costumes, having thoroughly read up on our destination! It feels luxurious![18]

**CHARLEY**     Was it really worth three weeks at that awful Abbey?

**DOCTOR**     The Abbot of Felsecar is the greatest authority on human genealogy in the Milky Way! And now we know that the first instance of the name Grayle appearing in the records in a British context was right here, on the payroll of this very Roman fort, in 305 AD, the year of the two Emperors, Constantius and Galerius.

**CHARLEY**     So we find Grayle, and shoot him.

**DOCTOR**     We do not shoot him.

**CHARLEY**     Or catapult him, or feed him to the lions!

**DOCTOR**     We find out if he's contacted his alien masters yet, and try to stop whatever he's doing.

**CHARLEY**     You do always go the pretty way. (*Pause*) I'm joking!

**DOCTOR**     Are you?

**CHARLEY**     Or we could stone him, or throw him off the wall of the fort...

**DOCTOR**     Charley...

**Scene Seven: Temple.**

*FX: Liquid being poured into a bowl.*

**LUCILIUS**     It's so much more than blood. It's a sacrament. A promise from Mithras that he won't allow the demon bull to ravage the world again as it did before. (*Pause*) Listen to me! I sound almost Christian, don't I?

**MARCUS**     I like the fact you're into it. For me it's just a good excuse for an amphora of wine and a song afterwards.

**LUCILIUS**     That's how most of the men think.

**MARCUS**     Don't you worry. You should talk to that Christian down in the village: the Greek. There's a fanatic for you. Do you know, he won't admit the existence of other gods!

**LUCILIUS**     They won't get very far like that.

**MARCUS**     I'm amazed they've got this far. A soldier can appreciate this Mithras chap. Persian: we all know what good lads they are. Fond of the sun. Perished in battle. All very noble. This slave Christ was hung on a... (*embarrassed*) you know.

**LUCILIUS**     That's the attraction of fundamentalism. You get to be a fanatic. Our society of comrades gets the common soldier. Not too religious: just looks out where the birds are flying and does a bit of hail Pallas Athena at the weekend–

**MARCUS**     It's the bathing in blood. All lads together. A great laugh. So who's the penitent tonight?

**LUCILIUS**     It's, erm, Decurion Gralae.

**MARCUS**     Oh no. I may be indisposed after all.

**LUCILIUS**     He's just a little... intense.

**MARCUS**     He's mad as the moon! Have you heard some of the stuff he comes out with? It's hardly Mithraism at all!

**LUCILIUS**     So let him do it his own way. What are we, Christians?

**MARCUS**     Listen, Marcus, I'll bet that as we speak, Decurion Gralae is in his tent, muttering to something under his breath. And I doubt that something is Mithras!

**Scene Eight: Tent.**
*FX: GRAYLE is muttering and humming to himself.*

**GRAYLE**     Oh, my great Lord, help me see you as you truly are... show me the truth...

**CHARLEY**     (*From outside the tent*) Well, go on then. Knock.

**DOCTOR**     (*From outside the tent, to Charley*) How exactly do you knock on a tent? Oh well, never mind. Erm, hello? Anybody in?

**GRAYLE**     Yes? Please, please... enter.

**DOCTOR**     Oh, hullo.

**GRAYLE**     Ave, strangers. I am Decurion Sebastius Gralae. How may I aid you?

**CHARLEY**     (*Whisper*) Is that him?

**DOCTOR**     (*Whisper*) A little younger, but yes! (*To GRAYLE*) I'm Ambrosius Clemencis, and this is my friend –

**CHARLEY**     Daisius Daisius.

**GRAYLE**     Odd to see a woman in camp at this time of night. I advise you to leave as soon as possible, the fort is no place for a lady after dark.

**CHARLEY**     Thank you for the warning.

**GRAYLE**     Lady, there is always danger in a military camp. Women are what make the best of men. They offer us absolution, forgive us, and give us a reason to aspire to greatness. Such as you must be protected at all costs. Let me say again, depart swiftly!

**DOCTOR**     I'm very pleased to meet you too, Decurion Gralae. Or have we met before?

**GRAYLE**     Why, no, I don't think so–

**DOCTOR**     Fantastic!

219

**GRAYLE**          What's this about? I have to go and officiate at the temple in a moment.
**DOCTOR**          Oh no no no! My friend and I have vital information about the Picts. This is much more important than anything else you might have got planned.[19]
**GRAYLE**          What sort of information?
**DOCTOR**          Tell him, Dasicus.[20]
**CHARLEY**          Daisius.[21]
**DOCTOR**          I call her that for short. Well?[22]
**CHARLEY**          The Picts are revolting, under a new war leader, King Caractacus.
**GRAYLE**          How do you come by this intelligence?
**DOCTOR**          We were travelling in the hills when we saw the ladies and the pages of the court of King Caractacus–
**CHARLEY**          Just passing by.
**GRAYLE**          That does sound urgent. But it can wait until after I've been to the temple.
**DOCTOR**          Why, Decurion? What's so special about tonight at the temple? Is there going to be a tombola?
**GRAYLE**          I... I... I have to go! Lady, follow my words and leave this place!
*FX: He bursts out of his tent and runs.*
**DOCTOR**          I'm going to follow him! Charley... search the tent!
*FX: HE FOLLOWS.*
**CHARLEY**          Oh, of course. It falls to me to sort through the used undergarments of an ancient Roman.[23]

**Scene Nine: Temple.**
*FX: Latin chanting.*

**MARCUS**          I seem to have misjudged Gralae. Far from being a fanatic, he's not here at all!
**LUCILIUS**          We're going to need someone to manhandle the entrails. And where's the ritual sword?! I can't do everything!
**MARCUS**          It's not on the altar already? Gralae must really have something on his mind. Ah, talk of the bullock...
**GRAYLE**          Sorry, I was disturbed.
**MARCUS**          (*Aside*) I'll say.
**LUCILIUS**          Fine, fine, you're here now, brother. Go and get the entrails. Marcus, if you collect the sword then we should be all set.
*FX: MARCUS walking away and of a chest being unlocked and opened.*
**DOCTOR**          Oh, hello, am I in time for the meeting?
**LUCILIUS**          Of course! Come in, brother! New comrades are always welcome.
**DOCTOR**          I'm not a comrade. I'm shopping around. Trying out all the different cults. Seeing what suits me.
**MARCUS**          Absolutely. The only sane thing to do. I still like a bit of the mysteries of Mercury every now and then.
**LUCILIUS**          There's a place in the third rank. You're just in time for the bloodbath.
**DOCTOR**          The story of my life. Nice sword, by the way. I don't think I've ever seen anything like it. Could I have a look?

**MARCUS**     You're welcome to, brother. I've not seen another like it in all my years in the legion, either. There's something of an aura about it. The story goes that it's Mithras' own sword, his weapon of rustless metal with which he killed the demon bull. It's certainly killed a few bulls here in its time.

**DOCTOR**     Fascinating. And who'll be using it tonight?

**LUCILIUS**     That fellow over there, Decurion Gralae.

**MARCUS**     Unfortunately.

**DOCTOR**     Should he be moving the statues around like that?

**MARCUS**     Oh, by Jupiter! Sorry. He's putting them in the wrong positions!

**LUCILIUS**     Leave him be. I'll have a quiet word afterwards.

**Scene Ten: Tent.**
FX: *A chest being hauled open.*

**CHARLEY**     Oof! If there isn't anything here, then I–

FX: *Bleeping and blooping.*

**NIMON**     (*Over communicator*) Gralae? Is that you?! Gralae?! Is it time yet?!

**CHARLEY**     (*Trying to sound male*) Erm, no! No, it is not time yet![24] Over and out!

FX: *She slams the chest shut.*

**CHARLEY**     Doctor...

**Scene Eleven: Temple.**
FX: *Latin chanting. Faster now.*

**DOCTOR**     So what happens now?

**MARCUS**     Lucilius announces the bloodbathing, and then Gralae carries it out.

**DOCTOR**     He looks a bit strange.

**MARCUS**     He's not supposed to still be wearing his armour. Got here in a rush, apparently.

**DOCTOR**     Where does he come from?

**MARCUS**     Oh, he's from Londinium, like us, of Briton stock. We're not high on the list of Roman tourist spots since we had that independence business. Gralae's a fellow Decurion, changed his family name from something barbarian, but born within the sound of Boudicca's Bells. He's not some Greek mystic, he's just got some wild ideas. He tried to talk to me about them, at the start of our tour of duty, back when he thought I'd listen.

**DOCTOR**     Like what?

**MARCUS**     He kept asking me if we were certain who we should worship. Mithras killed the demon bull, you see, to save us all. But he kept saying that the bull was the powerful one, a kind of cleansing force, that would wipe out our enemies and return the Empire to the glory it held during the realm of Emperor Hadrian. Instead of the mess we're in at the moment.

**DOCTOR**     Isn't that blasphemy?

**MARCUS**     What, like the Jews and Christians have? No, my friend, you believe what you want. If someone who was... (*embarrassed*) you know... can have a cult of his own, anyone can! Oh, now shh, Lucilius is ready to speak.[25]

**LUCILIUS** Dearly beloved, Mithras is with us.

**ALL** And we are with him.

**LUCILIUS** Before we proceed to the bloodletting, I have a few announcements. Centurion Severinus Paulus is getting married on Saturnsday, so let us wish him well in our prayers this evening... (*He continues, under...*)

**CHARLEY** Doctor!

**MARCUS** Oh no, that's quite out of the question I'm afraid, no women in the temple!

**CHARLEY** What?!

**DOCTOR** I thought you didn't believe in blasphemy?

**MARCUS** There's wild speculation on one hand and getting a woman near the blood on the other! Please!

**DOCTOR** Relax. We'll disappear outside for a minute.

### Scene Twelve: Roman Camp.

*FX: The sounds of the temple fade as they pop outside.*

**CHARLEY** You'd think we were in the Dark Ages!

**DOCTOR** Not for a couple of hundred years. Now what is it?

**CHARLEY** There's a device in Grayle's trunk. It looks like it's from the future. A sort of pointy thing, pulsing with light. And, Doctor, I think it must be a radio of some kind. It knew I was there, it spoke to me!

**DOCTOR** Did you bring it?!

**CHARLEY** Well, no. It spoke to me... well, rather angrily, and...[26]

**DOCTOR** They'll be a while with their announcements. Come on, let me see!

### Scene Thirteen: Tent.

*FX: The chest being opened.*

**CHARLEY** It's in here.

*FX: Bleeping and blooping.*

**DOCTOR** Wow!

**CHARLEY** What is it?

**DOCTOR** I have no idea. The technology looks familiar. It's definitely some sort of two-way transmitter. This must have been sent to Grayle by his alien friends. Which means he's already in touch with them. Hmm. Odd.

**CHARLEY** What?

**DOCTOR** It looks as though it should project a hologram as well, but you say it only spoke to you? No pictures?

**CHARLEY** None. So Gralae switched over to sound only?[27] Why would he do that?

**DOCTOR** I really don't know, Charley. Perhaps our Gralae isn't as certain of his masters as he will be in the future.

**CHARLEY** Plus he's wearing his armour wherever he goes: not something an immortal would do.

**DOCTOR** Yes, there's a distinct lack of trust there. And he didn't know who I was, of course. I think now would be the ideal time to put

Grayle off his stride. He's certainly more human than he was back in Singapore. We can use that.

*FX: Bleep!*

**NIMON**     (*Over communicator*) Gralae! The time approaches! Have the sacrifices at the appointed co-ordinates. We will switch to the psionic mind beam for the transfer of power. The first instalment of your immortality awaits you!

**DOCTOR**     Right you are! (*Whisper*) It's tonight! Tonight is when they, whoever they are, begin to make Grayle immortal!

**CHARLEY**     We have to stop it!

## Scene Fourteen: Temple.

**LUCILIUS**     And now let me hand you over to brother Gralae for the sharing of the blood and flesh of the bull that our lord Mithras destroyed that we might live.

**GRAYLE**     Thank you, brother Lucilius. (*Ritual*) I show you the amphorae of the blood. (*A shout*) And now let me show you where you have gone wrong!

*FX: He throws down the vases. They shatter. Uproar.*

**MARCUS**     Oh, how terribly dull. It's gone all over the place. (*Yell*) Will you please stop <u>believing</u> in things, Decurion?! It's very messy! Now where are you going? Oh, in the middle of the ceremony and everything!

*FX: The door slams and we hear bolts sliding home.*

**MARCUS**     I suppose I'll have to haul him back ins– It's locked! That mad old... He's locked us in! What in Hades is he doing?[28]

## Scene Fifteen: Just outside the Temple

**GRAYLE**     I worship the great bull that encompasses all time and space! Master, I can feel you in my head! I call on you to give me now the power that you promised me! I offer the lives of all the men in this temple as a sacrifice worthy of you!

*FX: Roar of building power.*

**CHARLEY**     I thought he was supposed to be in the Temple!

**DOCTOR**     That was for the ritual gesture. This is for the sacrifice proper. Don't you think it's a much more dramatic effect, here at the very centre of the fortress, open to the sky? That sound... The transfer must be starting already! We've got to stop him!

*FX: Sudden hum of power.*

**CHARLEY**     How?! Aaah! That light! What is it?

**DOCTOR**     Gravitic distortion. Gravitational lensing! They're phasing energy through the event horizon of a black hole, channelling it directly into his body. Oh pants![29]

**CHARLEY**     Is this what makes him immortal?

**DOCTOR**     Not quite. This will keep him going for another millennia at least, but he won't be truly immortal until he physically travels through a black hole. The energies are too powerful to be released through space. It looks as though he's quite happy to sacrifice everyone in there for just that much, though. Everyone inside that temple is in terrible danger. We have to get them out!

**CHARLEY**     He's bolted the door. Hold on...

223

*FX: Bolts released. Doors open.*
**DOCTOR**      Come on!

**Scene Sixteen: The Temple.**

**MARCUS**      Gralae, what do you think you're... Oh, it's you two. What's going on here?
**LUCILIUS**      Through the window, look at the sky! It's the colour of blood! It's full of light!
**DOCTOR**      Marcus, you've got to get your men out of here.
**MARCUS**      We are soldiers in the service of Rome! We do not...[30]
**DOCTOR**      If you stay here, you'll all die, for nothing! Facing things like this is my job.
**LUCILIUS**      Do as he says! I feel it in my bones, Marcus. This is not the place for this battle. Leave that for another time.
**MARCUS**      I knew you'd make a prophecy one of these days! Very well! (*To soldiers*) Retreat! Abandon the area! We will return in greater numbers!
*FX: The soldiers run off through the doors.*
**LUCILIUS**      You seem to know what this is about. Can I help?
**DOCTOR**      Erm... I don't know!
**CHARLEY**      Yes, Doctor, what are we going to do?
**DOCTOR**      I'm going to try talking to Gralae.
**CHARLEY**      Talking to him? But he's going to kill you!
**DOCTOR**      In the future. Possibly. But the laws of time are suspended, remember? There's still a chance that I can talk him down.
**CHARLEY**      I'm coming with you.
**DOCTOR**      No. I'm not going to put you in the firing line. Go with Lucilius and make sure that you both get a good distance away from the fortress.
**CHARLEY**      Doctor–
**DOCTOR**      Please Charley, I'm counting on you.
**CHARLEY**      All right. Let's go, Lucilius.
**LUCILIUS**      I just hope Marcus and the others have made it to the gates.

**Scene Seventeen: Roman Camp.**
*FX: Running Roman soldiers.*

**MARCUS**      Keep going men! We're nearly at the gate!
*FX: Roar of energy.*
**MARCUS**      Ignore the sky! It's just the aurora. It's a mirage!
*FX: Time portal FX from The Time of the Daleks. The soldiers react in horror.*
**MARCUS**      A demon! A metal demon! Oh, what has this got to do with anything?! Don't just stand there, attack it!
*FX: Dalek blast. A man screams and falls.*
**MARCUS**      Take it together! Put up your shields! Charge in the tortoise!
*FX: More blasts. More screams.*
**MARCUS**      Push it into the ditch!
*FX: A huge heave. A bash. The Dalek falls into the ditch and explodes.*
**MARCUS**      That's it lads! We killed it! Now come on, to the gates!

Help the servants and the other troopers out! Look to the wounded! Come on, get moving there...

## Scene Eighteen: In the centre of the camp.

*FX: Grayle is immersed in the beam of light.*

**GRAYLE**       I can feel... time and space opening up to me... Thank you, masters, for this grace! Until all time can be mine to inhabit, I will serve you faithfully, Lord!

**DOCTOR**       Gralae!

**GRAYLE**       You! The stranger!

**DOCTOR**       I'm not here to hurt you, Gralae. But I am here to stop you sacrificing the lives of all these people.

**GRAYLE**       They are lambs to be set on the stone! They worship gods which do not exist. Heroes and sprites! Their sacrifice will bring the true Lords into this world once again!

**DOCTOR**       How? How did you find them?!

**GRAYLE**       In my meditations on the nature of power. In my prayers to Mithras. How foolish I was, to imagine he was the centre of all things. As foolish as he, when he thought he had killed the demon bull. That demon called to me, with his fellows. They made me solid offers, came before me in visions. They will take me out of this ignoble place, so far from the fortune that should be mine.

**DOCTOR**       A fortune where? In Rome?

**GRAYLE**       In Londinium, where the eldest of all my brothers has inherited the villa. I changed my family name to distance myself from such humility. Now I know I shall outlive him, and claim my family's honours and possessions. All the wealth of an undying man!

**DOCTOR**       That's why you're going to doom an entire world? An entire universe?! For money?!

**GRAYLE**       As yet I know not what my masters desire of me. But I think you seek to mislead me, stranger. My masters will grant me power, the strength to make Rome glorious again.

**DOCTOR**       You really have no idea what you're doing, do you? Gralae, I travel in time. I have spoken to you in the future. Then you had already doomed the world. But it doesn't have to be like that.

**GRAYLE**       Enough! Soon my masters will come, and then my ascension can truly begin. Your lies will not deter me.

**DOCTOR**       No. You're wasting your time, Gralae. You're beaten already. The sacrifice you offered has escaped. Without the lives of those men, your masters will stay just where they are. You may live a few extra years, but immortality?[31] I don't think so.

**GRAYLE**       No! How dare you?!

**DOCTOR**       For the sake of this world and everyone who lives here, present and future. I can promise you, Gralae, every time you try to summon your masters I will be there to stop you.

**GRAYLE**       Perhaps I should remove you now then. I am a soldier, and you have declared war on me and the ones I follow. Is it not better to destroy you sooner rather than later?

**DOCTOR**       You're making a mistake, Gralae. Why can't you just live out your extra years and gain the fortune you want so badly? We need never see each other again.

**GRAYLE**     You underestimate me. Extra time is welcome, but it is not immortality. I will only be satisfied when I am immortal, seated among the gods, and my Lords have this world in their hands! If you seek to stop me, then you make yourself my enemy. Make your peace with <u>your</u> gods!

**CHARLEY**     Get away from him!

**DOCTOR**     Charley! I told you to –

**CHARLEY**     I won't let you hurt him, Gralae. Don't come any closer, or I'll use this thing, I swear I will!

**DOCTOR**     The sword from the temple. It looks a bit big for you.

**GRAYLE**     You hide behind women, now? When you know I would never harm a lady? You are not only my enemy, but a coward!

**DOCTOR**     I'm not hiding, Gralae –

**GRAYLE**     No matter. You have won this round, stranger. You have spoilt my sacrifice. But if you get in my way again, with the lady or without, next time I shall put an end to your meddling!

**CHARLEY**     Doctor, he's getting away!

**DOCTOR**     Let him. We've done all we can do here. Oh, and thank you for saving my life! But please don't make a habit of disobeying everything I say. I usually have a very good reason.

**CHARLEY**     You're welcome. I think I'll keep this sword. It's very jolly.

**DOCTOR**     (*Urgently*) But now, we've got to get going! Grayle ran off for a reason, and I don't think it was to return an overdue library book.

*FX: Collapse of masonry. Rumbling.*

**CHARLEY**     The temple's shaking! Doctor, what's going on?!

**DOCTOR**     Grayle's alien masters were trying to beam the sacrifices to their homeworld using a transmat beam. The shockwaves will destroy the rest of the fortress!

**CHARLEY**     You're right. We do have to get going![32]

*FX: more masonry falls to the ground. A low rumbling is heard.*

### Scene Nineteen: Roman Camp.

*FX: Steady roaring of building energy. Doctor and Charley running.*

**DOCTOR**     Come on! Back to the TARDIS! Tell me you got everyone else out!

**CHARLEY**     Lucilius was a bit of a straggler but I saw him on his way. They'll all be well clear by now. We're the only ones in danger, actually!

**DOCTOR**     Not far now...

*FX: Sound of raw power as a beam engulfs the temple. The temple collapses.*

**CHARLEY**     There goes the Temple!

**DOCTOR**     And us next! Come on! The shockwave is going to hit any moment...

*FX: Roar. Things start to explode.*

**CHARLEY**     The huts! The fences! The sky![33]

**DOCTOR**     Run![34]

*FX: Roar. More explosions, over the following.*

**DOCTOR**     We sprinted through the fort as the shockwave raced behind us. Buildings exploded into ash as it gained ground. Grayle's masters hadn't got the energy they needed that night, and the destruction was all in vain. When we reached the TARDIS, we were only seconds ahead of the blast.

**CHARLEY**      Doctor!
**DOCTOR**      Key... Key, key, key! Ah, there we are!
*FX: Unlocks the door.*
**CHARLEY**      Doctor! We're not going to make it in time!
*FX: A vast explosion of energy.*

**END OF PART ONE.**

# Part Two

## Scene Nineteen: (Reprise).

**CHARLEY**    Doctor!
**DOCTOR**    Key... Key, key, key! Ah, there we are!
*FX: Unlocks the door.*
**CHARLEY**    Doctor! We're not going to make it in time!
*FX: A vast explosion of energy. But under it we hear the TARDIS take-off sounds.*

## Scene Twenty: TARDIS Interior.
*FX: TARDIS interior noises.*

**DOCTOR**    That was close!
**CHARLEY**    I'll say! Doctor – oh no, your toga's on fire!
**DOCTOR**    What?! Quick, help me!
*FX: They beat out his toga.*
**DOCTOR**    And that was such a great toga, too. We only got away from that by the skin of our noses. Ow, look out where you're pointing that sword![35]
**CHARLEY**    Sorry. I'll put it in the umbrella stand. So what do we do now?
**DOCTOR**    Grayle seemed to think that he would get another chance at immortality. I don't think it'll be for a while though: he was pretty put out. I suspect his masters are limited by some astronomical alignment, something that lets them transfer their power only at certain times... We have to find the point in space and time where they try again.[36] A point where I can somehow sever the link between them. And here's how we find it!
**CHARLEY**    You're not going to need another sample, are you?
**DOCTOR**    No, no. I've set the TARDIS to trace the point of origin for that transmat beam.
*FX: Bleeping of TARDIS console.*
**DOCTOR**    Here we are. Look at this. The beam originated in the Ordinand system. A rather unlucky system by all accounts, got a black hole almost on their doorstep. That would make sense. Thanks to that black hole, and the sheer number of planets in the system, they can only transmit to Earth every...
*FX: Bleeping of calculation.*
**DOCTOR**    750 years or so! I think we can count on Grayle's masters having another go. Their window of opportunity is only open for a year, but that's more than enough time. How about paying Grayle another visit?
**CHARLEY**    Doctor, have you stopped to ask yourself... Why does Grayle want to kill you?
**DOCTOR**    Well I am a rather troublesome person. He probably just wants me out of the way. Actually... in Singapore there <u>was</u> a bit more to it than that...
**CHARLEY**    From what you said, he absolutely <u>hated</u> you. But he

didn't recognise you in the Roman fort. That was the first time you'd met. What if he's after revenge for you getting in the way just then? And for all the times we're going to do it again?

**DOCTOR**    So if I hadn't tried to stop him killing me, he wouldn't want to kill me?

**CHARLEY**    Yes.

**DOCTOR**    If you think about things like that and travel through time, Charley, you'll turn your brain into a spiral staircase. And I've heard of people who've vanished up staircases like that. 'Zagreus sits inside your head/Zagreus lives among the dead/Zagreus sees you in your bed/And eats you when you're sleeping', as mother used to say.[37]

**CHARLEY**    Zagreus?

**DOCTOR**    A character from a Gallifreyan nursery rhyme. A bad guy who was a know-all to boot.[38] But that's not important. Whatever Grayle's personal motives for wanting to see me dead, there's still the matter of his masters, who, as we speak, have fed upon the Earth and changed the whole timeline in the process. Those alien 'demons', whatever they are, might want me dead themselves.

**CHARLEY**    Point taken. So where are we going?

*FX: Bleeps from console.*

**DOCTOR**    Ah. One of my favourite times and places. London in the year 1055. The court of King Edward, known as the Confessor, during the time known as 'The Rule of Solomon'.

**CHARLEY**    So he was a very wise King Edward?

**DOCTOR**    Yes, but they didn't really mean that then. Solomon was known for being a <u>peaceful</u> man. This chap was very cunning. (*An uneasy thought*) And so was his wife. (*Brightening*) Still, they kept England at peace for decades.

*FX: The TARDIS stops.*

**DOCTOR**    Grab a gown from the wardrobe room, Charley.[39] We're off to hunt Sebastian Grayle in an era of harmony and tranquillity.

## Scene Twenty-One: Edward's Court.

*FX: Clattering of chains. Roaring of man in them.*

**EDWARD**    He's not going to calm down, is he?

**EDITH**    (*To captive*) Aelfgar, you have murdered and abused your subjects as Earl of East Anglia.

**EDWARD**    (*To captive*) Oh calm down! You're not some Irish Viking. Do try and act like an Anglishman.

**EDITH**    We hearby decree – (*To EDWARD*) Oh, sorry, you should do this bit.

**EDWARD**    I suppose. I wish you could. (*To captive*) Aelfgar of East Anglia, you are banished to the wilds of Scotland. Do not set foot upon any of the Earldoms of Angleland upon pain of death.

**EDITH**    (*To guards*) Take him away.

*FX: The sounds of horns. The thrashing and yelling prisoner is dragged away.*[40]

**EDWARD**    So who shall we give his Earldom to? Plenty of candidates. But who's the best tactical choice? Your brothers in the Godwin family have too many sons.

**EDITH**    It's a family trait. Present company excepted.

**EDWARD** (*Whisper*) Oh, my Edith, dear Swan Neck, I wish we could have a child... but...

**EDITH** (*Whisper*) I was joking, Edward. You know I could never hurt you with words like that. I feel able to play lightly with our misfortune.

**EDWARD** (*Whisper*) Misfortune? I haven't heard my nature called that before.

**EDITH** (*Whisper*) Well I call it a misfortune when you're off in chambers with William the Bastard of Normandy for a whole weekend.

**EDWARD** (*Whisper*) And didn't Harald Hardrada of Denmark entertain you enough over that time?

**EDITH** (Whisper) Ooh, they think you're <u>so</u> holy! They say that's why we have no heir. Your mind's on <u>higher</u> things.

*FX: The sound of horns again.*

**EDWARD** (*Whisper*) Shush, here comes the Bishop. Leofric of Exeter.

**EDITH** Oh. I like him.

**EDWARD** Don't provoke me, Edith.

**GRAYLE** Greetings, my King. My Queen.

**EDWARD** What is your message for us at this Court of Lent, your grace?

**GRAYLE** Only to say that my mines produce fine jewellry for my lieges, of which I humbly offer two pieces.

*FX: The tinkle of jewellry.*

**EDITH** Why, Leofric, this necklet is lovely.

**EDWARD** This chain is warm against my throat. Most comforting. London may be of our favourite courts, and this grand hall is magnificently decorated for our presence, but it does get a bit chilly.

**EDITH** What is this comfortable metal?

**GRAYLE** A new one, my lady, known only to the expert miners who have opened new shafts to my instructions in the south-westerly tip of Earl Godwin's Earldom.

**EDITH** This was most skilful of you, your grace. We shall talk later at supper.

**EDWARD** Now you are excused.

**GRAYLE** My lieges.

*FX: Horns.*

**EDITH** Most generous! Surely you agree that Leofric is ripe for Earldom.

**EDWARD** Yes. Bishops often make good Earls. They don't go stealing nuns like some of your family.

**EDITH** And he's not a Godwin. If you must ignore my kin.

**EDWARD** Take my arm, Swan Neck. We will go to our meal and ponder this further.

## Scene Twenty-Two: Elsewhere in the Court.

*FX: Curtain being swept aside.*

**DOCTOR** I think the old girl will be safe in there.

**CHARLEY** I like this dress. All these brooches.

**DOCTOR** Two things the Saxons were good at. Jewellery and politics.

| | |
|---|---|
| **CHARLEY** | But why couldn't I bring my sword? |
| **DOCTOR** | Because you're a lady. Do try and remember.[41] |
| **CHARLEY** | (*Shock*) Doctor! Look out! |
| **DOCTOR** | (*Whisper*) What?![42] |
| **CHARLEY** | Over there! The guards! |
| **DOCTOR** | They're just standing by the doors to the great hall. |

**CHARLEY**     Doctor, I know my Bayeaux Tapestry! The chaps with the funny nose pieces are Normans! The web of time must have been really fooled about with, they must have invaded early!

**DOCTOR**     Charley, Charley, Charley! Norman soldiers were garrisoned in Britain years before the conquest!

**CHARLEY**     They were?

**DOCTOR**     Yes. Edward and his wife Edith promised the throne to William of Normandy, Harald Hardrada of Norway, everyone who wanted it! They kept them at each other's throats for decades. Nobody wanted to invade, because they all thought they were going to inherit! This is a cosmopolitan court, full of Danes and Saxons and Angles and Jutes and Frenchmen and Normans and Norwegians and Irishmen and Scots and, most importantly, one rather ancient Ancient Briton.

**CHARLEY**     How do you know he's here?

**DOCTOR**     Well the TARDIS was picking up signs of transmissions from the Ordinand System to this city. But there's this as well.

*FX: Bleeps.*

**DOCTOR**     A power detector. There's a radioactive source in this building. I'd be willing to bet that Grayle's got something to do with it. I'll keep the detector switched off under my robes until we're free to explore. Which reminds me. Here, swallow this.

**CHARLEY**     What is it?

**DOCTOR**     Anti-radiation pill. It'll protect you from any harmful effects from the radiation, if we get close to it.[43] Now come on, let's go and say hello to the Royals over dinner.

## Scene Twenty-Three: Great Hall.

*FX: Conversation, Saxon music in the background, the thud and slice of primitive cutlery.*

**EDWARD**     (*Calling to a courtier*) An excellent lamb, freeman. Your culinary skills bring fame to this court.

**EDITH**     Have you given any more thought to Bishop Leofric taking over the Earldom of East Anglia?

**EDWARD**     I haven't given much thought to anything. I have an ache in my throat.

**EDITH**     Myself also. London's halls <u>do</u> bring chills. Why must they build these things right next to the river, it makes my bones ache and – [44]

**EDWARD**     But ho, look who's here! (*To all*) All of you! To your feet! Sound the horns!

*FX: Horns.*

**EDWARD**     It is the Reverend Doctor of Bruges, long of my acquaintance, and that of my father. Welcome, Doctor!

**EDITH**     (*Whisper to herself*) Oh no, not him!

**DOCTOR**     My liege. (*Meaningful pause*) My lady.

**EDWARD**     Rise, Reverend Doctor. This man, Edith, before you and

231

I met, helped treat my father Aethelred of a fever that would have dispatched him.

**EDITH**          (*Pretending she doesn't know the Doctor*) Really?

**DOCTOR**          Aethelred was unready to die that night! He fought like an ox. Speaking of which, this is the Lady Charlotte.

**CHARLEY**          I beg your pardon?!

**DOCTOR**          (*Whisper*) I mean you're a fighter. 'My liege, my lady' now, quick![45]

**CHARLEY**          My liege. My lady.

**EDITH**          Isn't she rather... young... to be travelling with... a physician such as yourself, Doctor?

**DOCTOR**          What she lacks in experience she makes up for in sheer gall.

**CHARLEY**          (*Whisper*) An ox with gall? I'm keeping a list of these, you know.

**EDWARD**          Sit and take wine and food with us. Had we heard of your coming, we would have sent messengers ahead to meet you.

**DOCTOR**          Thank you, my liege. (*Whisper to CHARLEY*) Do you see who's sitting over there, looking like he's smelt something nasty?

**CHARLEY**          (*Whisper*) Grayle! He hasn't aged a day.

**DOCTOR**          (*Whisper*) Oh, I think he has. A little tension around the eyes. You learn to see such details when you're used to the bitchiness of Time Lord society. (*To EDWARD*) My King, who is that fellow?

**EDWARD**          That's—

**EDITH**          Bishop Leofric of Exeter. Why do you ask?

**DOCTOR**          I've met him before.

**EDITH**          And was that a happy meeting?

**DOCTOR**          Perhaps I should ask him.

**EDITH**          Then it was not.

**DOCTOR**          Would the Queen excuse me?

**EDITH**          Indeed. (*Whispered aside*) I have before. (*To CHARLEY*) So, young Lady Charlotte, do take some wine.

**CHARLEY**          Thank you, my lady.

**EDITH**          Now, what of Bruges?

**CHARLEY**          Oh! It's... much the same as it was...

*FX: Table talk.*

**DOCTOR**          So, Grayle, or should I say Leofric? You've got yourself a grand old Saxon name now. Why are you at court? What are you planning?

**GRAYLE**          Doctor, is that what they called you? Doctor who?

**DOCTOR**          My enemies never ask me that. Isn't that terrible, that they know me better than my friends?

**GRAYLE**          You've travelled through time to come here. My masters have warned me to guard against your arrival. And now there you are! Before my eyes! You spoke truth that day in the fortress then, if this is no dream.

**DOCTOR**          Pinch me if you like.

**GRAYLE**          I will do more than that. It has been centuries since I saw you last. During that time you have sometimes been far from my thoughts. But never far from my heart. I spent eighty years in penitence and guilt in a community of monks on the Northern Isles. Only to see them all die of their years while I remained young. I have married twelve wives, but had no children, and watched every wife fade before my eyes into a crone. This world hangs around my neck as a stone at the throat of a drowning man. But whenever I looked up I remembered the words of my masters, telling me that this world would pass. And in that I was constantly reminded of you. Of the man whose interference insured that no season would pass for me without fear and pain. You prevented me from gaining the transcendence of a true immortal. And there you are now, the distance of my arm away. My hand wants to go to my mace and slay you, for all my seasons of fear. (*Furious and impotent*) The only thing that prevents it... the only thing...

**DOCTOR**      Is that you're well in with the royals and don't want to upset the dinner table. Do you still consider your masters to be gods?

**GRAYLE**      Blasphemer! Would I have taken holy orders if I did?

**DOCTOR**      Then... you and I don't have to be enemies at all! If you've found a faith–

**GRAYLE**      Faith in the power of the Lord, who smites his enemies. Faith that I am being courted by angels of providence, and offered a truly graceful lifetime to be a new messiah to these fallen children!

**DOCTOR**      Oh dear. You're still off your rocker.

**GRAYLE**      (*Roar*) Have a care, villein!

**DOCTOR**      Careful with the mace. No weapons at table. So you must be busy right now. You failed your masters last time. What have they asked you to do to regain their favour?

**GRAYLE**      I don't have to tell you anything!

**DOCTOR**      But you're a gloater, Grayle. I know you are.

**GRAYLE**      What have you against me, to follow me? To reappear now, when my ascension is nearly complete?

**DOCTOR**      Must we go through this again? Your actions will ultimately lead to the destruction of the planet Earth, the conquest of all time and space![46] I can't and won't allow that. Think again about what your masters are. For all our sakes.

*FX: Table talk.*

**EDWARD**      Fascinating, lady, fascinating![47] To hear you talk so fondly of your native city.

**EDITH**      Hmm. Next time we have visitors from Bruges I must dance this 'Charleston'.

**CHARLEY**      It's all the rage, my lady. I think you'd – (*Starts to cough and choke*)

*FX: Drops her goblet. Falls to the ground.*

**DOCTOR**      Charley!

**EDWARD**      She's ill! Call the apothecaries!

**DOCTOR**      Let me, my liege!

**EDITH**      The poor little girl! Whatever is the matter?

**DOCTOR**      She's got an accelerated heartbeat, she's sweating and she's unconscious. This isn't an illness, she was fine a minute ago! She's been poisoned!

*FX: A gasp from the courtiers.*

**EDWARD**      In our court! Who would dare?!

**EDITH**      We must make her expel the substance!

**DOCTOR**      No we mustn't! (*Remembering his place*) My lady. I have medicines in my travelling chest. Let me take her there.

*FX: He heaves her into his arms.*

| | |
|---|---|
| **EDWARD** | Clear his way! Let no man bar his path! |
| **DOCTOR** | Hang on, Charley! Just hang on! |

**Scene Twenty-Four: TARDIS Interior.**
*FX: The doors open.*

**DOCTOR**     The nanites of the TARDIS console room should be whizzing around your body right now, Charley! It won't take long. I'm sorry I said that about the ox. And the gall.
*FX: TARDIS doors open.*

| | |
|---|---|
| **GRAYLE** | A mighty magician's cabinet. I'm impressed. |
| **DOCTOR** | Grayle! How did you follow me in here?! Oh. Don't tell me... |
| **GRAYLE** | The door was open. |
| **DOCTOR** | You did this to her! |
| **GRAYLE** | Indeed I did. I thought you'd take her back to your vehicle. How spacious it is. |
| **DOCTOR** | She could have been killed! |
| **GRAYLE** | Yes. But what of it? Within sixty years or so she'll be dead anyway. |
| **DOCTOR** | Why is that important?! |
| **GRAYLE** | Because this world is designed by man and God on the basis of mortality. I returned to my inheritance, Doctor, and eventually I received it. My brothers died... without issue. |
| **DOCTOR** | And you had a hand in that? |
| **GRAYLE** | I don't remember. Tiny, short, lives. I've ceased to notice the way dust motes like that quibble. I concern myself now with no one but Earls, and Kings, and angels. |
| **DOCTOR** | Then no wonder you're as mad as they come! |
| **GRAYLE** | My new state, and the slow processes of influence and investment have given me a land of my own, a bishopric. And soon they will give me more. |
| **DOCTOR** | An earldom, perhaps? |
| **GRAYLE** | The world, Doctor. What less could one desire? |
| **DOCTOR** | As well as your immortality? Your masters are getting more generous by the second! How are you going to get hold of the world, then? |
| **GRAYLE** | My masters will bestow upon me the Earldom of Earth when they come at last. |
| **DOCTOR** | You're a fool to believe that. And I suppose they want nothing at all in return? |
| **GRAYLE** | It will be my efforts that will allow their entrance to this world. I have gathered the holy metal, followed their instructions. They are grateful enough for that. |
| **CHARLEY** | (*Weakly*) That thing you do still works, doesn't it? |
| **DOCTOR** | Charley, you're all right! |
| **GRAYLE** | Don't turn your back on <u>me</u> for the sake of a short-lived wench! |
| **DOCTOR** | (*Whisper.*) A short-lived – (*Roar of anger*) You...! (*He stops within inches of GRAYLE*) Oh dear. |
| **GRAYLE** | (*Shout*) Stop! Yes, I carry a blade as well as my mace! And you go unarmed! Why couldn't I kill you now?[48] |

234

**DOCTOR**     Because the King's servants will already be searching for me.

**GRAYLE**     And in this machine they will not find you. I closed the door behind me.[49]

**DOCTOR**     Because when first we met, you gave me the impression that you killed me at long range.

**GRAYLE**     Interesting! So we meet in the future, and I have done this deed? But I have free will, and would do it now!

**DOCTOR**     Because of the hatstand.

**GRAYLE**     The what?

*FX: Thump. GRAYLE groans and falls.*

**CHARLEY**     The hatstand.

**DOCTOR**     Thank you, Charley.

**CHARLEY**     Well, now he's tried to kill me, are you feeling more inclined to save yourself and the entire world by dropping him into a volcano or something?

**DOCTOR**     No. And I'm horrified that you're still suggesting that.

**CHARLEY**     I only say it because I know you won't do it. But –

**DOCTOR**     Yes?

**CHARLEY**     We could drop him off on some perfectly nice but deserted planet. Just get him out of the way.

**DOCTOR**     And then his masters, as soon as their alignment allowed, would either rescue him or pick a new disciple.

**CHARLEY**     Oh well. At least you got some information out of him.

**DOCTOR**     Yes, he's swapping metal for immortality. Not a very good bargain, I'd have thought. We need to find out what he's doing with the metal... but for now, we're expected back in the great hall.

**CHARLEY**     So what shall we do with him?

**DOCTOR**     I'd like to lock him in here for a while, but left alone he could do serious damage. Besides, in the end he would get out of any confinement. That's one of the most wonderful things about Lady Time, isn't it? How nothing's constant. How everything decays and changes.

**CHARLEY**     You call that wonderful?

**DOCTOR**     I call it absolutely beautiful. How would it be if everything was always the same? If you never got too big for your dresses, if you never got to pass them on to your sister... If the rainy autumn lasted forever and spring never came. At least I change. I'm stumbling my way through bodies like I own a particularly dangerous bicycle. Grayle never changes. Not inside. Not who he is. So time piles on top of him and kills everything good. No one should have to go through that.

**CHARLEY**     If we're going to help him, we're going to have to separate him from his masters. So we need to find out more about them, don't we?

**DOCTOR**     Yes. Sorry, was I soliloquising again? Filthy habit. Come on, let's get him outside and hide him in a corner somewhere.

**Scene Twenty-Five: Elsewhere in the Court.**
*FX: Curtain being swept aside.*

**CHARLEY**     He's heavy!
**DOCTOR**     Get him behind the... Ah.
**EDITH**     What have you done to our bishop?
**DOCTOR**     My lady! We only–

235

**CHARLEY**    Rendered him unconscious.

**EDITH**    You seem quite well now, young lady. You said earlier, Doctor, that yourself and Leofric had been enemies...

**DOCTOR**    Um. Doesn't look good, does it?

**EDITH**    Guards! Take them!

**DOCTOR**    Edith! Come on, I know what this is really about!

**EDITH**    Then you will have to find something else to ponder in our prison.

*FX: The DOCTOR and CHARLEY are hustled away by the guards.*

### Scene Twenty-Six: Cell.

*FX: The creak of chains.*

**CHARLEY**    I hardly credited it that all those cartoonists in Punch might have had it accurately, but it seems they did. We are actually manacled to a wall.[50]

**DOCTOR**    It's a form of torture.

**CHARLEY**    Odd, because it doesn't hurt.

**DOCTOR**    In a couple of days it will. If they leave us for a week we'll be in continuous agony.

**CHARLEY**    Oh.

**DOCTOR**    But cheer up. Look, there's a mouse!

**CHARLEY**    I am deeply cheered. So what did you mean? When you told Queen Edith that you knew what this was really about?

**DOCTOR**    Oh, she knows I wouldn't hurt her bishop. She's just upset because I left her at the altar.

**CHARLEY**    You... did what?

**DOCTOR**    Before Edward and Edith met, Edward was a puppet ruler, put on the throne by Edith's family, the Godwins. They decided they wanted an heir to the throne, so they married him off to their daughter, Edith, the most beautiful woman in England. Probably.

**CHARLEY**    Yes, but–

**DOCTOR**    But Edith turned out to be also the most intelligent woman in England. She and Edward really liked each other. And they spent the next few decades making all of England's enemies fall into their own traps.

**CHARLEY**    So you and she had a lot in common.[51]

**DOCTOR**    I met her at her father's court. Much as I met Edward at his. I really liked the idea of spending some time talking about politics with the most brilliant tactician of her age. Only Edith saw it a bit differently.[52] One leap year she asked me to marry her.

**CHARLEY**    And you said–?

**DOCTOR**    I must have mumbled. And then everyone was talking about a wedding, before her father returned to say no, and I couldn't see her beforehand, and none of her courtiers seemed to want to listen when I said I didn't want to marry her, and one thing led to another and...[53]

**CHARLEY**    And you did a runner!

**DOCTOR**    It was either that or become part of British history.

*FX: Door opening.*

**GRAYLE**    I hope you are both considering your immortal souls.

**CHARLEY**    You! I should have thumped you harder.

**GRAYLE**    The King is most displeased with you for attacking one of his clergy.

**DOCTOR**   If I could speak to him–
**GRAYLE**   But he's indisposed. An illness. I've been granted leave to take your confession, Doctor. To forgive you for your sins against me. I intend to hear you beg your contrition at great length, but first, let's see what tricks you have up your sleeve.
*FX: Rustle as he searches him.*
**GRAYLE**   What, for example, is this?
**DOCTOR**   It's a musical instrument.
**GRAYLE**   Then how does it play?
*FX: Bleeps and bloops. Then the roar of a geiger counter.*
**GRAYLE**   (*Yells*) It roars at me!
*FX: It thumps onto the floor and the roar reduces to a hiss.*
**CHARLEY**   (*Whisper*) Doctor, if that's the radiation detector...
**DOCTOR**   Just a harmless tracking device. Still a man of your age, eh, Grayle? Frightened of the great beyond. Don't your masters scare you, just a little bit?
**GRAYLE**   Of course they do. It is wise to fear the angels of the Lord. And it would be wise of you to fear me. And my blade.
**CHARLEY**   Doctor...
**GRAYLE**   First you will suffer slowly. Then the girl.
**DOCTOR**   Charley, close your eyes.
*FX: The DOCTOR screams in agony.*
**CHARLEY**   Stop! Please! Stop hurting him!
**GRAYLE**   Very well. Hmm, you are a short-haired wench, aren't you?
**CHARLEY**   I really... didn't mean... that you should hurt me instead.
**GRAYLE**   Unfortunately, that's exactly how I took it.
**DOCTOR**   (*Panting*) Grayle, if you harm her–
*FX: CHARLEY shrieks in pain.*
**GRAYLE**   Hush, that was just a nick on your ear. Men suffer worse at the barber.
**DOCTOR**   If you harm her I will show you suffering beyond anything you've experienced so far! Do you hear me, Grayle?!
**GRAYLE**   You dare?!
**CHARLEY**   No, Doctor, don't make him go to you, not for me–
*FX: The DOCTOR screams again. The door opens.*
**EDITH**   Leofric?
**GRAYLE**   My queen.
**DOCTOR**   Edith... Thank goodness...
**EDITH**   Do not thank anything yet, Doctor.[54]
**CHARLEY**   You're not here to free us?
**DOCTOR**   From the look of that smile, no, she isn't.
**EDITH**   His grace the Bishop has been a good servant to the crown. And the Doctor has been only a false traitor to me.
**DOCTOR**   Edith, I was very fond of you. I just don't do weddings.
**EDITH**   Leofric has offered me a way to keep Angleland safe for centuries hence. And when dear Edward dies... and somehow Leofric has made his way past all the servants and food tasters to bring the King to the brink of that condition... then myself and the new Earl of East Anglia will have a baby strong enough to keep the throne.
**GRAYLE**   My loyalty to my Queen is absolute, and the necklet she wears is testimony to it.

**DOCTOR** My lady, I can give you gifts too. The sparkling object on the floor, for instance...

**GRAYLE** No! Wait, my—

**EDITH** What, this?

*FX: She picks it up. Bleeps and bloops.*

**EDITH** An odd sort of gift. A lantern of tiny lights and chiming noises. The handiwork of Bruges is something to behold, but for what?

**DOCTOR** (*Realising something*) For England, my lady.

**EDITH** What does the knave – oh!

*FX: She stumbles.*

**GRAYLE** My lady! Take my arm!

**EDITH** My... throat... so warm... I feel so weak...

**CHARLEY** Doctor! Has the tracer done something to her?

**DOCTOR** Of course not.

*FX: She falls to the ground.*

**GRAYLE** My lady! My lady? (*Then more carefully*) My lady, can you hear me? No, no I think not... (*He starts to laugh*)

**CHARLEY** What have you done to her?

**GRAYLE** Exactly what I have done to her husband. The necklets they wear are made of a holy metal, mined in great quantity by my servants. The metal kills. It can kill you slowly, over months, like an illness, as my men discovered.[55] But then my masters deemed that we should stack it in a pile with peat and lead, and it emerged in a form that only I could handle safely, a form that burnt my servants like the sun, and killed them in hours.

**DOCTOR** Humans will call it plutonium.

**CHARLEY** (*Puzzled*) But, Doctor—

**DOCTOR** And you made two necklaces of it to kill the King and Queen. Are you hoping to take their place?

**GRAYLE** A hundred sail barges will arrive at the docks this night, each loaded with the deadly metal. Each controlled by a master who will be as dead as the ferryman across the infernal river, though he will know it not.

**DOCTOR** You're bringing them here.[56] A hundred sail-barges full of plutonium. That's a lot of raw power. But what do you intend to do with it, hmm?

**GRAYLE** I shall use it. It will bring my masters to me.

**CHARLEY** None of this is in the history books, is it?

**DOCTOR** No, but if it stopped now, it could be smoothed over. The court's been exposed to a lot of radiation. It'll persist for a few decades. But that would explain the mad genetics of... of the next few rulers.

**GRAYLE** Why so prim, Doctor? There is nobody here to be dismayed by your knowledge of the future.

**EDITH** Isn't there? What a wonderful plan you had. A pity it's going to fail.

**GRAYLE** What? You live!

*FX: The door crashes open.*

**EDWARD** She does, traitor! As do I! Do you think we have kept this throne so long by not recognising death when we feel it at our throats?

**GRAYLE** The necklets... replacements!

**DOCTOR** Which is why the Queen didn't set off the detector. She really does remind me of me.

238

**GRAYLE**   It matters not! You cannot stop me!

*FX: Sword drawn, scuffle.*

**EDWARD**   Guards! Gua – oh.

**EDITH**   Unhand me!

**GRAYLE**   Another word, my liege, and the Lady Edith is no more. My triumph is still at hand! I depart to enjoy it!

*FX: The door slams as he dashes out.*

**EDWARD**   Guards! Where are you? Useless lot. (*Calls again*) Pursue him! Pursue Leofric.

**DOCTOR**   Your guards won't be able to stop him! If plutonium doesn't harm him, he's pretty near invulnerable. Get me out of these manacles. That man is my responsibility.

*FX: The shackles are struck off.*

**EDWARD**   You know my wife well, it seems, Doctor.

**DOCTOR**   Only as well as you do, my liege.

**EDITH**   You two are the only men wily enough to see through my tricks.

**EDWARD**   Here, if you would pursue the villein, take my sword.

**EDITH**   For England, Doctor.

**DOCTOR**   I don't do swords, either, my Queen, there's always a better way. We have to stop those barges from unloading! Tell your men to expect a fight at the docks! Prepare them to defend the court! Charley, you go back to the TARDIS. I'll deal with Grayle!

**CHARLEY**   Be careful, Doctor!

*FX: The DOCTOR runs off.*

**EDWARD**   My dear Edith, do you ever think you married the wrong man?

**EDITH**   My dear Edward– (*Pause*) Shall we see to those boats?

## Scene Twenty-Seven: Battlements.

*FX: Windy view of the Thames far below.*

**DOCTOR**   I clambered out onto the roof of the hall and looked down. Along the river floated a necklace of bright jewels, each barge burning a lantern above its cargo of death. Power enough to do anything, but I already had an idea of what Grayle intended for it. It wasn't a comfortable thought. When I caught sight of Grayle, standing on the wall, he was surrounded by a nimbus of light. His masters had already started to send their power to him.

**GRAYLE**   Doctor. You are too late. Soon you shall see my masters face to face. They have already granted me another taste of their ultimate reward, and so much more is to come.

**DOCTOR**   No. I'm here to stop you.

**GRAYLE**   Stop me? You mean kill me. For what I did to your companion.

**DOCTOR**   I mean stop you. Any way I can.

**GRAYLE**   So you have a moral code? An aversion to killing? But not an aversion to dooming me to this half-life of a thousand years!

**DOCTOR**   Grayle, you doomed yourself. But you can save yourself just as easily. Don't do this.

**GRAYLE**   After all this work? I think not. See my machine, Doctor. My masters instructed me in its particulars, but I built it. Is it not a fine sight? The holy metal will lend its power, and I shall bring my masters to my side. The angels of the Lord shall walk upon the Earth once again.

**DOCTOR**      Those are not angels! Grayle, can't you see?! They are monsters, and they seek to turn you into one as well!

**GRAYLE**      Then at least I will no longer be the youngest son, the last promoted, the furthest banished!

**DOCTOR**      Look inside yourself! They're turning you into something inhuman! The Grayle I met at the Temple of Mithras would not act as you do now. He was misguided, but not evil. He would have spared the life of a lady. You were prepared to torture one.

**GRAYLE**      What is evil? What is morality to an immortal? You can keep your petty ethics, Doctor. See? The barges have reached the docks. My men are about to unload them. Soon the metal will be delivered to me!

**DOCTOR**      Ah no, actually. The plutonium won't get inside the castle. I've seen to that.

*FX: Shouts from below. The clash of swords.*

**GRAYLE**      My men at arms… are being held back! So. You obstruct me again!

**DOCTOR**      It's what I do.

**GRAYLE**      Not for much longer. I have the machine, Doctor. I can mine more holy metal from another source. And I will live long enough to fulfil my role, which is more than can be said for you! This time I will be sure of your death!

*FX: The DOCTOR grunts as GRAYLE tackles him.*

**GRAYLE**      (*Panting*) Do you know how to fly, time traveller? Shall we find out?

*FX: Scream as someone falls from the roof.*

**END OF PART TWO.**

# PART THREE

## Scene Twenty-Seven: (Reprise)

**GRAYLE** What is evil? What is morality to an immortal? You can keep your petty ethics, Doctor. See? The barges have reached the docks. My men are about to unload them. Soon the metal will be delivered to me!

**DOCTOR** Ah no, actually. The plutonium won't get inside the castle. I've seen to that.

*FX: Shouts from below. The clash of swords.*

**GRAYLE** My men at arms... are being held back! So. You obstruct me again!

**DOCTOR** It's what I do.

**GRAYLE** Not for much longer. I have the machine, Doctor. I can mine more holy metal from another source. And I will live long enough to fulfil my role, which is more than can be said for you! This time I will be sure of your death!

*FX: The Doctor grunts as GRAYLE tackles him.*

**GRAYLE** (*Panting*) Do you know how to fly, time traveller? Shall we find out?

*FX: Scream as GRAYLE falls from the roof.*

**DOCTOR** Not today, Grayle. Thanks all the same.

**CHARLEY** Doctor, what have you done?!

**DOCTOR** Hullo Charley.

**CHARLEY** You've killed him!

**DOCTOR** No. Look down there. That's him swimming away. A fall like that wouldn't even wind him. Thanks to his masters, Grayle is virtually indestructible.

**CHARLEY** Well unless he gets out of this city pretty fast I think Edith will do her best to put that right. With any luck.

**DOCTOR** I wonder if Grayle can be killed at all. I have no idea how far his invulnerability extends.

**CHARLEY** Not very far if I get my hands on him. What's this?

**DOCTOR** It's the machine that Grayle's master instructed him to make. Looks like a rudimentary transmat. Powered with enough plutonium to shift a reasonable mass all the way from the Ordinand System.

**CHARLEY** He was telling the truth then. He was bringing his masters to him.

**DOCTOR** Master in the singular, I think. Unless his masters are very small indeed I don't think this machine could handle more than one. Interesting.

**CHARLEY** Is it?

**DOCTOR** Very. That Grayle had to make a machine like this at all suggests that his masters no longer possess the energy to move anything between the systems themselves, whether that be sacrifices or themselves. They must be getting desperate. Until Grayle finds a way to take at least one of them away from the Ordinand System, they're stuck there.

**CHARLEY** So it's just him we have to deal with now then.[57] We throw

241

this machine off the tower and make sure that Grayle has his head chopped off or something and case closed!
**DOCTOR**    It's not quite that simple.[58]
**CHARLEY**    It never is, is it?
**DOCTOR**    The Grayle that I just threw off this roof wasn't quite the one that I met in Singapore. We meet each other at some point in the future. Besides, he's probably on his way out of the country as we speak. It'll take him a while, too long for this window of opportunity, but he can always make another machine and find the fuel for it. All we can do here is make sure the plutonium is properly dealt with. Then we find Grayle's masters' next opportunity and get in the way again! Shall we go?
**CHARLEY**    Doctor?
**DOCTOR**    Yes?
**CHARLEY**    The machine?
**DOCTOR**    Oh yes. Give us a hand, Charley.
*FX: Grunt of exertion from them as they push the machine off the tower. Distant explosion.*

### Scene Twenty-Eight: TARDIS Interior.
*FX: TARDIS take-off fades into TARDIS interior.*

**DOCTOR**    Thankfully, despite the drama of the last few hours the Court wasn't that ruffled. Intrigue comes with the territory when you spend much time around royalty.[59] I left instructions with Edith and Edward on how to deal with the plutonium, along with enough anti-radiation pills to protect anyone working with it. We took off as soon as politeness allowed. Probably sooner than that. As soon as I had the chance to relax, my body remembered that it had been rather roughly dealt with...
**CHARLEY**    Doctor, are you all right?
**DOCTOR**    No, Charley, I don't think I am. Oh dear. There's blood on my shirt.
**CHARLEY**    Come on, lean on me, we'll get you to the medical wing.

### Scene Twenty-Nine: TARDIS Medical Wing.
*FX: A medical sort of TARDIS hum. CHARLEY is running something that bleeps over the DOCTOR's chest.*

**CHARLEY**    So many small incisions. He really took a dislike to your chest.
**DOCTOR**    Mm. How's your ear?
**CHARLEY**    That's nothing. It's stopped bleeding on its own.
**DOCTOR**    I thought he was going to–
**CHARLEY**    But he didn't. Will you please just say what's on your mind? It's unnerving when you're quiet. Normally, there is not a single unexpressed thought.
**DOCTOR**    Charley, when we were fighting I really... I think I actually wanted to kill Grayle. I'm not sure I had his invulnerability in mind when I threw him from the roof. For a moment I hated him as strongly as he must hate me. I imagined I saw your blood on his hands...

242

**CHARLEY** And I remember expressing several violent thoughts about him. But I wouldn't do anything about them. He's a bounder. It's only natural to want to–

**DOCTOR** There's a difference between your words and my actions! I'm the Doctor. I can't do that sort of thing. But I might have done.

**CHARLEY** But you didn't. And I know you wouldn't. You're right. That's not who you are. All the same, there's something about Grayle that really upsets you, isn't there?

**DOCTOR** Yes. I don't know… it's just that his ideas are so small. He's timeless, but he's still a product of the times he's living in. And yet his plans are so huge.

**CHARLEY** So, you think he has ideas above his station![60]

**DOCTOR** Maybe there's a bit of Time Lord snobbery left in me after all. This isn't like when I run into the Master. He's got some self-knowledge, he knows that what he's doing is futile. He's just having fun, in his own way. Showing off to a universe that doesn't care. He always changes his mind when it looks like the cosmos is going to be destroyed. I'm rather fond of him. But Grayle… He'd destroy the universe because of the terms of his father's will.[61]

**CHARLEY** And now he's failed to get his immortality again. He's going to go another 750 years tied up in the details of the world. I don't think it's going to do much for his sanity.

**DOCTOR** I don't think it can get much worse. He's changed. He's become evil. The first Grayle, or should I say Gralae, wouldn't even understand what that means.

**CHARLEY** So we stop him. No problem. Put your shirt on.

### Scene Thirty: TARDIS Console Room.
*FX: TARDIS console room.*

**DOCTOR** It's fairly straightforward this time. We just look forward another 750 years and we find… Of course! The early nineteenth century. Georgian – one of my favourite periods.[62]

**CHARLEY** So how do we find him? He could be anywhere in the world!

**DOCTOR** I don't think so. He's been tied to Britain for so long, I think he'd get back to it as soon as he could. Probably the moment William invaded. And so he's had all this time to collect more plutonium for his machine.

**CHARLEY** Doctor, why do these masters, his angels or whatever, actually need a machine like this? I mean, they seem pretty powerful, why can't they get here in spaceships?[63]

**DOCTOR** You know, that's a very good question. A very good question indeed… (*trails off*)

**CHARLEY** Well?

**DOCTOR** I haven't a clue. Maybe this thing will provide an answer.
*FX: As tweaks and twiddles it over the next few lines.*

**DOCTOR** Hmmm, Grayle will need directions from his masters to build a replacement machine because I doubt he wrote down the instructions the first time. Mind you, he's had plenty of time by now so we better find him quickly.

**CHARLEY** In which case, we just need your detector… and the

TARDIS tells us he's in... oh, Buckinghamshire. Another wonderful opportunity to wear a nice dress.

**DOCTOR**     Wouldn't that be a bit conspicuous?[64]

**CHARLEY**     An opportunity for _me_.

### Scene Thirty-One: Caves.

_FX: TARDIS materialisation. Door opens._

**DOCTOR**     Caves. (_Voice fades_) Hang on, somewhere in the TARDIS I have (_voice approaching_) one of these.

_FX: A flaming torch ignites._

**CHARLEY**     Careful with that!

**DOCTOR**     Mind your petticoats. I really like this sword of yours. In terms of fashion, I mean. This was a time when it suited a gentleman to carry one. It's thin enough to pass for a rapier. Do you like the look?[65]

**CHARLEY**     I'd prefer it if I could carry it.

**DOCTOR**     Not in the year 1806. George III is on the throne, William Pitt is Prime Minister, and ladies fight with witticisms and the occasional fan, not with edged weapons. We've landed towards the end of the time the transmission channels are open.

**CHARLEY**     So Grayle's had a year to talk with his masters?

**DOCTOR**     Not forgetting the 750 years he's been left to his own devices. Knowing about radioactivity.

**CHARLEY**     Wonderful. Are you ever going to explain this plutonium stuff to me?

**DOCTOR**     Not much to explain. Tremendously rich source of energy, kills humans if you get near it unprotected, and frequently used in weaponry. Next?

_FX: High-pitched squeaks and flaps._

**DOCTOR**     Hey! Bats! Great!

### Scene Thirty-Two: Fields.

_FX: The distant calls of cattle and sheep. The cawing of ravens._

**GRAYLE**     Release the prey!

_FX: A bird flaps into the air._

**GRAYLE**     (_Yell_) Go on, Lucifer! Kill![66]

_FX: With a cry, a falcon takes to the air, and kills the bird._

**LUCY**     Your falcon is master of the air, Sir Sebastian.

**GRAYLE**     As I am master of these lands, Lucy. And soon so much more besides.[67]

**LUCY**     Such as?

**GRAYLE**     (_Laughs_) Your heart, for instance.

**LUCY**     My father has only an influence on my affections, sir. He does not buy and sell me like one of your shares.

**GRAYLE**     Ah, you talk of social niceties. I know nothing of these. All I care for is the power to rise above them. But you would not talk at all had you no interest in the matter, madam. Have I not shown you wonders, things from other worlds, secrets beyond human understanding?

**LUCY**     Indeed. I believe you are what you say you are, a man who stands above the rest. A man, however, is not a museum. There is the matter of his conscience.

**GRAYLE**     I have none. 'Do what thou will shall be the whole of my law.'

**LUCY**     And you have pride in that. That you are above the laws of man and God.

**GRAYLE**     And that, Miss Martin, is why you are here. This weekend, I would have an answer from you to the matter of my proposal.

**LUCY**     You will have your answer, sir. In time.

*FX: The falcon returns to GRAYLE's arm.*

**GRAYLE**     I tire of this sport. I have much to prepare for the meeting tonight. It is an important occasion in our calendar. I trust you and your father will attend?

**LUCY**     If women are allowed, sir.

**GRAYLE**     My dear Miss Martin, women are positively encouraged! Shall we?

## Scene Thirty-Three: Caves.

*FX: Dripping caves.*

**CHARLEY**     We're getting near to the surface. There's a light in the distance.

**DOCTOR**     And look at this!

**CHARLEY**     Another mouse?

**DOCTOR**     Oh. Sorry to disappoint you. It's just a door made of gold.

*FX: Door creaks open.*

**DOCTOR**     Oh, it's just some sort of dungeon!

**CHARLEY**     Well, we were in a dungeon just the other day, and that one didn't have chandeliers, candles, a dining table, or...

**DOCTOR**     Oh yes. (*FX: Pours himself a drink*) The Beaujolais Nouveau. Mmm.

**CHARLEY**     So this is Grayle's dining room?

**DOCTOR**     Buckinghamshire... Of course! We're in Wycombe Caves! One of the bases of the Hellfire Club!

**CHARLEY**     So this is the same organisation we encountered–?

**DOCTOR**     Yes, but a few decades past its golden years. Such renowned debauchees as Sir Francis Dashwood, the Earl of Sandwich and Benjamin Franklin disported themselves right here! We can't be far from Medmenham Abbey...

**CHARLEY**     Benjamin Franklin? The American president?

**DOCTOR**     President... scientist... magician. In those days you were allowed to be president and still be interesting.

**CHARLEY**     So what sort of things did they get up to in here?

**DOCTOR**     Oh. You know. Rude things.

**CHARLEY**     Like?

**DOCTOR**     They probably drank far too much. And look – they weren't too careful where they threw their chicken drumsticks.

**CHARLEY**     Did they have orgies?

**DOCTOR**     (*Shocked*) Charlotte Pollard!

**CHARLEY**     I went to an orgy once. There was a lot of melted cheese.[68] I didn't stay.

**DOCTOR**     Well, people said the Hellfire Club had orgies, but they

245

always say that when women are first admitted to any patriarchal political culture.

**CHARLEY**     Oh. How boring.

*FX: Dust sheet being pulled away.*

**CHARLEY**     What are these?

**DOCTOR**     Cretan urns.

**CHARLEY**     What's a Cretan urn?

**DOCTOR**     Less than a Grecian.

**CHARLEY**     I mean: how do you know they're Cretan?

**DOCTOR**     The designs. It's an entirely separate culture. And these are from the height of the Minoan civilisation.

**CHARLEY**     Quite a large collection. And there are blades: knives, swords, ancient coins...

**DOCTOR**     Again, all Minoan. Grayle hasn't lost his interest in *bos bovis.*[69]

*FX: Approaching footsteps.*

**DOCTOR**     Someone's coming!

**CHARLEY**     Where can we hide?!

**DOCTOR**     Let's not.

**CHARLEY**     What if it's Grayle?

**DOCTOR**     We're going to meet sooner or later. Sometimes the best way in is the front door.[70]

**CHARLEY**     You tried that last time, remember? And we ended up manacled to a wall?

**DOCTOR**     Ah.[71] Perhaps we should try sneaking then. Over here, behind the urns!

*FX: Door opening.*

**MARTIN**     You sir! Who are you?! What are you doing in here?!

**CHARLEY**     (*Aside*) So much for sneaking.

**DOCTOR**     I'm Sir Peter Pollard, sir! And I'm pottering! Your servant, sir! And you are...?

**MARTIN**     Colonel Richard Martin, sir. At your service, sir.

**DOCTOR**     The famous Richard Martin, eh? I thought you'd be older. An honour to meet you. I'd like to say a personal thanks for your brave actions at the Battle of Aboukir. This is my daughter, Charlotte.

**MARTIN**     (*A conman, worried at the DOCTOR'S knowledge of the man he's impersonating*) Well, I... Charmed to meet you, Miss Pollard. But–

**CHARLEY**     But now we are saved, sir! We were touring the caves, guided by a couple of local rogues. We were hoping that we would snag a fine stalactite or stalagmite. The rogues extinguished their torches and tried to rob us, but Daddy dear was too swift for them.

**DOCTOR**     Oh, I so was.[72] We ran in here and slammed the door. When we heard your footsteps we feared the rogues had returned. Hence the hiding. Very fine urns, by the way.

**MARTIN**     Rogues, you say?! One day someone will think to license the guides. May I ask, sir, where are you staying hereabouts?

**DOCTOR**     Why, sir, we have only just arrived.

**MARTIN**     Then, please, the young lady must be feeling faint. She is much the same age as my own dear daughter, Lucy, and I know to what weakness such frail things are prey. Oblige me and accompany me back to where I have my lodgings, with the owner of these very caves.

246

| | |
|---|---|
| **DOCTOR** | And that would be?[73] |
| **MARTIN** | Sir Sebastian Grayle. I'm sure when he hears your story he'll offer you every hospitality. |
| **CHARLEY** | Doubtless. |
| **MARTIN** | Allow me to lead the way. |
| **CHARLEY** | (*Whisper*) Sir Peter Pollard? |
| **DOCTOR** | (*Whisper*) Daddy dear? |
| **CHARLEY** | (*Whisper*) I can make this stuff up all day. I've read a lot of Jane Austen. |

### Scene Thirty-Four: Great House.
*FX: The ticking of a clock.*

| | |
|---|---|
| **LUCY** | So Sir Sebastian, have your completed your preparations? |
| **GRAYLE** | Indeed, Lucy. I have received messages by courier from every one of our brethren. And those of your own sex who form a sorority within the circle of hellfire. Tonight is the centre of our year, the celebration of the rising of the bull.[74] |
| **LUCY** | Please, sir, such talk would offend my maidenly ears. |
| **GRAYLE** | I would hope your ears would be maidenly. |
| **LUCY** | If that is a joke sir, I protest that I do not understand it. |
| **GRAYLE** | You may protest, madam. But– |

*FX: The door opens.*

| | |
|---|---|
| **MARTIN** | Sir Sebastian! Alone with my daughter! Do I take it she has answered your suit? |
| **LUCY** | No, Papa, she has not. |
| **MARTIN** | Well, that's most irregular, but– |
| **GRAYLE** | But anything for your wealthy future son-in-law, eh, Richard?[75] And you bring guests with you! Who might you have... Well. (*Laughs*) Doctor, we meet again! I feel I am duty bound to offer you my every hospitality. |
| **CHARLEY** | (*Whisper*) Great. More manacles. |
| **MARTIN** | I found the lady and gentleman in the caves as I was finding the horned goblet as you requested, Sir Sebastian. You know each other, then? |
| **GRAYLE** | Indeed. Will you not introduce yourself, Doctor? On my part I present to you my great friend and, if I may be so bold, my future wife, Lucy Martin. |
| **DOCTOR** | Delighted to meet you, Miss. |
| **MARTIN** | Doctor, you say? |
| **DOCTOR** | It is my privilege to be both a doctor and a knight, Mr Martin. |
| **LUCY** | Why, it is a delight to find some feminine company in this great folly. |
| **CHARLEY** | To what folly do you refer? |
| **LUCY** | Why, how many follies do you see around you? |
| **CHARLEY** | I would hesitate to be known as a girl who found folly where there was none. |
| **DOCTOR** | (*Whisper*) Oh, stop it! |
| **GRAYLE** | You seem to have acquired a new title since I met you last, Doctor. How invigorating. As you can see, I too have changed a little. |

247

**DOCTOR**      Well losing the beard was a good move.[76]

**GRAYLE**      Ah, I have missed your sense of humour! I think you should join me for dinner tonight, along with your lovely...?

**CHARLEY**      His daughter. Charlotte.

**GRAYLE**      Daughter? Oh how delightful.[77] There is no telling what hilarity may ensue!

**DOCTOR**      A splendid idea, sir!

**CHARLEY**      (*Whisper*) What are you doing? What is <u>he</u> doing?

**DOCTOR**      (*Whisper*) Later!

**GRAYLE**      Burroughs, my manservant, will now show you to the west wing, and prepare rooms for you. You will both stay the night and join my little... party, won't you?

**Scene Thirty-Five: Elsewhere in the Great House.**
*FX: Creak of stairs.*

**CHARLEY**      So... would you like to explain? He wasn't waving a sword at us, we weren't surrounded by huge scary men, and yet you cheerfully do what he tells you! Why?

**DOCTOR**      Because he wasn't waving a sword at us, or surrounding us with huge scary men. He's happy, and in the mood to talk.[78] We still don't know who his masters are. With Grayle acting like this, we can find out.

**CHARLEY**      And why do you think he's happy?!

**DOCTOR**      He's confident. He's invulnerable. He must be close to his goal. And he doesn't think I can stop him. He's ready to gloat. All the more reason to find out exactly what's going on. From the horse's mouth.

**CHARLEY**      Fine. You win. But I reserve the right to say, 'I told you so,' if we end up chained to a wall again.

**DOCTOR**      Granted. Come on, let's check over the rooms and then find out more over nibbles.

**Scene Thirty-Six: Great House.**
*FX: The chink of cutlery and murmur of conversation.*

**MARTIN**      Marvellous supper, Sir Sebastian.

**GRAYLE**      Thank you. I will endeavour to keep your daughter in similar style.

**LUCY**      Oh good.

**GRAYLE**      Will you not take venison, Doctor?

**DOCTOR**      Thank you, no. I rarely touch meat.

**GRAYLE**      A very spiritual point of view.

**CHARLEY**      I would have thought, Sir Sebastian, that you would be most interested in spiritual viewpoints?

**GRAYLE**      I was once. Now I am of the opinion that the world and all that is in it merely exist to serve me. I intend to change this country for ever, and, as Mr Martin knows, I have the means to do so.

*FX: Polite laughter.*

**DOCTOR**      So you acknowledge no master?

**GRAYLE**      Every man must acknowledge one master, Doctor.

**DOCTOR**      I thought that you had renounced God and His holy angels, sir.

248

**GRAYLE**      I may have moved beyond the limits of what used to be my holy order, but I retain the loyalty to my masters, Doctor. As you must realise.

**LUCY**      You held holy orders, Sir Sebastian? Which one? Were you a monk?

**GRAYLE**      I was, dear Lucy, once the Bishop of all Cornwall!

*FX: Polite laughter.*

**MARTIN**      (*Laughing*) We never know when you are joking, sir!

**DOCTOR**      (*Whisper*) It's as I thought. He's willing to talk about anything.

**CHARLEY**      (*Whisper*) Because he thinks he's invincible.

**GRAYLE**      Doctor! What are you whispering about? You insult the rest of the table with your secrets!

**DOCTOR**      I have little to hide from you, Sir Sebastian. But the things I could reveal may shock the ladies. Perhaps we should discuss them in private?

**GRAYLE**      What have you that would shock my dear Lucy? Do you offer her insult? Have a care, sir, lest I see cause to defend her honour!

**DOCTOR**      You see no such cause, I promise you!

**GRAYLE**      You call me blind, now? Unable to see your words for what they are?

**DOCTOR**      Of course not...

**GRAYLE**      Then you call me a liar?

**DOCTOR**      Now I see what you're up to. Very clever, Grayle. Very civilised.

**LUCY**      My dear... Perhaps my father and I should leave? You and this gentleman seem to have some history that has disturbed you, perhaps?

**MARTIN**      Yes. It may be that this trouble would be better resolved without our presence. Come, my dear...

**GRAYLE**      No. Stay. I wish you to see this. Doctor, I call you out. You have offered me, my house, and my lady insult. A duel is the only answer to this slur. Immediately, sir!

*FX: Gasps of horror.*

**MARTIN**      Sirs, please! Cannot both of you forgive and think of your fellow man?

**DOCTOR**      Sir Sebastian, I have no reason or desire to raise arms against you. Please forgive my words. I meant no insult.

**GRAYLE**      Your meaning was clear, sir! Are you a coward then, that you will not accept my challenge?

**DOCTOR**      You have called me that before, I recall. And it was as untrue then as it is now.[79] I accept your challenge, sir!

**CHARLEY**      Doctor, no! That's just what he wants!

**DOCTOR**      I take it that the choice of weapons is mine?

**GRAYLE**      Of course.

**DOCTOR**      Then I choose swords.

**GRAYLE**      Burroughs will bring torches to the hundred acre field! And may honour be satisfied!

**Scene Thirty-Seven: Fields.**

*FX: The hooting of owls. The crackling of torches.*

**DOCTOR**      I stood under an old oak tree in the darkness as Grayle's servants fussed around, clearing a formal area in the field for the duel. The house staff and guests stood at a distance, looking on.

**CHARLEY**      Doctor, are you sure you know what you're doing?

*FX: Swish of sword.*

**DOCTOR**      This sword you picked up has got a really nice weight to it. Do you want to have a go?

**CHARLEY**      No I do not. What do you think you're doing?

**DOCTOR**      Grayle's idea of toying with me is to pull me down to his level. To kill me using the manners of history. He set me up at dinner, and now he wants to finish me off before the meeting tonight.

**CHARLEY**      Are you any good with a sword?

**DOCTOR**      I've had my moments. (*Pricks himself*) Ow! This thing is sharp!

**CHARLEY**      And how are you going to deal with the small matter of your opponent being invulnerable to all harm?

**DOCTOR**      With style, of course. Ah, good evening Miss Martin. If you'll excuse me, ladies, I have a feeling I should be warming up or something.

**LUCY**      Your papa seems to have played out his hand.

**CHARLEY**      And your papa is nowhere to be seen.

**LUCY**      He is horrified by this duel, and will not be seen at it.

**CHARLEY**      And yet you are not?

**LUCY**      Indeed. Is that not peculiar?

**CHARLEY**      To which 'hand' of my papa's did you refer just now?

**LUCY**      Credit me for some intelligence, Miss Pollard. The bad history between your father and Sebastian is obvious. They made no attempt to conceal it. And yet you expect me to believe that you found yourself stranded at Sebastian's country house completely by chance?

**CHARLEY**      I confess that there may have been motive behind our appearance. But I can assure you, Lucy, that my father's hand is no more played out than yours.

**LUCY**      So. We seem more alike than I first thought. May I speak frankly with you, Charlotte?

**CHARLEY**      I would not have it that you spoke to me otherwise.

**LUCY**      I have no intention of marrying Sir Sebastian Grayle. I did so when first we met. But one can only hear so much about the purifying power of male cattle before one is completely put off one's supper.

**CHARLEY**      So why are you still here?

**LUCY**      Because I have my manners. And because I am waiting. Oh look, they are about to begin.

**GRAYLE**      (*Call*) Are you prepared, sir?

**DOCTOR**      I expect so.

**GRAYLE**      We will stand back to back. Then we will march forward ten paces, to the beat of the drum. On the tenth pace, we turn and move to the attack. Do you accept these rules?

**DOCTOR**      Is it too late to suggest a round of bridge?

**GRAYLE**      Raise your sword, sir. And begin your last walk!

*FX: The drums begin beating their ten beats.*

**CHARLEY**      Oh no...

**MARTIN**      Ah, there you are, daughter.

**LUCY**      Papa. You have changed your mind as to seeing this spectacle, then?

**MARTIN**      Why no! I have... arrived to insist you accompany me back to the house.

**LUCY**      Of course, father, I –

**CHARLEY**      You can't just walk away! Not when the Doctor could be about to die!

**MARTIN**      The Doctor? That is a strange way to refer to your father.

**CHARLEY**      He's not my father. He's my best friend. Or he was...

*FX: The drums stop.*

**GRAYLE**      Halt! Turn, Doctor! En garde!

**DOCTOR**      I turned. Of all humanity's weapons the sword is their favourite. Different forms of it persist throughout their history, and consequently I've taught myself to become expert in its use. Unfortunately Grayle had been alive even longer than I had, and had even more time to practise. We closed to a sword's length apart and steel clashed for the first time.

*FX: Clash of swords. They speak over the sound of metal on metal.*

**GRAYLE**      You're good, Doctor, but skill won't save you.

**DOCTOR**      And you, Grayle, are overconfident. Pride comes before a fall and all that.

**GRAYLE**      You hurled me from a roof and could not kill me. You know I have a certain advantage in this duel. You can't hurt me, but I...

*FX: The DOCTOR screams as GRAYLE stabs him.*

**CHARLEY**      Doctor!

**LUCY**      He is not badly hurt, Charlotte. Be brave.

**GRAYLE**      I can hurt you! This will be such satisfying sport. You will scream for death before I'm finished with you.

**DOCTOR**      (*Panting*) Not... if I finish with you first!

*FX: An explosion sucking of energy. GRAYLE cries out. His sword clatters to the floor.*

**GRAYLE**      You only touched me, but it... it burned!

**DOCTOR**      It sucks the alien energy from your body, Grayle. It's a rustless weapon! The ancients who constructed it knew what they were doing! Are you feeling your age yet?

**GRAYLE**      You cannot kill me, Doctor. You are too noble for that!

**DOCTOR**      Yes. A nobility that you once possessed. You were very like me once. You were dissatisfied with what you had. You searched for something more. You sought the freedom to roam space and time. The first Grayle even had the humility to recognise a greater power, the capacity to love! We could have been friends, Grayle. Cut off from your masters, we could still be.[80] I don't have to take all your energy. Just enough to frustrate their plans. You have a woman ready to marry you! Isn't one life enough?!

**GRAYLE**      Not for you! You arrive to make my life painful at every point! You won't allow me the freedom you crave for yourself!

**DOCTOR**      Not at the expense of others.

**GRAYLE**      But it is the only freedom I can have, the freedom to go beyond! You say I have a bride here, but I do not. I do not aim to keep her any more than I intend to keep anything else from my life here! I will have something better!

**DOCTOR**      Grayle, listen to me. If I hold this sword to your throat for long enough, the years will exact their rightful toll. Do you want to know what it feels like to be fourteen hundred years old?

251

| GRAYLE | I will... I will not allow— |
| DOCTOR | I won't let you let go! I can't! |
| GRAYLE | Then... you will die! |
| CHARLEY | He's got a knife! |

*FX: The DOCTOR screams.*

| CHARLEY | Doctor![81] |
| GRAYLE | Come here, Miss Martin! |
| LUCY | Doctor! Father! Help! |
| CHARLEY | He's got Lucy! |
| GRAYLE | I... may have lost my vigour... but I can get it back... |

when my masters arrive. When I give them the final thing they need... my bride! Come near me and she dies! Another sacrifice is easy enough to come by! Let us away!

*FX: A whinny of a horse. It gallops off.*

| MARTIN | He's taking Lucy with him! We must follow! |
| CHARLEY | I don't think the Doctor's quite ready for that. A moment |

ago, you were ready to leave him to fight. Funny isn't it how you want his help now.

| DOCTOR | It's all right, Charley. Err... have I... changed? |
| CHARLEY | No, still the same. |
| DOCTOR | Oh. Good. Takes more than a few stab wounds to... finish |

me off. A couple of bandages and I'll be... Oh no!

| CHARLEY | What?! |
| DOCTOR | This shirt is full of holes! Can't I even keep one of them |

intact?!

| MARTIN | Never mind your shirt, sir! What about Grayle?! |
| DOCTOR | Grayle. Yes. He's taken Lucy to give to his masters. He'll |

have rebuilt the transmat, probably got the plutonium to power it too.

| MARTIN | Sir, if this 'transmat' is the means by which Grayle said |

he would change this country for ever, then I know where it is kept. The caves, where I found you. That is where the party is to be held tonight!

| DOCTOR | Then let's go! To the caves![82] |

## Scene Thirty-Eight: Caves.

*FX: Dripping of caves.*

| LUCY | Let go of me! |
| GRAYLE | As soon as I have attached you to the sacrificial stone— |

*FX: Chink of manacles on stone.*

| GRAYLE | Then I'll gladly let go of you. |
| LUCY | The sacrificial...? What are you planning to do to me? |
| GRAYLE | Once they arrive through my machine my masters |

require one more thing of me. They require the binding energy of organic compounds. Such energy as is found in your body! The journey through the black hole saps their energies. They need to feed upon their arrival.

| LUCY | This is more of your magic. I know not of what you speak. |
| GRAYLE | Once I felt the same way. But then they showed me the |

worlds they inhabit. Their palaces of infinite consumption. Their great journey of life. Once they are here, Lucy, all will become clear. They will consume this world, give me true immortality, and allow me the freedom to depart for the very stars. I was going to wait for the rest of my Hellfire

Club to arrive, to provide more sustenance, but one body should be a good start. Why don't we set things in motion...

*FX: He clicks a button. A whirring and beeping.*

**GRAYLE**  Right now?

## Scene Thirty-Nine: Cave Entrance.

*FX: Owl hooting. General night sounds.*

**DOCTOR**  Come on!

**MARTIN**  He's placed a great rock against the door. How is that possible?

**DOCTOR**  He's using up the last of his energy. Which means he's getting ready for the end.

**CHARLEY**  You must have really hurt him with that sword.

**DOCTOR**  Yes. I drained him of so much power I should think he's feeling rather vulnerable now. I was very lucky, really. It was Marcus that gave me the idea, but it took me a while to think of it. This is the sword with which Mithras slew the demon bull. Or a recreation of it. A rustless weapon.[83]

**CHARLEY**  Pure iron! In stories, magical creatures are always afraid of that!

**DOCTOR**  Exactly. If it worked for Mithras, I thought, it'll work for me. It wasn't just his chivalry about ladies that made Grayle run from us at the Roman fort. (*To MARTIN*) Is there another way into the caves?

**MARTIN**  Well, there's the chimney... It's a narrow crevice, leading down to where we build a fire, but–

**DOCTOR**  I can get down there. Show me.

**CHARLEY**  I'm coming too. Don't even try to say no.

**DOCTOR**  Wouldn't dream of it.[84]

## Scene Forty: Rocks.

*FX: The DOCTOR, CHARLEY and MARTIN scramble up to the crevice.*

**MARTIN**  Here it is. Last weekend I had to follow the smoke through the woods and throw a bucket of liquor down there to make the fire bellow during one of Grayle's ceremonies.

**DOCTOR**  No fire now. Let's get down there.

**CHARLEY**  Wait a moment. I can't go climbing like this.

*FX: Ripping of dress.*

**MARTIN**  Oh I say.

## Scene Forty-One: Caves.

*FX: Increasing bleeping.*

**GRAYLE**  Masters, I call you. Hear me through your device. I am opening the gateway now and creating a beacon.

*FX: Trickling of dust and pebbles.*

**GRAYLE**  The sacrifice is ready. You will be able to feed as soon as you arrive.

*FX: Stream of falling rocks. The DOCTOR and CHARLEY fall in with a cry.*

**DOCTOR**  Hello, Grayle! Feeling mortal, are we? You don't look a day over seventy!

**GRAYLE**    Stay back! I may have lost my invulnerability, for the present, but my flintlock can still protect me, and I no longer care what my servants think of me. Drop the sword, Doctor, and kick it over here.
*FX: Sword clatters as it hits the floor and skitters across it.*
**GRAYLE**    I'm glad to see you have retained your senses.
**CHARLEY**    You don't care about your servants because they're not going to be around for much longer, right?
**DOCTOR**    But not you. You think your masters will spare you from their hunger?
**GRAYLE**    Why shouldn't they? They have proved loyal to me so far.
**DOCTOR**    But now they're on the point of getting everything they need! Do you really think that once you've opened the way for them, they'll want to spend any of their energy on granting you immortality?[85]
**GRAYLE**    They will give me a place in their kingdom. I will finally have somewhere that is mine! A home!
*FX: A futuristic trumpet blast.*
**GRAYLE**    They have heard my summons! They are arriving!
**LUCY**    Help me!
**GRAYLE**    Don't go near her! I can kill every one of you!
*FX: Wibbling of spacetime.*
**GRAYLE**    The gate opens! My masters have arrived on this planet!
**DOCTOR**    Good grief! You have been busy, haven't you? That's a time corridor! Transmats not good enough for you now?
**LUCY**    What is appearing there?!
**CHARLEY**    It's like some giant metal egg!
**DOCTOR**    Oh dear. I've seen one of those before. I really should have worked this out a bit earlier.
*FX: The wibbling halts.*
**DOCTOR**    (*Whisper*) We have to do this now. When those things get out nobody will be able to stop them. Charley, save Lucy.
**GRAYLE**    A moment, my masters, a moment while I free you!
**LUCY**    Charlotte, quickly!
*FX: Smashing of shackles.*
**CHARLEY**    There! Get up!
*FX: GRAYLE turns the wheel to open the pod.*
**DOCTOR**    Let go of that wheel, Grayle! I won't allow them to feed on this world!
**GRAYLE**    My masters will be –
*FX: He grunts with exertion and the door of the pod opens.*
**GRAYLE**    Free! My masters are free!
*FX: Hiss of capsule opening. The heavy hooves of the Nimon.*
**NIMON**    Free to feed on this delicious world!
**CHARLEY**    Doctor, what are they?!
**DOCTOR**    (*To NIMON*) Do you want to introduce yourselves, or shall I do it for you?
**NIMON**    Foolish Time Lord. We are the Nimon. And you are our prey![86]
*FX: Nimon blast.*

**END OF PART THREE.**

254

# PART FOUR

**Scene Forty-one: (Reprise)**

**LUCY**          What is appearing there?!
**CHARLEY**       It's like some giant metal egg!
**DOCTOR**        Oh dear. I've seen one of those before. I really should have worked this out a bit earlier.
*FX: The wibbling halts.*
**DOCTOR**        (*Whisper*) We have to do this now. When those things get out nobody will be able to stop them. Charley, save Lucy.
**GRAYLE**        A moment, my masters, a moment while I free you!
**LUCY**          Charlotte, quickly!
*FX: Smashing of shackles.*
**CHARLEY**       There! Get up!
*FX: GRAYLE turns the wheel to open the pod.*
**DOCTOR**        Let go of that wheel, Grayle! I won't allow them to feed on this world!
**GRAYLE**        My masters will be –
*FX: He grunts with exertion and the door of the pod opens.*
**GRAYLE**        Free! My masters are free!
*FX: Hiss of capsule opening. The heavy hooves of the Nimon.*
**NIMON**         Free to feed on this delicious world!
**CHARLEY**       Doctor, what are they?!
**DOCTOR**        (*To NIMON*) Do you want to introduce yourselves, or shall I do it for you?
**NIMON**         Foolish Time Lord. We are the Nimon. And you are our prey!
*FX: NIMON BLAST.*
**CHARLEY**       Doctor!
**DOCTOR**        Ow. That hurt.
**NIMON**         If we had desired your death, Doctor, you would be dead. We will feed on you now.
**GRAYLE**        Yes, masters. Take the binding energy of their forms. Feast on their wretched corpses! I shall prepare the horned goblet.
**CHARLEY**       Not very technological.
**NIMON**         The binding energy oscillator.
**DOCTOR**        It's not a goblet at all, but a product of their psionic technology. The Nimon rely on the design sense of other races. I should have realised, there were so many clues!
**GRAYLE**        I have it here in this... But... Martin gave it to me! I placed it in this bag, and... The gold coins! The jewelled scabbard! Centuries of treasures – they're all gone!
**DOCTOR**        It seems someone else shares your love for money, Grayle.[87]
**LUCY**          And now he will hopefully be far from here!
**CHARLEY**       Your papa isn't your papa either, is he?
**LUCY**          The two of us have seen me married to some of the richest men in the country. And left them all at the altar while we take what you might call our dowry.

255

| DOCTOR | I thought he didn't look much like Richard Martin. |
| GRAYLE | But... my masters! |
| NIMON | Find him, you fool! Find the oscillator! |
| GRAYLE | Immediately, Masters! |

*FX: He runs out.*

| DOCTOR | Oh dear, poor Nimon, can't you feed without it? |
| NIMON | We can still kill you! |

**DOCTOR**   Yes, but then you don't get your takeaway dinner. And you need all your energy after passing through a black hole, don't you? How long before you have to retreat back to the last planet you've butchered?

**NIMON**   We have enough energy to... to...

*FX: A roar and a thump.*

| CHARLEY | Doctor! |

## Scene Forty-Two: Rocks.
*FX: GRAYLE scrabbles over rocks.*

**GRAYLE**   Martin! Where are you?! I see you! You can't run from me, old man!

**MARTIN**   (*Scared*) Sir Sebastian! Take back your riches! Here, you can have it all! As long as dear Lucy is safe—

**GRAYLE**   I care not for any of these baubles, wretch. Only... here it is, the horned goblet![88]

*FX: Whirr of power.*

## Scene Forty-Three: Caves.
*FX: The Nimon roars weakly and stumbles.*

**DOCTOR**   I don't call that very hard! It was like being thumped by a wet sock! You're weak as a kitten!

**NIMON**   In moments... you will feel our strength!

**DOCTOR**   If you say so. Meanwhile, you don't mind if I take a look inside this pod of yours, do you? (*Pause*) Ah, you've changed the design! Self-directional! That's a nice touch! The power came from Grayle's machine, of course, but still...

**CHARLEY**   Doctor, what are these creatures?

**DOCTOR**   The Nimon are like interstellar locusts, going from planet to planet, absorbing their energy. (*To NIMON*) You've been trying to get your hands on this world for ages, haven't you?

**NIMON**   It is at a focal point in space and time. A point from where we would have access to millions of other worlds. From where we could launch many ventures of conquest at once!

**DOCTOR**   So that's how you gained your mastery of space and time. Or will gain. Or hopefully won't. Unlike you to work in a big mob like this.

**NIMON**   This world is vital. Our people are spread throughout the cosmos. A scout to each promising planet.

**DOCTOR**   (*To NIMON*) But this time it went wrong, didn't it? Your scout was sent here, and thought he'd struck gold. A planet covered in people, full of the raw radioactive sources you need to power your machinery. He made friends with the Persians, gave them a few trinkets based on his pod... a sword, for instance, that would never rust, made

256

from material that had travelled through a black hole! That's where the whole pure iron myth comes from! Always a bad mistake, to assume you're never going to be at the pointy end of your own weapon. Mithras, or whoever his legend was based on, didn't know anything about earthing temporal energy. But he knew that magical beasts are killed with magic swords, so he went ahead and did just that! After that, you must have given up hope. (*To CHARLEY*) That Nimon passed into legend, became a metaphor, a memory of the nightmare that waited for humanity out there amongst the stars...

**NIMON**      Your mockery will serve no purpose, Time Lord. The scout was destroyed, but we were not defeated. We found Grayle.

**DOCTOR**      Oh yes, after waiting around two millennia or so. What kept you?

**LUCY**      You talk to them as if they are objects of fun. Are they really so weak that we may ridicule them in safety?

**CHARLEY**      It's just his way, Lucy.[89]

**DOCTOR**      (*To NIMON*) You know, I think you've got a bit fatter, as a species, since we last met. You're big monsters, but you're out of shape.[90]

*FX: Growling roar of Nimon.*

**DOCTOR**      (*Whisper*) And yes, Lucy, if these creatures gain their full power and numbers, they'll be dangerous enough to destroy the whole planet and from there rule the entire cosmos, and then I won't be laughing.

**LUCY**      (*Whisper*) Doctor, the golden door...

**DOCTOR**      (*Whisper*) Already checked it. Someone went and locked it. We're not getting out that way.

**Scene Forty-Four: Rocks.**

*FX: MARTIN backs away across sliding gravel.*

**MARTIN**      You have everything I have taken.[91] Surely there is no point in harming me? Are you going to let me go?

**GRAYLE**      Over here, to the chimney! Yes, you weakling scum! I <u>am</u> going to... 'let you go'!

**MARTIN**      What? No!

*FX: He screams and falls.*

**Scene Forty-Five: Caves.**

*FX: Bleeps.*

**DOCTOR**      This pod's really a fascinating craft. Nippy. Tight round cosmic corners. Capable of quite some–

*FX: MARTIN's scream cuts out as he falls into the room and hits the ground, dead.*

**LUCY**      Papa! Oh... papa.[92]

*FX: A clatter as a hoard of objects falls into the room.*

**LUCY**      Our booty. Including the golden blade! Stay back, creatures, or I shall–

**DOCTOR**      A <u>golden</u> blade wouldn't be much use against anything Lucy, let alone something with the hide of a Nimon. Only certain types of weapons will get through that. But some of those gold coins might be useful if I can... quickly, give me a handful!

| NIMON | The oscillator! Seize the oscillator![93] |
|---|---|
| CHARLEY | They've got it, Doctor![94] What can we do?! |
| LUCY | There's no way to escape! |
| DOCTOR | Oh yes there is! Come on, now they're distracted, into the pod! |
| CHARLEY | We're not going to go to the Ordinand system, are we? It'll be crawling with Nimons! |

*FX: Bleeps, getting the pod ready.*

| DOCTOR | Nimon, Charley. The plural's the same as the singular. And no, we're not.[95] Help me with this door! |

*FX: They heave. The pod door swings closed.[96]*

| NIMON | We have the oscillator! Now... feed on them! |

*FX: Nimon blast. But the sound of pod dematerialisation has started.*

## Scene Forty-Six: Nimon Pod.

*FX: Bleepings of journey.*

| LUCY | I fail to see how hiding in here will inconvenience our foes for very long. |
|---|---|
| DOCTOR | Ah, you're in for a surprise![97] |
| CHARLEY | Can you fly this thing, Doctor? |
| DOCTOR | Oh yes. It's still operating on the power coming from Grayle's beacon. He must have loaded enough plutonium into that thing to fuel half the universe! But we're not going that far, just– |

*FX: Materialisation noise.*

| DOCTOR | A few hundred yards. Come on, quickly! |

## Scene Forty-Seven: Caves.

*FX: Nimon pod door opens.*

| DOCTOR | The coast is clear. |
|---|---|
| LUCY | We are... somewhere else! |
| DOCTOR | Now, if you thought that journey was impressive, Lucy, that was just the branch line. All aboard for the express! |
| CHARLEY | We call it the TARDIS. Prepare yourself for a shock. |

*FX: Rattling of keys. TARDIS door opens and closes.*

## Scene Forty-Eight: TARDIS Interior.

*FX: TARDIS interior.*

| LUCY | Why, it's– |
|---|---|
| DOCTOR | Obviously. |

*FX: Bleepings of controls. TARDIS take-off.*

| CHARLEY | Doctor? Are we... running away? |
|---|---|
| DOCTOR | Everyone's calling me a coward today. Of course not. |

Grayle has opened a portal between this world and the Ordinand system. As long as the plutonium lasts they'll be able to bring over as many pods as they want. It's very inefficient though. If the Nimon run true to form, then that advance party will construct a black hole somewhere close enough for use, and use it as a hyperspatial gateway. Then they'll come here in their millions.

**CHARLEY**     So what do we do?

**DOCTOR**     First of all we close Grayle's portal. It may be an inefficient use of energy, but they could probably bring across a hundred or so other Nimon before Grayle's plutonium runs out. We're not going to risk that happening.

**LUCY**     How do you plan to do that?

**DOCTOR**     By diving right into the space/time corridor they're using and getting in the way![98]

**CHARLEY**     But Doctor, might this not be the death to which Grayle referred? He killed you at a distance, without being able to see your body...

**DOCTOR**     We'll just... have to take that chance. Hang on!

*FX: The TARDIS plunges into the time corridor.*

**Scene Forty-Nine: Caves.**

*FX: Roaring of Nimon.*

**NIMON**     There are... no sacrifices... for us to consume!

**GRAYLE**     But the Doctor?! You let him escape?!

**NIMON**     Do not presume to chide us. He took our pod a short distance.

**GRAYLE**     No, I'm sorry masters.

**NIMON**     We require... sustenance!

*FX: Approaching crowd noise.*

**GRAYLE**     Of course! A moment, my masters. You will have it!

*FX: He unlocks the door.*

**GRAYLE**     Ah, my fellow Hellfire Club members. Right on time. Please, come on in.[99] I can promise you a banquet to remember.

**NIMON**     Ah! A feast indeed!

*FX: Nimon blasts. A lot of screaming. Silence. This sequence of effects has got to go on for a little while, or it's a bit silly and Pythonesque.*

**GRAYLE**     Did they please you, masters?

**NIMON**     They sustained us. I will call the chosen warriors waiting in the Ordinand System.

*FX: Bleeps.*

**NIMON**     They are ready to begin the Great Journey of Life. But there is something blocking the space/time corridor! Another craft!

**GRAYLE**     The Doctor!

**NIMON**     Find the pod! We shall pursue him, and destroy him!

**Scene Fifty: TARDIS interior.**

*FX: TARDIS interior.*

**DOCTOR**     We're safe! And inside the time corridor. Blocking it up. As long as we stay here, the Nimon can't invade.

**CHARLEY**     They're not going to be happy about that, are they?

**DOCTOR**     Absolutely not.

*FX: Bleeps. A scanner.*

**DOCTOR**     And here they come. They've taken the pod from the Earth end of the tunnel. They're heading straight for us. Prepare for ramming!

**LUCY**     How do I do that?

**CHARLEY**     As if I know!

**DOCTOR**     Hang on to something!

*FX: The pod hits the TARDIS. Everybody goes flying. Materialisation noises.*

**CHARLEY**     Doctor! The pod! It's materialising inside the TARDIS!

**DOCTOR**     It was just a feint! They used the possibility of ramming us to get inside the ship!

*FX: The Pod opens.*

**GRAYLE**     You thought you could stop me, Doctor?! I have lived and lived to defeat you, and I still live now. And now you are about to die!

**NIMON**     Take this vehicle out of the time corridor! Now!

**DOCTOR**     Oh no, if you're threatening me and my friends, then I suppose I'll just have to do as you say.

*FX: Bleeps of TARDIS controls.*

**DOCTOR**     (*Whisper*) Lucy, when I say hippo, hit that switch.

**LUCY**     (*Whisper*) Why are you asking me?

**DOCTOR**     (*Whisper. Lie*) Because I have... something else for Charley to do. And remember, to tell her for me: 'Fast return switch, three times fast'. (*Out loud*) There! We're ready to move out of the time corridor.

**NIMON**     Then do so!

**DOCTOR**     Well, Grayle, it looks like you've won. As I said, we could have been friends. You could have been an honourable man. You were certainly a worthy adversary.

**GRAYLE**     I spit on your worthiness. On your honour. They are worth nothing.

**DOCTOR**     Well. Here's where we find out. Hippo.

**LUCY**     Oh!

*FX: The click of a switch. The doors open. The roar of the vortex outside.*

**CHARLEY**     Doctor, the doors!

**NIMON**     No! The time vortex! It is pulling at us! We are— No!

*FX: The roars of the Nimon spiral off into the distance.*

**CHARLEY**     Doctor, the vortex is dragging us in! I can't hold on!

**LUCY**     Grab my hand! There!

**DOCTOR**     Goodbye Charley! Take care of Lucy!

**CHARLEY**     Doctor, no!

**DOCTOR**     Geronimo!

*FX: His voice fades into the distance of the vortex.*

**GRAYLE**     Fool! I have but to reach that lever, and—

*FX: Doors close.*

**GRAYLE**     And I am safe! My masters may have been swept away, but their fellows await to invade in numbers. If I contact them, they will be able to advise me on how to move this craft out of their way! Your mentor was a coward, girl, to take his own life rather than swallow this defeat!

**CHARLEY**     He... was not a coward. He was worth ten of you!

**GRAYLE**     But who lived longest? This is the moment! This is the moment he spoke of! The moment when I have killed him!

**CHARLEY**     (*Agreeing, devastated*) Killed him... and be unable to gloat over his body.

**GRAYLE**     Indeed. Well, I shall make sure I do that! I shall ask my masters how I may manage it. After they have returned my immortality to me. Now, where is the signalling equipment?

**Scene Fifty-One: Time Vortex.**
*FX: Whizzy, psychedelic effects over the Doctor Who theme.*[100]

**DOCTOR**    The butterfly colours of the vortex stormed around my head. I could feel them wanting to pull my psyche apart and sacrifice me on the altar of time. And they would have done: only very powerful beings can survive unprotected in the vortex. Except when those beings have set up a vortex tunnel especially to get them to a specific destination. I slid my limbs into a Gallifreyan lotus and focussed on the task at hand. I'd come up with this idea a few seconds before the Nimon had arrived in the TARDIS. And right now it seemed twice as mad as it had then.

**Scene Fifty-Two: TARDIS Interior.**
*FX: TARDIS interior.*

**LUCY**    Charlotte, I am sorry. The Doctor told me–
**CHARLEY**    I know. He was standing right by the doors. He had to be, to sell them that bluff. He got you to do it because he knew I wouldn't sacrifice him.
**LUCY**    He... had some last words for you.
**CHARLEY**    I'm not sure I want to hear them yet, Lucy. I think I'd rather save them for when we find out what Grayle and the other Nimon have in mind for us.
**LUCY**    Very well.

**Scene Fifty-Three: Time Vortex.**
*FX: Vortex effects and underlying theme.*

**DOCTOR**    I let my mind drift off across time and space... and found the mental signature at the end of this path that I'd expected when I created this wormhole at the TARDIS console. I made my mind swim in that direction, knowing that that was where the Nimon I'd hurled into the vortex were going to end up. I had to get there first. (*Out loud*) Wa-hey!
*FX: His voice spirals off into the vortex.*

**Scene Fifty-Four: TARDIS Interior.**
*FX: TARDIS interior.*

**CHARLEY**    He smelt of honey. He always let his tea cool for far too long before he drank it. And he let me win at *Cluedo*. I think.[101]
**GRAYLE**    There! I have contacted the Ordinand System, and my masters will be here in moments! I'm sure they will enjoy consuming you before they move this vehicle out of their path and conquer Earth. They have said they will teach me how to use it, give me freedom over all time and space![102]
**LUCY**    (*Whisper*) Are you sure you would not like to hear those last words of the Doctor's now, Charlotte?
**CHARLEY**    (*Whisper*) I think now would be a good time.
**LUCY**    (*Whisper*) I'm sure in the culture you both come from they are passionate and meaningful words, but I confess I do not understand them. The Doctor said: 'Fast return switch, three times fast'.

| | |
|---|---|
| **CHARLEY** | (*Whisper*) Why didn't you tell me that before? |
| **LUCY** | (*Whisper*) You asked me not to! |
| **CHARLEY** | (*Whisper*) Never mind. Do you think you can distract Grayle? |
| **LUCY** | (*Whisper*) Well, what do you think? After all, in the last year I've only persuaded eight different men to marry me. (*Out loud*) Sir Sebastian? Chase me! |

*FX: She runs off. Inner door being slammed.*

| | |
|---|---|
| **GRAYLE** | What? Where are you going?! You cannot escape! |
| **CHARLEY** | Simple but effective. Now then, which one is... Oh. How nice of him to clearly label something for once. |

*FX: She flicks the switch three times fast. Dematerialisation sounds.*

| | |
|---|---|
| **CHARLEY** | Let's hope it's a quick journey. |

## Scene Fifty-Five: Roman Camp.

*FX: Whinnies of horses, distant commands, distant trumpets, etc.*

| | |
|---|---|
| **MARCUS** | Ave, Lucilius. Cold night, eh? |
| **LUCILIUS** | Ave, Marcus. This rain! You wonder what's going to fall out of the sky next! |

*FX: The DOCTOR falls from a great height, yelling, and lands on a tent, which crumples beneath him.*

| | |
|---|---|
| **DOCTOR** | Ow. Ow. Ow. Ah! Lucilius! |
| **LUCILIUS** | Do I... do I know you?![103] |
| **DOCTOR** | No, but I know you, good servant! I'm a messenger from mighty Mithras, a being of the sun fallen from the sky. |
| **MARCUS** | By Jupiter! I mean, by Mithras! It's all true! |
| **LUCILIUS** | What would you have me do, messenger? |
| **DOCTOR** | The demon bull has returned. And he brings friends. They will appear within moments. Take Mithras's sacred sword from the temple and hold them back... until I do what I have to do! |
| **LUCILIUS** | A chance to battle evil! A chance to kill the demon bull! Thank you, messenger! |
| **DOCTOR** | Thank me when you've seen the bull. (*Calls as he runs off*) Now, excuse me, I have to pay a visit to an old friend! |
| **LUCILIUS** | Marcus, we must wake the centurions, call the legion to arms! |
| **MARCUS** | What shall we tell them? |
| **LUCILIUS** | Tell them there are Picts in the camp! Anything! But we must gather our forces! This could be the most important battle we will ever fight! |

## Scene Fifty-Six: Tent.

*FX: GRAYLE is muttering and humming to himself. This is GRAYLE/ GRALAE when we first met him.*

| | |
|---|---|
| **GRALAE** | Oh, my great Lord, help me see you as you truly are... show me the truth... |
| **DOCTOR** | Hello! You don't know me, but I promise you, I'm the best friend you're ever going to have. |
| **GRALAE** | What?! Who are you?[104] |
| **DOCTOR** | I represent the light, Decurion Gralae. I know you've been |

talking to the dark. But I should have realised that the words I first heard from you were your last appeal to the light you thought had failed you.

**GRALAE**      How do you know?

**DOCTOR**      Come with me. We have much to do.

**GRALAE**      Very well. But be warned, I have my sword.

**DOCTOR**      You won't need it. Now come on, quickly!

### Scene Fifty-Seven: Roman Camp.

*FX: Calls to arms. trumpets.*

**GRALAE**      The men are being called to arms! I must–

**DOCTOR**      They're being called to fight the beast you've conjured up. The demon you've been talking to, the owner of the magical item which it uses to talk to you.

**GRALAE**      You do know everything. Are you... Are you my lord Mithras?

**DOCTOR**      I'm here to do his work. And I know the contents of your heart.

**GRALAE**      My lord, forgive me! I am sorry! I was... merely interested... inquisitive as to the nature of the gods!

**DOCTOR**      And inquisitive about your family inheritance.

**GRALAE**      I sought time, always more time! And then to have a real voice, a real item in my hands! I did not mean to desert you! I have wronged you!

**DOCTOR**      But you can right that wrong, Gralae. Starting right now.

### Scene Fifty-Eight: TARDIS Interior.

*FX: TARDIS interior. GRAYLE runs after LUCY. She cries out as he grabs her.*

**GRAYLE**      Got you, you vixen! Large as this ship is, there's no escape here for you. Would that I could kill you too, but for the needs of my masters.

**LUCY**      You are bound to fail, wretch!

**GRAYLE**      You run, you struggle... It is almost as if... But no, what plan could she possibly? (*He realises*) Come on!

*FX: He drags her off, still fighting. Interior door sound. TARDIS travelling sound.*

**CHARLEY**      There you are. You certainly gave him a run for his money, Lucy!

**LUCY**      He did get a bit out of puff.

**GRAYLE**      The central column is moving! Does that mean... yes, we are travelling! What have you done, girl?

**CHARLEY**      It just started moving on its own. Maybe the Nimon are controlling us.

**GRAYLE**      Perhaps, but I do not like to stake my life on it. Come here, both of you!

**CHARLEY**      I can't operate that console any more than you can. We're going to end up where we're going whether you like it or not!

**GRAYLE**      Indeed, but with you at the end of my pistols, at least we shall be ready for whatever awaits.

**Scene Fifty-Nine: Roman Camp.**
*FX: Alarms and trumpets.*

**GRALAE**       I don't understand your words, lord.
**DOCTOR**       Get up off your knees. See these gold coins? Have you ever seen this much gold in one place before?
**GRALAE**       No, lord.
**DOCTOR**       And is it worth more than the villa of your father? Would it give you a villa of your own and a comfortable place in the world?
**GRALAE**       Yes, lord.
**DOCTOR**       Then here, it's yours. You were going to own it anyway.
**GRALAE**       Lord, thank you! Now I have the money to marry my beloved Julia.
**DOCTOR**       You have a girlfriend?
**GRALAE**       Her father would not allow her to marry a man so lacking in inheritance. And I feel that every moment in this fortress is a waste of the time we could be spending together, back home.
**DOCTOR**       That's how ridiculous money is. By moving it from one place to another you can save a world, buy back your honour. But it can only solve the problems that it created in the first place. Now leave the fort, buy out your commission tomorrow, leave for home, marry the girl and never talk to demons again!
**GRALAE**       Yes, lord! I happily do as you bid–
*FX: TARDIS materialisation sound.*
**GRALAE**       Lord, what is that?! Is it another miracle?
**DOCTOR**       It's my lift home, assuming I can deal with what's inside. Now, hurry, you have to get away from here before you meet–
*FX: TARDIS doors open.*
**GRAYLE**       Get away from... (*Amazed at the sight of his old self*) From me! Or I kill the women!
**CHARLEY**      Don't listen to him, Doctor![106]
**DOCTOR**       Oh dear.[107]

**Scene Sixty: Temple.**
*FX: Vortex noises.*

**NIMON**        We live! We have merely been displaced in time! We are on the world which we will soon invade, and we will feed!
*FX: Roman soldiers rush in.*
**LUCILIUS**     There they are! The symbol of all evil! Here to defile our temple! But I have the sword of Mithras to stand against them!
**MARCUS**       Forward, men! For Mithras! For the legion! For the emperor!
*FX: The soldiers attack the Nimon. Roaring. Nimon blasts. Hacking. Nimon and humans screams. The clash of sword of hide.*
**LUCILIUS**     I have you, beast! I have you in the heart!
*FX: Nimon roars and dies.*
**MARCUS**       They are demons but they can die!
**LUCILIUS**     Second rank, throw your pilla!
*FX: Spears flying through the air. Screaming of Nimon.*
**NIMON**        Destroy the humans! Destroy them all!

264

**Scene Sixty-One: Roman Camp.**
*FX: Distant battle.*

**DOCTOR**        You hear that, Grayle? The legion are dealing with your masters! Oh, and meet your former self. Gralae... this is Grayle.
**PAST GRALAE**   Is he... me? How is that possible?
**GRAYLE**        I am your future. This man would deny you one.
**PAST GRALAE**   But he has just given me everything I need.
**GRAYLE**        Because he knows that on my path you can have so much more! You can conquer all of time and–
**PAST GRALAE**   And hold women at the point of a weapon! How have I come to that?
**GRAYLE**        Because women, like men, are but insects who die in a season!
**PAST GRALAE**   My Julia is not!
**GRAYLE**        Oh, but she was. She soon lost her looks and her wit, and finally her life. I've forgotten what she looked like.
**PAST GRALAE**   I would have given anything to spend my life together with her!
**GRAYLE**        I <u>did</u>.
**DOCTOR**        Are you quite finished talking to yourself?
**GRAYLE**        A fascinating encounter, Doctor, but it is of no importance. I have a clear field of fire on you now.[108] It is fitting that I kill you now, in the small space before my masters grant me their power once more. It is fitting that I will kill you while I am also mortal!

**Scene Sixty-Two: Temple.**
*FX: Sounds of battle continue.*

**MARCUS**        There is only one of the beasts left! Charge!
*FX: Massed yell of Roman soldiers.*
**NIMON**         We have killed so many of you! I will kill all!
*FX: Nimon blast meets roar of soldiers.*
**LUCILIUS**      You... will... kill... no... more!
*FX: Gurgling roar of dying Nimon.*
**NIMON**         The others... will... feed... on your world!
*FX: With a final roar, the NIMON dies and falls to the floor.*
**MARCUS**        Lucilius, the beast is dead!
**LUCILIUS**      Thank mighty Mithras. We have won this day.
**MARCUS**        And covered the temple floor with the biggest blood sacrifice it has even seen. Five of the beasts. Five dozen of our comrades.
**LUCILIUS**      But it was the best of battles, Marcus, my friend. For the best of causes. Somehow, I know it. What we did here today has made a difference to the future. The beast is slain. What is best in mankind can prosper in our little time, without fear of the future.
**MARCUS**        Come, let's to the injured. We have many wounds to heal.

**Scene Sixty-Three: Roman Camp.**
*FX: The distant sound of cheering men.*

**DOCTOR**        By the sound of it, I think the legionaries have won.
**GRAYLE**        It doesn't matter, Doctor. With your vehicle out of the

tunnel between worlds, my masters will still swarm to feed on the Earth of the future.

**PAST GRALAE** What?!

**CHARLEY** It's true!

**LUCY** He's planning to destroy the world!

**GRAYLE** But first I shall do what I have ached to do for centuries. I will destroy you, Doctor! Pray to whatever gods you have!

**DOCTOR** I do that every day.

**CHARLEY** Doctor, please! Run!

**GRAYLE** Die, Doctor!

**PAST GRALAE** No! This will not be!

*FX: Sound of sword striking. A scream from GRAYLE.*

**DOCTOR** Grayle...

*FX: The body falls to the ground.*

**LUCY** Grayle, you killed... yourself!

**PAST GRALAE** He... was evil. The worst kind of man. I couldn't let him kill you. How could I turn into that... that thing?! No honour, no love, no humanity!

**DOCTOR** I don't think you need worry about becoming him now. History is changing as we speak.

**CHARLEY** This means Gralae won't be energised by the Nimon, doesn't it? He won't be their agent, none of what we've been through will happen! (*To GRALAE*) You've saved more than the Doctor. You've saved the world!

**DOCTOR** The world isn't quite saved yet, Charley. Gralae, there's a couple of things still to be done.

**PAST GRALAE** Anything to end this nightmare.

**DOCTOR** You've got to destroy the communications device. And you've got to begin an evacuation. The Nimon will still try to transmat the sacrifices. They didn't wait for you to confirm that with them in the last version of history, and they won't now! The temple and the camp will still be destroyed.

**PAST GRALAE** It shall be done.

**CHARLEY** Doctor, doesn't this create a paradox? Aren't we about to land here and try to find Gralae?

**DOCTOR** Not with the temporal disruption that the Nimon caused. It's allowed this new version of history to quietly replace the old one, and never mind how we got here. Time heals itself like that.

**CHARLEY** (*To herself*) Sometimes...

**LUCY** I will never be able to tell anyone of this story.

**DOCTOR** Come on, into the TARDIS. We'll drop you off in your home time period.

**LUCY** Oh, yes please!

**DOCTOR** Thank you, Gralae. By sacrificing a possible future of your own, you've opened ours to us again. You've created a new world.

**PAST GRALAE** A better one, I think, that does not contain that shadow of myself. Goodbye Lord Doctor, a safe journey and long life to you and yours!

**DOCTOR** And to you, my friend. Come on ladies. Our carriage awaits.

**CHARLEY** Doctor, my head... it's full of different memories. Contradictory ones.

**DOCTOR** That'll last until you sleep. And then you'll know some of them as memories, and some of them as stories, and some of them as dreams. Don't worry, everything will be taken care of. The tides of time wash us all clean.[109]

*FX: TARDIS door closes. TARDIS take-off. Fade into...*

## Scene Sixty-Four: Singapore Gardens.

*FX: The lap of water, the distant sounds of ships and the blare of loud gamelan music. A party is going on. Fireworks, applause and laughter.*

**CHARLEY**      I'm glad we got back to Singapore to see the end of the New Year celebrations.
**DOCTOR**      And this time in the good old-fashioned original timeline! Time Classic, I call it.
**CHARLEY**      So the disruption to time is all sorted out? It had nothing to do with me being?
**DOCTOR**      (*Too fast*) Of course it didn't! Mind you, the TARDIS still didn't seem too keen on coming back here. Probably some dust in the old girl's circuits.
**CHARLEY**      Lucy seemed happy to be home.
**DOCTOR**      I was quite offended. Most people get one ride in the TARDIS and want to keep on doing it!
**CHARLEY**      Well, she did have to attend to the funeral of her partner in crime.
**DOCTOR**      Yes, I suppose she did. So shall we go and find your boyfriend Alex and have dinner?
**CHARLEY**      He is not my boyfriend. And yes, let's.
**DOCTOR**      And we don't have to avoid mentioning his embarrassing relatives. We can talk about his noble ancestors. Oh! Hey! Charley, do you know what the most wonderful thing of all is?
**CHARLEY**      What?
**DOCTOR**      I've got through this whole business without referring to the horns of a dilemma, or exclaiming 'holy cow', or–
**CHARLEY**      But you have now.
**DOCTOR**      Yes! Isn't it nice that things are back to normal?

## Scene Sixty-Five: Int TARDIS.

**DOCTOR**      ...and I truly believed that they were, which just goes to show how wrong you can be, my Lord.
**RASSILON**      I am not sure I like the use of the word 'You' there, Doctor.
**DOCTOR**      My apologies. 'How wrong I can be'. Poor Lucy. If she hadn't accompanied me in the TARDIS...[110]
**RASSILON**      You care for the life of yet another individual as you do the welfare of the universe, which is to be admired. Yet conversely, you assumed that the Nimon were responsible for the chaos that now threatens us all when they actually made use of conditions that existed because of your own actions. It is sad, Doctor, but there is fault and blame in your actions.
**DOCTOR**      But... I honestly believed that Grayle was behind the time disruption.[111] That with his redemption, I need worry no longer. I meant every word I said to Charley. I should have known better.

267

**RASSILON**     Indeed! And what else do you have to tell me?

**DOCTOR**     I think the rest of the story can speak for itself, my lord. Let's just say, not long after we left Singapore, Charley and I discovered that our troubles were only just beginning...

*NB: This scene to be recorded as Scene 60 of* Neverland, *with the relevant portions being used there and here.*

## Scene Sixty-Six: Country House.

*FX: The ticking of a clock. A door cracks open.*

**LUCY**     Papa? Oh no. Force of habit. I half expected you to be there. I don't know how I shall go on without you, when I–

*FX: She screams.*

**MARTIN**     What is it, Lucy?! What's wrong?! I just popped out for a moment to get the port. My dear, you look like you've seen a ghost!

**LUCY**     I think I have! (*Recovers for a moment*) But how?!

**MARTIN**     I've been worried sick myself, waiting for you to return. I went down the caves to look for you, after that I fought off that oaf Grayle, but you had gone. Thank goodness you're all right!

**LUCY**     There are times when it is as good to see you as it would be to see my real dear papa, in his grave all these years.[112] Was this a trick, then? Have I organised your funeral as part of our greatest charade?

**MARTIN**     I don't know what you –

*FX: A sound like a drain gurgling, played backwards. Everything shakes and the two people wail in fear. There is a rumbling that remains constant under the following, and LUCY and MARTIN must sound as if they are in danger of losing their balance.*

**ANTI-CHARLEY** Ahhh (*as if getting comfortable in a new dress*)... how pleasant...

**LUCY**     Charlotte! Or is that Charlotte? But you left, with the Doctor...

**ANTI-CHARLEY** Doctor? Charley Pollard? Is that who I am? Who I... will be... yes. Yes, of course it is. I can see her now, her memories are forming inside me...

**LUCY**     I... I don't understand...

**ANTI-CHARLEY** Do excuse this disturbance – I shouldn't be in your universe, we don't... like each other very much. Look on me as a visitor, a tourist doing a spot of Christmas shopping at Liberty's. I think that is how Charley Pollard would regard it.

**LUCY**     But you're Charley...

**ANTI-CHARLEY** No. Not quite. But I may be – oh! Oh yes, you, young human, are tainted. You have residual chronon energy about you. How delightful, I'm feeling... peckish. You've been time travelling – with the Doctor no doubt. Come here. I... hunger.

**LUCY**     No... no, I... ahhhhhh!!!

*FX: Drain gurgle again as LUCY is sucked screaming into whatever ANTI-CHARLEY is. It fades.*

**ANTI-CHARLEY** And you? You, sir, are a paradox, equally touched by Lady Time's graceful fingers. You are a product of disruption, as am I. You should not be here at all.

**MARTIN**     Young lady, I know not of that which you speak... but please, I beg of you... do not hurt me... please...

*FX: His begging is swallowed up by his scream as he, too, is sucked drain-like into ANTI-CHARLEY.*
**ANTI-CHARLEY** Yes. Yes, I now know all I need. I am coming for you, Charlotte Pollard. And you, Doctor.
*FX: Drain-noise again as she goes, laughing. The rumbling settles and all that remains is an eerie silence, and a slight breeze upon which we can hear faint laughter, mixing into:*
*Closing theme.*[113]

**THE END**

# Hidden Bonus Track:

**DOCTOR**     He is impulsive, idealistic, ready to risk his life for a worthy cause. He hates tyranny and oppression, and anything that is anti-life. He never gives in, and he never gives up, however overwhelming the odds against him. The Doctor believes in good and fights evil. Though often caught up in violent situations, he is a man of peace. He is never cruel or cowardly. In fact, to put it simply, the Doctor is a hero. These days there aren't so many of them around...[114]

# NOTES

**N.B.** The cast credits in the CD booklet were slightly different in order to disguise certain characters' true identities. Robert Curbishley was credited as playing Grayle's Masters' Voices, whilst Don Warrington was listed as playing The Auditor. (Also, India Fisher played Anti-Charley, but was uncredited.)

## PART ONE

**1.** Line changed to: 'Her journey on the *R101*, where I'd met her, had been with the intention of keeping an appointment with a **chap** called Alex.' *Gary Russell: 'Paul McGann and I felt that "boy" made Alex sound too young and also made the Doctor sound prejudicial, so we changed it to the more anodyne "chap".'*

**2.** Line changed to: '~~He~~ sounds like a man after my own heart.'

**3.** '**No**,' said twice.

**4.** Deleted dialogue – DOCTOR: '~~I think she was just being nice.~~'

**5.** Line changed to: 'The **chap** took Charley's arm, and showed her his buttonhole.'

**6.** Line changed to: 'There was **still** quite a bit of coverage.'

**7.** Line changed to: 'Thinking it was Charley, ~~as she'd forced me to say I'd join the two of them in the celebrations at midnight~~, I didn't even glance up.'

**8.** Added dialogue – a WAITER: 'Certainly, sir.' The WAITER was played by sound designer Gareth Jenkins.

**9.** '**Yes**,' added at the start of the line.

**10.** Line changed to: 'It's... **it's** possible.'

**11.** Line changed to: 'We can prevent this ~~from~~ happening!'

**12.** Added dialogue – DOCTOR: 'Hmm.'

**13.** Line changed to: 'Look over **there**!'

**14.** Line changed to: 'Masters who feed on the energy of worlds, **they** have tremendous power if they can indulge their slaves so much as to create a whole new timeline for them.'

**15.** Deleted dialogue – DOCTOR: '~~That's why he went to the trouble of getting his masters to do that.~~'

**16.** Line changed to: 'We're never going to have **that** major battle against the Picts, are we?'

**17.** Line changed to: 'Wait a minute, I'm trying to keep my **stole** out of the mud.'

**18.** This exchange was altered to:

**DOCTOR** ~~So am I! Now, you're certain my bottom doesn't look big in this?~~

**CHARLEY** ~~Doctor... We really do have more important things to think about.~~

**DOCTOR** ~~Of course, of course!~~ **Now** just take a moment to consider how well we're doing! For once, we've arrived somewhere in exactly the right costumes, having thoroughly read up on our destination! It feels luxurious!

*Gary Russell: 'No disrespect to Paul Cornell or Caroline Symcox, but on the day of recording both Paul McGann and India Fisher felt the script generally had too many cultural references to the 20th century, this being one of them. I agreed and so this is the first of a small number of similar slightly post-modern references you'll see cut out.'*

**19.** Line changed to: 'This is much more important than anything else ~~you might have got planned~~.'

**20.** Deleted dialogue – DOCTOR: '~~Tell him, Dasious~~.'

**21.** Deleted dialogue – CHARLEY: '~~Daisius~~.'

**22.** Deleted dialogue – DOCTOR: '~~I call her that for short. Well?~~'

*Gary Russell: 'Not sure why these lines were cut - perhaps we felt the Daisias Daisias stuff was over-egging it a bit.'*

**23.** Line changed to: 'It falls to me to sort through the used undergarments of an ancient **Briton**.' *Gary Russell: 'We thought that as Gralae was a Briton and Charley knew his descendant's family to be English, she'd have known he wasn't Roman.'*

**24.** Line changed to: 'No, it is not **the** time yet!'

**25.** Line changed to: '~~If someone who was... (embarrassed) you know... can have a cult of his own, anyone can! Oh now~~, shh, Lucilius is ready to speak.'

**26.** Line changed to: 'It spoke to me... well, rather angrily, ~~and~~...'

**27.** Line changed to: 'So **Grayle** switched over to sound only?'

**28.** Line changed to: 'What ~~in Hades~~ is he doing?'

**29.** Deleted dialogue – DOCTOR: '~~Oh pants!~~' *Gary Russell: '"Oh pants" did not go down well with Paul McGann. I think chronologically it was the first bit we recorded where he just refused to say it and began the process mentioned in Note 18.'*

**30.** Line changed to: 'We do not **run away**.'

**31.** Line changed to: 'You may live an **extra few** years, but immortality?'

**32.** Deleted dialogue – CHARLEY: '~~You're right. We do have to get going!~~'

**33.** Deleted dialogue – CHARLEY: '~~The huts! The fences! The sky!~~'

**34.** CHARLEY says this line, rather than the DOCTOR.

## PART TWO

**35.** This opening exchange of this scene was altered to:

**DOCTOR**   That was close!
**CHARLEY**   I'll say! ~~Doctor – oh no, your toga's on fire!~~
**DOCTOR**   ~~What?! Quick, help me!~~
~~FX: They beat out his toga.~~
**DOCTOR**   ~~And that was such a great toga, too.~~ We only got away from that by the skin of our noses. Ow, look out where you're pointing that sword!

**36.** Line changed to: 'We have to find **out** the point in space and time where they try again.'

**37.** Line changed to: '"Zagreus sits inside your head/Zagreus lives among the dead/Zagreus sees you in your bed/And eats you when you're sleeping", as **momma** used to say.' The *Zagreus* rhyme was written by Alan Barnes.

**38.** Deleted dialogue – DOCTOR: '~~A bad guy who was a know all to boot~~.' *Gary Russell: 'Paul just felt 'to boot' was not his Doctor and in the end the whole line came out.'*

**39.** Line changed to: 'Grab a gown from the wardrobe ~~room~~, Charley.'

**40.** Added dialogue. At this point, the PRISONER says: '**No. You can't send me away**...' The PRISONER was played by Gareth Jenkins.

**41.** Line changed to: 'Do try **to** remember.'

**42.** Deleted dialogue – DOCTOR: '~~(Whisper) What?!~~'

**43.** Line changed to: 'It'll protect you from any harmful effects ~~from the radiation~~.'

**44.** Line changed to: 'Why must they build these things **so close** to the river, it makes my bones ache and –

**45.** Line changed to: '(*Whisper*) I mean you're a fighter. "My liege, my lady" ~~now~~ quick!'

**46.** Line changed to: 'Your actions will ultimately lead to the destruction of ~~the planet~~ Earth, the conquest of all time and space!'

**47.** Line changed to: 'Fascinating, **my** lady, fascinating!'

**48.** Line changed to: 'Stop! Yes, I carry a blade ~~as well as a mace~~! And you go unharmed! Why **shouldn't** I kill you now?'

**49.** Line changed to: '**They won't find you in this machine**. ~~I closed the door behind me~~.'

**50.** Line changed to: '**I can't believe we're actually manacled to a wall. I thought they only did that in cartoons**.' *Gary Russell: 'We tweaked this line in studio because we couldn't be sure Charley was a regular* Punch *reader and thought a more generic "in the cartoons" seemed better.'*

**51.** Line changed to: 'So you and she **have** a lot in common.'

**52.** Line changed to: 'Only Edith saw it a **little** bit differently.'

**53.** Line changed to: 'And then everyone was talking about a wedding, before her father returned to say no, and I couldn't see her beforehand, and none of her courtiers **wanted** to listen when I said I didn't want to marry her, and one thing led to another and...' *Gary Russell: 'One of my favourite things ever here – the idea that the Doctor and Edith nearly got married is pure Cornellian and very, very funny. We had a ball with Sue Wallace and Len Greaves in this story. I'd worked with Len before, in Paul Cornell's previous play,* The Shadow of the Scourge, *and we got on terribly well – he was also a director and had directed Nick Pegg's pantomimes up in Harrogate. In talking to Nick as we were preparing this run of Eighth Doctor stories, I said I was thinking of Len for Edward, and Nick suggested Len's wife as Edith. I had no idea he was married to Sue, who I'd worked with back in 1988 on a BBC show called* Making Out *and of whom I was terribly fond. We had a laugh doing these scenes – both Sue and Len have very dry, very droll senses of humour and every so often they, plus Paul, India and Steve Perring, would do a whole scene in the style of a* Carry On *film.*

*Which wasn't too surprising as the double-entendres in this episode skate perilously close to the best of Talbot Rothwell!'*

**54.** Line changed to: 'Do not thank **me for** anything yet, Doctor.'

**55.** Line changed to: 'It can kill you slowly, over months, like an illness, as my men **have** discovered.'

**56.** Deleted dialogue – DOCTOR: '~~You're bringing them here.~~'

## PART THREE

**57.** Line changed to: 'So it's just him we have to deal with **for** now then.'

**58.** 'I'm afraid,' added at the beginning of the line.

**59.** Line changed to: 'Intrigue comes with the territory when you spend ~~much~~ time around royalty.'

**60.** Deleted dialogue – CHARLEY: '~~So, you think he has ideas above his station!~~'

**61.** Line changed to: '~~Maybe there's a bit of Time Lord snobbery left in me after all. This isn't like when I run into the Master. He's got some self knowledge, he knows that what he's doing is futile. He's just having fun, in his own way. Showing off to a universe that doesn't care. He always changes his mind when it looks like the cosmos is going to be destroyed. I'm rather fond of him. But Grayle...~~ He'd destroy the universe because of the terms of his father's will.' *Gary Russell: 'This seemed too much like self-referential continuity at the time and slowed down the plot so chop chop chop we went...'*

**62.** Line changed to: 'We just look **ahead** another 750 years and we find... Of course! The early nineteenth century. ~~Georgian – one of my favourite periods.~~'

**63.** Line changed to: 'I mean, they seem pretty powerful, why can't they get here in **a spaceship**?'

**64.** Line changed to: '**Be a bit conspicuous**, **wouldn't it**?'

**65.** The first three lines of Scene Thirty-One were changed to:

**DOCTOR** Caves. ~~(Voice fades) Hang on, somewhere in the TARDIS I have (voice approaching) one of those.~~
~~FX: A flaming torch ignites.~~
**CHARLEY** ~~Careful with that!~~
**DOCTOR** ~~Mind your petticoats.~~ I really like this sword of yours. In terms of fashion, I mean. This was a time when it suited a gentleman to carry one. It's thin enough to pass for a rapier. Do you like the look?

*Gary Russell: 'I had this one cut in post-production as I never felt entirely comfortable with the takes we did and it didn't damage the plot by losing it.'*

**66.** Line changed to: '**Lucifer**! **Seek**!'

**67.** Line changed to: 'And ~~soon~~ so much more besides.'

**68.** Deleted dialogue – CHARLEY: '~~There was a lot of melted cheese.~~'

**69.** Line changed to: 'Grayle hasn't lost his interest in **his** bos bovis.'

**70.**   Line changed to: 'Sometimes the best way **is in** the front door.'

**71.**   Line changed to: 'Ah, **yes**.'

**72.**   Line changed to: '**Ah, yes**. **I was**.'

**73.**   Line changed to: 'And that would be **whom**?'

**74.**   Line changed to: 'Tonight is the **night** of our year, the celebration of the rising of the bull.' *Gary Russell: 'A delightful episode this, the best of the four I think. My suspicion is that a lot of the dialogue is Caroline Symcox's – India and Justine had great fun playing it. Justine sent me her tape after a mutual friend told her about the plays. She was  smashing and gave 110% to the role of Lucy. I had agreed with Paul Cornell right at the start that we'd do a play with a lot of characters but as each episode was self-contained, we could double up on actors (I usually abhor doing this). Thus Stephen Fewell was both Lucilius and Martin in this story, whilst Bob Curbishley was both Marcus and the voice of the horned beasts! Of all the stuff Steve Fewell has done for Big Finish, I think his Richard Martin is his best. Very well observed and his sparring with Paul McGann on the day was great fun to watch – I think they both liked having such good dialogue.'*

**75.**   Line changed to: 'But anything for your **future wealthy** son-in-law, eh, Richard?'

**76.**   'Yes,' added at the start of the line.

**77.**   Line changed to: '~~Oh~~ how delightful.'

**78.**   Line changed to: 'He's happy, and **he's** in the mood to talk.'

**79.**   Line changed to: '~~And~~ it was as untrue then as it is now.'

**80.**   Line changed to: 'Cut off from your masters, we could still be **friends**.'

**81.**   This and the following three lines are replaced by:

| CHARLEY | Doctor! **No**, **Lucy, come back**! **He'll be all right**. |
| LUCY | Doctor! **Oh**, **papa**, help! |
| CHARLEY | **Grayle, let Lucy go**! |

*Gary Russell: 'We developed this a bit in studio, just to emphasise exactly what was going on as it might not have been entirely clear from these lines as scripted. Paul and Caroline were being right and proper and not giving anyone exposition to speak, but on this occasion it think it was needed so we put it in. That's my justification and I'm sticking to it!'*

**82.**   Line changed to: 'Then let's go! ~~To the caves!~~'

**83.**   Line changed to: 'This is the sword which Mithras **used to** slay the demon bull. ~~Or a recreation of it~~. A rustless weapon.' *Gary Russell: 'I cut the recreation line because it sounded like the Mithran Bull was recreated, not the sword!'*

**84.**   'I,' added at the beginning of the line.

**85.**   Line changed to: 'Do you really think that once you've opened the way for them, they'll want to spend any of their energy ~~on~~ granting you immortality?'

**86.**   *Gary Russell: 'I showed everyone a clip or ten of* The Horns of Nimon *so they could see the things and Bob could perfect the voice. (There are some out-takes of these scenes where he did them as William Hague, who was clearly the politician de jour at the time!) On seeing the Nimon, Paul McGann sat down, muttering how glad he was he was doing* Doctor Who *on audio. Justine, I remember, needed* *persuading that this story had actually been transmitted. Like everyone else, she couldn't quite believe the Nimon had ever been considered acceptable for TV! I was too busy saying, "Yes, I know they look rubbish but they're a great concept and have fab voices which'll work on audio." I think this was the argument I'd used on Paul Cornell when first asking him to put the Nimon into a script. Bob got the voice really well and combined with Gareth Jenkins's sterling work in post-production, made them seem really quite terrifying. Finally, Bob had worked for me a couple of times previously on* Doctor Who *and Benny audios but this, and his role in* The Chimes of Midnight *done earlier in the same week, were his biggest parts. A fabulous actor who became briefly recognisable because he introduced his "parents" to the joys of MacDonalds in a TV commercial shortly afterwards.'*

## Part Four

**87.** Line changed to: 'It seems someone else shares your love **of** money, Grayle.'

**88.** Line changed to: '**Keep it**! ...here it is, the horned goblet!'

**89.** 'Oh,' added at the beginning of the line.

**90.** Line changed to: '~~You're big monsters, but you're out of shape~~.' *Gary Russell: 'One of a couple of* Get Carter *references that were exorcised when Paul McGann gave me a questioning look during recording. He never said a word. He just stopped, looked at me and slowly shook his head. I felt sorry for Paul Cornell, who was in the gallery with Alistair Lock and hearing these little moments dropping out of his script with a silence that spoke volumes!'*

**91.** Line changed to: '**You have your horned goblet! Let me keep the rest**.'

**92.** Line changed to: 'Oh... ~~Papa~~.'

**93.** Line changed to: 'The oscillator! **Where is** the oscillator?'

**94.** Line changed to: '**They've got it, Doctor**!'

**95.** Line changed to: '~~Nimon, Charley. The plural's the same as the singular. And~~ no, we're not.'

**96.** Added dialogue – GRAYLE: (***Rushing in***) '**Masters! I have your goblet**!' *Gary Russell: 'I thought it was important to bring Grayle back into the scene here with the goblet otherwise it was a tad confusing as to who had what and when. We also dropped the Nimon/Nimons line which was the result of an in-joke between Paul Cornell and myself. It'd been funny in a pub, less so in a studio with time running out.'*

**97.** Line changed to: '~~Ah,~~ you're in for a surprise.'

**98.** Line changed to: 'By diving **straight** into the space/time corridor they're using and getting in the way.'

**99.** Line changed to: 'Please, come ~~on~~ in.'

**100.** *Gary Russell: 'We pay for the* Doctor Who *theme by the second and I've always forbidden musicians from incorporating it into their scores (I think there's one play which does it early on in our run) – hence Paul's cute idea never happened here.'*

**101.** Line changed to: 'And he let me win at ***Scrabble***.' *Gary Russell: 'I wasn't convinced that* Cluedo *wasn't a post-R101 Thirties invention and thus thought* Scrabble *might be more Charley's thing!'*

**102.** Line changed to: 'They have said they will teach me how to use it, **giving** me freedom over all time and space!'

**103.** Line changed to: '~~Do I...~~ do I know you?'

**104.** Line changed to: '~~What!~~ Who are you?'

**105.** Line changed to: 'It's my lift ~~home~~, assuming I can deal with what's inside.'

**106.** Deleted dialogue – CHARLEY: '~~Don't listen to him, Doctor!~~'

**107.** Deleted dialogue – DOCTOR: '~~Oh dear.~~'

**108.** Line changed to: '~~I have a clear field of fire on you now.~~' *Gary Russell: 'Steve Perring played both Grayles simultaneously. This was my first time working with Steve but was not to be the last. He has a great voice for a villain in the smooth George Sanders/Peter Cushing mode rather than a "Bwa ha ha" moustache-twiddling mode. The next time we were in Bristol recording with Mr McGann, I made a point of getting Steve back in a semi-regular role as the Croaker.'*

**109.** Line changed to: 'The tides of time **will** wash us all clean.'

**110.** The first three lines of Scene Sixty-Five were deleted. *Gary Russell: 'I don't know why these three lines were dropped – maybe they didn't fit in with what they had to slot around in* Neverland. *Don Warrington wasn't there and indeed his dialogue wasn't recorded for another nine months when he did all his lines for* Seasons of Fear, The Time of the Daleks *and* Neverland *together.'*

**111.** Line changed to: '~~But...~~ I honestly believed that Grayle was behind the time disruption.'

**112.** Line changed to: 'There are times when it is as good to see you as it would be to see my **own dear late** papa, ~~in his grave all these years~~.'

**113.** There is no closing version of the *Doctor Who* theme in Part Four. *Gary Russell: 'The first six lines of Scene Sixty-Six are by Paul and Caroline, the rest were written by me to set up the Anti-Charley/Sentris stuff for* Neverland. *I don't think Paul and Caroline even knew of them until the play came out, but I could be wrong. I quite like this little scene.'*

**114.** The Hidden Bonus Track was cut from the finished play. *Gary Russell: 'Paul Cornell begged me to do this – he thought Paul McGann reading it would sound magnificent and he would have been right, but I felt it was inappropriate and irrelevant, and pulling my producer's hat on ever tighter, flatly refused. I believe it was the right decision, to go from the Anti-Charley moment to this would have seemed really out of place. And I don't think Paul McGann was keen either...'*

# APPENDICES

This section of the book contains supplementary material for each of the four scripts featured. Iain McLaughlin's original version of The Eye of the Scorpion is presented in its fullest form: the first one and a half episodes. Also included are some of Iain's notes sent to producer Gary Russell during the scriptwriting process.

Crossroads in Time was a rejected pitch for an audio story from Gareth Roberts and Clayton Hickman; also in these appendices are The One Doctor's original proposal, the script for its trailer and the scripts for two items that became hidden bonus tracks on the CD.

Before Dust Breeding, Mike Tucker was writing a different script for the Master – Dark Rising, the only completed episode of which is presented here. Also, Seasons of Fear's original outline is included.

# EYE OF THE BEETLE

## PART ONE

**1. Int.**
*Inside his shack, an Egyptian (circa 1400 BC if we could see him) is
dishing up food. We can hear him pottering with pots, bowls and testing
his own cooking – a noisy slurp. His name is AMENK.*

**AMENK**     Not bad. Not bad at all.
*The sound of the door being hurled open and a small boy noisily runs in.
The boy is TARSHISH.*
**TARSHISH**     Father! FATHER! FATHER!
**AMENK**     I knew you could smell food, Tarshish. Your nose is
sharper than a Nile crocodile. Sit and eat. What is it? What's frightened
you? What have you seen? If you have been stealing figs from Mulak
again, not even Pharaoh could save your hide from my belt.
*Footsteps enter.*
**YANIS**     The boy saw me.
**AMENK**     Why…? Who are you?
**YANIS**     Yanis. Warlord of the Scorpion tribe.
*Slicing blows. AMENK dead, TARSHISH soon after.*
**YANIS**     And soon to be Pharaoh of this miserable country.
*Sips the food.*
**YANIS**     Not bad.

**2. Inside the Temple at Thebes.**
*SHEMEK, an elderly priest is observing the stars and tutting. He is joined
by FAYUM, a member of the Royal Court. Fayum is much younger. They
are friends but talk as if at war – baiting each other. If their tone wasn't
friendly, you'd think they loathed each other.*

**SHEMEK**     This is not good. Not good at all.
**FAYUM**     Still muttering and watching the night skies, Shemek?
How are the omens? No, don't tell me – they're bad.
**SHEMEK**     Yes. The gods send signs in the skies that speak only of
terrible things to come.
**FAYUM**     Spare me your nonsense, Shemek. We are safe inside
Pharaoh's own palace. Nothing can harm us here.
**SHEMEK**     We shall see.
**FAYUM**     Your ramblings may impress the concubines and hesets
but I see through them and I see through you, you old charlatan. Sleep
well, old friend.
*FAYUM's footsteps echo into the distance.*
**SHEMEK**     (*Softly*) And I see what awaits you, my impetuous friend.
The same death awaiting us all.

### 3. TARDIS interior.

*The FIFTH DOCTOR is giving PERI the ten bob tour of his beloved ship. (This is directly after* Planet Of Fire, *so PERI is still pretty green at this time and space travel malarkey.)*

**PERI**      I still can't believe you can fit all this into one little blue box.

**DOCTOR**      Oh, we've barely started the tour.

**PERI**      Barely started? We've been at it for hours. And if my mother heard me say that to a guy I'd just met she'd have a coronary on the spot.

**DOCTOR**      What was that?

**PERI**      Nothing. I was just saying that we'd been wandering these corridors for hours.

**DOCTOR**      I thought you wanted to know your way around.

**PERI**      I do, believe me, but I lost my bearings six corridors, three floors and two hours ago.

**DOCTOR**      It just takes a little getting used to, that's all. You'll know your way around in no time.

**PERI**      So you really know what all these doors are?

**DOCTOR**      Naturally. For instance, this is the small library.

*He opens the door and we hear waves crashing on the shore.*

**PERI**      The books are going to get wet.

**DOCTOR**      Ah.

*He shuts the door.*

**DOCTOR**      Of course, sometimes the TARDIS moves things about. Still, not to worry. A little redecorating never hurt anybody.

**PERI**      A little redecorating? You've got a lake in there.

**DOCTOR**      Yes, I know. I much preferred it where it was. Where to next?

**PERI**      I don't suppose you've got a restaurant stashed away here? My stomach thinks my throat's been cut.

**DOCTOR**      There should be a food machine around here someplace. I haven't used it much since Susan left...

*A thud as the TARDIS lands.*

**DOCTOR**      We've landed. Let's see where we are. We can carry on the tour later. Come on. This way.

*He hurries off.*

**PERI**      *(Mutters)* Great. We'll just pick this up later, will we?

**DOCTOR**      *(Calling)* Peri...

**PERI**      Coming.

### 4. TARDIS Console Room.

*The DOCTOR is busy working the controls when PERI hurries in.*

**PERI**      Doctor...

**DOCTOR**      Sssh.

**PERI**      Do...

**DOCTOR**      Ssssh. Ah. Excellent.

**PERI**      From that 'Ah!' and 'Excellent!' I take it I don't have to ask if you know what happened.

**DOCTOR**      We've materialised.

**PERI**        You're gonna have to teach me how these controls work.
**DOCTOR**      Perhaps. I remember what happened the last time I let Tegan drive. Come on. Let's take a look outside...
**PERI**        You male chauvinist...

## 5. Ext. The Egyptian desert.
*PERI hurries out of the TARDIS after the DOCTOR.*

**PERI**        ...porker. Where are we?
**DOCTOR**      From the gravity and atmosphere (*sniffs*) I'd say Earth. No industrial by-products in the air? Definitely Earth. Egypt, roughly 1400BC.
**PERI**        Oh, come on. Even you can't tell all that from the air.
**DOCTOR**      True, but the hieroglyphs on the wall of that house behind the TARDIS are a bit of a giveaway.
**PERI**        Great. Even the Egyptians had graffiti.
**DOCTOR**      Hmm. (*Thoughtful*) Can you hear something?
**PERI**        Like what?
**DOCTOR**      Horses... Like...
*A young woman (late teens) is yelling and shouting for her horses to stop. Her chariot is a runaway. She is HATCHEPSUT.*
**HATCHEPSUT** Slow down. Whoa. Slow down, damn you.
**DOCTOR**      Like that.
**PERI**        Her chariot's out of control.
**DOCTOR**      She's being chased. There's another chariot.
*All through we hear HATCHEPSUT and her horses getting closer.*
**PERI**        They're firing arrows at her. We have to do something.
**DOCTOR**      I'm thinking.
**PERI**        Think faster. They're almost on top of us.
**DOCTOR**      Here. Grab that rope. Tie this end round the TARDIS.
**PERI**        What are you going to do?
**DOCTOR**      Take the other end to the far side of the breach in the wall and yank it tight after the first chariot is through. Hurry.
**PERI**        I wish I had paid more attention at summer camp. This stuff's so slippery.
**HATCHEPSUT** Steady. Steady.
**DOCTOR**      Over here. This way. Peri, are you ready?
**PERI**        Nearly.
**DOCTOR**      Hurry. She's almost through. Quickly.
*The pounding of the horses is almost on top of them.*
**PERI**        There. Done. She's through. Pull it.
*The sound of the rope going taught and then a shocked yell, followed by the sound of a man in armour hitting the ground hard.*
**PERI**        You got him.
*The fallen man groans. HATCHEPSUT is yelling for her horses to stop.*
**HATCHEPSUT** Stop. Slow now. Stop. Whoa.
*No use. The horses thunder on.*
**DOCTOR**      Her horses have been scared out of their wits. She can't control them. Keep an eye on our friend there.
**PERI**        What?
**DOCTOR**      I don't have time to argue. Someone has to stop those horses. Tell your friend I borrowed his chariot for a few minutes.

*The sound of the reins being flicked and the chariot moving off again.*
**DOCTOR**　　　Hya.
*The fallen man groans and mumbles.*
**MAN**　　　Wha...?
**PERI**　　　I hope this isn't an antique.
*The sound of a pottery jar being smashed over the man's head. Another groan and he hits the dirt hard for the second time in under a minute.*
**PERI**　　　Sorry. That's really gonna hurt.
*Out in the desert, the DOCTOR's chariot is chasing HATCHEPSUT's. If we could see them the horses would be sweating up a foam as they charge across the desert. Their hooves are pounding loudly.*
**DOCTOR**　　　Hya. HYA!
**HATCHEPSUT** WHOA. SLOW DOWN. STOP!
**DOCTOR**　　　I'm almost there. Hang on.
**HATCHEPSUT** Whoa. Slow now..
**DOCTOR**　　　Here. I'm bringing my chariot alongside. You'll have to step across onto it.
**HATCHEPSUT** No.
**DOCTOR**　　　Your horses are too frightened to stop. I'm not going to hurt you. I'm almost there. Just a little closer.
*On top of the horses pounding hooves, the sound of wheels touching and sparks flying. Both HATCHEPSUT and the DOCTOR yelp.*
**DOCTOR**　　　A little too close. Gently. Gently. Now. Step across. Hurry, I can't hold the chariots this close for long. Take my hand. Take it! Now jump. It's just one step. Step now.
*The sound of HATCHEPSUT leaping over and landing on the DOCTOR's chariot.*
**DOCTOR**　　　Got you. It's all right. I've got you. Whoa now. Whoa.
*The chariot pulls to a stop.*
**DOCTOR**　　　Are you hurt?
**HATCHEPSUT** Stay away from me.
**DOCTOR**　　　It's all right. Put the knife away. I'm not going to hurt you. Though I can't say the same for the chap I borrowed this chariot from.
**HATCHEPSUT** Where is he?
**DOCTOR**　　　Back there. Unconscious.
**HATCHEPSUT** Good. Get me away from here.
**DOCTOR**　　　I don't suppose you'd care to tell me why he was trying to kill you?
**HATCHEPSUT** You don't know?
**DOCTOR**　　　If I knew I wouldn't ask, would I?
**HATCHEPSUT** You are a stranger here. Or an idiot.
**DOCTOR**　　　Of the two, I'd rather be a stranger. I've been to Egypt before but I don't think I've been here recently...
**HATCHEPSUT** Take me to Thebes.
**DOCTOR**　　　You haven't answered my question.
**HATCHEPSUT** No, I haven't. When we are safe in Thebes, I will see that your questions are answered.
**DOCTOR**　　　All right. Hold on. Hup. Giddup.
*The horses pull the chariot away.*

**6. The desert.**
*In the desert, by the TARDIS, the DOCTOR's chariot pulls up by PERI.*

**DOCTOR**        Whoa.

**PERI**        Doctor, am I glad you're back! I'm almost out of pots to clobber this guy with.

*The man groans. Another pot smashes and he hits the ground hard again.*

**PERI**        But I've still got one left.

**DOCTOR**        You enjoyed that too much, young lady.

**HATCHEPSUT**        I hoped he would be dead.

*The sound of HATCHEPSUT giving her would-be killer a real good booting – well, sandaling.*

**DOCTOR**        Stop. There's no need for that. Beating up an unconscious man won't solve anything.

**HATCHEPSUT**        I owe him and his kind a hundred times worse.

*Knife pulled again.*

**DOCTOR**        Give me that knife.

**HATCHEPSUT**        Let go of me. Give it back. Why do you protect this filth? Are you one of their number? Are you a mercenary?

**DOCTOR**        A doctor. The Doctor, actually. And I'm protecting him because I despise meaningless death.

**HATCHEPSUT**        (*Conceding unhappily*) Get me back to Thebes. Now.

**PERI**        You got her, then.

**DOCTOR**        So it would seem.

**PERI**        So who is she? Why were they trying to kill her? I thought this guy might have been a bandit but that's battle armour he's wearing.

**DOCTOR**        Yes, I spotted that as well. She's not exactly the most communicative of people. We'll take her to Thebes. Rip Van Winkle with the headache as well.

**PERI**        Four of us on that chariot is gonna be cramped.

**DOCTOR**        We'll be all right. These war chariots were built for two passengers and I don't think Sleeping Beauty will mind if we hang him over one of the horses.

**HATCHEPSUT**        We must leave now. By now he is bound to have been missed.

**DOCTOR**        That might be a good idea. I've had more than enough excitement for one day.

**HATCHEPSUT**        Hurry. Or I will leave you both here.

**PERI**        That's gratitude for you.

## 7. The desert.

*Two more of the would-be assassins are observing. These are scouts.*

**SCOUT 1**        The stranger has rescued her.

**SCOUT 2**        Do we attack them now?

**SCOUT 1**        With what? We have no arrows left. Besides, the chariot would reach the outer defences of Thebes before we could catch it. We would be tortured for answers like they will torture that poor fool.

**SCOUT 2**        So what do we do?

**SCOUT 1**        Report that she escaped. And hope that our chief spares our lives.

## 8. Thebes.

*The chariot rattles and chunters towards Thebes.*

**DOCTOR** There it is.

**PERI** Wow.

**DOCTOR** Yes, it is impressive, isn't it?

**PERI** If Howard could see me now. He always moaned that I didn't have any interest in history.

**DOCTOR** Where to?

**HATCHEPSUT** The palace.

**DOCTOR** The palace? If this is an enemy chariot, I don't think they'll exactly welcome us with open arms.

**HATCHEPSUT** That will not be a problem, Doctor.

**PERI** Doctor... have you noticed the people...

**DOCTOR** ...are all kneeling?

**PERI** And bowing.

**DOCTOR** Excuse me. I don't think you told us exactly who you are.

**HATCHEPSUT** No. I did not. Stand proud and firm.

**PERI** We've got company.

**DOCTOR** Whoa there. Whoa.

*The chariot halts. More chariots rattle to join them.*

**PERI** I don't like the look of those swords, Doctor.

**DOCTOR** I'm not too keen on the spears either. Best behaviour, Peri.

**PERI** You patronising...

*A man's voice cuts across her. He sounds mid-forties – ANTRANAK, head of the palace armies. A younger man is with him – SENENMUT.*

**ANTRANAK** Mighty one. We sing praises to the gods for your safe return.

**SENENMUT** I warned you against that ride in the desert, Hatchepsut.

**DOCTOR** Hatchepsut?

**PERI** Mighty one?

**HATCHEPSUT** Remember who you are speaking to, Senenmut. Be very careful. Escort us to the palace, Antranak. We have a great deal to do but this is not the place to do it.

**ANTRANAK** As you command, mighty Pharaoh.

**PERI** Pharaoh? Oh, God.

**DOCTOR** I should have known. Why else would they be attacking her?

**PERI** Should I be bowing or curtseying or something?

**HATCHEPSUT** Yes, but refrain from doing so. The chariot is quite small – and it would be unseemly for someone accompanying Pharaoh to fall off in public.

**PERI** Whatever you say.

**HATCHEPSUT** I would wager, Doctor, that you did not expect anything like this when you first saw my chariot being chased.

**DOCTOR** Er, not really, no.

**HATCHEPSUT** And yet you saved me without knowing who I was. Would you have done anything differently if you had known I was to be Pharaoh. I don't think so. Am I right?

**DOCTOR** I was under the impression that divine Pharaoh is always right.

**HATCHEPSUT** I think I would do well to avoid sparring in word games

with you, Doctor. You have no fear of me yet you don't seek my favour either. You are a most unusual man.
**DOCTOR**      Thank you.
**HATCHEPSUT** Now smile and wave to my people. Let them see that their divine Pharaoh is unharmed.

## 9. The desert.
*The two scouts who watched the DOCTOR rescue HATCHEPSUT are back at their camp. Waiting for them is YANIS.*

**YANIS**      Where are the two spineless dogs who let the whelp of a girl escape? Bring them in here.
*Sound of the two SCOUTS being hurled into the tent. When they speak they are terrified and babble, often talking over each other and continuing the others sentences.*
**GUARD**      Here, sire.
**YANIS**      Well, dogs? Do you have an explanation of how the Egyptian pup escaped from a squad of over a dozen chariots? Make your answer good or I will stake you in the sand and watch the buzzards feast on your eyes and innards.
**SCOUT 1**    It wasn't our fault, sire.
**SCOUT 2**    We plead for mercy.
**YANIS**      Save your pleading. I want answers. How did she escape?
**SCOUT 2**    She had a large escort. Six...
**SCOUT 1**    No, ten chariots. We killed all the rest – we even got her driver.
**YANIS**      And still she escaped? Imbeciles! Worse – cowards.
**SCOUT 2**    No, great sire. She had help.
**YANIS**      What help?
**SCOUT 1**    A man with long fair hair and strange clothing...
**SCOUT 2**    And a violent girl who repeatedly attacked one of our men even when he was unconscious.
**YANIS**      A girl should be no match for a man – not even one of you idiots. Tell me about the man.
**SCOUT 2**    He knocked our warrior from his chariot as if by magic.
**SCOUT 1**    Pharaoh's horses were running wild but this fair haired man took our fallen comrade's chariot and caught up.
**YANIS**      Even though the Pharaoh girl's horses were charging out of control?
**SCOUT 2**    He drove like a demon. I have never seen better. Except for you, of course, mighty Yanis.
**SCOUT 1**    He even lifted the Pharaoh from her chariot with one hand.
**YANIS**      Strong, is he?
**SCOUT 1**    Yes. The strength of ten men,
**SCOUT 2**    And tall. A head taller than most.
**YANIS**      So you were afraid of this mighty, fair giant? That is why you didn't attack.
**SCOUT 2**    No, great chief. They were too far away. We could never have caught them before they reached Thebes.
**SCOUT 1**    We thought it best to return and tell you what had happened.

**YANIS**      What has happened is that now that inbred whelp who calls herself Pharaoh knows that we are here and she knows that we will attack sooner rather than later. She is wily as a fox. She will be preparing for us. Get out. All of you.

**GUARD**      Yes, great chief. What of these two?

**YANIS**      Slit them open and let the dogs feed. They are worse than useless.

**SCOUT 1**      No, great Yanis. Mercy, please.

**SCOUT 2**      I have a wife and four children at home. Let me live. I will not fail you again.

**SCOUT 1**      And I am loyal. I have always been loyal to you.

**YANIS**      And to my predecessor who, as I remember, you helped me murder. Guard, leave them here. I will let them live – but at a price.

**SCOUT 1**      Anything.

**SCOUT 2**      Yes, but please. Please let us live.

**YANIS**      Guard, go.

*Sound of tent flap rustling as the Guard leaves.*

**YANIS**      So you want to live?

**SCOUT 2**      Yes, sire.

**SCOUT 1**      We'll do anything...

**YANIS**      One of you will live.

*Sword drawn. Thrown into the ground.*

**YANIS**      Fight – to the death. I will let the winner live.

**SCOUT 1**      Fight each other?

**YANIS**      Or will I have you both sliced open?

**SCOUT 2**      I... we...

*Sound of the two men suddenly leaping for the sword – a fight. Yanis hugely enjoys the spectacle.*

**YANIS**      If you provide some entertainment you might prove to be of some use.

*Fight continues.*

## 10. The Palace at Thebes.
*The DOCTOR is calling for PERI.*

**DOCTOR**      Are you ready yet?

**PERI**      I'll be out in a minute.

**DOCTOR**      Do try to hurry. It's considered bad form to keep the ruler of the known world waiting in her own palace.

**PERI**      Okay, okay. Here I come, ready or not. Well? What do you think?

**DOCTOR**      You've been busy.

**PERI**      Not me. I've had half a dozen servants helping me bath – and that was only hugely embarrassing – dress, put this stuff on my eyes...

**DOCTOR**      Kohl. It's used to make the sloe-eyes shape.

**PERI**      I know. My stepfather is an archaeologist, remember? This dress shows a bit more... you know... than I'd like, but hey. When in Egypt. I see you've made absolutely no effort to blend in.

**DOCTOR**      I don't know what you mean. This jacket is a classic.

**PERI**      At least you didn't have servants trying to shave your head.

**DOCTOR**      It's the fashion. Shall we?

**11. The Palace at Thebes.**
*There are the rumblings of a large gathering.*

**PERI**        Now this is what I call a party. Is this all for us?
**DOCTOR**      Shush. I think we're on.
*Music is played – a fanfare.*
**SENENMUT**    *(Grandly)* The great and mighty queen, daughter of the stars. All bow to Pharaoh Hatchepsut, divine and eternal, the living god.
**DOCTOR**      *(Quietly)* Peri, kneel.
**PERI**        I'd like to see you kneel in a dress this tight – actually, no I wouldn't.
**SENENMUT**    Rise and approach Pharaoh, Doctor.
*Slight delay while the DOCTOR and PERI approach the throne.*
**HATCHEPSUT** The Doctor and Peri have done great service to your Pharaoh and to Egypt. As thanks, Doctor, I give you this cartouche bearing my divine name. It marks you as friend of Pharaoh and under my divine protection.
**DOCTOR**      You do me great honour, mighty Pharaoh.
**HATCHEPSUT** Now let the banquet begin.
*A walloping great gong.*
**HATCHEPSUT** You will sit by Pharaoh, Doctor.
**DOCTOR**      Thank you.
**PERI**        Yeah. Me, too.
**HATCHEPSUT** If you wish. Eat. You could do putting some flesh to your bones. Men do prefer something more substantial, wouldn't you say, Doctor?
**DOCTOR**      I... never comment on a lady's appearance. I find it much safer that way.
**PERI**        Thanks a lot.
**HATCHEPSUT** You amuse me, Doctor. A warrior with a wit? I have not known such a man since my husband.
**PERI**        You're married?
**HATCHEPSUT** *(Very icy)* Not any more.
**DOCTOR**      *(Quickly)* Please forgive Peri's ignorance, Majesty. We have been travelling for a considerable time. She had not heard of your divine husband's passing.
**HATCHEPSUT** I will forgive her lapse this time, Doctor, because you ask it.
**DOCTOR**      You are most generous, Majesty.
*Shemek, the old astronomer and priest, speaks to Fayum, renewing their banter. Senenmut is there as well.*
**SHEMEK**     This cannot sit well with you, Fayum. An outsider sitting at Pharaoh's right hand.
**FAYUM**      I imagine it sits less well with Senenmut.
**SHEMEK**     He's a smart lad, that Senenmut, but he should learn to be a bit more subtle when it comes to women. It doesn't do to let them see you're too keen. Especially when she's Pharaoh and she's got the temper of a trapped scorpion.
**FAYUM**      And when she's so interested in this newcomer.
**SHEMEK**     You spotted that as well?
**FAYUM**      I'm young, not blind. I think everybody with eyes in the court has noticed it.

**SHEMEK**　　He's certainly an odd-looking sort. That fair hair – and that pale skin. Must come from far to the north. And stop staring at his woman, Fayum.

**FAYUM**　　She's very beautiful.

**SENENMUT**　　She is indeed.

*Yelps from Fayum and Shemek.*

**SHEMEK**　　Senenmut! Must you creep around like that? I forget – you're a politician. Of course you have to creep. How long have you been skulking there?

**SENENMUT**　　Long enough to hear you talk about me in ways I'd rather you didn't. At least in as public a place as this.

**FAYUM**　　Oh.

**SHEMEK**　　Don't deprive me of my gossip. At my age, it's one of the few pleasures I can still manage.

**SENENMUT**　　You may fool other people with that decrepit-old-man act, Shemek, but this is me you're talking to. You don't fool me.

**SHEMEK**　　And you won't fool anyone either if you don't stop glaring at the Doctor.

**FAYUM**　　You don't like Pharaoh showing favour to this outsider.

**SENEMUT**　　Pharaoh makes her own decisions.

**SHEMEK**　　And you do not like them?

**SENENMUT**　　(*Seething*) To say that would be to admit treason. Everyone knows that divine Pharaoh is infallible. She is a living god, and as she so often points out, I am not even royal.

**SHEMEK**　　(*Laughing*) And I thought you a better liar than that.

**SENENMUT**　　Go back to your stars, old man. Or are even they tired of your prattle? The truth is that I am worried – for Hatchepsut – and for all of us. These are strange days.

*Back at the top table, PERI is obviously having a bit of a look round.*

**PERI**　　I wish I'd brought a camera to this shindig.

**DOCTOR**　　And how would you explain it to the developer?

**PERI**　　Never been to a toga party?

**DOCTOR**　　Well, there was that bash Nero threw...

*Music starts up. Obviously music for the dancing girls.*

**PERI**　　What now?

**DOCTOR**　　The entertainment.

**PERI**　　Dancers? Oh my gosh. They're topless.

**DOCTOR**　　Well, yes they are I suppose. It's the custom. Just ignore it if it bothers you.

**PERI**　　Easy for you to say. You're not being letched at by that black toothed priest over there. If he asks me to dance I'll punch him.

**DOCTOR**　　You'll do no such thing.

**PERI**　　I'm joking. Just joking. Those other topless girls – are they the next dancers?

**DOCTOR**　　Ah... well, no. Actually, they're a different kind of entertainment.

**PERI**　　Singers? (*Dawn of realisation*) You don't mean... hookers? These people need a cold shower.

**DOCTOR**　　You may find some of their activities offensive but remember, you're seeing them from a 20th century perspective. By this time's standards, being a palace servant, even in this capacity is quite respectable.

**HATCHEPSUT**  Are you enjoying the banquet, Doctor?
**DOCTOR**      Very much, your majesty. Aren't we, Peri?
**PERI**        Having a great time.
**HATCHEPSUT**  Do any of the hesets find favour in your eye, Doctor?
**DOCTOR**      (*Uncomfortable*) They're charming. I suppose. But I don't think I should... you know...
**HATCHEPSUT**  You do not wish to insult Peri in public. Perhaps later.
**DOCTOR**      Er, yes. Perhaps. (*Changing the subject*) The food is splendid.
**HATCHEPSUT**  You must try the roast boar. It is absolutely excellent.
**DOCTOR**      Why not?
**HATCHEPSUT**  (*Claps hands to slave*) Bring boar for my guest.
**PERI**        Is now a good time to remind you that I'm a vegetarian? Doctor, that slave with the boar...
**DOCTOR**      What about him? Wait, I see what you mean. His clothes don't quite match the others.
*Sound of a heavy plate being thrown aside.*
**PERI**        He's got a knife!
**SLAVE**       Death to Hatchepsut!
**DOCTOR**      No!
**SENENMUT**    Guards!
**PERI**        Doctor!
*There are yells and general noises of confusion and struggle, including a cry of pain from the DOCTOR.*
**HATCHEPSUT**  You have saved me again, Doctor. Senenmut, Antranak! The guards are worthless! Send them to the House of Pain.
**PERI**        You're bleeding.
**DOCTOR**      (*Obviously in a bit of pain*) It's nothing much. Just a flesh wound, really. The knife only grazed my hand.
*The slave laughs.*
**HATCHEPSUT**  Tell me what is so funny. It will be the last thing you say before your tongue is ripped from your head.
**SLAVE**       I will not die alone. The dagger was coated with poison. He has only minutes to live.

[*End of Part One.*]

# EYE OF THE BEETLE

## PART TWO

**1. Recap from Part One.**
*At the banquet. Sounds of general banqueting.*

**HATCHEPSUT** (*Claps hands to slave*) Bring boar for my guest.
**PERI**  Is now a good time to remind you that I'm a vegetarian? Doctor, that slave with the boar...
**DOCTOR**  What about him? Wait, I see what you mean. His clothes don't quite match the others.
*Sound of a heavy plate being thrown aside.*
**PERI**  He's got a knife!
**SLAVE**  Death to Hatchepsut!
**DOCTOR**  No!
**SENENMUT**  Guards!
**PERI**  Doctor!
*There are yells and general noises of confusion and struggle, including a cry of pain from the Doctor.*
**HATCHEPSUT**  You have saved me again, Doctor. Senenmut, Antranak! The guards are worthless! Send them to the House of Pain.
**PERI**  You're bleeding.
**DOCTOR**  (*Obviously in a bit of pain*) It's nothing much. Just a flesh wound, really. The knife only grazed my hand.
*The slave laughs.*
**HATCHEPSUT**  Tell me what is so funny. It will be the last thing you say before your tongue is ripped from your head.
**SLAVE**  I will not die alone. The dagger was coated with poison. He has only minutes to live.
**PERI**  Doctor!
**DOCTOR**  Actually, I am feeling a little queasy, Peri.
**HATCHEPSUT**  Take him to my private chambers. And be gentle with him.
**DOCTOR**  Wait. What kind of poison was it?
**HATCHEPSUT**  Tell him.
*No answer. A hefty thump.*
**SENENMUT**  Answer Pharaoh.
**DOCTOR**  Never mind. Give me his knife.
**SENENMUT**  Here.
*The Doctor sniffs.*
**DOCTOR**  Scorpion venom? Let's have a taste.
*Sound of Doctor running finger along the blade and licking the venom.*
**DOCTOR**  Definitely scorpion.
**PERI**  What are you doing? That's poison.
**DOCTOR**  Yes, I know. Fresh, too.
**SLAVE**  How can you take that poison and still stand?
**DOCTOR**  Well, it would be bad manners to keel over at Pharaoh's feet.

**SENENMUT** This pig will not speak here, Majesty.

**HATCHEPSUT** Torture this creature. I want to know why he tried to kill me and who sent him. Find out who dares attack Pharaoh.

**DOCTOR** Is that really necessary? No one's actually been hurt.

**HATCHEPSUT** He attacked me, Doctor. You may have saved my life twice but that does not give you leave to talk to me in that manner. Senenmut, I told you to torture this animal. Find out what it knows.

**SLAVE** You will learn nothing from me.

**HATCHEPSUT** We shall see. Begin with castration.

**SLAVE** Before coming into the palace I took a smaller dose of the same poison that was on the knife. It is more than enough to kill me. Already I feel this world slipping away from me but I have no regrets.

**HATCHEPSUT** Who sent you?

*A slap.*

**HATCHEPSUT** Answer me! Answer!

*Another slap.*

**SLAVE** (*Fading*) The true Pharaoh.

*Sound of the slave hitting the floor, followed by the buzz of whispered conversation. The comment about the true Pharaoh has got a reaction from the cheap seats at the banquet.*

**SENENMUT** What should we do, Pharaoh?

*No answer.*

**ANTRANAK** Pharaoh?

*There's an air of anticipation.*

**SHEMEK** (*Quietly, to himself*) Pharaoh...

**DOCTOR** Hatchepsut, you must give an answer.

**HATCHEPSUT** (*Confident – raging but confident*) Discover what you can about this scum then throw the corpse into the Nile. And interrogate the chariot driver I captured today. Or must I do that part of your job as well? Then let the crocodiles have him. I will be in my chambers. You will accompany me, Doctor.

**SENENMUT** Take this dead scum to be examined.

**FAYUM** Senenmut. What did the killer mean when he said 'the true Pharaoh'?

**SENENMUT** How should I know?

**FAYUM** It will be the gossip of Thebes within the hour.

**SENENMUT** I don't doubt it.

**FAYUM** Then you must discover what he meant by true Pharaoh.

**SENENMUT** I don't need a junior priest telling me what I have to do. I don't like this. Mercenaries in the red desert, an assassin in the palace – and all when this Doctor arrives.

**FAYUM** How could he eat poison as if it was a sweet-meat?

**SENENMUT** I don't know. But I'll find out.

## 2. Hatchepsut's Chambers.

*PERI and HATCHEPSUT have arrived. A PHYSICIAN is tending the Doctor.*

**HATCHEPSUT** Doctor? Doctor, are you ill?

**DOCTOR** Just the poison in my system.

**PERI** But you're going to be all right. Right?

**DOCTOR** It's giving me terrible heartburn. I'll be right as rain after an hour or two's sleep.

**HATCHEPSUT** You. Slave. Assist the Doctor to my bed.

**DOCTOR** There's no need.

**HATCHEPSUT** You said yourself that you need rest. Lie down.

**DOCTOR** All right.

*Sound of the Doctor being lugged across and put on the bed.*

**HATCHEPSUT** Do you need anything?

**DOCTOR** Something to drink wouldn't go amiss. My throat is a little dry.

**HATCHEPSUT** I will have wine brought.

*Footsteps head away.*

**PERI** I don't suppose you'd tell me how you managed that trick with the poison?

**DOCTOR** That? Oh, my physiognomy is a little different from yours. The poison's not lethal to me – it's just given me a terrible tummy ache. (*Sounding tired*) I'll be fine when I wake up. Absolutely... fine...

**PERI** Doctor? Doctor?

*No answer.*

**PERI** (*Disgusted*) Zonked.

**HATCHEPSUT** Ah, he is asleep.

**PERI** Yep. He'll probably be snoring his head off any minute now.

**HATCHEPSUT** He is a brave man.

**PERI** Can't deny that. Sometimes I wish he'd think before he acts.

**HATCHEPSUT** The brave do not have time to sit and think. They must act to seize opportunities when they come.

**PERI** It's acting without thinking that's left him needing to sleep off the poison. Not that I'm complaining that he stopped the assassin. I just don't want him getting hurt, that's all.

**HATCHEPSUT** Your care for him does you proud. Even though you are some years younger than him, I imagine he is a fine husband to you.

**PERI** Husband? Oh, no. We're not married.

**HATCHEPSUT** What then? (*Peering down her regal nose*) Are you a slave? Or a concubine?

**PERI** I'm nobody's slave. Or concubine for that matter.

**HATCHEPSUT** What then?

**PERI** We're friends. We travel together because we want to. Simple as that.

**HATCHEPSUT** Even though you are not his woman?

**PERI** I don't think travelling alone appeals to him much. And I get to see the world. And anywhere else for that matter.

**HATCHEPSUT** You make no sense.

**PERI** A lot of people say that.

**HATCHEPSUT** You share a great affection with the Doctor, though.

**PERI** He can be a pain sometimes but it's hard to stay mad at him for long.

*Knock at door.*

**HATCHEPSUT** Enter.

*Door opens and footsteps come in.*

**SENENMUT** Pharaoh. I am honoured to be...

**HATCHEPSUT** (*Cutting across*) From that grovelling start I assume you haven't discovered anything.

**SENENMUT**    Not as much as I would have hoped.

**PERI**    Have you found anything? Like, how did he get in for a start?

**SENENMUT**    That we do know. At least in part. One of the hesets saw him coming from the Palace of Concubines. She thought he was one of the eunuchs.

**HATCHEPSUT**    If he had lived, I would have personally turned him into one before he was executed.

**PERI**    Have you asked at the... what's it called?

**HATCHEPSUT**    Palace of Concubines.

**PERI**    Yeah. There.

**SENENMUT**    That is not permitted. Other than concubines and eunuchs, only Pharaoh may enter the Palace of Concubines.

**PERI**    So you're not going to question them?

**SENENMUT**    That would be an unacceptable breach of our laws.

**HATCHEPSUT**    And if I say it is allowed?

**SENENMUT**    Pharaoh's word is law.

**HATCHEPSUT**    You may enter the Palace of Concubines on this occasion, Senenmut. Peri, you will accompany him.

**PERI**    Me?

**HATCHEPSUT**    The Doctor is your friend. Don't you want to know how this happened?

**PERI**    I guess.

**HATCHEPSUT**    And I think you will be less likely to be cowed by the concubines. They have lofty opinions of themselves.

**PERI**    Okay. The Doctor will be okay here?

**HATCHEPSUT**    I will see that he is tended to.

**SENENMUT**    With your leave, Majesty.

**HATCHEPSUT**    You may go.

**SENENMUT**    My queen. Come.

**PERI**    I'm not a pet dog. What next? Sit? I won't be long, Doctor.

**HATCHEPSUT**    He can't hear you.

**PERI**    I wanted to say it anyway.

*Footsteps go. Door closes.*

**HATCHEPSUT**    You. Slave. Have Antranak join me at once. Perhaps Peri will be spending more time with the concubines than she expects.

[*End of draft.*]

# THE EYE OF THE SCORPION: SCRIPTING NOTES

## By Iain McLaughlin

---

E-mail: Iain McLaughlin to Gary Russell – Friday 8 December 2000
*More>>>*

---

Okay, I've just read through your notes a couple of times. For the most part I agree with your points. Some of the dialogue is ghastly and cumbersome – getting the point over but without any subtlety. I don't remember them being so duff when I wrote the thing, but in hindsight, some of the dialogue is a bit, well, crap (and I'm probably being kind to myself there). That can be fixed.

If you think the Doctor's dialogue has strayed from Peter Davison to Colin Baker, then that's a bad mistake I'll need to fix. I thought the Fifth Doctor was gutsier in Peter Davison's last year (admittedly in *The Caves of Androzani* it was because he knew he was going to peg out), but all through that year I thought he was a stronger, firmer character and I tried to push him that way. But if I've cocked it up, it needs to be fixed.

Peri's dialogue can be fixed as well. Less cocky, more intelligent? Less cheap gags? Stronger and pushing the action more. How about if she pushes for the investigation of the Palace of Concubines, and cajoles Erimem into joining her? With a bit of tweaking, the scenes in the tunnels and Palace of Concubines could change emphasis so that Peri is more of the driving force. When she gets taken as a hostage in Part Three, instead of having Peri turfed off the chariot, if she broke free and jumped she'd be freeing herself without need for rescue.

You mentioned that you wanted a less linear plot and some kind of interaction between Peri and Antranak. Rather than have him develop a crush on her, how about if he's wary of both Peri and the Doctor? He's been Erimem's adviser thus far, and now she's got new favourites. He's not jealous of Erimem (who's 17, by the way) showing them favour, but they arrived just at the right time – and that's a bit lucky for his liking. He doesn't know anything about these people, which makes him uncomfortable. So he could be wary of Peri, try to get some answers from her about who she is, where she and the Doctor came from, etc. It would all be to protect Erimem but it would give a bit of edge to him from the listener's point of view – he's got a problem with Peri, so maybe he's a bit iffy. This would give Peri the chance to stand up to Antranak when he's niggling at her. I'd also like to add a scene where the Charioteer (the Scout) is being interrogated (tortured). Peri thinks it's barbaric (inwardly, Erimem probably agrees) but Antranak thinks Peri's objections to torture are a bit shady. Why doesn't she want this enemy to be forced to tell what he knows? And when the Scout escapes, he suspects Peri even more. (Obviously it's the Horus character who lets the Scout go.) If Antranak's character is that wee bit greyer and edgier, when he's accused of the killings, for a second, we might think, yeah, it's possible he did it to protect Erimem. The extra plot-line should make scene changes easier, particularly in Parts Two and Three.

As for Horus, the chief priests of each god's temple took the name of that god and were usually addressed by the god's name. However, I take your point about Horus being associated with Sutekh and the Osisrians in *Doctor Who*. The priests still retained their own names (even if they rarely used them) so there's no hassle with calling the character by his own name (how does Horemshep sound?) – all that would need would be an early mention of him being the High Priest of Horus, and leader of the Council of Priests. (I did think about calling him Anubis, but again, that's a god's name, which might make folk think of the Osirians, and besides, everyone associates Anubis with death, so it'll be a bit of a giveaway that he's the bad guy.) Early on, there should probably be a scene showing the enmity between Horemshep (?) and both Antranak and Fayum. (Maybe before the banquet?) This would build up both Antranak and Horemshep (and make them both greyer, rather than obviously good guys or bad guys) and it would help to establish who they are within the Palace hierarchy. Fayum would be quite low down the pecking order – but obviously basically a nice bloke who's known Erimem all her life, which would give his turn to villainy later on a bit more oomph.

Apart from ropy dialogue, the two main problems you mention are the ending and the idea of the Doctor using a component from the TARDIS's telepathic circuits. I didn't explain it all that well in the script, but the Doctor sensed the telepathic presence while unconscious and realised that the component would be needed. I got the impression from your notes that you weren't convinced by this bit at all. However, if we bin the idea of him nabbing a bit of the TARDIS *en route*, maybe he could use part of the stasis box for a similar purpose. The box must have had some kind of telepathic inhibitors to keep the creature dormant. Would using that disorient Yanis and his crew long enough for an escape? And he could tinker with it so that it would amplify his own thoughts out to the TARDIS (blocking the sun, etc.). From memory, I recall a few of the Virgin novels mentioning the link between the Doctor's mind and the TARDIS's telepathic circuits.

The mind creature will be explained in more depth early in Part Four, when the Doctor and Erimem are on the chariot. There's already a small scene where the Doctor briefly goes over what the creature is. He'll now go into detail, explaining that the creature exists totally in the minds of biological hosts. No matter how many people (or creatures) are infected, it remains a single creature, spreading out and looking for new hosts. It isn't particularly vicious – evolution has just left it with this as its way of propagating and surviving. If needs be, to protect itself, the creature can abandon minds. (But should this be mentioned? It's a great big sign-post of things to come. Personally I'd rather not use it – or at least make sure it's a throwaway and not handed much significance in the speech.)

The ending is the big problem. You hate it. Which is a pretty major problem really. You were clear that it's the violence in it you didn't like. Too much solving of problems just by somebody getting a thumping. Okay. Reading through it, I had a few problems with it myself – the Doctor wouldn't look to bury someone alive as easily as he did here. He'd try something smarter than that. So here's an alternative ending:

The storyline goes along the same path until the Doctor and Peri head down into the tunnel under the Sphinx. Up top, the battle is being lost by the Egyptian troops. They are being converted in mass numbers. Erimem is grabbed and dragged down, after Antranak's chariot crashes. The Doctor and Peri have reached the end of the tunnel, which he opens only to save Erimem's life. He plays the scene as if he's only just discovered that Peri is infected. If he let on that he knew days earlier, they'd know he was up to something. Erimem will be killed (or infected) if he resists Horemshep passing the creature on to him. He agrees, but the fragment of the creature present in Horemshep can't get a grasp on his mind – it's too big. It's the Doctor's plan – he's trying to pull all the different strands of the creature into one place so that he only has one enemy to deal with. To do that he has to let the thing get an idea of how much effort it would take to capture a Time Lord's mind. When the creature comes together in one body – Peri's – the Doctor's plan is starting to go a bit pear-shaped. He'd expected it to be Horus or Yanis, where it has a stronger hold. But the creature knows the Doctor won't kill his friend – or anybody else if he can help it. He has to act quickly – the human brain can't deal with the sort of mental energy Peri's having to process. His plan was to lure the mind creature here and then use the telepathic inhibitor to disorient the host. Unfortunately, the inhibitor can't handle the sheer volume of mental energy present in Peri and burns itself out. The Doctor knows he has to get the creature in Peri talking before it can take his mind. He asks it questions – lots of questions. He gets Erimem to do the same. Everyone present throws questions at the Peri host. The strain of trying to process so many questions throws the creature into distress. At first Peri can answer the questions, throwing the answers back with arrogance and disdain, but as the questions come quicker, she is in pain and the creature finds itself struggling with the limitations of the human brain. It has the memories of so many people that it can't help knowing the answers – but the human brain can't deal with all that information at once and Peri's brain shuts down after a barrage of questions. And so everything's sorted – until a rat scuttles over and sniffs at Peri. A fragment of the creature is passed to the rat. The Doctor plonks a (canopic?) jar over the rat, trapping it. The Doctor has to get Peri and the rat to the TARDIS quickly – he can draw the mind parasite from them and store it safely until he can deliver it to the appropriate authorities. The creature makes a final bid for freedom – trying to take control of the TARDIS through the telepathic circuits, but screams in pain when it realises how vast the ship's mind (for want of a better word) is. It's out of its depth. The Doctor comments that the TARDIS will lock it away safely in a corner of her memory until it's ready to go to the authorities. (Is this TARDIS scene overkill? A cop-out? It's just that, given the Doctor's hatred for taking any life, he'd probably try to keep the creature safe, no matter what instinct had made it do. But I'm not sure if the scene in the TARDIS would be necessary. Maybe it would, just to show Peri recovering and letting Erimem see a glimpse of the reality behind the Doctor's stories. Or perhaps the Doctor could comment on the creature trying to take the ship, knowing that it doesn't have a hope? He's not even slightly worried.)

From here, Peri recovers and gets to see the celebrations. Erimem knows she can't be Pharaoh and decides to slip away. Peri suggests that she leave in the TARDIS – there's nowhere on Earth in that period that won't know who Erimem is. The Doctor takes some persuading and lets Erimem know she probably won't have the chance to come back and that wherever or whenever she settles it won't be like anything she's ever known. He tells her of the risks and the downside of such a drastic move, but she wants to go, to learn, and so they go, leaving a badly hurt (broken leg? Arm?) Antranak and Fayum to walk in on the dematerialising TARDIS. Confirmation that Erimem was indeed a god. He doesn't know it yet, but Fayum's going to be Pharaoh. By the way, Yanis is dealt with by Fayum (it's kind of redemption for him after the parasite abandons his mind). He takes up a sword and deals with Yanis (quickly – I guess a swordfight would be dull on audio). Maybe it's not a swordfight at all? Maybe Fayum just cuts a rope or uses the sword to set off one of the traps in the tunnel/tomb, or uses it to topple a statue on top of Yanis. However he does it, Fayum should deal with Yanis (who'll be in a foul temper, knowing that his chances of taking Egypt are gone and because he realises that the creature has been manipulating him). The quiet priest defeats the warlord and shows himself worthy of being Pharaoh.

This ending's pretty much violence-free (except for the Fayum/Yanis bit, which won't be actual fisticuffs or anything like that) and I think it's more of a *Doctor Who* ending. The Doctor's thinking his way out rather than fighting. He doesn't relish the thought of one human brain having to deal with what it'll have to go through (particularly when he finds out it's Peri's) but the creature needs to be in one host to be defeated.

From your notes, I wasn't sure if you liked the setting for the ending or not. It needed to be somewhere isolated but close to the action, and the sink-shaft in the story really does exist, as does the tunnel at the bottom of it. According to myths recounted in various Graham Hancock and Robert Bauval type books, the tunnel leads to a giant chamber between the front paws of the Sphinx, and also branches off into the pyramids. Whether it does or not, I've no idea, but I thought it was worth using the myth. It felt like the right sort of place for a *Doctor Who* finale, and made sense from the Doctor's perspective in the story. But, if you don't like it, we could shift to a temple or even a necropolis. It's just that almost everybody already know the pyramids and the Sphinx, so we don't have to take too much time setting up the location for the ending.

Obviously, the ending's still in pretty rough form here, but it's probably best to let you have a shufti now, rather than plough on and find you're after something totally different.

---

**E-mail: Iain McLaughlin to Gary Russell – Monday 10 July 2001**
*More>>>*

---

The points you raised in no particular order.

It wouldn't be common for women of this era to read but it wouldn't be unheard of either. A lot would depend on where the women came from. Some of the tribes of the time would make sure their noble-women could read to make them more appealing to whoever they were going to wind up getting married off to. The nature of the Pharaoh involved comes into it a lot as well. If Pharaoh wanted to keep his women uneducated, well, that was that really. No reading, no learning, no chatting about anything interesting – just lie back and think of Egypt whenever old Pharaoh got the horn and decided it was number 47's turn. Given that Erimem can read and fight, I think we can assume that her dad was a pretty reasonable Pharaoh, who didn't have a problem with women learning and probably encouraged it.

The world being round was first proven by an Egyptian smart-arse by the name of Eratosthenes. He was an astronomer, historian, geographer, philosopher, theatre critic, poet and mathematician. A right bloody clever clogs. Anyway, he worked out that the world was round by using big sticks, the movement of the sun during the day and the difference in time of sunset on the same days in different locations. He worked out the Earth's diameter and circumference to within a few percent of the exact figure. He was a good bit later than Erimem's era but he did work from other people's suggestions and ideas going back to Erimem's time and before, so it's feasible that the idea was being bounced about at the time by a local brainbox.

Pronunciations. Okay, here goes.

| | |
|---|---|
| Erimemushinteperem | Erimem-oosh-in-tep-er-em |
| Kohl | pronounced like 'Coal' |
| Hatchepsut | as it's written Hat-chep-soot |
| Smenkhare | Smen-carry |
| Heset | hes-set |
| Maab | Mab |
| Maat | Mat |

Seth          as *Emmerdale* as it sounds – became Set at some point in history but I used Seth to avoid *Pyramids of Mars* ideas.

| | |
|---|---|
| Rhaoubak | Roo-back |

Priest's speech      As it's written I suppose. It's not a real prayer. I made it up. It was just something to sound authentic before the priest got a doing.

| | |
|---|---|
| Cheops | Key-ops |

names          As they're written. I made them up and they're not used again anywhere.

By the way (WARNING – high boredom factor ahead), stating that Smenkhare was female is taking sides in a contentious debate amongst Egyptian scholars. Traditionalists go with the idea that Smenkhare was a noble who succeeded Atenakhen and that's that, so there and yah-boo-sucks. A more modern idea is that Smenkhare is actually Atenakhen's wife, Nefertiti. At first her name was just Nerfertiti, then she changed it to Nefer-Nefer-Nuahu-Nefertiti (fit that on a cheque). She disappeared totally from history at the exact time that the co-ruler, joint Pharaoh (and lover if we go by the smutty carvings) of Atenakhen appeared. This co-ruler was Smenkhare-Nefer-Nefer-Nuahu. So, one side says it's the same person. The other side shouts 'bollocks' and the intellectual debate contuinues. It's not really a big thing – but I reckoned that *Doctor Who* would always come down backing the controversial side of an argument like this one.

# CROSSROADS IN TIME

## By Gareth Roberts & Clayton Hickman

### PART ONE

A strange incident aboard the TARDIS... The Doctor tells Melanie they've been hurled into the far distant future. But when the doors open they find themselves outside Traveller's Halt, a Midlands motel that seems completely normal.

The Doctor's very confused; according to the TARDIS, there's no way this can be present-day (i.e. late 1980s) Earth. Prosaic-minded Mel can't see how it can be anywhere else.

The Doctor and Mel are welcomed by receptionist Carol Chance, who heavily hints that the Doctor and Mel ought to find somewhere else to stay. David Darling, manager of the Motel, then appears with his wife Jane and Carol's demeanor changes at once. She begins to book them in and the suspicious Doctor plays along. Mel overhears the Darlings having something of a marital crisis, with Jane accusing David of infidelity with waitress Denise Perks.

The Doctor decides he needs to take more readings while Mel explores Traveller's Halt. Outside, however, he is not happy to see that the TARDIS is missing. An apologetic Darling arrives and tells him the Council took it off in a skip. He's sure everything can be sorted out later.

Mel talks to the waitress, Denise, who tells her of her romantic past; she's been jilted at the altar twice, stalked by a serial killer, and been married four times. Her first husband was killed by a falling chimney; the second ran off with another man; the third was shot in a Post Office raid; the fourth went missing in Venezuela. Mel's amazed – but friendly Denise seems to think this is all very normal.

Mel departs and Denise calls Darling to the dining room – and they're soon in a clinch. Denise demands to know when David's going to leave Jane, kick her out and let Denise in to take over the motel. Darling placates her and hurries away. Denise is distracted by a strange crackling noise in one corner of the room – there's an odd liquid seeping through one wall. Denise cleans it away – but gets some on her hands...

Mel comes across Norman, the motel's somewhat slow handyman, who's raking the leaves on the drive. Norman confesses to Mel he's been in love with Denise for years – since 1988. Mel points out the year is 1988. Norman tells her it seems like it's been a very long year...

The Doctor is searching for Carol but she seems to have vanished. Examining some pamphlets in the lobby showing the locality, the Doctor decides he needs to find the TARDIS. He distracts Jane in order to steal her car and then tells Mel he's going to drive into the nearest town, Crotten, and get the TARDIS back. Mel, angry at his refusal to accept that life can just be ordinary for some people, nevertheless jumps in with him.

Jane discovers her car's been stolen, and complains to David. The Doctor is a lunatic. David assures her everything is under control. Denise stumbles up to them – she needs help. Her skin where she touched the liquid is turning silver.

Outside, the Doctor and Mel see Crotten in the far distance but, as they drive on, a car suddenly appears in their path. There's the sound of screeching brakes. Mel screams…

## PART TWO

The Doctor and Mel have collided with another car. Luckily they are not hurt and clamber out to help the other driver. Mel's gobsmacked – it's her old school sweetheart, Danny…

Back at Traveller's Halt, Denise is confined to bed. Norman brings her flowers and wonders why her eyes are glowing silver. The Doctor and Mel enter with the injured Danny. Mel and Danny talk – a lot's happened since they were together. Mel admits she's thought often of Danny but she now seems a little uncomfortable around him…

The Doctor is becoming ever more concerned, particularly about Denise. He tells Darling she's been contaminated by some kind of alien biotechnology, which is altering her genetic make-up. Darling scoffs, and sends Denise off to the (unseen) motel nurse. Jane reckons the Doctor should be locked away, but Darling thinks he's a harmless – and entertaining – eccentric. Jane immediately agrees with her husband, who seems to exert an almost hypnotic control over her.

The Doctor chats with Norman, and asks if he's noticed anything strange recently – odd lights in the sky, that sort of thing. Norman hasn't. But the way he talks intrigues the Doctor. People say he's stupid, but Norman reckons he notices a lot of things nobody else has – like it's been 1988 for what seems like forever and nobody's getting any older.

Danny tells Mel he was on his way back down to Brighton to see his parents and thought he'd stop the night at the Motel. Mel pulls out a map from Danny's luggage and points out that the Motel must be miles out of his way. She asks him to point out where it is. Danny knows the Motel's near Birmingham but he can't show her precisely where. Mel thinks he's just shaken up by the accident – but she can't find Crotten anywhere on the map.

The Doctor bursts into Darling's office where he is talking to Jane, demanding to know if they'll listen to what he has to say. Before he can get any further, Mel and Denise enter. Denise reveals that her medical exam has confirmed only one thing – she's pregnant by Darling.

There is an unearthly screeching, like heavily distorted music. Mel and the Doctor cover their ears but everybody else immediately freezes. The Doctor tells Mel he's convinced this is the beginning of an invasion – some powerful alien force is stranded on Earth and it's flailing out illogically, trying to defend itself – and somehow it's affected Denise. That's what drew the TARDIS off course and now it seems to be affecting time itself.

Everyone suddenly springs back to life, picking up where they left off, shocked by Denise's announcement. The Doctor tries to alert them to the time distortion but they look at him as if he's mad and continue with their own arguments, leading to a distraught Denise running out of the office with David and Jane in hot pursuit.

Alone in the office, the Doctor asks Mel to check Denise's entry on the staff database but Mel is perplexed to find that the computer is just a screen and an empty case, with no drive inside at all. Suddenly they are disturbed by a strange woman dressed exactly like Carol Chance. The Doctor asks who she is and is told that she is Carol Chance – despite bearing no resemblance to the woman they met earlier.

Jane, Denise and David stand in reception, rowing about the pregnancy and David's affair. Jane screams that David can have Denise if that's what he wants and storms out. An upset Denise runs outside. The phone rings and David answers it. A distorted, mechanical voice announces that the Doctor is fulfilling his role satisfactorily, but that something must be done to ensure that Mel follows hers. David agrees.

The Doctor tells Mel that he is going to go and get the TARDIS back as things are getting dangerous. Mel says that she'll keep an eye on things here and anyway, she wants to talk to Danny. They walk out into reception, the Doctor heading out of the doors and Mel approaching Darling who is still on the phone. He passes the receiver to her, saying that Danny is calling from his room for her. Mel is suddenly overcome by an unearthly electronic sound, which begins to invade her mind…

Outside, the Doctor begins to walk down the gravel drive towards the main gates but finds the huddled form of Denise, curled up in his path. He dashes to her assistance but suddenly a terrifying transformation occurs. Denise becomes a slavering monster and leaps for his throat…

## PART THREE

The Doctor is amazed when the echoing sound comes again and Denise just freezes, mid-pounce. He runs off.

Inside, the Doctor confronts Mel – now he understands, or thinks he does. Traveller's Halt might not be a real place at all. Mel scoffs – she's not really listening to him and is suddenly full of the joys of getting back with Danny. The Doctor is gravely worried.

He finds Jane and David locked in an argument about David's infidelity with Denise. He breaks it up, and tries to hypnotise Jane, but gets nowhere – she can only quote things that have happened since she's been at Traveller's Halt. Everything before is a blank.

In the back room, Mel's amazed when Danny suddenly proposes to her – isn't this going a bit fast?

The Doctor changes tack and attempts to probe Darling – it looks like he's made a breakthrough, but suddenly Darling's voice changes and tells him not to interfere. Walking in, Jane reacts; she's heard that voice before. Urgently, the Doctor asks her where, but before she can reply the Denise-monster enters and slays her. The Doctor attempts to hold the creature back while Darling goes into a strange, corny soliloquy for his wife – then Denise returns to normal, and she and Darling instantly decide that perhaps they'll be better off without Jane. The Doctor watches this in horror and then runs off.

Danny tells Mel they can get married tomorrow if she wants. Suddenly seeming very unlike her old self, Mel agrees and they embrace.

The Doctor collars Norman, and regresses him. He succeeds in breaking the barrier and Norman reveals he's not a gardener, he's an actor. He's been playing

301

Norman in a daytime soap opera called *Traveller's Halt* for fifteen years. He remembers the series being axed, and going in to film the final episode – but nothing else, as if his life stopped right there.

Things suddenly begin to slot into place in the Doctor's mind. The time breaks weren't that at all – they were some sort of commercial break – and they're all trapped in a time loop, with the inhabitants forced to play characters for some unknown purpose.

With Norman in tow, the Doctor tries to get through to Mel that this is all some kind of fictional simulation but she won't listen. She and Darling tell the Doctor he's invited to their double wedding.

The Doctor, in despair at being trapped here forever, pleads with Norman; was there a place in the Motel that was never seen in the programme? Norman reckons that's easy – the kitchens. The Doctor races there – but Darling is waiting.

Suddenly threatening, Darling tells the Doctor no one may enter the kitchens. The Doctor grabs Norman and pushes past him – and they fall into a screaming void…

## PART FOUR

The Doctor and Norman emerge into a huge machine/organism. The Doctor postulates that if this is the kitchen, they must be cooking up something huge! They find a row of suspended animation pods – and inside are some non-speaking extras, the original Carol Chance and the – supposedly dead – Jane, now almost fully recovered.

Mel and Danny are preparing for their wedding. Mel is behaving as if this was the most natural thing in the world. Darling tells them and Denise that today will be the happiest day of their lives. Nothing can possibly go wrong. Romantic music swells.

The Doctor's amazed by the technology he's found – it's more advanced than anything he's ever encountered. He discovers the Central Intelligence, and interferes with its workings – and they hear the voice of Darling…

Darling's voice tells them they are inside all that remains of one of the oldest, mightiest civilizations in the universe. A race that existed longer than any other and evolved into immortal beings of pure thought. They were so jaded and full of ennui that they had no knowledge left to uncover – all that kept them going in the end was the Earth soap opera *Traveller's Halt*. When it was axed they used their phenomenal brains and their science to transport the cast to a time bubble on the day the last episode was filmed, built an environment for them and reprogrammed them using a powerful artificial intelligence created for this purpose. Then they were left to play out randomly generated storylines for all eternity.

Back in the motel, the weddings are about to start when Darling receives a signal and leaves.

The Doctor is startled when all the extras, and the reprogrammed (original) Carol Chance – all now dressed in wedding gear – silently leave their pods, and head for the portal.

Norman wonders what's happened to the aliens. The Doctor postulates they couldn't save themselves, and melted away – this machinery is millennia old – but they built the controlling intelligence too well and it is still fulfilling its original programming. Suddenly the Doctor grasps it – when he and Mel turned up, it scanned them and worked out the best way to incorporate them into the plots. Hence he started fighting monsters – because that's what he does best – and Mel was presented with an impossible, romantic affair with somebody from her distant past.

Danny and Mel tie the knot and Mel is blissfully happy. They set off for their honeymoon suite – in Traveller's Halt, of course.

The Doctor discovers the enormously complex machine that generates the (deceptively simple) storylines for the soap. They show that he has been written out and will die off screen, and Mel will be murdered by Danny on her honeymoon night.

Suddenly Darling enters, now fully under the control of the Central Intelligence. He advances on the Doctor with murderous intent – now for his off screen death. The Doctor quickly activates Jane's pod. She emerges as her real self – and furiously confronts Darling – he's kept her in *Traveller's Halt* for fifteen billion years. Reacting to her anger, the real Darling is brought out of his trance long enough for Norman to punch him out and shove him into the portal, where he vanishes back to the motel.

Silencing their myriad questions, the Doctor tells Jane and Norman that the only way he can save them all is for them to go back in to the simulation. They reluctantly obey.

Alone, now, the Doctor frantically starts rewriting the storylines – and concocting the last ever episode of *Traveller's Halt*…

In their room Danny and Mel celebrate with champagne. David suddenly picks up the bottle like a club and advances on the terrified Mel – then, just as quickly, he drops the bottle and claims it was just a joke – the Doctor is exerting his control. Mel, snapping back to her real self, flees the room.

Darling, now back under the influence of the storylines, is about to marry Denise when Jane appears, claiming she faked her own death. Darling falls into her arms – and a distraught Denise is comforted by Norman, who proposes to her – and she accepts. Mel arrives in the midst of this and Norman tells her not to worry – the Doctor is sorting everything out and they're quite safe…

But with plots being created and resolved so quickly, the delicate logic circuits of the Central Intelligence begin running too fast and the Doctor suddenly realises he's in terrible danger. As the machine begins to smoke and spit he quickly writes in the appearance of the TARDIS outside the motel and runs through the portal to the lobby. He appears as a big businessman who's bought Traveller's Halt to develop into a nature reserve. He pays off the whole staff with huge sums of money and the unearthly music starts up again – it's the closing theme and the very end of *Traveller's Halt*…

The ground begins to shake and the sets begin to collapse. The actors sink to their knees, and begin to pass out as the influence that has controlled them for so long is finally lifted. Only Mel, Norman and Jane seem able to snap out of it and they help the Doctor to drag the unconscious actors into the TARDIS, which disappears just as Traveller's Halt finally disintegrates

Cut to Earth, Birmingham, 1988 – the TARDIS appears in the deserted canteen of the TV studios and, having placed the dozing actors in the chairs to await their (real) final bow, the Doctor and Mel make their farewells to a bemused Norman and Jane.

The Doctor explains that, for them it'll be like they've been asleep only fifteen minutes in the canteen – not fifteen billion years in a black hole.

As they leave, Norman and Jane are astonished to find that the money the Doctor conjured up for them is still real. It doesn't matter that they're about to be axed – they could buy the whole TV company now if they wanted!

Back in the TARDIS, Mel – still in full wedding attire – is somewhat upset that Danny wasn't for real. She knew he was too good to be true and despite it being fictional, the whirlwind romance was still rather wonderful. Smiling, the Doctor reckons there's only room for one man in her life – him!

The TARDIS sets off for new adventures.

# THE ONE DOCTOR:
# OUTLINE

By Gareth Roberts and Clayton Hickman

> 5.45
> *Doctor Who*
> Starring **Colin Baker**
> and **Bonnie Langford** in
> *The One Doctor*
> A four-part story by
> GARETH ROBERTS and
> CLAYTON HICKMAN
> 1: The Doctor's shocked
> when he discovers
> somebody's taking his
> name in vain

## PART ONE

The far, far future. A very few millennia from the end of time itself, where virtually the whole universe knows everything there is to know. Time travel is as *passé* as space travel by this time, and some races treat travelling through the fourth dimension like a game. It's not an era the Doctor is fond of. Therefore when he and Mel pick up a faint distress signal from 'the vulgar end of time' as the Doctor describes it, he only grudgingly agrees to investigate…

The TARDIS lands in a crowded concourse on the planet Xarfos in the middle of a street party. The citizens are ecstatic – they've been saved! The Doctor and Mel discover from a young citizen, Sokkery, that the seventeen worlds in the Xarfos System were lately threatened by the evil Skelloids. Luckily for the Xarfoss, the famous mysterious Time Lord known only as the Doctor was visiting and, together with his assistant Sally-Anne, defeated the Skelloids. They're being feted in the Great Hall of Xarfos even now.

The Doctor's baffled – he's never been to Xarfos. Mel suggests he might be on the tail of a future self. The Doctor's sure he's not. He can't sense any time distortion. And there's something not quite right about any of this – he's certainly never heard of the Skelloids.

In the Great Hall of Xarfos, the Great Leader Potikol is thanking the Doctor and Sally-Anne. The 'Doctor' (who we will recognise as Biggins) has a small request of the Xarfoss – he needs money to buy a new stock of the crystals that power his TARDIS. Diamonds to be exact. Potikol is taken aback, but has to agree.

When Potikol's out of earshot, the 'Doctor' and Sally-Anne confer. Sally-Anne

305

reckons this job's been a pushover – the Xarfoss have been the doziest mugs yet. She steals a kiss from the 'Doctor', as they crack open another free crate of space beer.

The Doctor and Mel can't get into the Great Hall, which is being mobbed by grateful Xarfoss. No pass, no entry. The Doctor grabs Sokkery's copy of the *Xarfos Evening Visi-Echo*, and sees an image of 'the Doctor'. He's never seen that face before, but it certainly isn't him…

Potikol greets the now somewhat merry 'Doctor' and Sally-Anne. There's a problem – the computer links to the Great Bank of Xarfos have been interfered with by a piece of space flotsam that's crept into the system. A dredger's been sent up to clear it out of the way – then all will be well and the diamonds delivered. Sally-Anne's worried, but the 'Doctor' tells her to keep a steady heart. She thwacks him as he pinches the bottom of a passing servant girl.

The real Doctor hypnotises a guard and slips into the Great Hall with Mel. Mel thinks this is all crazy.

Potikol gets a message from the dredger – it's been destroyed by the UFO!

The Doctor and Mel burst in on the 'Doctor' and Sally-Anne. The Doctor accuses his namesake of deliberate impersonation, and after verifying he's not even a Time Lord, demands he stops his scam right now. The 'Doctor' gets nasty – this quadrant of space is his patch, so bugger off. The Doctor fumes – he's the Doctor, the genuine article. The 'Doctor' scoffs – yeah, right.

Sally-Anne calls for guards. The Doctor and Mel are unceremoniously bundled away and dumped in the cells to cool off. Potikol sweeps in, alarmed – the destructive alien object has changed course and it's heading straight for Xarfos. Only the Doctor can save them now! The 'Doctor' gulps.

In the cells, Mel tries to persuade the Doctor that the two con-artists aren't doing much harm. The Doctor's fuming when suddenly a wave of alien sonic energy descends upon the planet. It's destroying their minds!

## PART TWO

The soundwave dissipates and an evil alien voice is heard. It's coming from the UFO. It demands 'TRIBUTE'. The three most precious objects from the Xarfos system must be provided within six hours, or it will destroy the entire system.

Potikol is distraught, and begs the 'Doctor' for help. The 'Doctor' is surprisingly calm; he tells Potikol to bring the TARDIS to the Great Hall. Sally-Anne's pleased. They're going to do a runner, then? The 'Doctor' is miffed. Hasn't she twigged? This alien voice is the other feller's version of the Skelloids – part of his scam. They've got to find him and get rid of him; he's a threat to their whole operation.

Mel reckons the Voice must be a part of the false Doctor's scam – but the real Doctor certain that it's kosher. Potikol, very distracted, comes in to see them, and authorises their release. The Doctor begs him to listen, but Potikol isn't interested in their ravings – he must supervise the delivery of the TARDIS to the Great Hall. The Doctor's intrigued – this he must see.

The 'Doctor' and Sally-Anne argue – Sally-Anne reckons they should clear out. The Doctor and Mel enter, left to wander in all the confusion. The impostor compliments the Doctor on his technique, and then angrily tells him to clear off. The Doctor tries to convince him they're in genuine danger. Suddenly the Voice is heard again –

TRIBUTE IS REQUIRED! To prove its point, it devastates the eleventh planet, a small mining colony. Suddenly, the 'Doctor' is rather worried.

The 'TARDIS' is brought in – it's a simple teleport capsule in disguise. The impostor goes in, telling Potikol he'll be back when he's completed the three tasks set by the Voice. Potikol gives him a list of the three greatest treasures of Xarfos. Sally-Anne follows. The Doctor grabs Mel and they dash in just as the capsule is about to leave.

The capsule dematerializes but won't go far. The Doctor tells the impostor it's the UFO – it's immobilized all rudimentary computers in the system. He takes control, materializing the capsule – inside the real TARDIS. They can use it to find the tribute. The Doctor also discovers that the ship has effectively sealed the entire system. Nothing can get in and out and no time travel is possible. They really do have only a few hours to complete their tasks. The impostor wants out but the Doctor's having none of it. They need all hands if they're going to crack this one

The TARDIS lands on Xarfos 8, where Mel and Sally-Anne are paired off to accquire the first Great Treasure; then the Doctor and the Impostor set off. They'll collect the girls later.

Xarfos 8 is home of Xarfos's most successful export business – the entire planet has become a furniture and DIY emporium run by robots. No human has dared to venture here in centuries, since the robot Assemblers took over. Potikol's list specifies Shelving Unit XZ419 as the Great Treasure. The enthusiastic Mel and the unenthusiastic Sally-Anne begin to search the storage bays… but they are not alone.

The Doctor and the Impostor arrive on Xarfos 3, home of the second Great Treasure – the Intelligence Mentos, an immortal artificial brain that can answer any question. But they seem to have arrived backstage in a TV studio. They wander onto the brightly coloured set – and find themselves in front of a vast audience. A woman starts to ask them pointless and embarrassing personal questions over techno music. The Doctor protests – where is Mentos? This is urgent! The woman huffs. She *is* Mentos.

Mel and Sally-Anne are creeping round the bays. Mel's sure she's found the right item when suddenly they are surrounded by Assemblers…

## PART THREE

Mel tries to explain their mission to the Assemblers. The First Assembler rejects the advice of the Second Assembler, that the intruders are organic spies and must be killed. He has a better idea. If they want Item XZ419, they can have it. His words have a dark subtext.

The Doctor tries to explain his mission to Mentos, but Mentos is more interested in his personal life and keeps deflecting his questions with crude innuendo. She blindfolds them and asks them to feel various protuberances of alien species and thus identify them in her top rated show 'Touch the Tentacle'. The Doctor despairs. He tells the Impostor that Mentos must have tired of its great knowledge and dedicated itself to doing the stupidest possible thing it could. The Impostor has an idea. He joins in with gusto.

The First Assembler tells Mel and Sally-Anne they have one hour to assemble Item XZ419. Something no puny organic could ever do. If they fail, the Assemblers will disassemble them as a warning to all their fleshy kind. Sally-Anne despairs – they'll never do it. Mel's determined – she'll use her capacity for total recall and computer programming skills. But she despairs when she starts to read the instructions – it's going to be tough.

The Impostor flirts wildly with Mentos as the game goes on. The Doctor's very disapproving – this is getting them nowhere.

Mel's puzzled. She's sure some parts of the Shelves keep appearing and disappearing – and the instructions keep changing too. Sally-Anne slumps in a maudlin heap.

The Impostor's doing very well, with some help from the Doctor. Until the final round, when he claims what he's holding is a Zarbi. Mentos says he's wrong – it's a Navarino. The Impostor is furious, accusing Mentos of being wrong. Mentos fumes – she is never wrong. She is Mentos! The true personality of the Intelligence breaks through. Full of shame, she agrees to come with them. The Impostor turns smugly to the Doctor – one up to him.

Mel realises the Shelves are a cheat. Parts of them keep slipping into other dimensions – they can never be fully assembled. It's this unique property that makes them such a Great Treasure; the Assemblers have learnt to manipulate dimensions in an astonishingly complex and beautiful way. Sally-Anne reckons their number's up. Mel sees a glimmer of hope.

Mel tells the Assemblers she's completed the task. The confused Assemblers examine the Shelves. Mel confuses them using their own instructions. The TARDIS appears, and Mel grabs Sally-Anne and the Shelves. She explains – the Shelves of Infinity have never been assembled, so how could the Assemblers know she was lying? By the time the Assemblers realise they've been tricked, the TARDIS is on its way.

In the TARDIS, the four travellers examine the list of Treasures. The quest for the third will take them to the dead planet Xarfos 10 – the Third Great Treasure is the Great Jewel of Xarfos – the largest diamond in the galaxy.

The TARDIS lands and the four travellers emerge. The Great Stone is in clear view, totally unguarded. The Doctor steps forward – and a huge, monstrous jelly monster lurches from hiding and gobbles him up…

## PART FOUR

Mel pleads with the Monster and explains the danger they're all in and it spits the Doctor out. It introduces itself as the Guardian of Xarfos, last survivor of the jelly creatures that lived here. The Jellies were incredibly long-lived single cell organisms; he was the youngest, and has lived for seventy million years of unendurable boredom. He has arranged for the delivery of a home entertainment link from a distant star system inhabited by similar beings. They will deliver at any time in a forty thousand year span, and he's getting annoyed waiting for them.

The Doctor and co explain their pressing need for the Great Jewel. The Jelly understands the situation, and will gladly hand it over – the only trouble is, he must roll over the hill to personally switch off the force field that protects the Jewel. And if he moves, he's sure that the delivery craft will appear – it's sod's law. The Doctor assures him all will be fine. If the craft turns up they'll tell the deliverers to wait. The Jelly rolls off to switch off the force field.

Back on Xarfos 1, Councillor Potikol is startled by the Cylinder Voice. It tells him they have just ten minutes left. Potikol urges the Doctor on.

As they wait, Sally-Ann complains to the Impostor. She wants out – this is their last scam. The Impostor is distracted by a buzzing insect but tells her to keep quiet – she's got no nerve.

The Jelly rolls back into view, and the Doctor, Jewel in hand, thanks it. The Jelly gets distraught; it's been left a telepathic message by the deliverers saying it wasn't in. The Doctor realises the Deliverers were what they thought was a buzzing insect – they're only a micron long. The Jelly bemoans its luck and, as the Doctor sympathetically listens, the Imposter makes a grab for the crystal. With Sally-Ann in tow, he dashes into the TARDIS and dematerialises. He'll get the glory for this little job, and who knows what the rewards from the Xarfoss will be?

The Doctor is livid. Is there nothing to which that man will not stoop? The Jelly, sullen and sulky, intimates that he might have a solution. Mel coos and clucks over him until he finally suggests they might like to make use of his transmat portal, by which the deliverers arrived. It should get them back to Xarfon 1 sharpish.

Aboard the TARDIS, the Imposter is attempting to pilot the craft to the throne room and having a little difficulty. Sally-Ann is ever more annoyed at his behaviour. She quite liked the real Doctor.

The Cylinder is now hovering over Xarfon city. Despite Potikol's protests and desperate pleas for more time, it extends its deadly Destructor Ray. The TARDIS appears and the Imposter rushes out with the Three Great Tributes. The Cylinder examines them and is pleased. Just then the Doctor and Mel materialise in the throne room and the Imposter calls on Potikol's guards to surround them. The Cylinder voice suddenly booms out. It wonders who found these objects; they should be rewarded. The Impostor steps forward – he did. The Voice asks his name. The Impostor says he is known as the Doctor. Mel's furious; the Impostor's going to take all the credit. The Doctor shushes her.

The Cylinder urges the 'Doctor' to step forward and then it fixes him in a force field. This was a test – only the legendary Doctor could have completed the tasks in the time. And its (unnamed) creators want to punish the elusive Doctor for thwarting their plans all through time. He has fallen into their trap. The Doctor, Mel and Sally-Ann watch in horror as the Impostor, now protesting he is not the Doctor, is sucked into the Cylinder, to be imprisoned forever in a time bubble. It disappears and the Xarfon system is freed.

Potikol is distraught. What an awful fate to befall their saviour – but at least the Treasures are safe. The Doctor tells Mel he'd worked out what was happening when he saw the Cylinder close up just now; he recognised the technology of a race of his old enemies. Mel reckons he can be too clever for his own good now and again.

Sally-Ann tells the Doctor she's at a loose end without her boyfriend – and she'd quite like to become a real companion as she thinks it might be 'a laugh'. Just then she is distracted as Potikol and his council roll up to pay tribute to her. The Doctor quickly bundles Mel into the TARDIS and dematerialises. He'd rather be imprisoned in a time bubble than have to travel with Sally-Ann!

Mel asks after the Imposter – he wasn't really all that bad, she protests. The Doctor half-heartedly agrees. He's sure they could affect some sort of rescue. He smiles. 'In time…'

# THE ONE DOCTOR:
# DOCTOR WHO AND MEL'S CHRISTMAS

### Hastily written by Clayton Hickman

*FX – Jingle Bells-y music. Would be nice if it vaguely echoed the Doctor Who theme. Fade up TARDIS in-flight hum. DOCTOR WHO and MELANIE are seated in armchairs before a blazing fire.*

**DOCTOR WHO**　That was absolutely splendid, Mel.[1]
**MELANIE**　Thank you Doctor.
**DOCTOR WHO**　The best nut-roast I can remember.[2]
**MELANIE**　It took me a while to get to grips with that peculiar oven back there, but it wasn't bad, was it?
**DOCTOR WHO**　Delicious. The food machine is a useful device, but lacking in panache if you fancy anything more adventurous than bacon and eggs.[3]
**MELANIE**　So what would you like to do now?
**DOCTOR WHO**　Well, this is your Christmas Day, remember?
**MELANIE**　Yes. This was a very good idea of yours, actually.
**DOCTOR WHO**　That's the thing with time travel – it's so easy to let things slip. I forgot to celebrate my birthday for two decades, once. (*Conspiratorially*) Still, it means that nobody knows how close to the big nine-four-oh I really am.[4]
**MELANIE**　Your secret's safe with me, Doctor! (*Sighs*) You know, this rather reminds me of the Christmasses back home in Pease Pottage. Presents, lunch, a roaring fire. Bliss!
**DOCTOR WHO**　Shame about the temporal drift compensators.
**MELANIE**　They'll soon dry out. And it was a lovely thought to make it snow in the control room.
**DOCTOR WHO**　But not very practical, eh? I never could resist showing off! (*He chuckles*) But anyway, what shall we do now?[5] What was the form back home?
**MELANIE**　We'd just sit around, perhaps have a sherry and watch the Queen's speech.
**DOCTOR WHO**　Well the sherry's no problem. It is Christmas, after all.
*FX – He uncorks a bottle and pours two glasses.*
**MELANIE**　(*Taking a sip*) Oh that's lovely.
**DOCTOR WHO**　And as for the other...
*FX – He gets up.*
**MELANIE**　Where are you off to?[6]
**DOCTOR WHO**　(*Sightly off-mic*) Ah, here we are.[7]
*FX – DOCTOR WHO wheeling something in on squeaky castors. He puffs and pants a little. It's large and heavy.*
**DOCTOR WHO**　What do you think, Mel?
**MELANIE**　What is it?
**DOCTOR WHO**　Oh, I'll take the dust sheet off.
*FX – He does so.*
**MELANIE**　Um. What is it?[8]
**DOCTOR WHO**　This, Miss Bush, is the Time/Space Visualiser.[9] We can

tune into any event anywhere in the universe and anywhen in history. The Queen's Speech should be a doddle.[10]

*FX – A radio-esque whine of static.*

**DOCTOR WHO**  Now where did I put that remote control? Are you sitting on it, Mel?

*FX – She rummages down the side of her chair.*

**MELANIE**  Is this it?

**DOCTOR WHO**  Aha!

*FX – He sits down again.*

**DOCTOR WHO**  Now, let's see...

*FX – He presses some buttons on the remote. The whine of static changes in pitch.*

**DOCTOR WHO**  The Queen's speech...

*FX- The static begins to clear.*

**MELANIE**  Something's beginning to come through...

*FX: The static resolves itself.*

**QUEEN ELIZABETH I**  ...may have the body of a weak and feeble woman, but I have the heart and stomach of a king!

*FX: A crowd cheers.*

**MELANIE**  (*Laughs*) I think you might have gone a little too far back, Doctor!

**DOCTOR WHO**  (*Mildly huffy*) Well, if your country will have two Queen Elizabeths, what do you expect?[11]

**MELANIE**  I suppose it won't be Top of the Pops next, either?

*FX- The static returns in B/G.*

**DOCTOR WHO**  Perhaps we shouldn't risk it, eh?

**MELANIE**  (*Laughs*) Oh, Merry Christmas, Doctor!

**DOCTOR WHO**  (*Laughs*) Merry Christmas, Mel![12]

*FX – The clink of their sherry glasses.*

**DOCTOR WHO**  And, incidentally, a very Merry Christmas to all of you at home![13]

*Fade up the Jingle Bells-y theme. Mix in TARDIS vworping off to new adventures.[14] FADE.*

## NOTES

**N.B.** This scene was included as a hidden bonus track on the CD issue of *The One Doctor*. Colin Baker and Bonnie Langford played DOCTOR WHO and MELANIE, whilst QUEEN ELIZABETH I was played by Jane Goddard. *Gary Russell: 'Clayton wrote this at my request. My only suggestion was that it end with the "And a very Merry Christmas" joke.'*

1.  Line changed to: '**Oh**, that was absolutely splendid, Mel.'
2.  Line changed to: '**Quite** the best nut-roast I can remember.'
3.  Line changed to: 'The food machine is a useful device, but **it lacks** panache if you fancy anything more adventurous than bacon and eggs.'
4.  Line changed to: 'Still, it means that nobody knows how close to the big nine-**three**-oh I really am.'
5.  Line changed to: '~~But~~ anyway, what shall we do now.'
6.  Deleted dialogue – MELANIE: '~~Where are you off to?~~'

**7.**    Deleted dialogue – DOCTOR WHO: '~~Ah, here we are~~.'

**8.**    Line changed to: '~~Um~~. What <u>is</u> it?'

**9.**    Added dialogue – MELANIE: '**Ah**…'

**10.**    Line changed to: 'The Queen's Speech should be **no problem**.'

**11.**    Line changed to: 'Well, if your country will have two Queen Elizabeths, ~~what do you expect?~~'

**12.**    In this and the preceding line, "Merry Christmas" is replaced by "Happy Christmas".

**13.**    Line changed to: 'And, ~~incidentally~~, a very Merry Christmas to all of you at home!'

**14.**    The TARDIS dematerialisation noise is absent.

# THE ONE DOCTOR: 'SUPERBRAIN' QUESTIONS

By Gareth Roberts & Clayton Hickman

**The grandson of Earth's greatest ever politician negotiated a non-aggression pact with Ambrox 9 in 2110. Name him.**
Robbie Williams III

**A stassit is to the Turbrons as a Karbol is to which race?**
The Meethropods

**Which comedian once said, 'You can take a Pescaton to water, but you can't make him sink'?**
Gantax Nondrian

**From which planet do the famed Master Bakers run their patisserie empire?**
Barastabon

**What comes next in this sequence: S4 Z4 L1 K3?**
B14

**The Argons hail from which planet?**
Arg

**And for a bonus point, name their leader.**
The Great Rangdo of Arg

**The protective shells of which race are used to make Feltahm Paste?**
The Hisperas Collective

**Which team did the Shivron support in 'Beelzegg'?**
The Shavro of Shivron.

**Who fought the Mingons?**
The Thrabes of Gingolo.

**Whose battle cry was 'Death to the Frotes'?**
The Nancek.

**Where was the Treaty of Venus signed?**
Mars.

**Who described his mother as 'a single-celled amoeba of no repute or import'?**
Fara the Fierce.

**What was the immediate effect of the Vibrations of Vaal on the citizens of Stannos?**
Their hair began growing again.

**What is the best time for planting dokes?**
During the Season of All Drains.

**Pop music – who had a hit with *Din-fo-pok*?**
Normak Pring.

**Politics – with whom did the Great Chair Creature of Galactikos conduct an extra-marital affair?**
Norm of Taan.

**What was unusual about the Elevation of Deimos's eleventh and twelfth periods of office?**
They were non-consecutive.

**Name the inventor of Ocean Juice.**
Odysseus Potato.

**Which visistar was reported to have said, 'Is that a staser in your holster or have you erupted into pustules'?**
Morgana Kart.

**'The magnification of the moons of Xex' was the first instalment in which blockbusting inter-trilogy?**
The Frab Saga.

**How was X-Zimpli of Tench killed?**
She drowned in a pool of her own life fluids when her pod sac burst.

**Which race was described by Zartian 5 as 'a transparent opacity'?**
The Poets of Koj.

**How long did the seventy-year war of Harat last?**
Seventy-one years.

**Who fired the opening shot in the Arrowmaster Conflict?**
The Jamary.

**Why was the Derby of Phinta cancelled?**
A hoax bomb threat made by Phintan separatists.

**In needlework – is the urk a forestitch or a backstitch?**
A backstitch.

**Which regiment of Vri were sent to the Graj frontline last?**
The tenth.

# THE ONE DOCTOR: TRAILER

## By Clayton Hickman

*Outer-space 'rumble'.*[1] *Mysterious, menacing music through this whole sequence. The voice-over should be of the deep, American-accented, overly dramatic variety.*

**VOICE-OVER**   A deadly danger from the depths of space...[2]
*Then, as if over an echoey PA:*
   *(Scene 16)*
**CYLINDER VOICE** Citizens of Generios, you will listen.
*Cut to interior of TARDIS:*
**VOICE-OVER**   And only two people stand between it and the innocent populations of seventeen planets...
   *(Scene 1)*
**MELANIE**       These readings... the TARDIS is way off course...
**DOCTOR WHO**   Way, way off course... we've drifted millennia into the far future...[3]
*Back to outer-space atmos:*
   *(Scene 16)*
**CYLINDER VOICE** I have been sent to collect Tribute!
*Back to TARDIS atmos:*
**VOICE-OVER**   SHE!... was a computer programmer from Sussex...
   *(Scene 3)*
**MELANIE**       So – where exactly are we?
**VOICE-OVER**   HE!... was a Time Lord from Gallifrey...
**DOCTOR WHO**   The vulgar end of time.
*Back to outer-space atmos.*
**VOICE-OVER**   But can they save millions of lives... alone?
   *(Scene 16)*
**CYLINDER VOICE** I must have the three greatest treasures of the Generios System. Or I will destroy you all!
*Dramatic sting.*
**VOICE-OVER**   Coming soon from Big Finish Productions, a story of suspense...[4]
*Cut to exterior of Generios. Party atmosphere:*
   *(Scene 4)*
**DOCTOR WHO**   What's happened? We've only just arrived. We picked up a distress call.
**SOKKERY**       Sorry... wasted journey.   *(Cut dialogue)* We've been saved... the Skelloids are vanquished...
**DOCTOR WHO**   So – what became of these 'Skelloids'?
**SOKKERY**       The Doctor sorted them out for us, didn't he?
**DOCTOR WHO**   ...did you say the Doctor?[5]
*Another dramatic sting.*
**VOICE-OVER**   A story of modesty and understatement.[6]

*We hear the crowd chanting 'WE WANT THE DOCTOR!', loudly. This fades into the echoing atmos of the Council Chamber.*

*(Scene 5)*

**POTIKOL**        *(Combines several lines)* Doctor, Doctor... you've done so much for us – saved the seventeen planets from certain annihilation... How can we ever repay you *(CUT: for saving us?)*[7]

**BANTO ZAME**  I don't expect repayment – the work I do is reward in itself. Anyway... Sally-Anne and I really must get back to the STARDIS.[8] *Back outside. Atmos less important now.*

**VOICE-OVER**   A story of stoic concern...[9]

*(Scene 4)*

**MELANIE**       You're really rattled, aren't you?

**DOCTOR WHO**  Yes. Because if I didn't save this planet from the evil Skelloids – who is the Doctor that did...?[10]

*Echoey metallic background FX:*

**VOICE-OVER**   And a story of fairly challenging DIY...[11]

*(Scene 32)*

**MELANIE**       'Slot stanchion G into the base unit...'   Hold on, I'm certain I've already done that...

**BANTO ZAME**  That was stanchion D, and it wasn't the base unit, it was the central support stand![12]

*Appropriate clangs. Fade this out.*

*Back to spacey atmos. Bring stirring music up:*

**VOICE-OVER**   Colin Baker... Bonnie Langford... and Christopher Biggins in a story which proves that two's a crowd.

*(Would be nice to mispronounce and mis-stress the names: e.g. COElin Baker. Bonnie LangFORD. ChrisTOFFer Biggins...?)*

*Any B/G will do:*

*(Scene 21)*

**BANTO ZAME**  Listen, do I have to get nasty?

**DOCTOR WHO**  I wouldn't advise it![13]

**VOICE-OVER**   *Doctor Who – The One Doctor.* Coming this Christmas to a CD player near you. There can be only one...[14]

*Music builds to crescendo:*

*(Scene 43)*

**CYLINDER VOICE**  Bring me the Tribute! The Tribute, I say!

*In, quick:*

*(Scene 5)*

**BANTO ZAME**  What a plank!

*Final, comedic 'sting'. A-la the end of* The Holy Terror *trailer.*

# NOTES

**N.B.** This trailer first appeared at the end of the Big Finish *Doctor Who* CD *Colditz*, released in October 2001. A second, reworked version appeared on the following month's release, *Primeval*. In November 2002, incidental music from *The One Doctor* was featured on *Doctor Who: Music From The Sixth Doctor Audio Adventures*, and was prefaced on that CD by the second trailer, with a couple of minor tweaks. All edits were based on the above script. Unless specified, the VOICE-OVER was performed by Alistair Lock.

**1.** Added dialogue. In the first version of the trailer, there is an opening VOICE-OVER: 'Coming soon from Big Finish Productions – *Doctor Who: The One Doctor...*' In the second version, it's changed to: 'Coming soon... Coming soon... Coming soon...' (For the version used on the *Music* CD, the opening is performed by Nicholas Briggs: '*Doctor Who... Doctor Who...*')

**2.** In the first edit of the trailer, all of VOICE-OVER's scripted lines are absent.

**3.** In the second edit of the trailer, this line is changed to: 'Way, way off course... ~~we've drifted millennia into the far future...~~'

**4.** In the second version, line changed to: 'Coming soon from Big Finish Productions, a **tale** of suspense...' (In the *Music* edit, the phrase 'Coming soon' is replaced by '**Available now**'.)

**5.** In the second version of the trailer, this clip was changed to:

**DOCTOR WHO**  What's happened? ~~We've only just arrived. We picked up a distress call.~~
**SOKKERY**  ~~Sorry... wasted journey. (*Cut dialogue*) We've been saved... the Skelloids are vanquished...~~
**DOCTOR WHO**  ~~So – what became of those "Skelloids"?~~
**SOKKERY**  The Doctor sorted them out for us, didn't he?
**DOCTOR WHO**  ...did you say the Doctor?

In the first edit, DOCTOR WHO's line is different (as it is in Part One of *The One Doctor*): 'So – what **happened to** these "Skelloids"?'

**6.** In the second version, line changed to: 'A **drama** of modesty and understatement.'

**7.** In the first edit, line changed to: '(*Combines several lines*) Doctor, Doctor... you've done so much for us – ~~saved the seventeen planets from certain annihilation...~~ How can we ever repay you (*CUT: for saving us?*)' In the second version, the entire line was deleted.

**8.** After this line in the first version, the following was added:

(*Scene 4*)
**MELANIE**  Looks like you've already saved the day, then. Beaten yourself to it.
**DOCTOR WHO**  I somehow doubt it. I've never been to Generios before.
(*Scene 7*)
**SALLY-ANNE**  You don't reckon they've rumbled us? We ought to get out of here.
**BANTO ZAME**  And lose our chance of a hundred million credits?

In the second version, the line was changed to: 'I don't expect repayment – the work I do is reward in itself. ~~Anyway... Sally-Anne and I really must get back to the STARDIS.~~'

**9.** In the second edit, line changed to: '**An epic legend** of stoic concern...'

**10.** In the first edit, this line is as in the script. In the second version, this line was replaced with:

**DOCTOR WHO** Yes. ~~Because if I didn't save this planet from the evil Skelloids – who is the Doctor that did…?~~
*Echoey metallic background FX:*
**VOICE-OVER** A fable of unbridled passion.
  *(Scene 23)*
**DOCTOR WHO** Sally-Anne, is it?
**SALLY-ANNE** Yeah.
**DOCTOR WHO** You can take your hands away now.
**SALLY-ANNE** Oh.
**DOCTOR WHO** Thank you.

**11.** In the first version of the trailer, everything from this point until CYLINDER VOICE's line, 'Bring me the Tribute! The Tribute I say!' is deleted. In the second version, this line was changed to: 'And a **compelling** story of fairly challenging DIY.'

**12.** In the second version, deleted dialogue – BANTO ZAME: '~~That was stanchion D, and it wasn't the base unit, it was the central support stand!~~'

**13.** In the second version, added dialogue –
**DOCTOR WHO** I'm quite capable of defending myself.
**BANTO ZAME** *(Louder)* Oh *yes*? Yes, yes?
**DOCTOR WHO** *(Louder, over BANTO ZAME's line)* Yes! Yes, yes!
**MELANIE** *(Yelling)* Quiet!

**14.** In the *Music* version of the trailer, line changed to: '***The One Doctor* – the one soundtrack. Available in a few seconds on this CD.** There can be only one.'

# Dark Rising: Episode One

## By Mike Tucker

### 1. INT. DRAKEFELL'S OFFICE. EVENING.

**HAL TOLLER**  Damn you, Drakefell, I cannot believe that you are being so insensitive about this!

**DRAKEFELL**  And I cannot believe that you are being so ignorant.

**HAL TOLLER**  Ignorant? How dare you! Have you any idea what it is you're doing here?

**DRAKEFELL**  I am perfectly aware of what I'm doing, Mr Toller. Ensuring that industry carries on into the twenty-second century.

**HAL TOLLER**  For God's sake man, there's little enough work here at the best of times. Tourism is all that keeps the village going and your plant...

**DRAKEFELL**  Is a necessary addition to this community.

**HAL TOLLER**  Is a prefabricated monstrosity that is driving the visitors away in their droves! You're destroying this community! It's not as if you've even taken on any staff – that at least would show some responsibility!

**DRAKEFELL**  I can see that this discussion is not going to get us anywhere.

**HAL TOLLER**  Oh for heaven's sake, surely you can see...

**DRAKEFELL**  This meeting is at an end, Mr Toller. I am a busy man and I really haven't got any more time to spend on endless debate. I'm sorry that you can't see what we are trying to do here, but I'm afraid that there is nothing that you can do to stop it. You might as well stop trying to fight it.

**HAL TOLLER**  Right, well we'll see about that. Good day, sir!

*A door slams.*

### 2. INT. THE PUB. NIGHT.

*There is the babble of conversation from the bar. The door opens and we hear the barking of a large dog.*

**HAL TOLLER**  Good boy, Saladin, good boy, down now. He's behaved himself, George?

**GEORGE**  Good as gold.

**MARY**  How did you get on, Hal?

**GEORGE**  Hold on there, girl, let the man get a drink inside him first.

**MARY**  Oh come on, Mr Toller, what did he say?

**GEORGE**  Get the man a pint, for God's sake!

**MARY**  All right, all right! What'll it be, Hal?

**HAL TOLLER**  A pint of Best please, Mary.

**GEORGE**  I remember a time when bar staff knew their place...

**MARY**  Yes, and men dragged their womenfolk around by the hair. Times change, George.

*Mary thumps a pint of bitter onto the bar.*

**MARY**  There you go, Hal.

**HAL TOLLER**   Ah, you're a life saver, you really are.
*He drinks.*
**MARY**   (*Impatient*) Well?
**HAL TOLLER**   Oh, it's a complete waste of time. Talking to that idiot Drakefell is like talking to a brick wall. He cares nothing for the village, and even less for the impact his blasted plant is having on the environment.
**MARY**   But you told him about the fish, about the pollution...
**HAL TOLLER**   Yes...
**MARY**   And about the disease that the foxes have been catching...
**HAL TOLLER**   I told him everything, Mary. As I said, the man just isn't interested.
**MARY**   But they must see the impact that the plant is having, they must!
**HAL TOLLER**   The brutal fact, young lady, is that the demise of another small Welsh fishing village is seen as a small price to pay for cheap unlimited fuel. You've seen the news reports. It gets worse every day.
**MARY**   But these plants of Drakefell's are causing chaos. You saw the Greenpeace report about his Australian refinery.
**HAL TOLLER**   And saw how quickly they covered it up.
**MARY**   So you're just going to give up? Hal, you can't...
**HAL TOLLER**   Hold your horses! Now did I say anything about giving up? I just think that I need to go higher than Drakefell, that's all.
**GEORGE**   Going to head over to Cardiff then, are you?
**HAL TOLLER**   I think so. Try and talk some sense into the local political mafia. I'll go on to London if I have to.
**MARY**   When?
**HAL TOLLER**   Tomorrow. The longer we hang around, the more damage Drakefell and his machines are going to do to the coast.
**MARY**   I'll come with you.
**HAL TOLLER**   No, Mary. You're a little too outspoken for the political arena. I think that I'd do far better on my own.
**GEORGE**   She's a little too outspoken behind the bar as well if you ask me.
*There is a ripple of laughter in the pub.*
**MARY**   Now listen, Hal...
**HAL TOLLER**   (*Interrupting*) You would be far more use to me compiling some more evidence of exactly how much impact this project is having on the area. We're going to need all the ammunition we can muster if we're going to have a hope in hell. (*He takes another swig of beer*) You would also be far more use to me if you could put in an order for one of Derek's steak and kidney pies!

## 3. INT. DRAKEFELL'S OFFICE. NIGHT.
*A phone rings.*

**DRAKEFELL**   Drakefell. (*A pause*) Yes... Really. To London indeed. No... No, that's quite all right. Leave everything to me.

## 4. EXT. THE PUB. NIGHT.
*From inside the pub we hear the tinkle of a bell.*

**MARY**        Come on, you lot. I want those glasses.
**HAL TOLLER**    Right. I've got a bag to pack and some phonecalls to make. Hopefully I'll see you tomorrow night.
**MARY**        Good luck.
**GEORGE**    Goodnight, Hal
**HAL TOLLER**    Night, George. Come on, Saladin.
*We hear the bark of a large dog.*

### 5. EXT. PUB CAR PARK. NIGHT.
*The pub door opens and HAL TOLLER crosses the car park. He fumbles with his car keys. The dog snarls.*

**VICAR**        You've had a pleasant evening, I trust, Mr Toller.
**HAL TOLLER**    *(Startled)* Good God...
**VICAR**        Ah... Not quite.
**HAL TOLLER**    *(Embarrassed)* Oh, I... Yes, well you gave me quite a shock, vicar.
**VICAR**        I do apologise. I'm afraid that the robes of office don't make me the easiest person to see at night.
**HAL TOLLER**    And I wasn't really expecting to see you in a pub car park at midnight.
**VICAR**        Ah, well I had some... business to attend to, and I was hoping that I would catch you, Mr Toller.
**HAL TOLLER**    Really?
**VICAR**        Yes. I understand that you were up at the new fuel plant today.
**HAL TOLLER**    Yes, that's right.
**VICAR**        Did you have any joy?
**HAL TOLLER**    No, I'm afraid I did not. The company director is the most unpleasant son of a...
**VICAR**        Quite. What will you do now?
**HAL TOLLER**    I'm heading over to Cardiff in the morning. I've got some friends in the National Assembly, I can let people know what is going on here, if nothing else.
**VICAR**        And if they won't listen?
**HAL TOLLER**    Then it's on to London.
**VICAR**        London. You are determined, Mr Toller. Well, I'll leave you to it, you have a long walk across the moor to your house.
**HAL TOLLER**    No that's fine, Vicar, I've got the...
**VICAR**        And I'm sure that you weren't intending to drive. I understand that our local bitter packs quite a punch.
**HAL TOLLER**    Yes. Yes, you're quite right, vicar, and I'm sure Saladin will appreciate the walk. Won't you boy? Good night Reverend.
**VICAR**        Good night, Mr Toller. I will think of you in my prayers.

### 6. EXT. STONE CIRCLE. NIGHT.
*The chanting of a coven. Low and sinister.*

### 7. EXT. PUB CAR PARK. NIGHT.

**VICAR**        Ah, George, there you are.
**GEORGE**    Give a man a heart attack you will, creeping around like that.

| VICAR | You've got what you promised? |
|---|---|
| GEORGE | Yes, I've got it. |
| VICAR | Good. |
| GEORGE | It's not right, vicar. What you're asking. It's not right, |
| VICAR | You're not going to go back on your word now, are you, George? |
| GEORGE | No, no I suppose not. Here... |
| VICAR | Excellent. Then I'll see you in church tomorrow. Goodnight, George. |

## 8. EXT. STONE CIRCLE. NIGHT.
*The chanting increases.*

## 9. EXT. MOORLAND. NIGHT.
*HAL TOLLER stumbles through the bracken. There is a distant rumble of thunder.*

**HAL TOLLER**   Wretched man. He'll be trying to make me give up smoking yet. Hold on there Saladin. I want to get a light.
*The dog starts to bark wildly.*
**HAL TOLLER**   Saladin! Come here!
*More barks.*
**HAL TOLLER**   Wretched dog!
*The barks become painful yelps. Then a long drawn out howl*
**HAL TOLLER**   Saladin?

## 10. EXT. STONE CIRCLE. NIGHT.
*The chanting reaches a creccendo.*

## 11. EXT. MOORLAND. NIGHT.
*There is no sound from the dog now, only the crunch of bracken as HAL TOLLER searches.*

**HAL TOLLER**   Saladin? Where are you boy? Saladin?
*There is a low snarl.*
**HAL TOLLER**   There you are. What the devil got into you?
*The snarls become vicious, terrifying.*
**HAL TOLLER**   What's the matter, boy? Saladin!
*The snarl becomes a horrifying semblance of human speech, guttural and low.*
**SALADIN**   Human filth.
**HAL TOLLER**   I don't believe... No... Stay back...
**SALADIN**   All of you will die! DIE!
**HAL TOLLER**   No... no... NO!!!
*There is a horrible scream of terror interspersed with snarls and roars, then silence...*

## 12. EXT. MUSEUM. DAY.
*The sound of the TARDIS materialising. The door opens and ACE emerges.*

**ACE**   (*Exasperated*) Professor! I thought we were meant to be in the Cretaceous.

| | |
|---|---|
| **THE DOCTOR** | (*From inside the TARDIS*) And? |
| **ACE** | There's a mammoth out here. |
| **THE DOCTOR** | (*From inside the TARDIS*) So, I'm a little late. |
| **ACE** | A fake mammoth! |
| **THE DOCTOR** | (*From inside the TARDIS*) Ah! |
| **ACE** | A bad fake mammoth! We're in a museum! |
| **THE DOCTOR** | (*Coming out and locking the door*) Fascinating places, museums. |
| **ACE** | Not from this side of the glass they're not. |
| **THE DOCTOR** | Ah, no. The TARDIS must have got a little confused. |
| **ACE** | You're telling me. How are we going to get out? |
| **THE DOCTOR** | Oh, this lock won't take me long to open. It's not as if they're expecting any of the exhibits to try and get out. |
| **PRIDDY** | No, our usual problem is people breaking in. |
| **ACE** | (*Surprised*) Gorden Bennett! |
| **THE DOCTOR** | Ah, good morning. Assuming it is morning. I'm the Doctor, and this is my friend Ace. I don't suppose you could... er... |
| **PRIDDY** | Let you out? Of course, of course. I must say your arrival was quite fascinating. |
| **THE DOCTOR** | Yes, well I suppose that does require some explanation... |
| **PRIDDY** | I mean transportation of matter is perfectly feasible of course, but I didn't expect the manner of transport to be a metropolitan Police Box. |
| **THE DOCTOR** | (*Nonplussed*) Er, quite... |
| **PRIDDY** | Where did you get it? I've been after one for our twentieth century gallery for quite a while. Police box that is, not matter transporter, and whilst it does look very good next to Algernon... |
| **ACE** | Who? |
| **PRIDDY** | Algernon. The mammoth. Quite a good replica, don't you think? Oh, he's getting a little tatty, I know, but we had a moth problem last year, you see, and... |
| **THE DOCTOR** | (*Interrupting*) Excuse me, Mr...? |
| **PRIDDY** | Priddy, Basil Priddy, chief curator. |
| **THE DOCTOR** | Delighted. Well excuse me, Mr Priddy, but you don't seem very concerned with the manner of our arrival. |
| **PRIDDY** | And I don't expect that you are at liberty to tell me much about it. Official secrets and all that. You work for some kind of government agency I imagine? |
| **THE DOCTOR** | Something like that. |
| **PRIDDY** | Ah, I knew it. Matter transference, UFOs, psi powers – they're all government black ops projects. There have been articles about their existence for years. I know all about them. Never thought that I'd get a chance to see one, though. |
| **THE DOCTOR** | Mr Priddy, you said that you've had problems with people breaking in...? |
| **PRIDDY** | Yes, couple of weeks ago. Couple of fascinating Celtic pieces taken. Still no clue as to where they've gone. |
| **THE DOCTOR** | Celtic? |
| **PRIDDY** | Yes, from our Celtic collection. Would you care to see? |
| **THE DOCTOR** | Yes, I would. |
| **ACE** | Professor, I though we were going to the cretaceous. |
| **THE DOCTOR** | Ace! |

**PRIDDY**      Cretaceous? Time travel as well? You government boffins really have been busy haven't you. Knew it was possible of course, I mean that's how they went back and assassinated Kennedy. Wish you were allowed to talk about it. Never mind. I must give you my card, perhaps you could pick up some specimens for me. The Celtic gallery is this way. *He bustles off.*

**ACE**      Professor! What are we doing? He's mad. A UFO nut.

**THE DOCTOR**   Mr Priddy is a little eccentric I'll admit, but I'm intrigued as to why anyone would break into a museum to steal Celtic artifacts. Come along, Ace.

## 13. INT. CELTIC GALLERY. DAY.

**PRIDDY**      Here you see, or rather you don't see, what was stolen. This used to house one of the finest selections of Celtic gold in the principality.

**THE DOCTOR**   Ah, we're in Wales then.

**PRIDDY**      Yes, on the coast. Not far from Swansea.

**ACE**      In other words somewhere wild, remote, wet and populated entirely by sheep.

**THE DOCTOR**   Ace!

**PRIDDY**      Not a bad description, actually. We are rather isolated here. I expect that's why you chose us for your experiments.

**THE DOCTOR**   Yes, quite. A lot of the gold is still here, though.

**PRIDDY**      Yes, only two pieces went. Not the most valuable, but still of enormous scientific value.

**THE DOCTOR**   Hmm... *(He peers at something)* This is fascinating.

**ACE**      It's just graffiti. Your thieves are just bored kids, I expect.

**THE DOCTOR**   Bored kids with a grasp of ancient Celtic runes.

**ACE**      You what?

**THE DOCTOR**   These runes are written in a form of Gaelic almost forgotten in this time period.

**PRIDDY**      Yes, it's a runic alphabet that has completely baffled me, I'll admit.

**ACE**      So the vandals are sophisticated around here.

**THE DOCTOR**   And they're written in blood.

**ACE**      Blood?

**PRIDDY**      Yes, the police aren't quite sure what to make of it. I've told them about the coven, but they don't seem to take me very seriously.

**ACE**      You do surprise me.

**PRIDDY**      I'll show you the police report. Won't be a jiffy.

*Priddy shuffles off.*

**THE DOCTOR**   Honestly, Ace!

**ACE**      Oh, come on, Professor, our local curator is a *Fortean Times* junkie with a line on every conspiracy theory going, this coven is probably just the local women's institute out on a jolly and this theft is just a publicity stunt. There's nothing going on here!

## 14. INT. CHURCH. DAY.

*The congregation comes to the end of a hymn – 'We Plough the Fields and Scatter' would be good. There is much shuffling of hymn sheets and coughing as the VICAR starts his sermon.*

**VICAR**        Harvest. A time when we gather in the bounty of the Earth. A time for celebration. But a time when we also remember that man was cast out of the Garden of Eden. Even here in this village, there is sin, hidden deep in the hearts of each of you.
*There is a sudden and terrifying rumble. Everything starts to shake. The congregation start to panic.*
**VICAR**        Judgement is upon us!

### 15. INT. PUB. DAY.
*Glasses and bottles smash, the rumble is terrifyingly loud.*

**GEORGE**        What in God's name?
**MARY**        It's an earthquake!
**GEORGE**        Come on, woman. Get out from behind there!
*Bottles start to smash down.*

### 16. INT. CELTIC GALLERY. DAY.
*Display cases rattle (a fire alarm goes off?).*

**ACE**        What's happening, Professor?
**THE DOCTOR**        Feels like an earth tremor.
**ACE**        In Wales?
**THE DOCTOR**        If you've a better explanation then I... AHH! (*He gives a cry of pain*)
**ACE**        Doctor?
**THE DOCTOR**        It's all right, I'm just... AHH!
**ACE**        Doctor, what's wrong?
**PRIDDY**        (*Coming back into the room*) Well this is turning out to be quite a day for... Good lord, is he all right?
**ACE**        I don't know. Help me get him to a chair.

### 17. INT. PUB. DAY.
*The rumble stops, slowly the glasses and bottles stop rattling.*

**MARY**        I think it's stopping.
**GEORGE**        Yes. Yes I think you're right.
**MARY**        Well now they're going to have to do something.
**GEORGE**        What?
**MARY**        The government. Oh, come on. George! You're telling me that that had nothing to do with the plant?
**GEORGE**        But surely...
**MARY**        We don't know what damage they're doing out there. I just hope that Hal can get someone to listen to him.

### 18. INT. DRAKEFELL'S OFFICE. DAY.
*A door bursts open.*

**COWLEY**        What the hell was that?
**DRAKEFELL**        Ah, Miss Cowley. Nice of you to knock.
**COWLEY**        You're lucky that you still have a door to knock, Drakefell.
**DRAKEFELL**        Discourtesy isn't necessary, Doctor.

**COWLEY**    I'm sorry, director. I'm a little shaken – literally. What happened?

**DRAKEFELL**    A minor earth tremor, an unfortunate side effect.

**COWLEY**    Side effect! We weren't exactly the most welcome of guests before, now...

**DRAKEFELL**    Now we will carry on exactly as before, this plant...

**COWLEY**    Is vital to the fuel crisis, I know all that, Director, you can spare me the propaganda.

**DRAKEFELL**    Then can you please let me know if any of our workers were injured during out little... incident.

**COWLEY**    There are no other workers Mr Drakefell. It's a Sunday, everyone is in bed or in church. It's just you and me.

## 19. INT. CHURCH. DAY.
*The hear the babble of the congregation. The rumble fades.*

**VICAR**    And lo there was a great earthquake and the sun became as black as sackcloth, and the moon became as blood...

## 20. INT. CELTIC GALLERY. DAY.
*The rumbling and shaking fades to nothing.*

**ACE**    Get a lot of earthquakes round here, do you?

**PRIDDY**    That's the first to my knowledge.

*There is a groan from the Doctor.*

**THE DOCTOR**    Urgh.

**ACE**    Hey, he's coming round. Professor? Are you okay? What happened to you?

**PRIDDY**    Here, Doctor. I'll fetch you a glass of water.

**ACE**    Doctor?

**THE DOCTOR**    I'm all right, Ace, I'm all right. How long was I unconscious?

**ACE**    Only for a couple of seconds, just as long as the earthquake lasted.

**THE DOCTOR**    Yes, the earthquake... That's when it started.

**ACE**    What started?

**THE DOCTOR**    An enormous pressure in my mind, the awakening of something... massively powerful – ancient.

*PRIDDY re-enters the room.*

**PRIDDY**    Here you are, Doctor.

**THE DOCTOR**    Thank you, Mr Priddy.

*He drinks.*

**PRIDDY**    Poor Algernon hasn't survived very well, I always thought those tusks were too fragile.

**THE DOCTOR**    I rather think that damage to a badly stuffed replica mammoth is going to be the least of your problems, Mr Priddy.

**ACE**    I was wrong, wasn't I, Professor? There is something going on here.

**THE DOCTOR**    Yes, Ace, there is. Something dangerous. I think that I should get back to the TARDIS and run a few tests.

**PRIDDY**    TARDIS? Your ship.

**THE DOCTOR**    Yes. (*Mischievously*) Would you like to see inside my top

secret, experimental, government black ops police box?
**PRIDDY**          But surely... Official secrets and all that...
**THE DOCTOR**      Oh, I'm sure we can count on you to be discreet.
**PRIDDY**          Well, if you think that it would be all right.
**ACE**             (*Accusingly*) Professor...
**THE DOCTOR**      Come along, Ace.
**ACE**             What do you think caused that tremor?
**THE DOCTOR**      Well I'm not going to know that until I've run my test, am
I? Ah, I see what you mean about the mammoth, Mr Priddy. Still, I might
have a spare tusk I could let you have...
*The TARDIS key rattles in the lock.*
**THE DOCTOR**      Odd...
**ACE**             Come on, Professor.
**THE DOCTOR**      The door won't open.
**ACE**             Have you got the right key?
**THE DOCTOR**      No, Ace, you don't understand. It's the TARDIS. She isn't
letting me in!

## 21. INT. THE PUB. DAY.

**GEORGE**          Lord, what a mess.
**MARY**            I'm going to phone Hal.
*She picks up the receiver. Nothing.*
**MARY**            Dead. (*Putting the phone down*) Hold the fort here a
minute, George.
**GEORGE**          Hey, where are you going?
**MARY**            (*Calling back*) The phonebox on the green. I've got a
horrible feeling that all the phones are out.
*The door shuts.*
**GEORGE**          I'll just check that the beers survived then.

## 22. EXT. THE GREEN. DAY.
*Birdsong, a distant police siren? MARY opens the phonebox door and picks
up the phone. Again, nothing. She presses the switch a couple of times.*

**MARY**            Damn.
*Something slams into the glass.*
**HAL TOLLER**      (*Horribly loud*) The Earth is hungry, all will die!
*MARY screams.*

## 23. INT. MUSEUM. DAY.

**ACE**             But this is daft, Professor. She can't just lock you out.
**PRIDDY**          I'm afraid the local locksmith doesn't work Sundays.
**THE DOCTOR**      I really don't think your local locksmith...
*There is a scream from outside.*
**PRIDDY**          Good Lord.
**ACE**             Now what?
*There is another scream.*
**THE DOCTOR**      Come on!

**24. EXT. GREEN. DAY.**
*THE DOCTOR, ACE and PRIDDY run over.*

| | |
|---|---|
| **PRIDDY** | Mary? Mary are you all right? |
| **MARY** | Oh, Mr Priddy, he just came out of nowhere. |
| **PRIDDY** | Good Lord. It's Hal Toller. What the devil has... |
| **THE DOCTOR** | He's been badly mauled, some kind of animal. He's in shock. Is there somewhere we can take him? |
| **MARY** | The pub. Over here. |
| **THE DOCTOR** | Come on. You two give me a hand with him. |

**25. INT. PUB. DAY.**
*HAL TOLLER is manhandled inside. He moans weakly.*

| | |
|---|---|
| **GEORGE** | What the devil was that screaming about, Mary? Good God. |
| **MARY** | Clear a space for us, George. |
| **GEORGE** | Over here old man, here you go. |
| **HAL TOLLER** | The Earth... angry. |
| **MARY** | It's all right, Hal. It's all right. What's wrong with him? |
| **THE DOCTOR** | I don't know. Shock certainly, but there's something else. He needs a doctor. |
| **PRIDDY** | But I thought you were a doctor... |
| **THE DOCTOR** | Not a medical Ddoctor. Is there one in the village? |
| **MARY** | You're from the plant aren't you? You're one of Drakefell's men. |
| **THE DOCTOR** | Plant? |
| **MARY** | Well, look what your bloody experiments have done... |
| **ACE** | Hey, cool it missus! |
| **THE DOCTOR** | I'm afraid that I don't have the slightest... |
| **MARY** | Oh, don't you start with all your hush hush... |
| **GEORGE** | Steady now, Mary. Let's get Hal sorted. |
| **MARY** | They've done enough damage. |
| **PRIDDY** | Oh, don't be ridiculous, girl, he needs help. |
| **THE DOCTOR** | Will someone tell me what this plant is? |
| **PRIDDY** | There's a new mining and refining installation along the coast, Doctor. Experimental. Caused a fair bit of... friction in the village. |
| **THE DOCTOR** | Then they're bound to have a medical bay! |
| **MARY** | We don't need them... |
| **THE DOCTOR** | Phone them! |
| **MARY** | I can't. |
| **PRIDDY** | Oh for heavens sake, Mary. |
| **MARY** | No, I mean really, I can't. The phones are dead. That's why I was checking the phonebox. |
| **ACE** | The earthquake? |
| **THE DOCTOR** | Possibly... |

*HAL TOLLER groans again.*

| | |
|---|---|
| **GEORGE** | Well we've got to do something. |
| **THE DOCTOR** | This plant. How far is it? |
| **GEORGE** | A mile or so. Look, who the devil are you? |
| **THE DOCTOR** | There will be time for introductions later. Now, who's got a car? |

**MARY**         Most of the cars in the village are out of action because of this fuel crisis.
**PRIDDY**         I could drive you over there, Doctor. My car is still running.
**THE DOCTOR**    Excellent, Mr Priddy! Ace, go with him.
*The door swings shut.*
**THE DOCTOR**    Right, you'll need to keep him warm. I don't think his injuries are life threatening, but I'm worried about infection. Can you get some towels Miss...
**MARY**         Reynolds. Mary Reynolds
**THE DOCTOR**    We need to try and clean some of these wounds, get some of the earth out.
*There is the blast of a horn from outside.*
**THE DOCTOR**    That sounds like my lift.
**MARY**         Doctor. I'm sorry... Thank you.
**THE DOCTOR**    I'll be as quick as I can.
*He exits the pub.*

### 26. EXT. THE GREEN. DAY.
*The spluttering of an engine.*

**ACE**          It's a real boneshaker, Professor.
**THE DOCTOR**    Another exhibit, Mr Priddy?
**PRIDDY**         It serves its purpose, Doctor, and in the current fuel crisis it can manage a considerable number of miles to the gallon. Hold tight now.
*The car roars off.*

### 27. INT. PUB. DAY.
*Toller continues to moan.*

**MARY**         It's all right, Hal. Help is on its way. George, can you give me a hand a moment. George! George?

### 28. EXT. PUB CAR PARK. DAY.

**VICAR**         A doctor, you say.
**GEORGE**        Yes, got a girl with him. They've headed off to the plant with Priddy. Look, I've got to get back. Mary'll be looking for me.
**VICAR**         Thank you George. Perhaps it was a good thing you didn't come to church with us this morning, hmm?

### 29. EXT. THE MOOR. DAY.
*The car puttering along.*

**PRIDDY**         There's the plant, Doctor, across the bay.
**THE DOCTOR**    Hmm. They haven't exactly gone out of their way to make it blend in, have they?
**ACE**          A right blooming mess if you ask me.
**PRIDDY**         The environmentalists are up in arms, and I can't say I blame them. But Drakefell maintains that it's the only way to end this fuel crisis quickly.

**THE DOCTOR**   Drakefell?

**PRIDDY**   Edward Drakefell. Company director and the man who discovered this miraculous new fuel source.

**THE DOCTOR**   (*Thoughtful*) Really... Look out!

*The car screeches off the road. There is a horrible snarl.*

**ACE**   What was it, Professor?

**THE DOCTOR**   Something very large and very savage.

**PRIDDY**   I'd read all about the sightings of moorland beasts, but I had no idea we had one here.

**ACE**   Is that what attacked Mr Toller?

**THE DOCTOR**   More than likely, don't you think?

**ACE**   It looked like some kind of dog.

**PRIDDY**   Hal Toller had a dog, a Great Dane called Saladin.

*There is a horrible snarl from nearby.*

**THE DOCTOR**   I rather think that it's more than just a Great Dane now. I think you should start the car, Mr Priddy.

*The engine turns over but fails to catch.*

**PRIDDY**   I'm trying, Doctor, I'm trying.

**ACE**   Give it more choke!

*The snarls get louder.*

**THE DOCTOR**   Mr Priddy...

**SALADIN**   Human scum. All will die...

*The end titles mingle with the howl of the dog.*

# SEASONS OF FEAR:
# OUTLINE

## By Paul Cornell

The Doctor and Charley keep Charley's appointment in Singapore to meet with Alex Carthy, a boy Charley knew in school. The Carthys are an old Sussex family, interlinked and intermarried with Charley's family over the ages.

But while Charley and the boy have a happy tea together, the Doctor is surprised when a suave man approaches him, knowing who and what he is. He introduces himself as Sebastian Carthy, Alex's father. He's here to gloat. He represents certain universal powers, powers that have granted him immortality. The Doctor, by saving his son's friend from the *R101*, gave these powers their opportunity. The web of time is broken. Now anything can happen. And it has: because Sebastian has killed the Doctor. Many years ago. He sired a son, had him develop a friendship with Charley and set up this appointment merely so he could gloat over his victim.

Carthy departs the shocked Time Lord and throws a newspaper onto Charley's table as he leaves. The headline tells of the destruction of the dirigible with everybody onboard killed. The Doctor grabs Charley and whisks her off to the TARDIS. But she's already guessed the truth: she's supposed to have died.

The Doctor tells her that where there's life there's hope. He explains his predicament as best he can, and asks for information on Carthy. He refuses to let Charley sacrifice herself to put the situation right. He's not even sure it would. They journey back to Charley's childhood home, a sprawling country house, and there the Doctor finds photos and mementoes of the man. And photos of members of the Carthy family down the ages that have all been him.

The Doctor reasons that since the web of time has been breached, he can interfere himself. If he can stop Carthy ever contacting these infernal powers, deprive him of his immortality... even just find out more about his enemies... He gets Charley to interact with the TARDIS console. It explores her bloodline, and takes them back in time to the earliest meeting between the Carthys and the Pollards.

That was towards the end of the Roman occupation, where Severinus Carthacus was an Irish legionaire and Charley's male ancestor was a priest of Mithras. The Doctor and Charley investigate the secretive legionaire, and finally try and interfere when Severinus, following ancient texts he'd discovered in Iran, corrupts a Mithraic ritual to summon the great foe of the god Mithras, a demon bull. The demon consumes a Roman camp, and the Doctor and Charley escape, as does Severinus.

The Doctor finds himself fading away at intervals. The 'demon' has set off a time storm. The Doctor sends the TARDIS to a point where the influence is weakest. He discovers Carthy living as one of Edward the Confessor's counsellors, trying and failing to set up a cult to sacrifice to his demon. The Doctor finds a single victim, dying of a lack of energy, and raises the King against the cult, the King's wife, Edith, being Charley's ancestor. But Carthy's demon now has the energy it needs and

Carthy escapes. The Doctor sets off into time once more, and he and Charley find Carthy in the eighteenth century, a point the TARDIS scanners indicate as one where the web of time is especially weak. Carthy is by now a rich landowner, and his Hellfire Club are terrorising the countryside. The Doctor takes advantage of a slip in etiquette at a vicarage ball and challenges Carthy to a duel with muskets. Muskets that Carthy has enhanced with his secret knowledge. This could be the point when Carthy kills him! But no, the Doctor knows that Carthy could gloat here. He wounds Carthy, and shows the locals, led by their priest, Charley's ancestor, Carthy's advanced technology. They burn down the Club's caves and meeting place. But not before the Doctor has seen Carthy whisked away in a pod.

The TARDIS pursues the pod, and the Doctor and Charley encounter Carthy during the Blitz. Carthy has set a trap for the Doctor, diverting the courses of V2 rockets onto particular areas, using a device to manipulate gravity. That was the moment Carthy spoke of: when a rocket hits the house the Doctor has rushed into. But the Doctor is saved... by the Doctor! Now the laws of time can be broken, and he's journeyed back to this place on many occasions to form a whole team of himself to capture Carthy. But not before Carthy has concentrated the energy of an entire night of bombing into an energy broadcasting device.

Carthy calls for his masters, and they arrive in multiple travel pods. These are the advance guard of the Nimon: they're going to feast on Earth, and Carthy has now provided them with enough energy to do it. Desperate, the Doctor and his duplicates link hands at the controls of Carthy's energy broadcast device. A flash of potential energy explodes. The web of time is broken into pieces, and the Nimon's link to Earth is destroyed with it. The Doctor and Charley find themselves back where they started, in the Raffles Hotel, only with no company but each other.

The Doctor thinks that he's put things right: that time has repaired itself. But as the two friends walk back to the TARDIS, unseen by them, something sinister and relevant to the next play happens...